OUR WOMAN IN MOSCOW

ALSO BY BEATRIZ WILLIAMS

Her Last Flight

The Wicked Redhead

The Golden Hour

The Summer Wives

Cocoa Beach

The Wicked City

A Certain Age

Along the Infinite Sea

Tiny Little Thing

The Secret Life of Violet Grant

A Hundred Summers

Overseas

OUR WOMAN IN MOSCOW

A Novel

Beatriz Williams

wm

WILLIAM MORROW
An Imprint of HarperCollins*Publishers*

OUR WOMAN IN MOSCOW. Copyright © 2021 by Beatriz Williams. All rights reserved. Printed in the United States of America. No part of this book may be used or reproduced in any manner whatsoever without written permission except in the case of brief quotations embodied in critical articles and reviews. For information, address HarperCollins Publishers, 195 Broadway, New York, NY 10007.

HarperCollins books may be purchased for educational, business, or sales promotional use. For information, please email the Special Markets Department at SPsales@harpercollins.com.

FIRST EDITION

Designed by Nancy Singer

Library of Congress Cataloging-in-Publication Data has been applied for.

ISBN 978-0-06-302078-8 (hardcover)
ISBN 978-0-06-309439-0 (international edition)

21 22 23 24 25   LSC   10 9 8 7 6 5 4 3 2 1

To Deo
(1902–1988)

OUR WOMAN IN MOSCOW

RUTH

When we were eight years old, my twin sister, Iris, saved my life. I'm serious. I had a fever and a terrible stomachache, and our parents were out at some party. The nanny was one of those no-nonsense types you get, and I was not then—nor am I now— someone who likes to air her private miseries for the delectation of others.

Iris was the one who noticed my gray, shining face, as I curled up in bed and tried to read a book. Twin sisters and all. She just *knew* something was awfully wrong. She made the nanny call up 21, or wherever it was, and have the maître d' send for our parents. Of course, Mother told Nanny she wasn't coming home for any silly stomachache, and really Ruth should *know* better than to seek attention that way. She'd thought *better* of me. Nanny relayed this message with an air of triumph. I said *Fine* and curled back up, shivering as you shiver when a fever's come on.

So what did Iris do? My sweet, small, timid, delicate flower of a sister? She called up the ambulance service all by herself, that's what she did, and a half hour later they burst into our apartment, swept past poor astonished Nanny, and swiftly diagnosed a probable case of acute appendicitis. Within the hour, they were wheeling me into the operating room at the Hospital for the Relief of the Ruptured and Crippled on East Forty-Second Street. Mother burst hysterical into the waiting room in her fur coat, I'm told, though by then I was under some combination of nitrous oxide and chloroform, so I can't say for certain.

Anyway, my point is Iris saved my life that day, so it seems I owed her one.

WHERE WAS I? MY mind's wandering a bit. It's been a long day, and it's not even noon yet, and I'm afraid I've already drunk the best part of a bottle of English gin in order to cope. I'm sitting inside the fuselage of some type of military aircraft—don't ask me what *kind*, for God's sake—in the company of a United States army doctor and a pair of army nurses. We're on our way to evacuate an injured American citizen. It's an important mission. He's an important citizen, a genuine twenty-four-carat hero. I'm not allowed to tell you where we're going—that's top secret—and I'm probably not allowed to tell you his name, either.

Still, now that I think about it, they didn't specifically say I *couldn't*.

All right. I'll whisper it, so pay attention.

Charles Sumner Fox.

Nice name, isn't it? So distinguished. On his business card, it reads C. SUMNER FOX. That's because of his mother. He told me the story once, when we were in Italy together. It goes like this. His father's from Savannah, and his mother's from Boston, and they met in western Massachusetts where Mr. Savannah attended Amherst College and Miss Boston attended Smith. Some mixer, I guess. They fell in love somehow. She agreed to marry him and start a new life in Georgia, but she insisted on naming their firstborn after a famous abolitionist, just to make a point. Look for Charles Sumner in your encyclopedia and you'll see what I mean. Senator from Massachusetts during all those squabbles and treaties before the Civil War, the ones you learned about in school and forgot. Once, while he was on the Senate floor delivering a speech against slavery, some congressman took his cane and beat Charles Sumner until he almost died. I'm serious. Grievously injured, all because he stood there on the floor of the United States Senate, if you will, and called the congressman's cousin a *pimp for Southern interests.*

Men. I tell you.

Anyway, as a result of these shenanigans, Charles Sumner became the hero of Massachusetts, where the good citizens reelected him even though he couldn't actually attend the Senate, on account of being beaten so badly, so that his empty desk could stand as a noble reminder, et cetera. All the world loves a martyr. As time went on, mothers named their sons after him, just to make a point.

But listen to this. It's sort of funny. After Charles Sumner Fox was born, his mother decided he didn't look like a Charles after all, so she called him Sumner. And he's been Sumner Fox ever since, to the world and to me. If the name rings a bell, it's because he once played football for Yale, where he was considered one of the greatest fullbacks ever to carry a pigskin. So you probably heard of him.

I'M BUCKLED INTO A seat across from the doctor and nurses. They're wondering who I am and what I'm doing here, and why I stink like a gin distillery. They won't look me in the eye. That's all right. I light a cigarette and offer the case to them. They accept gratefully. I light them up one by one with a fine gold Zippo loaned to me by my sister's lover, who doesn't actually smoke. Have you ever noticed how every single doctor and every single nurse smokes like a damn chimney? Not that I blame them. You see enough death and sickness and grievous injury, you need something to keep your nerves in order.

We sit smoking, not looking at each other. Smelling the human stink of the inside of a troop transport, the scorch of engine oil and aviation fuel. I wonder if they know who he is, this patient. Like I told you, it's all top secret. And believe me, the US government is going to keep this one under lock and key for some time to come. It's a daisy, all right.

I turn my head to stare out the window at the thick clouds below. My foot keeps tapping against the deck of the airplane—I think the doctor and nurses are annoyed. But I can't seem to stop. I'm a bundle of raw nerves that no quantity of English gin and cigarettes can soothe. And it comes to me, as I sit there strapped into my metal seat, blowing smoke from my parched mouth, that maybe this is why my sister saved my life all those ages ago, when we were eight years old.

Iris saved me for this moment.

And what I have done this summer, I have done to repay my debt—the debt I owe her, the debt I owe people like Sumner Fox, the debt I owe to civilization itself—to all who came before me and saved me without my knowing it.

Outside the window, the great humming engine changes key. The airplane drops. I stub out my cigarette and close my eyes. Within the hour, I'll know how our story ends.

ONE

Love is whatever you can still betray.
Betrayal can only happen if you love.

—*John le Carré*

LYUDMILA

MAY 1951
Moscow

When she was six years old, Lyudmila Ivanova watched as a trio of men in dark suits searched her family's tiny apartment in the middle of the night and arrested her father for the crime of owning a set of English novels. He was a professor of literature, and the books were Russian translations. Still, English novels were decadent, and when his case went before the tribunal, her father refused to admit his crime and repent. Lyudmila still remembers his straight back and clear voice as he addressed the three judges on the dais before him. He was sentenced to ten years' labor in some work camp in Siberia. The family never heard from him again.

When Lyudmila was sixteen, her older brother Piotr was recalled from Paris, where he had run a network of local intelligence agents supplying information to the international Communist Party, although everybody knew that Comintern was actually run by the Soviet espionage agency. Six months later, he was arrested because he had lived in the West and his ideological purity had therefore been corrupted. This time there was no trial. Lyudmila later learned that he had been executed by firing squad.

Two years after that, another brother simply disappeared while working for Soviet intelligence in Germany, and as a result, when Lyudmila joined the intelligence service herself—at the time, it was called the NKVD—she underwent a rigorous interrogation. Miraculously, she survived. The fact that she had been the one to denounce her brother to the NKVD worked in her favor, as did her extensive knowledge of Marxist theory, her avowed disgust of bourgeois capitalist society, and her exceptionally ascetic lifestyle.

That was in 1932. Since then Lyudmila has survived the purges of the late 1930s and the slaughter of the Great Patriotic War, from which nobody else in her entering class at the NKVD—by now reformed into the KGB—was left alive. Lyudmila survives not because she's extraordinarily brilliant, or strategic, or well connected. She survives because she has two rules. The first is not to attract attention to herself. Comrade Stalin doesn't know her name. Beria of the secret police doesn't know her name. She serves them quietly, anonymously. Others who clamored for recognition are now dead, or starving to death in a Siberian gulag. Not Lyudmila. She does all the dirty work. She finds girls to supply Beria's particular needs, for example, and she finds ways to silence the grieved family members who demand some explanation. When it comes to sniffing out heretical thoughts, nobody has a more sensitive nose than Lyudmila. She's particularly good at extracting confessions. Never once has she claimed credit for any of these acts of patriotism. She lets others claim the credit and then watches as they, too, fall victim to some denouncement. Some discovery of impurity in thought or deed. They all fall eventually.

The second rule is even more important: trust nobody. Trust nothing! Every single person she meets, inside the KGB and outside of it, is suspect. Every piece of information that crosses her desk, gathered from networks within the Soviet Union and without, is suspect. Lyudmila has one faith—the Communist state. Everything else falls sacrifice to this one idea, even herself.

LYUDMILA DOESN'T TRUST *THIS* particular man one bit, even though he's supplied the KGB and its predecessors with valuable information from the British Foreign Office for the past twenty years. His name is Guy Burgess, and he's recently arrived from London with a fellow spy named Donald Maclean. They defected together, just ahead of the authorities who were about to unmask them at last.

Lyudmila knows who tipped them off. She knows where all the Soviet Union's diligent moles have built their hills and tunnels in the great institutions of the West—political, academic, military, scientific, you name it. She knows the almost laughable fact that one of Britain's top spy catchers is, in fact, a Soviet spy himself. She knows their code names, and what they've done and what they've produced, over the years and last week, and exactly how much alcohol they drink to dull the psychological pain of committing treason against a country and a culture that consider a gentleman's honor so sacrosanct as to be taken for granted. (Quite a lot, even by Russian standards.)

She carries all this information in her head as she sits across the table from Burgess, who lounges in his chair and chain-smokes the British cigarettes they've provided for him.

"I don't know what you're talking about," he's telling her. "If there were some clever high-level plot to infiltrate Moscow Centre—

American or British—I'd have heard about it. Philby gets all that intelligence right from the source, and I happened to be living in Philby's own bloody basement in Washington, not one month ago."

"Perhaps this operation is taking place above STANLEY's head," she says, in her nearly flawless English—taking pains to use Kim Philby's code name, as good tradecraft requires.

Burgess shakes his head. "Nothing takes place above Philby's head. MI-6 trusts him like a priest. My God, they handed him the Volkov defection case, didn't they? About as hush-hush as it gets. He speaks to the CIA head on a daily basis. He and Jim Angleton are like brothers."

"Nevertheless. They will have been made suspicious by these telegram decryptions. They will have realized our network has penetrated their agencies and their government departments at the highest level. It is possible and even likely that they will have undertaken an operation outside of the intelligence service itself, to root out everyone who has been disloyal."

"That's your own paranoia talking," Burgess says. "I assure you, the British don't see it that way. They can't conceive a Cambridge man passing along secrets to a foreign country. They'll go on assuming it was some cipher room clerk from Reading who needs the money to pay off his bookie."

Lyudmila stares at him with distaste. He's slovenly, this man. His shirt collar is stained, his teeth are indescribably yellow, his skin is slack and paunchy from incessant drinking, from overindulgence in rich food, from scorn for physical exercise. Possibly he's the most undisciplined man she's ever met, at least in this profession, and what's worse, he's an open homosexual who makes no effort at all to disguise or control his voracious carnal appetites. But while Lyudmila is suspicious and puritanical, she's also fair.

Burgess possesses a brilliant intellect and exerts enormous charm, when he chooses. He also knows everything about everybody.

She decides to lay a single card on the table.

"We have recently intercepted a communication from here in Moscow to a contact named ASCOT in London. Do you know who this ASCOT might be?"

He flicks some ash from his cigarette into the overflowing tray at his elbow. "Not the slightest idea. I've never heard of an agent named ASCOT. Where was the communication directed?"

"To a private address. A flat in West London that seems to be owned by a shipping company called Lonicera. We have the flat under surveillance at the moment, but we have not been able to determine anything of significance. We suspect, however, that this communication may be the key to a number of recent security leaks, for which we have been unable to identify the source."

"Lonicera, eh? Doesn't ring a bell."

As an intelligence agent of nearly two decades' standing, Burgess is a practiced liar. Still, Lyudmila can't detect any sign of deception in his voice or his affect. He looks so at ease, he might be sprawled in his own living room, except Lyudmila suspects that Burgess's living room—the one he left behind in London, anyway—is equally as squalid as Burgess himself.

"Very well," she says. "You will, of course, inform us immediately should your memory ring a bell, after all?"

"With pleasure. I'm eager to be of service."

If she were alone, Lyudmila's mouth would curve with contempt. Defectors! Really, they're such a nuisance. They know too much, they're altogether too *eager to be of service*. Don't they understand that *defection* means *retirement*? What use can a defector possibly be? He's already given up all his information. He can't go

back to his home country for more. His only value is publicity—
the triumph of Soviet intelligence. Otherwise, he's just a drain on
the state. You have to find him some job that will keep him out of
trouble. You have to give him a nice apartment and access to luxury
Western goods, so he doesn't complain. You have to keep a close
eye on him, to make sure he's not getting restless and disillusioned.

In fact, Lyudmila can think of only one defector whose assimi-
lation has gone smoothly, without any headaches for her—a happy,
contented Soviet citizen with his happy, contented family.

Almost as if he can read her mind, Burgess stubs out his cigarette and says, "By the by, how's Digby coming along?"

Lyudmila gives him a hard stare. "*HAMPTON*," she says, with
emphasis, "has been a model citizen. He and his family are now living in Moscow. He serves us as an academic and adviser on matters
of international affairs."

"Given up the booze, has he? That's what I hear."

"Where do you hear this?"

He shrugs as he lights another cigarette. "Here and there. Well,
that's fine news. He and I were chums for a moment or two, back
in London. Good chap, for an American. Wife's a trifle uptight for
my taste, but the children were charming."

"Yes." Lyudmila checks her watch. "Now, if you'll excuse me,
Comrade Burgess, I'm afraid I have other demands on my time
this afternoon. My colleagues will arrive shortly to continue the
debriefing."

Burgess props the cigarette in the ashtray and stands to shake
hands. He is, after all, an English gentleman.

LYUDMILA MAKES HER WAY to her afternoon appointment, which
is of such long standing that she doesn't have to think about her

route as she navigates the Moscow streets. She thinks instead about Burgess—so pleased with himself, so delighted to have created such an international ruckus. The world's press is in the middle of an apoplexy right now over the missing English diplomats, and Burgess is enjoying every moment.

Still, for all his faults, Burgess has always been loyal. More mercenary than the others, to be sure, but only because he has expensive tastes and a Foreign Office salary. He's provided a wealth of priceless information over the years. Not once has any of that information proved false. Nor did he display so much as a hint of the classic signs of deception, throughout the course of the interview.

Lyudmila has to conclude—provisionally, at least—that he doesn't know anything about the ASCOT operation, including its existence.

Which only goes to support her hypothesis. This operation, after all, seems to have as its objective the systematic exposure of Soviet moles burrowed within the most secret inner corridors of Western intelligence—all those Burgesses and Macleans and Philbys and Hisses, so carefully recruited and managed over years and even decades.

It stands to reason, therefore, that it's being conducted from outside the formal intelligence service, by some renegade officer or officers who—like her—have finally learned to trust nobody.

A man code-named ASCOT.

And the agent whom ASCOT has boldly sent into Moscow, into the heart of the Soviet state, to uncover the traitors, one by one.

RUTH

From the perspective of my desk, parked outside the deluxe private office of our president and chief executive officer, Mr. Herbert Henry Hudson, you can see just about everything that goes on within the premises of the world-famous Hudson Modeling Agency.

This is no coincidence, believe me. I like to keep an eye on everything, always have.

On the day Sumner Fox walks past the glass double doors—an ordinary hot afternoon in late June, a steady stream of fresh new-mint high school graduates eager to commence their modeling careers, God bless them—I've been running the agency for about four years, depending on your definition of the term, and I have no intention of going anywhere. I like my job. I like my way of life, more or less. I wear my usual uniform of white button-down shirt and black gabardine slacks, hair pulled back in a neat gold knot, red lipstick and nothing else. I prop my feet on my desk and drink my seventh cup of strong black coffee while I flip through the portfo-

lio of some vampy fifteen-year-old from Elizabeth, New Jersey—
claims eighteen, the pretty liar, but I'm a better judge of age than
a horse trader—and *God knows* I have no time at all for the bull-
shouldered fellow who stands at the reception desk like a heavy-
weight boxer who's taken a wrong turn at Albuquerque.

My telephone rings. Reception.

I direct an eyebrow of disapproval toward Miss Simmons from
above the frame of my reading glasses. She shrugs and tilts her head
toward the beef standing in front of her desk.

I lift the receiver. "Macallister."

"Miss Macallister, Mr. Sumner Fox from the FBI is here to see
you." She says *FBI* in a hushed, secret voice, enunciating each letter
separately.

I open my mouth to tell Miss Simmons to tell the so-called
FBI to get lost, but she tacks on another sentence before I get the
words out.

"He says it's about your sister."

AS I SAID, I like to keep everything at the agency within view—with
one exception, to which Mr. Fox and I repair now.

He's impressed, I believe, as most people are when they step
inside the boardroom of the Hudson Modeling Agency. The room
itself is nothing—just a big old committee table, the usual chairs
of dubious comfort—but the *view*, my word. There's this particular
corner of the twenty-sixth floor that opens out unobstructed across
the East River and all the way down to the Brooklyn Bridge, if you
don't mind a kink in your neck, and that wall is made of nothing
but glass, glass, glass, cleaned regularly by a well-trained team of
daredevils. Now, Sumner Fox isn't the kind of man who betrays

anything so vulnerable as an emotion. (In this, we are equals.) But he does walk across the width of the room and smash his fists into the pockets of his trousers and sort of roll up and down on his big flipper feet as he stares upon that stupefying expanse of metropolis.

I take the opportunity to stare him up and down. As I said, he's a large fellow, not exceptionally tall but built like an Angus steer, all shoulders, square rawboned head on which a bare half inch of extremely pale hair bristles up like a field of mowed hay. No residual tail, thank God, but the position of his fists in his pockets strains the back flap of his jacket upward just enough to reveal a fine muscular bottom, which pleases me. You don't go into my line of business without some appreciation for the aesthetics of the human form. Now that I consider the matter, I wonder if he allows me to inspect him on purpose.

Whether he means to impress me or to warn me, I don't pretend to guess.

I know enough about these sorts of encounters to allow the other person to introduce the conversation. After I've looked my fill, I fold my arms across my chest and wait for him to address me. Which he does, after a minute. Pivots in a military manner and says—gravelly midsouthern baritone—"Miss Macallister. I do appreciate your taking the time to meet me like this, without a prior appointment."

"I'm just a secretary, Mr. Fox. You don't need an appointment to meet with me."

"*Just* a secretary?" He actually smiles, displaying a set of neat white teeth. "That's not the word on the street."

"Oh? Which street is that?"

"Why, the street that says you run the whole show. That poor old Mr. Hudson is what you might call a puppet, and you're what might be called a puppeteer."

"Now, that's just slander," I reply. "But as it happens, I *am* a busy woman, and I like a man who gets right to the point. You were saying something about my sister? Has she perhaps made her whereabouts known to the world at last?"

"That's an excellent question, Miss Macallister. Maybe you could answer it for me."

"Me? I don't think you know the facts of the case. Do you smoke, Mr. Fox?"

He blinks his pale eyes. "No, thank you."

"Then I hope I don't offend you." I stalk around the other side of the table to the console, where the agency keeps a selection of cigarettes for the refreshment of the august members of the board of directors. I light one with a match, old-fashioned damsel that I am. By the time I turn back to face Mr. Fox, I feel I have the situation in hand.

"I must confess, I'm mystified. Why come to me now, after all these years? I mean, I haven't heard a word from the FBI, not since that first week after they disappeared."

"And yet most families would be beating down our door, demanding an explanation, when a diplomat goes missing on a foreign posting with his wife and children."

"Well, we aren't most families." I blow out a stream of smoke. "To be perfectly honest, I hadn't seen or heard from my sister in years. Long before the State Department lost track of her."

"How many years?"

I stare at the ceiling and count my fingers. "Twelve. Why, it's

June, isn't it? That makes twelve years *exactly*. I ought to bake a cake or something."

His frown is not a frown of disapproval or of sadness or anything subjective like that. I think he's just pondering the meaning of it all—twin sisters estranged for a dozen years—what could possibly have caused such an unnatural divorce? He might also be disappointed. Clearly there's not much you can learn about a woman from a sister who's better acquainted with her dry cleaner.

"So you see," I continue, hoping to shut down the entire conversation, "you're barking up the wrong tree, if you want the lowdown on whatshername."

"Iris."

I snap my fingers. "That's it."

"Do you mind if we sit down?"

"Yes, I do, rather. Stack of work sitting on my desk. Dictation to type up, telephone messages to deliver."

He cracks the smallest smile. "Now I *know* you're just pulling my leg. Have a seat, Miss Macallister, and I'll do the same. The sooner we finish this conversation, the sooner you can get back to your secretarial duties."

I suppose I realize I've met my match, when it comes to stubbornness of character. And really, I'm not offended. After all, we *want* our FBI men to be tough, stubborn, unrelenting sons of bitches, don't we? At least when they're not after *us*.

I take the chair he gallantly pulls out for me and wait for him to take the seat opposite. Drag an ashtray from the center of the table and make myself comfortable with it.

"I hope you don't mind if I study your face," I say. "It's an occupational habit."

"Not much to study. I've been told I'm no picture portrait."

"That's true. You look as if somebody carved you from a tree with a blunt axe. But beauty isn't everything when it comes to photographs. If you've been in this business long enough, why, beauty's sort of boring. Like Tolstoy. Beautiful people are all alike, but the ugly . . ."

"Now, that's an interesting observation, coming from a beautiful woman."

"Pshaw." I tap a little ash into the tray. "I thought you intended to move things along?"

"As you like. You don't mind if I take notes, do you?" He pulls a small leather notebook from the inside pocket of his jacket.

"Be my guest. I do take shorthand, if you need a break or something."

"That would be against protocol, I'm afraid. You say you last saw your sister in June of 1940?"

"That's correct."

"And since then you haven't spoken at all? Letters, telegrams?"

"Not a word."

He set down his pen. "You don't have any idea of her whereabouts, from June of 1940 until November of 1948? What she was doing? Husband and children and any of that?"

"Of course I do. Our aunt kept me filled in, from time to time."

"That would be Mrs. Charles Schuyler, wouldn't it?"

"My stars, you *have* done your homework, haven't you? We know her as Aunt Vivian, of course."

"I'm glad to hear it. So Mrs. Schuyler represents your only source of information on Mrs. Digby's whereabouts—"

"And our brother, Harry. I believe he dropped in on them, from time to time, at whatever diplomatic post they'd been sent to."

He casts me a sharp look, as if there's some hidden meaning in this. "Until November of 1948, of course, when Mrs. Digby and her family vanished from their flat in London."

"That's right. I read all about it in the papers."

"Just the papers?"

"Well, it was a sensational case, wasn't it? Once the press got their hands on it. No signs of struggle or burglary or anything like that. They just packed their suitcases and left, and nobody's heard from them since. Isn't that right, Mr. Fox?"

"Not necessarily. Don't you think Mrs. Digby might have tried to find some way to send word to those she loves?"

"I wouldn't know. I don't believe I fall inside that category, I'm afraid. All I've heard is what's been reported in the press. One outlandish theory after another."

"And do you have an opinion on any of them, Miss Macallister?"

"They all seem a little farfetched to me." I tap some ash into the brass ashtray. "I'm sure you'd know much more about that kind of thing than I do. What do you think? I'm dying to know. Was Digby *really* a spy for the Soviets? Were they killed, or did they defect?"

If he's shocked, he doesn't show it. He doesn't even blink. "I don't deal in speculation, Miss Macallister. I deal only in facts."

I lean a little closer. "Come on, now. I promise I won't spill the beans to the papers or anything. She *is* my sister, after all."

You must understand that my heart's beating like a dynamo. I hope he's not the kind of fellow who looks at your neck to determine your pulse. I think I manage to keep the cigarette from shaking between my fingers, but it's a question of mind over matter, believe me—of a self-control honed over years spent sitting across from men at desks and restaurant tables and boardrooms like this one. I raise the cigarette to my lips and stare inquisitively at the dent between Mr. Fox's thick, straight eyebrows while I wait for him to speak. That's harder than it sounds, by the way. Most human beings would rather swallow a live goldfish than a lump of silence.

Mr. Fox leans back in his chair. He wears a dark suit and a dark, plain tie, just in case you can't guess what he does for a living. His shirt collar is white and crisp around his thick pink neck. "Let's return to the known facts," he says. "Mr. and Mrs. Digby lived overseas almost without pause since their marriage in June of 1940. Mr. Digby's work took them to various US embassies and consulates around the world. Their last leave stateside occurred in 1947, just before Mr. Digby took up the post in London."

"Is that so? I must have missed her. Shame."

"But you did say that Mrs. Schuyler gave you regular reports on Mrs. Digby's whereabouts and style of life, didn't you?"

I shrug. "I didn't always listen."

"I doubt that."

"It's true. Anyway, they were always moving from country to country, those two, mingling with princes and popping out babies. How many was it? Three?"

He glances at his notebook. "She was expecting her third when she disappeared."

"How lovely. Say." I lean forward and frown. "If they're in some kind of trouble, you're not going to make me adopt the offspring, are you? I don't get along well with children."

"I'm happy to say that's not a matter within the scope of our powers at the FBI, Miss Macallister. Returning to the matter at hand. You say you haven't had any communication with her at all? Nothing recent, for example? Letters? Postcards?"

"Why should I? After all these years?"

"You tell me."

I lean back again and cross one leg over the other. The chair squeaks agreeably. "You should talk to Aunt Vivian. She's the one who used to get all the letters."

"I already have."

"Harry? Our brother? He's out in Alaska somewhere, last I heard."

"I've spoken to Mr. Macallister, yes."

"What about her husband's family? He's got a mother or something, I seem to remember. And the father's a real piece of work, from what I hear. Mr. Digby Senior, some kind of bigwig in oil."

"Miss Macallister, you might be surprised to know that the FBI actually knows how to conduct a thorough investigation without recourse to any of your useful suggestions."

"Touched a nerve, did I? Everything coming up dry? You've come to the end of the line?" I stub out the cigarette. "The end of the line being me, of course. Deadest of dead ends. I'm so sorry I couldn't be of more use to you."

"Yes, I can see the regret in your eyes, Miss Macallister." He closes the notebook and replaces it in the inside pocket of his jacket. As he does so, I catch a glimpse of a mammoth chest.

I snap my fingers.

"Sumner Fox! Of course. Football. You were all the rage for a few years. Some college or another, wasn't it?"

"Yes," he says. "Some college or another. Here's my card, Miss Macallister. I urge you to contact me at the earliest possible instant, should you receive any word at all from your sister."

I take the card from his meaty fingers and slip it into the pocket of my slacks. "Life or death, is it?"

He squints at me carefully, as if my head's turned into a sun. "Just call that number, please, as a matter of urgency. And Miss Macallister? You'll understand this conversation should be kept strictly confidential."

I zip my lips. "You can trust me, Mr. Fox."

"Thank you," he says. "I'll show myself out."

AFTER HE LEAVES, I light another cigarette and take my time settling my vital humors. I stand right before that great wall of glass and stare between the monoliths toward my narrow section of the East River—all the miniature boats inching along the glittering summer water, all the acres of close-packed buildings stretching out beyond them. I think about how many people live inside those buildings. I think about the buildings beyond those buildings, the buildings beyond those, the parks and yards and nice suburban houses of Long Island, old Roosevelt Field where Lindbergh took off for Paris early one morning. It took him thirty-six hours to get there, which is perseverance, if you ask me. I admire perseverance. You find yourself some purpose and you stick to it, like a dog with a bone, no matter how many times the world tries to yank that bone away.

Now, was Lindbergh right to do it? Well, of course he was. But only because he made it to Paris.

BY THE TIME THE cigarette burns out, my heart's resumed its ordinary cadence. I no longer feel the twinge of every nerve. I return to my desk and flip through the stack of telephone messages left there by Miss Simmons, ignoring all the beady sideways appraisals from every direction. I mean, I can't blame them. Wouldn't you be curious, too?

One by one, everyone returns to work. Herbert and I conduct a couple of interviews in his office, brand-new girls who show some real promise, maybe, even if the poor bunnies are hopelessly naïve in their brave red lipstick and their enthusiasm. We offer contracts to both, which they want to sign right away, God bless them. I tell them to take the paperwork home and read it carefully first. *Don't sign anything you haven't read,* I tell them, and they nod earnestly and stick the contracts in their pocketbooks.

By six o'clock, the office has cleared out. I help Herbert with his hat and coat and shuffle him out the door to the limousine waiting for him outside. While waiting for the elevator, I remind him of his dinner engagement and kiss his soft cheek good night.

The elevator arrives, Herbert steps inside, and I'm alone at last.

I return to the reception area and switch off the lights. The glow of an early summer evening pours through the windows. I'm due for dinner in forty-five minutes, and under ordinary circumstances I'd take the opportunity to walk the twenty-two blocks through this golden light. I'd set aside the worries of the day and enjoy the hubbub, the hurry, the joy of people headed home in weather like this—the way a summer evening can transform even dirty old Manhattan into a city of translucent wonder. Instead I duck into Herbert's office and help myself to a glass of twenty-year-old single-malt scotch, no ice.

THERE ARE THOSE WHO claim that I slept my way to my current position, just outside the office of Mr. Herbert Hudson of the Hudson Modeling Agency, and I will allow there's a grain of truth to that rumor, as there are to most.

I first met Herbert when I was seventeen years old, just before Iris and I graduated from Chapin. He was the father of a friend of mine, we'll call her Rosie. Nice girl, Rosie. She and I performed in the school play together, that spring of our senior year. We put on *The Pirates of Penzance*—she played Mabel and I played the major-general, twirling my mustache to great acclaim—and Herbert hosted a little cast party afterward at his handsome Park Avenue apartment, in the course of which he cornered me on the roof terrace and asked me if anyone had ever told me I should model for photographs, that he was the president of maybe the biggest modeling agency in the world and he would love nothing more than to launch my career as a world-famous fashion model.

Now, even at seventeen I was no idiot. I understood that I was no more than ordinarily pretty, not the stuff of the world famous, and what was more, I perfectly comprehended the nature of the proposal Herbert was laying out for me. Finally, and most importantly, I was seventeen years old and had no intention of losing my virginity to Rosie Hudson's portly, red-nosed fifty-four-year-old father, and long story short, Herbert found a more gullible girl to keep him company that night, and I lost my virginity some years later to a genuine Russian prince, I kid you not.

By the age of twenty-three, however, I took a less romantic view of sexual relations, and a greater interest in what lay underneath the skin of another person. Chance placed Herbert next to me at a dinner party one evening, where I discovered that Rosie Hudson's lascivious father spoke four languages, collected Tintoretto, and had trained as an architect before his own chance encounter—those peculiar, dazzling points of inflection that determine our fate—led to the creation of the Herbert Hudson Modeling Agency. Then he said enough about him, what about me. I told him about Rome, about my brief spell as a fashion model—he laughed and said I must have caused a real sensation among his Italian colleagues—and about the war and my opinions on it. He walked me home through the New York drizzle. He was between wives at the moment, he told me, and I said I hoped he didn't mean to audition me for the role, because I wasn't cut out to be anybody's wife. He laughed some more and said he couldn't afford me, anyway, and because I happened to stand at a crossroads in my life, because I was sick and tired of gorgeous, faithless young men, I agreed to go to dinner with him the following Saturday. We went out to dinner eight times before we slept together, which was probably a record for me if I bothered to count, but it was not until after we drifted apart that he offered me a job as his secretary.

So whatever people might say about me—and they say a lot—I haven't been sleeping with my boss, at least not since he *became* my boss. And if I feel myself entitled to a glass of his private reserve from time to time—why, it's only because I am.

I SLING DOWN THE scotch and clean the glass myself. By the time I'm done with all the housekeeping, I've got twenty-eight minutes to make my way to the Fifth Avenue apartment of my aunt Vivian and uncle Charlie, and I'm unlikely to find a taxi at this hour. I should skedaddle right out the door, but I don't. I leave Herbert's office and lock the door behind me—walk to my desk to retrieve my pocketbook from the lower right-hand drawer—but I don't continue straight to the glass doors that open to the elevator lobby.

Instead I sit in my chair and reach deep into the open drawer for the hidden compartment at the back. To be clear, I inherited this interesting secret from the previous owner of the desk—whoever he was—so I can't take credit or blame. Still, it's there, and it's sometimes useful, and on the few occasions when I have nothing better to do, I ponder what my predecessor kept in there. Booze, probably. Prohibition was the mother of so many inventions.

But I came of age after the blessed repeal, so I don't have much use for this compartment. Just money or jewelry, when I need a temporary stash for either. And now this thing. This slim rectangle featuring a photograph of St. Basil's Cathedral on one side and a short, handwritten note on the other, which I haven't read.

This foreign postcard, which I received about a week ago, here at the office.

Now I stare at this flat cliché rendering of the onion-shaped domes, the black-and-white stonework, and consider whether I dare to turn it over and read the message on the other side. Whether I'm better off tearing that postcard to shreds and dropping it in the wastebasket for the night janitor to consign to oblivion.

In the end, I turn it over, if only to confirm the suspicion that Sumner Fox has planted in my head. The funny thing is, I'm not surprised at all by what it says. I've always known it would come to this. I've always known Iris would wind up in the worst kind of trouble there is, ever since Sasha Digby walked into her life on a spring day in 1940 and smashed us all to pieces.

IRIS

LATE MARCH 1940
Rome, Italy

The woman flailed against the giant who held her against his ribs. His hands snatched at her waist and her naked thigh with such force, his fingers sank into the tender flesh. How she fought him! With one hand, she pushed his head from her breast. Her curls flew into the air. But she didn't stand a chance, did she? Not a chance in the world against all that bulging muscle, all that solid, masculine bone.

Iris couldn't strip her gaze away. She stood hypnotized before the white limbs—the living skin—the long, curling ropes of hair. The robes that fell from waist and hip and shoulder. If she reached out to touch the marble, she would surely find it warm beneath her fingers. She'd feel the thrum of emotion—fear, desire, revulsion, passion, triumph—inside her own pulse. Once a week she visited the gallery, sometimes twice, and she couldn't decide whether it was hatred or rapture that drew her back to this particular statue. Whether she was mesmerized by the beauty of the human shapes—the struggling Proserpina, the mighty Pluto; whether she was repulsed by the violence, by Proserpina's helpless struggle; whether she was ashamed because she couldn't stop staring into this intimate, brutal act. She wanted to stop it somehow, to wrest Proserpina from Pluto's arms. But sometimes she caught herself in Pluto's thoughts, so consumed by lust for this tender flesh that he couldn't let her go—he couldn't *survive* without Proserpina's warmth in his cold, dark underworld, even though she hated him.

Some other visitors trickled around her. Iris didn't really notice them. That was why she visited in the middle of the week, or on a rainy afternoon, so there weren't as many people around to witness her in her trance, or to wonder why the small, young American virgin couldn't turn away from that riot of licentious marble. Today was a Tuesday, and a delicate spring rain pattered on the windows. Also, there was a war on, didn't you know. Only Americans went on vacations anymore, and even Americans weren't exactly thick on the ground. So nobody bothered Iris, and Iris didn't bother anybody, and when at last she broke the trance and turned to leave the gallery, she almost missed the bright blond head studying *The Rape of Proserpina* from the other side.

Almost, but not quite. You couldn't really miss a mane like that, especially in Italy—sleek and gold, propped up high on a pink neck, its pink ears tucked neatly back. Iris couldn't see the rest of him very well, hidden on the other side of all that writhing stone, and anyway she was on her way out and pretending not to look. All she could make out was a tall suit of dark blue, and a hand shoved in a trouser pocket, before she passed out of the room.

That was all. A glimpse of a golden head and a blue suit. So why did Iris feel as if she'd lost something precious, as she stood before another sinuous Bernini in the next room? A maiden who held the radiant sun in her hand as some invisible force pulled away the drapery that covered her.

He was just a stranger in a museum. She was never going to see him again, anyway.

BUT AS IRIS MOVED from room to magnificent room, she *did* see him again. And again! Well, maybe that was to be expected. They were floating down the same river, after all—following the same prescribed path around the ground floor of the Villa Borghese, taking in the masterpieces one by one. That head bobbed in and out, moving above the little clusters of other visitors, and Iris now saw the body it was connected to, tall and lean and long armed. The beautiful tailoring of his blue suit made the most of his rangy shoulders. When he stopped to contemplate a painting or a statue or an ancient Roman bowl, or the gorgeous decoration of the ceiling, he shoved his hands in his trouser pockets and tilted his head thoughtfully.

Once, Iris passed him straight on, when she left a room just as he was entering. She had just an instant to see his face, which was plain and no-nonsense, a prominent brow over a pair of wide-set eyes, maybe thirty years old. So near as Iris could tell, he didn't notice her, but then she took care not to catch herself looking at him, either. Were they playing a game, or not?

Oh, of course they weren't. It was all in her head. A silly, lightning infatuation. For a stranger! Iris stared at a David holding out the severed head of Goliath. The last room on the ground floor, and it was nearly four o'clock in the afternoon.

A woman stood next to Iris's right shoulder, a man to her left.

The woman stepped away, and for a minute or two, Iris and the man contemplated the painting in silence.

"We seem to be interested by the same pieces," the man said.

Iris startled and looked to her side.

The man with the golden hair.

He stared straight ahead. He had a long, sharp nose and a firm jaw.

"Do we?" Iris said.

"Pluto and Proserpina," he said, tactfully avoiding the word *Rape.* "*Truth Revealed by Time.* David and Goliath."

"Isn't everyone interested by those? They're the masterpieces."

He nodded to the painting in front of them. "You'd think the artist would model David after his own face, if he were going to model himself at all, but actually that's Caravaggio on the Goliath."

"Yes, I know."

The man turned his head and looked at her sheepishly. Beneath those heavy brows his eyes were very blue, almost ultramarine. "Sorry. Didn't mean to condescend. I was just trying to make conversation." He smiled. "We've met, you know."

"Have we?"

"Don't remember?" He stuck out one enormous, bony hand. "Sasha Digby. I work with your brother, at the embassy."

"Oh! Of course." She shook the hand.

"Party last month? At the ambassador's residence? You were there with Harry and your sister. Of course you don't remember. It was the end of the evening before I introduced myself. I guess we all had a little too much champagne."

Iris tried to recall the party, but Mr. Digby was right. She *had* drunk a lot of champagne that night, and she wasn't used to it. Her memories of the evening were . . . well, *kaleidoscopic* was a nice way to put it.

"I'm awfully sorry. I *should* remember you."

He laughed. "Yes, I do stick out in a crowd, don't I?"

"It's just that I don't usually have so much to drink. They kept refilling my glass when I wasn't looking."

"Ah, well, they do it on purpose. Without wine there would be no diplomacy. Anyway, I should have introduced myself earlier."

"Why didn't you?"

"Because I'm *shy*, Miss Macallister."

"No, you're not! Didn't you just walk up to me and introduce yourself?"

"Only after spending an hour wandering around after you, working up the nerve."

"Oh," Iris said.

Mr. Digby looked at his watch. "Say, I'd ask you to coffee, but I've got a silly appointment coming up."

"Then you shouldn't be late."

"No, I can't, I'm afraid. But I'm glad I spotted you here. I mean, I'm not surprised to see you in a place like this. I knew there was something different about you."

His ears were pink. A bright raspberry stain covered his cheekbones.

"I'm glad too, Mr. Digby," she said.

"Sasha."

"Sasha. I'm Iris."

"I know." He glanced again at his watch. "I'm late. I'm sorry, I don't mean to be rude."

"Go. Don't be late."

"You'll remember me at the next party?"

She shook his hand a second time. "I certainly will."

AFTER SASHA DIGBY RUSHED off, Iris floated upstairs to the first floor. (Not to be confused with the *ground* floor—this was Italy, after all.) Because marble was so extraordinarily heavy, you didn't find any mesmerizing Bernini statuary up there, just paintings and ancient Roman artifacts and some splendidly decorated rooms. Iris knew them all well. She came here often. A gallery like that was like an opium den for her, packed with pleasure and revelation.

Today, however, she drifted from room to room and didn't notice a thing. Her heart skipped and raced. She was bubbling over with some giddy froth of emotion she hardly dared to name. It was like the way a child felt on Christmas Eve, if Christmas were a tall, golden-haired man who already knew your name, who thought you were *different* from the other girls, who'd spent an hour working up the nerve just to say hello. She stopped in front of a painting of a woman who held a small, perfect unicorn in her lap, like a cat, and she stared at that woman and thought, *I know exactly how you feel!*

The rain let up. Sunshine lit the windows, the watery sunshine of springtime. Iris looked out onto the gardens below, the manicured hedges in their perfect, symmetrical designs. She could almost smell the damp green scent of the dripping leaves, the wet gravel, the rich earth. A patch of blue hung above. Everything glittered, so new and promising.

On a bench along one of the side paths sat a man and a woman, part hidden by the pattern of hedges. The man wore an overcoat and a fedora. The woman wore a raincoat and a plain, round black hat. They had crossed their legs, his right and her left, to form an intimate V. They seemed to be talking to each other, even though they were staring straight ahead, into the hedge across the path. The man was long and lean, and his suit was dark blue underneath his unbuttoned overcoat. Iris couldn't see his hair beneath that fedora, nor the color of his eyes or the shape of his nose. She couldn't even see the pinkness of his neck.

But she saw his hands, folded on top of his thigh, bony and enormous.

After a minute or two, the man rose and held out his hand to the woman, who took it and rose too. They walked off together, down the gravel path and out of sight behind a line of plane trees.

FROM THE BORGHESE GARDENS, it was a reasonably short walk down the grand, curving Via Vittorio Emmanuel to the US embassy, where Iris's brother, Harry, worked, processing visas for desperate Jews (though never nearly enough).

Farther down the road, and around a corner or two, Iris's twin sister, Ruth, was modeling dresses for some fashion magazine. Unlike Iris, Ruth was tall, blond, and angular, as Aryan as they came, and she'd made quite a stir among the Italian houses since the two of them joined Harry in Rome last October. Ruth had said something over breakfast about the Spanish Steps, if the weather cleared, so they were probably setting up the cameras and the lights right now. Ruth told Iris she could come and watch, if she wanted. Iris said *Sure, maybe*. (When Ruth turned away to sip her coffee, Iris rolled her eyes.)

But Iris *had* to go somewhere. The zing of the Villa Borghese had gone flat for her, and God knew she couldn't go walking around the gardens. With her luck, she'd run bang into Sasha Digby and his female companion. Maybe she'd find a café somewhere and order an espresso and take out her sketchbook. She marched out the entrance of the villa—nodded to the porter, who recognized her—down the steps, *clickety clack*, and no sooner did her foot hit the gravel than what do you know, a raindrop hit her smack on the nose.

By the time she reached the traffic whizzing down the Via Pinciana, the rain had decided it meant business. Iris stopped to open her umbrella and imagined the photography crew at the Spanish Steps rushing to pack up their equipment, while beautiful Ruth leapt for cover beneath a nearby awning.

Iris didn't even notice the motorcycle tearing around the bend in the road until she stepped off the sidewalk to cross to the other side.

RUTH

To be clear, my dinner engagement with Aunt Vivian and Uncle Charlie already existed in my appointment book before Sumner Fox paid me a visit this afternoon, so it's not as if I've sought them out particularly to talk things over. It's a regular appointment, dinner at their apartment on Fifth Avenue on the second Thursday of the month, assuming everybody's in town—not because we're particularly close but because none of us can figure out a way to break the habit without causing offense. Families, you know.

I'm only five minutes late when I hurry into the lobby and wave hello to the doorman—he's got a thing for me, always lets me run straight up—but Aunt Vivian isn't amused. She kisses me on both cheeks and says something snide about the sliding morals of the young.

"That's rich, coming from you," I reply.

Uncle Charlie stands at the liquor cabinet, mixing my martini. He's always glad to see me, even if he doesn't approve of career girls.

He hands me the drink and asks if anything's the matter, because I'm looking a little pale.

"Oh, nothing your martinis can't fix, Uncle Charlie." I collapse on a chair and light a cigarette. "Just an FBI agent turning up, asking about Iris."

"Iris? The FBI? What the hell do they want with her, after all these years?"

"Ask your wife. The agent says they already spoke to Aunt Vivian."

"Vivian? What's this?"

Aunt Vivian flicks the ash from her cigarette. "It's nothing, Charlie. I told them exactly what I imagine Ruth told them— nothing at all. There's been no word from Iris in four years. I can't imagine why they're looking into the whole mess again."

"Maybe they've found some trace of her," I said.

"Well, they're not going to find out anything new from *you*."

I gaze across the room at the windows that overlook Central Park, where sunset's begun to gather in the skies above New Jersey. "It's a funny thing, though. She sent me a postcard a week ago."

Aunt Vivian nearly drops her glass. "A *postcard*? From Iris?"

"Claims to be, anyway."

"From where?"

"Moscow."

Uncle Charlie swears. "I'll be damned! They defected! I knew it! Didn't I say he'd defect, the damn Communist?"

"What did the postcard say?" Aunt Vivian asks calmly.

"You don't seem all that surprised."

She shrugs. I rise and cross the room to the sofa where I flung my pocketbook. I rummage around until I find the postcard tucked inside. *"Dear Ruth,"* I read. *"Things are awfully busy here in Moscow. We're expecting another baby in July. More soon. Love always, Iris."*

"That's strange," Aunt Vivian says.

"Strange? That's putting it mildly."

"I mean it doesn't sound like Iris at all. She doesn't talk like that, let alone write like that. What did the FBI fellow say?"

I tuck the postcard back in my pocketbook. "I didn't tell him."

Uncle Charlie sputters into his scotch. "You're not saying you *lied* to a federal investigator, are you? Ruth? Are you?"

"I might have. I don't remember one way or another."

"Sure you don't," says Aunt Vivian.

"As your *lawyer*—"

"Oh, shimmy off that high horse, Uncle Charlie. You'd have done the same. Iris and I may not be the closest of pals—"

Aunt Vivian snorts.

"—but I'm no snitch, not even to my worst enemy."

"It's hardly snitching to tell the nice FBI man you've received a postcard from your sister in Moscow," says my aunt. "Under the circumstances."

"Please. Something's fishy, or he wouldn't have turned up now, after all these years. Digby's gotten her into a mess of some kind, and I don't just mean having another baby."

"What kind of mess?" demands my uncle. "They've already defected. What more mess could there be?"

I dangle my glass at him. "You know, these martinis are really terrific. I don't suppose you'll allow me another before dinner?"

When Uncle Charlie rises to refill the martini glass, Aunt Vivian sits back in her chair and drags from her cigarette. "Odd, about that postcard. Is she really having another baby, do you think?"

"I suppose she must be. Unless it's some kind of code, but why write something obviously false? I mean, they must have censors or something, watching the mail."

"You know she has a terrible time having babies. I don't know why she allows that man near her anymore."

"Love finds a way, I guess."

Aunt Vivian watches the movements of her husband's arms as he mixes and shakes at the liquor cabinet. "He drinks, you know."

"Everybody *drinks*, Aunt Vivian."

"Maybe she's finally leaving him."

"Then why defect with him in the first place?"

"I don't know. Tell me, why *did* they defect? You *did* stay with them in England, that summer before they left. You and the girls."

Aunt Vivian sits back in her chair and crosses her long legs. "Never mind. Tell me about this FBI man."

"What's there to tell? He looks the part, if that's what you mean. Sumner Fox. Do you remember him, Uncle Charlie? He played football somewhere."

"Sumner Fox. Christ. *The* Sumner Fox?"

"How many could there be?"

He hands me the glass. I lick the drops from the edges.

"He played fullback for Yale, mid-'30s," says Uncle Charlie.

"Then what happened?"

"Flew torpedo bombers off a carrier in the Pacific. Crashed on an island somewhere and spent the rest of the war in a Japanese prison camp. Don't you read the newspapers?"

"Only the news I like."

"*Well?*" says Aunt Vivian. "Is he handsome?"

I throw up my hands. "For the last time. Not every girl needs a husband. For God's sake, look what it's done to you! No offense intended, Uncle Charlie."

He settles in his chair and picks up a newspaper. "None taken."

NOW, I FORGOT TO mention that Aunt Vivian and Uncle Charlie have children of their own. Three of them, to be exact, all of whom come tumbling into the dining room at the appointed hour and spoil our hard-won cynicism. Don't tell anyone, but I've always liked Tiny best. Pepper and Vivian are so goddamn exhausting and far too much like me. Tiny turned thirteen a few weeks ago and her personality's changing by the minute. She's always been a serious child, always worried about beggars and stray animals and the atom bomb, and now she spends all her time buried in schoolbooks and newspapers. At dinner she's awfully quiet while her sisters yammer on about *Singin' in the Rain*, which they've just seen for the ninth time, and how Pepper's going to be an actress when she grows up. Over dessert, I ask Tiny what's wrong, and she says she's been worried about the missing diplomats.

Which missing diplomats? I ask.

"The Englishmen," she tells me. "Mr. Burgess and Mr. Maclean. They've been gone a year now. Didn't you see the story in the *Times?*"

I don't know what she's talking about, of course, and I'm just drunk enough not to pay much attention when she tells me. What's a pair of British diplomats to me?

Still, something bothers me about the incident, though I can't say what. Coming so adjacent to the postcard and the FBI visit, possibly. When I stagger home to my apartment in Sutton Place, I stop by the little grocery around the corner to buy the usual quart of milk, and at the last instant I pick up a newspaper, too.

Mike the doorman nods as I swing through the revolving door. I collect my mail from the slot and climb the stairs as a form of exercise, as is my habit, in order to maintain my maidenly figure. Inside my apartment, I pour the milk into a glass and spread out the newspaper on the table. The story about the diplomats appears on page 7, below the fold.

STILL NO WORD FROM MISSING BRITISH DIPLOMATS, runs the headline.

A year has now passed since the disappearance of Mr. Guy Burgess and Mr. Donald Maclean, both of the British Foreign Office, caused an international uproar, and the British government admitted yesterday there is still no definitive word on their fate. The two men were last seen boarding a pleasure cruise aboard the ship *Falaise* in the English Channel on Friday, May 25th of last year and went ashore during a brief stop at the French port of Saint Malo, at which passports are generally not checked, according to the French government. Clothing and personal effects of both men were discovered in their cabin when the schooner returned to port at Southampton the following Sunday morning, and the alarm was raised when Mr. Maclean did not report to work as usual on Monday morning. His wife, Mrs. Melinda Maclean, who was then expecting their third child in a matter of weeks, apparently saw nothing amiss and did not inform his superiors at the Foreign Office until . . .

By now my memory is jogged. Burgess and Maclean—of course. What a fuss *that* was. I recall—now, don't laugh—my first thought was one of pity for poor Mrs. Maclean. At the time, it was perfectly clear to my dirty mind that the two missing diplomats had, in fact, run off together to liberate themselves from the disapproval of a Puritan world.

A year later, though, other details strike me. I don't know, maybe I didn't notice them before. For one thing, there's something odd about this business of the passports, and the clothing and personal effects left inside the cabin of the good ship *Falaise*. Why not take them with you? And my God, what kind of monster skips out on two children and a wife so very pregnant as that, unless he absolutely *has* to? Sex is lovely, all right, but surely Maclean could not have been so deficient in basic decency, even if he *was* a diplomat.

I fold the paper back up and finish the milk, and it's not until I wash the glass and return to the table that I turn my attention to the day's mail. I'm not much of a correspondent, I'm afraid, and I tend to receive few letters of a personal nature. Just the usual brusque envelopes from banks and charities and insurance companies, the occasional missive from some government department of this or that, hardly the kind of communication you rip open with trembling fingers.

So I'm surprised to discover a slim, light envelope tucked between the usual correspondence, marked PAR AVION on one side. I flip it over and find no return address, just my own name in beautiful handwriting, and my own address. I don't think to look at the postmark before I open it. Tug out a single, tissuelike sheet of airmail paper, folded over once, and unfold it. A square black-and-white photograph falls out, three children posing against a fence in what seems to be a zoo.

I return to the letter itself and begin to read.

Dearest Ruth,

I'm so sorry not to have written sooner. The time has simply slipped away from me. I thought perhaps you might like to see how your sweet nephews and niece are growing, so I took this photo of the children at the local zoo.

I'm writing to ask if you wouldn't mind coming out here to lend me a hand with the baby's arrival. I am so drained by the pregnancy, and as you remember, these ordeals are always difficult for me. I know you're busy with your own work, and I wouldn't ask if I didn't need your help so desperately.

Your loving sister,
Iris

P.S. Our apartment here reminds me so much of the one we shared in Rome, all those years ago. Do you remember how happy we were then? I was just thinking of what you said to me that last day. Am I too late to admit that you were right?

IRIS

APRIL 1940
Rome, Italy

Ruth was matter-of-fact, as you would expect. "All things considered, you're pretty lucky. A broken ankle is nothing."

"Don't forget the stitches," said Harry.

"Still, the ankle's the worst part, because she can't walk. Thank goodness that fellow was there to snatch her out of the way. What's his name again, Harry?"

"Digby. Sasha Digby. Works in the visa section with me."

"Well, I'll be sure to write him a note." Ruth patted the blanket covering Iris's leg. "Where is he, anyway?"

"Digby? He's gone back to the embassy. He's a hard worker, stays late every night." Harry took out his cigarette case.

"Put that away," Ruth said. "We're in a hospital."

"So?"

"So what if you light up an oxygen container by accident?"

Harry flicked his Zippo lighter. "I'll take my chances, all right? If ever a man needed a cigarette . . ."

Ruth turned back to Iris. "What were you *thinking*, pumpkin? I mean *honestly*. Isn't it just *like* you to cross the street without looking first. Head in the clouds."

"I didn't mean to."

"Of course you didn't *mean* to. You never do. Harry, what about this Digby fellow? Would it be all right to ask him to dinner or something? I feel *something's* called for."

"Sure, why not? He's a good man. They say—"

A soft knock sounded on the door. A blond head poked around the edge.

"Hello? Mind if I join you? Nurse said it was family only, but I talked my way through."

"Digby! Man of the hour. Come on in, it's a real party."

Sasha Digby stepped inside the room, looking exceptionally tall and golden. He lifted his hands, which both held bottles of champagne. "Managed to smuggle these in for the invalid. How is she?"

"Just fine," Iris croaked.

"Broken ankle, sixteen stitches, and black and blue all over," said Ruth. "*Otherwise* she's just fine. Thanks to you."

"Just grateful I happened along at the right instant." Sasha looked tenderly at Iris with his ultrablue eyes. "Fright of my life when I saw you step off that curb."

Possibly Iris was going to die of humiliation. She lay there on her white hospital sheets—in her green hospital pajamas—*trapped* beneath Sasha Digby's sympathetic blue gaze. Thank God she hadn't looked in a mirror yet. Meanwhile, Ruth was still wearing the tangerine dress from the fashion shoot, scarlet lips, blond hair curled and glossy.

"I'm so sorry," Iris said.

"Sorry? Sorry for what? *I'm* sorry." He held out his hand to Ruth across the bed. "Sasha Digby. We met at the reception a couple of weeks ago."

Ruth half rose from her armchair to take his hand. "What reception was that?"

"You remember, Ruthie. At the residence." Harry winked at Sasha. "Too sauced, I guess."

"No, I remember now. Right at the end, wasn't it?"

Sasha shrugged his rangy shoulders, set down one of the champagne bottles, and removed the foil from the other. "I arrived late, I'm afraid. Cups anywhere?"

"What are we celebrating, exactly?" Ruth asked.

"We are celebrating *life*, Miss Macallister." Sasha eased out the cork with the gentlest of pops. "The fact that we're all still in it."

Harry, having scrounged cups from the tray on the bedside table, held one out beneath the neck of the bottle. "I'll drink to that."

Sasha poured champagne into each glass—Harry ducked into the corridor and came back with a third and a fourth—and everybody cried joyously, *To life!*

IRIS SPENT A WEEK and a half in the hospital, because the nice Italian doctor didn't trust her not to overdo it on her broken ankle, which he'd set with such care and attention. In all that time, she never once looked in the mirror, although she read four novels and sketched portraits for all the nurses.

Nearly every day, right around noon, Sasha Digby arrived with a bouquet of flowers. Each time, it was a new variety—tulips, lilies, orange blossom, roses the most beautiful shade of blush pink. He pulled up a chair and asked how she was feeling, told her the news, shared funny stories about Harry in the embassy—*a real clown, your brother, but a good man, smarter than he lets on*—and that kind of thing. Day by day their conversation went a little deeper, edged a little closer to the intimate. Exactly one week after the accident, Sasha folded up the *Herald-Tribune*—he was reading aloud a review of an art exhibition recently opened in Florence—and said, "I'm awfully sorry about your mother. Harry told me what happened."

"Thank you."

"You must miss her."

"It's not as bad as it used to be. She wasn't herself after Da— after our father died. My grandparents raised us, really. And then our aunt got married and took over a little."

"That would be Vivian Schuyler, wouldn't it?"

Iris was startled enough to look him right in the eyes. "How did you know?"

"Oh, small world. I guess you've met my mother, Elsie Adams. She's a van der Wahl by birth. Practically grew up with your uncle."

Iris felt a little dizzy. "Then you know everybody back home."

"Oh, not everybody. We moved around when I was young. My father's in the oil business. He and my mother divorced when I was ten or eleven, I guess."

"I'm sorry."

"We all have our sorrows, don't we? Yours greater than mine, I think."

"It doesn't matter how great they are. Sorrow's sorrow."

He sat back in his chair.

"What's the matter?" she asked.

"*You.*"

But he caressed the word. Iris looked at the window and then down at her lap. She thought Ruth would handle this so much better. Ruth would know what to say. *Ask him about himself,* that's what Ruth would tell her to do, if Ruth could whisper in her ear right now.

"*Sasha.*" Iris paused. "That's not your real name, is it?"

"Hold on a moment."

Sasha set aside the newspaper and walked to the door, which he closed without a sound. He crossed the room to the window, opened it halfway, sat back down, and lit a cigarette. Only when he'd taken a long drag and exhaled again did he contemplate the ceiling and say, "My real name—and you can't tell a soul—*promise me, Iris.*"

"I promise."

"Cross your heart."

Iris crossed her heart.

He leaned his head toward her and spoke in a stage whisper. "Cornelius Alexander Digby."

"That's awful."

"Named for my father, who was named for my grandfather. Father being the old throwback he was, there wasn't any question of naming me something else. But my mother insisted on calling me Sasha. Probably it's why they divorced, in the end. The affairs he could pretend not to notice, but the nickname just rankled."

Iris couldn't help laughing. It was the tone of his voice, as if he were gossiping about film stars or something, not his own parents. She thought it was almost worth breaking her ankle to sit in a private room with this tall Apollo and laugh, the way you laughed with a friend of long standing—someone you trusted. Then the laughter died away. Iris glanced at his face—the thoughtful way he dragged on his cigarette, looking at her.

"You'd better put that out," she said. "The nurse will come back any minute, especially if she sees the door closed."

"Oh, hang the nurse." But he rose anyway and stubbed out the cigarette on the windowsill.

"You're awfully sweet to visit me like this. I hope you're not feeling guilty."

"I *am* feeling guilty, but that's not the reason I visit you." He tossed the spent cigarette out the window and came to sit on the edge of the bed. With his thumb he brushed the bruise on her cheek. "You have a black eye, did you know that?"

Iris gasped and threw her hand up to cover the eye in question. "Nobody told me!"

"Don't worry, I've seen worse. It wasn't a direct hit. Anyway, you still look beautiful." Now he touched the bandage on her forehead that covered eight stitches near her hairline. "The thing about growing up everywhere, you don't feel you belong anywhere. You see things, terrible things, people living—no, *existing*, hardly even that—just *surviving* in the most abject conditions, and when you return to a place like East Hampton, for example, and the Schuylers and the van der Wahls playing endless tennis at the club, drinking endless silly cocktails and having conversations that—well, you know what I mean, don't you? It's as if they can't see anything beyond their little world and the little people in it—"

"Yes, I know!" she said eagerly.

Sasha let out a long sigh, almost like relief. "I thought you would. Anyway, that's why I come to visit you. I knew—when I saw you at that party, the very first moment—I thought I recognized it."

"Recognized what?"

"You were different, that's all. You'd understand."

Before Iris could ask *what* she was supposed to understand—she thought she knew, but she wanted to hear him say it—Sasha made a tiny, sad smile, smacked his palm against his thigh, and stood up.

"I've got to be back at the embassy, I'm afraid. Say, when do they let you out of here? I'd go nuts, if I were you."

"Soon, I hope."

He stared down at her face, and for a moment Iris thought he might bend down and kiss her. Then he *did*—so swiftly that later she'd wonder if she only imagined it.

"See you tomorrow?" he said.

BUT HE DIDN'T COME back the next day, or the next. Iris stared at the vases of flowers, all lined up on the metal nightstand next to the bed, and wondered if Sasha regretted that instant of intimacy. Maybe he'd realized he'd shared too much of himself, or worried he'd led her to think he was in love with her, when of course he wasn't. How could he be? They hardly knew each other.

On the second Friday after the accident, Ruth carried in a pair of crutches and announced that the hospital was kicking Iris out to make room for some poor slob having his appendix removed. She helped Iris change into a dress, brushed her hair, applied some lipstick. She packed up Iris's things, including all the vases of flowers—she shoved them all into one vase, as if they weren't important—and carried them capably out the door and down the corridor to the taxi waiting outside the hospital, while Iris hobbled along beside her, small and mortified and crippled.

✦ ✦ ✦

SIX MONTHS HAD PASSED since Iris and Ruth arrived in Rome, and still Iris caught her breath whenever they turned the corner of Via dei Polacchi and their apartment came into view. They were here because of Harry. Last September, on the first anniversary of Mother's death, Harry had sent a telegram that went something like

HAIL SISTERS STOP STATE DEPT REQUESTS YOURS TRULY REMAIN ROME ANOTHER YEAR STOP HOW ABOUT YOU JOIN ME STOP YOURS EVER HARRY

Iris had looked at Ruth and Ruth had looked at Iris. The two of them lived together in the family's old apartment in Sutton Place, and it happened to be a chill, rainy, hopeless Thursday, and they had been counting the days until Harry would return home from his two years' overseas assignment in Rome, the standard Foreign Service appointment. Now Europe had declared another war on itself, and Harry wasn't coming home, and Iris thought she couldn't stand another New York winter like the last one, all raw and grief-frozen, Ruth going out nightly to anesthetize her sorrow while the empty apartment echoed with memories. *Should we go?* Ruth asked, and Iris said, *But there's a war on*, and Ruth answered, *Not in Italy, and at least we'd all be together.* What she didn't say, but what they both understood, was that their parents would have wanted it that way—the three of them together.

The next day Ruth and Iris had walked down to the steamship office and booked passage (second class) for Rome, and when they arrived three weeks later Italy was still so warm and fragrant and vivid, Iris felt like a flower coming to life after a year of winter. She would sit on a bench overlooking the Tiber, say, or a chair in some darling café, and close her eyes to imagine her petals unfurling to the sun. They had taken this apartment on Via dei Polacchi—two bedrooms, a tiny bathroom and a tiny kitchen, and a parlor with a tiny balcony overlooking a tiny courtyard—and every morning Iris opened her eyes to the ancient fresco on the ceiling and thought, *I am in Rome!*

Because she'd been away for a week, the street looked new— the building just a bit unfamiliar. She'd forgotten that particular smell of stone and paint and sunshine. Spring had invaded every corner, and Ruth had planted flowers in all the chipped terra-cotta pots, so the balcony and the windows had come back to colorful life.

The apartment was on the second floor (Italian style) and Ruth followed behind patiently with the flowers and the carpetbag while Iris climbed both flights, step by step, planting her crutches on each stair before she hoisted herself up.

When they arrived at the door at last, Iris imagined she heard a noise, but still she was perfectly shocked when Ruth swung the door open and everybody yelled *SURPRISE!*

WHAT A SWELL PARTY! All of Harry's embassy friends were there, and all their neighbors, and several people Iris didn't even recognize, and Sasha Digby's golden head floated above them all. The guests drank wine or gin and tonic and nibbled from the platters of cheese and crackers and prosciutto. Say what you would, Ruth had always known how to throw a real bash.

In the center of the room squatted a big, comfortable, second-hand armchair and a mismatched footrest (*I took up a collection,*

Ruth said) where Iris propped her ankle in its plaster cast and sat like a queen on a throne. Everyone took a turn in the stool next to her, refilled her drink and her plate, and wished her well. By evening, she was drunk and sick from too much cheese and utterly happy. The guests filed out, and pretty soon only Harry and Ruth and Iris and Sasha Digby remained. Ruth sat on the stool while Sasha and Harry sprawled on the floor. The apartment was a shambles and reeked of wine. A bottle of cheap Chianti stood on the floor and Harry kept refilling everyone's glass, except for Ruth, who drank gin and tonic. Iris said how perfectly lovely it had been, hadn't it been a perfectly lovely afternoon? Couldn't they just spend all their afternoons like this?

Ruth stretched her long legs. "Not once Hitler invades France. Then all hell's going to break loose, isn't it?"

"Is he really going to invade? Everybody's been so well behaved."

"Pumpkin, it's a *war*, remember? Of *course* he's going to invade. Isn't he, boys? I'm shocked he hasn't launched across the French border already. It's already April."

Harry lifted his thumb and forefinger to the corner of his mouth and solemnly zipped his lips.

"Sasha?" Ruth reached out with her toe and nudged his knee. "What've you got to say about Hitler? Anyone have the nerve to stop him?"

"I don't know." Sasha finished his wine and lit another cigarette.

"Irritable, are we?"

"Not at all. I just think there's no point speculating."

"Just because your old buddy Stalin's abandoned the anti-Fascist cause—"

"Don't talk garbage, Ruth. Christ."

Ruth rattled the ice in her glass. "Sasha's a Communist."

Harry snorted. "Says who."

"No, it's true. He's been to Spain and everything. Haven't you, Sasha?"

Harry looked at Sasha. "Digby? I didn't know that."

"I was working for a *newspaper*," Sasha said witheringly.

Ruth laughed and collected her cigarette from the edge of the ashtray. "Anyway, ask him about the dialectic and the failures of capitalism. He'll tell you all about it."

Iris looked at Harry lounging on his elbow—Sasha glaring at Ruth—Ruth in her red silk dress, calmly smoking a cigarette, tiny smile at the corner of her mouth. "It sounds as if everyone's been having a terrific time together."

"Don't be cross. We've gone out for a few laughs, that's all. Haven't we, Harry?"

Harry leaned back until he lay on the floor, arms crossed contentedly over his stomach, smoke trailing from the cigarette between his fingers.

"Anyway," Ruth said, "last night Sasha tried to stick up for Stalin and got his intellect all tied up in knots. This treaty's put him in a real pickle."

"What treaty?" Iris asked

"The Molotov treaty. Don't you read the newspapers? Nazis and Soviets in bed together. It goes against everything, doesn't it?"

"Don't be stupid," Sasha snapped.

"You see what I mean?"

"Aw, lay off him, Ruth," Harry said from the floor. "Everybody was a Communist in college. You grow out of it, that's all."

"But *has* he grown out of it? That's the question."

"You're deliberately misrepresenting me," said Sasha. "All I said was that capitalism has its problems, that's obvious, and at least the Soviet system shows a way forward."

"Yes, a shining way forward, all us good little workers marching in lockstep, dressed alike and thinking alike. If you ask me, communism and fascism aren't all that far apart."

"You're wrong. They couldn't be further apart."

"They're coming at tyranny from different angles, that's all. But you both end up in the same place."

Iris looked at Sasha's pink, angry face. He opened his mouth, glanced at Harry, and stuffed a cigarette between his lips instead.

"I think communism sounds very noble," Iris said. "I don't think it's wrong to have ideals."

"Of course not. You can make a beautiful argument for communism, right until you put it into practice and end up with bolshevism." Ruth crossed her ankles—she'd toed off her shoes long ago—and admired her long, elegant feet. "How many heretics has Stalin purged this year, Sasha?"

Sasha stood up and stalked to the kitchen.

"You shouldn't," Iris said.

"Oh, he's all right. He's just the type of fellow who doesn't like having his opinions challenged."

"Where'd you hear that about Stalin?" asked Harry. "Purges, I mean."

"Because you get a lot of Communists in my line of work. Artist types and all that. And a lot of them know a lot of Russians who disappeared, the last few years." Ruth snapped her fingers. "Just like that."

"But there must be some explanation," Iris exclaimed. "Maybe they went to work on a farm or something."

"Oh, honey." Ruth looked at Iris the way you might look at a kitten.

Harry sat up. "The reason I ask is because we've heard a lot of rumors, too. So if any of your friends might have information—"

"I'm not a snitch, Harry Macallister, and neither are my friends."

"I don't mean snitching. I mean it's something we need to know about."

"A snitch is a snitch, that's all. The lowest of the low." Ruth rose gracefully to her feet and bent to stub out her cigarette in the ashtray next to Iris. When she straightened, she caught sight of Sasha, who stood in the kitchen doorway holding a glass of either water or gin, just watching the three of them. Iris couldn't tell the color of his face, and whether he was still mad. She wished she could jump up and run to him and put her arms around him.

"I guess I ought to be going," he said.

"No, don't. I'm sorry. I'm a troublemaker, that's all." Ruth held out her hand. "Friends?"

He took her hand and shook it briefly. "Friends, sure."

"Aw, don't let her bust your chops, Digby. Nobody thinks you're some kind of goddamn Red."

"'Sall right." Sasha swallowed back the rest of whatever was in his glass, and Iris decided it was probably gin, after all. He turned to her and smiled. His eyes were awfully blue and not that steady. He made an extravagant bow before her and lifted her hand from her lap. "Pleasure to see you out of the sick bay and looking so smashing, Miss Macallister."

"I do *not* look smashing. I look *smashed*."

Sasha kissed the back of her hand. "When the soul is as beautiful as yours, madam, the face needs no adornment."

"Digby! You dog. Stay away from my sister with that kind of malarkey."

"Oh, be quiet, Harry," said Ruth. "Can't you see he's being sincere?"

Iris stared at the rumpled gold hair and the loose collar—the blue eyes beneath the slight overhang of his brows. His lips were wet with gin. He still hadn't let go of her hand.

"He's just teasing," she said softly.

Sasha winked and straightened. "What do you say, Macallister? Are you maybe headed to the Gallo d'Oro?"

"I'm game if you are. Ruth?"

Ruth leaned her elbows on the back of Iris's armchair, pure dynamite in her red dress, barefoot and long limbed and just shapely enough. Her red lipstick had long since faded to pink, but on Ruth it looked natural instead of cheap. *Smashing*—that was Ruth, not Iris. Not exactly beautiful, but striking in a way that was better than beauty and—more importantly—photographed extremely well. The tendons rippled in her throat as she finished her drink. "You two go without me. I can't leave poor Iris alone on her first night home, and anyway, I've got to clean up after you swine."

"Oh, don't stay on my account!" Iris exclaimed.

Ruth sent Sasha a funny look and tapped out another cigarette from the pack next to the ashtray. "Believe me," she said, "I'm not."

OF COURSE, THE TELEPHONE did eventually ring and some friend or another persuaded Ruth to go out after all. Iris fell asleep at eleven o'clock to an empty apartment and woke up after ten hours of monumental slumber, rich with dreams. She checked the other bedroom, where Ruth lay on the bed atop the covers, facedown, wearing nothing but her satin slip.

Iris hobbled into the kitchen on her crutches and made coffee. While the percolator got going, she found an overlooked glass or two, and a piece of discarded cheese crawling with ants. She cleaned them up. On her way past the front door, she spied a small white note on the floorboard. It was addressed to her and went like this:

Dolce Iris, is it too much trouble to meet a fellow for coffee in some scurvy dive where we won't be interrupted by motorcycles or siblings? I propose the Vespri Siciliani on Via del Plebiscito at 11. It's only a short walk from your place but if you'd rather not, no hard feelings. I'll wait until noon. Yours ever, S.

RUTH

JUNE 1952
New York City

Nine mornings out of ten, I'm the first person to report for duty at the Herbert Hudson Modeling Agency, and the day after Sumner Fox's visit I believe I set some kind of record, charging through the glassy lobby at twelve minutes to seven—this in a business where people regularly stagger to their desks at eleven o'clock, still drunk from the night before.

I flip on the lights and make coffee, and when the coffee's good and hot I sit at my desk, light a cigarette, and flip through the morning papers, because nothing distracts you from your woes like the woes of other people.

But my luck is out, I guess. First off, my eye catches some headline to do with those missing English diplomats. ONE YEAR LATER, MACLEAN WIFE AND CHILDREN CARRY ON, it laments. I suck down some coffee and turn the page, but you know how it is when a particular item of news fascinates you. You can turn the page, all right; you can force your attention on all kinds of worthy stories about corruption at City Hall and the plight of refugees in some war-stricken country you've never heard of. But your brain wants what it wants, does it not?

Eventually I give in. I flip back to the column on Maclean's family—a blurred photograph of the Maclean children ducking through the school gates, one of his wife, Melinda (who happens to be American, it seems), gazing haughtily from the doorway of their house in the English suburbs. I learn that Mrs. Maclean, who delivered their third child only three weeks after her husband's disappearance, gives short shrift to any insinuations that Maclean has defected to the Soviet Union. "I will not admit that my husband, the father of my children, is a traitor to his country," she insists.

HERBERT WALKS IN AT half past eight. I rise to take his coat and hat and usher him into his office. Bring him his coffee and cigarettes and arrange myself in the chair before his desk for our usual morning chat.

Most people are not aware that Herbert Hudson suffered a stroke in the summer of 1945, in between the capitulation of Hitler and the capitulation of Tito. I'm telling you now so you'll understand why his attention wanders from time to time, as we review the day ahead, and why he sometimes sticks the wrong word in the middle of a sentence or two. I figure as long as I understand his meaning, who cares about the delivery?

This morning Herbert's having a little trouble lighting his cigarette—the right side of his body being a touch clumsier than the left, though you'd have to know him extremely well to notice—so I lean forward and help to steady his hand until the end of the cigarette flares comfortably orange. He nods his thanks and asks how Barbara's getting along.

"The headshots are out of sight." I rummage through the manila folder in my lap. "Bunny said she was an absolute professional, instincts and everything."

Herbert removes the cigarette from his mouth and brings the photograph up close. He studies her for some time. Herbert's got an eye, stroke or not—I mean his aesthetics never missed a beat. And I don't mean dirty, either; Herbert always could separate his libido from his professional judgment. For example. You can take a girl who absolutely drips sex appeal, or a girl so beautiful she might have been sent on loan from the archangel choir, and stick this girl in front of a camera and get absolutely nothing. I would put my sister in that category, by the way; not that Iris is as beautiful as the angels, maybe, but she has looks—at least she *did*, before she dropped all those kids—and also this winsome, sugar-cookie appeal that makes you want to tuck her into your arms and (if you're a man, I guess) sire ten thousand children with her. But in photographs she looks so ordinary she's almost plain. There's simply no angle and no light that translates her particular beauty into two flat dimensions.

Of course, if you're not interested in a modeling career, this is no hindrance at all. Miss Barbara Kingsley, on the other hand, is hell-bent on landing the cover of *Vogue*, and if this world were a just world she should, because those headshots aren't just out of sight, they're practically out of the whole goddamn universe. The best test shots we've ever taken. But this world is not a just world, and Barbara happens to be a Negro. So after a while Herbert sets down the photograph and sits back in his chair to smoke.

"Shame," he says.

"You just watch. I'm going to make her a sensation, I tell you, if I have to sleep with every ad man and magazine editor in town."

"America isn't ready for a girl like that."

"I'm counting on it. I say we use it to our advantage. She'll be a surprise—she'll be a scandal. The *publicity*, Herbert. Nothing ever got publicity because it was the same as what came before." I reach over his desk and pluck back the photograph. "Besides, she's drop-dead gorgeous. She's got a *look*, Herbert. What was the first thing you taught me? The look is everything. The *next* look, not the same old. She's the *next look*. She's the face of the *future*."

I'll say this for Herbert, he's no bigot—at least no more than we human animals can help, having bigotry bred into our blood, it seems. Certainly, he isn't against a Negro model on principle, and the professional in him would have to be blind not to see Barbara Kingsley's potential. But he doesn't want the trouble, not at his age. And he doesn't want *me* to have the trouble because he loves me.

"Besides, she needs this," I continue, knowing Herbert to be kind of soft in the region of his heart. "She's got a sick mother, comes from nothing. She'll work hard and keep herself clean. She knows what's at stake, she knows she'll have to be better and smarter and cleaner than any other girl in the shop, and she's willing to do whatever it takes. We've got a chance to make a real difference for her, Herbert."

"Shit," he says.

"Good. That's settled. I'll get the prints made and start working the phones today. And now I've got a question for you."

Herbert makes a resigned gesture of his good arm.

"What's your opinion of this McCarthy fellow?"

"McCarthy?"

"You know who I mean. The senator with the bee in his bonnet about the Communists, holds all the hearings. The Hollywood blacklist. Him."

Herbert makes a noise of disgust.

"Me too." I reach for his cigarettes and light one for myself. "But you know, there's a grain of truth there. For example, I personally knew at least one Communist working for the US government. The foreign diplomatic service. He was stationed at embassies around the world. And I can't say for certain he wasn't passing on information to the Soviets, all that time."

The funny thing is, Herbert makes no sign of surprise whatsoever. He just asks, "How do you know this fellow?"

"Met him when I was in Rome."

"How do you know he's still a Communist? A lot of us were Communists."

"Herbert! You don't say!"

He shrugs in his lopsided way. "Seemed like the humane way forward. Came to my senses when I saw what that goddamn thug Stalin was up to."

"Well, this fellow's different. He's a true believer. He'll rationalize anything." I pause to inhale. "He's also married to my sister."

Herbert tries to purse his lips for a whistle. Doesn't quite succeed. "Why haven't you said anything?"

"Because I'm not a snitch, Herbert, for all my many faults. I make no windows into men's souls, as a wise woman said before me, and anyway he's my brother-in-law, for God's sake."

"So what gives now?" Herbert asks. "Maybe something to do with Sumner Fox walking through my office yesterday?"

"How'd you know that?"

"Walls made of glass, my dear." He waves his hand. "And you can't mistake Sumner Fox, not if you're a Yale man."

"Well, I'm not a Yale man, nor yet a football lunatic. I never could see the point of grown men smashing each other up on a grass field for no good reason. But I do pay attention when the FBI wants to ask me a question or two about my sister."

"You need a lawyer?"

"Don't worry, the family's lousy with them. I was just thinking about the Rosenbergs."

Herbert makes another noise. "Fixed trial if I ever saw one."

"Well, maybe it was. But there must be a whole stack of evidence they couldn't reveal in a public court of law, because it's top secret. That just stands to reason. And you can't deny the Soviets exploded an atom bomb in—what was it, '49?—anyway, long before anyone expected they could. You can't tell me there weren't scientists leaking information, probably a whole network of them, whether the Rosenbergs were in it or not. The thing is, most of those traitors probably didn't consider themselves traitors at all. Just smart, well-meaning men like my brother-in-law, who thought they were doing the world a favor by bringing forward the great Communist revolution."

Herbert stubs out his cigarette and folds his arms at me. "So what's your point, doll?"

"I don't know what my point is. I guess I'm just trying to figure something out."

The morning sun leaks through a corner of the modern plate glass behind him. My God, he looks so much older than he did when we first met—so much older than when I started working for him. I used to take dictation at this desk, pencil poised, while Herbert rattled off a mile a minute. Now his face sags to the right and his eyes have that rheumy sheen to them, so you wonder if he can really see you at all. Over the years, his attitude toward me has taken on an avuncular quality, which might strike some of you as distasteful since we began as lovers. But nothing ever stays the same, does it? The accumulation of age and experience changes us daily. If it doesn't, you'd better worry.

Still, Herbert's changed more than most. He drinks his coffee with an unsteady hand and contrives to light another cigarette while the wheels spin in his head, manufacturing advice to his unruly protégée.

At last he speaks in his slow, halting voice.

"Do as you think best, doll. That's why I hired you."

I KEEP MYSELF BUSY as best I can. I order the prints for Barbara's portfolio and make at least two dozen calls on her behalf. By lunchtime, I've found my stride. I prop my feet on the desk and call up Barbara herself to deliver the good news. I feel like Santa Claus.

"That's nice, sugar," she says, "but I'll wait to celebrate once I see my face on something bigger than an Aunt Jemima advertisement."

"Now, Barbara. That's the wrong way to look at things. Sunny side up, I always say. In the first place, that's a big account, Aunt Jemima. In the second place, we've got the ball rolling, haven't we?"

"Sure we do. Just like that Sisyphus fellow."

"Say, I'll tell you what. I'll take you out tonight, champagne and everything, some nice club where we can listen to good music and get our picture in the paper."

"Have you got rocks for brains, sister? Just what club do you think is going to let the pair of us in, like one of those black-and-white cookies?"

I stub out my cigarette. "I see what you mean."

"Think you can just snap your white fingers and say *abracadabra?*"

I swing my feet to the floor and lean into the receiver. "You think I can't? Is that some kind of challenge, Miss Kingsley?"

"I got five bucks says we end up uptown at Smalls where they aren't so particular about pedigree."

"You're on. Meet me outside the Palmetto at eight thirty on the nose in your best dress. Some number that looks good in photographs, say."

"Oh, you think you got a plan, boss lady?"

"Miss Kingsley," I say, "we can't miss."

ALL RIGHT, SO I like to manage things. I like to take charge of people's affairs—it's one of my many talents. *Boss lady,* Barbara called me, and what's the matter with that? Someone has to be the boss, or nothing would get done. I've managed the careers of dozens of women—a few men, too—and nobody's complained about the results, at least not to my face. The fact is, most people are too softhearted, or they lack a certain clarity of vision, or they don't want to make mistakes, or—this is the big one—*they're afraid of what others will think of them.* They don't want to take that kind of responsibility. It's hard work and requires you to make decisions people won't like. But I'll tell you what, there's nothing like the satisfaction of a plan brought off to perfection, of knowing you've led your flock to greener pastures.

It would make a nice, neat story to say that I became this way because of my father dying when I was eleven years old, and my mother sort of absolving herself of any further parental responsibilities because she had her grief to contend with. But I'm afraid I've always been a managing person, the kind of girl who brings home animals and organizes the canned vegetables according to the alphabet and puts together the neighborhood stickball teams.

And there's Iris. I was always protective of her, when we were growing up. There was the time we started at Chapin, a school far above our social standing as it then was, and while nobody dared to snub me they had no trouble snubbing Iris, so I spent that entire first year blackmailing girls to play with my sister and invite her to parties and that kind of thing. Iris never knew. Or when we used to summer with my grandparents in Glen Cove, Long Island, and Iris was afraid of every little thing, sailing and swimming—in the Sound, that is, instead of a nice safe swimming pool—and especially strangers.

Anyway, her tender heart was staggered when Daddy killed himself. Mother had discovered the body first thing in the morning, so there was a terrifying fuss of screaming and telephones and ambulance men. Harry was off prepping at Hotchkiss by then, so it was just the two of us kids, Iris and me. She started having these strange shivering fits, so I took her into our room and crawled into bed with her to keep her warm. In those days nobody told you what to do with news like that—grief like that. Maybe a doctor would give you a sleeping pill or something, but otherwise you were just supposed to swallow it whole and not bother anybody else with the awkwardness of your sorrow. Fine for somebody like me, but for Iris? So I just held her and stroked her hair—didn't say a thing. In the morning she came to and drank a little milk that I fetched for her, and a week later she marched bravely into St. James Episcopal Church on Madison Avenue for the funeral, holding my hand. She wore the navy blue dress and coat I picked out for her at Bergdorf's. I was so proud of her. On our backs, I felt the prurient gazes of all the assembled so-called mourners, and I just thought to myself, *You will never understand what a wreck she was, only a week ago.*

You know, I met a shrink at a party once who said I had a God complex, whatever that meant, and for a long time afterward our entire conversation made me indignant, whenever I thought about it. For the record, I don't think I'm God, or even one of His archangels. Just a mortal woman doing her best with what's entrusted to her care.

But I do understand the frustration God feels when He shows us the right way forward, time and again, and what do we poor mortals do? We go the opposite direction, almost to spite Him, and sure enough we come to grief.

ANYWAY, YOU CAN'T SAY Barbara Kingsley doesn't follow my instructions to the letter. When the taxi screeches to a halt outside the Palmetto at eight thirty-two, out pops the most ravishing woman you've ever seen in your life, wearing a coat of white fox and a sequined dress that could bring sight to a blind man. I step forward and pay the driver myself, and he scoots right off. I turn back to gather my bevy of sirens and there stands Barbara, hands on hips, laughing her head off.

"All right, boss lady," she says. "I think I see your plan. Where do I fit in?"

"Right at the front, Miss Kingsley."

I won't lie, it took me all afternoon and a couple of years' worth of favors to round up a cast like that one. I won't name any names, but you've heard of them. I take Barbara's arm and proceed straight up to the maître d' at his elegant mahogany podium. "Reservation for eight, front row. Macallister party."

The maître d' looks at me and at Barbara and at me again. He leans forward and says, under his breath, "There seems to have been some mistake."

"No mistake. A celebration dinner, a case of your best champagne at least."

"Miss Macallister, I don't think you understand."

"What's to understand? Are we not dressed in the approved style?"

"No, your dress—your *dress*"—he's trying to avert his eyes from Barbara—"your dress is—well enough—but we have other rules, madam, for the comfort of our customers—"

"Oh. Oh, dear. I see what you mean. How careless of me." I turn to the group behind me. "My darlings, there seems to be some trouble. Apparently somebody in our party isn't quite up to snuff when it comes to the strict moral standards of the Palmetto Club. I expect it's *you*, M—."

Everybody laughs. I spin back to the maître d', who's caught a glimpse of the faces assembled behind me and turned a fine shade of strawberry pink.

"Don't worry, Mr. Billings. We quite understand your predicament. In fact, I feel certain that none of us will trouble you for entry into this"—I cast a supercilious glance around the lobby—"this fine old establishment, ever again. Will we, ladies?"

"Certainly *not*," says M—.

"And we'll pass the word to our friends, as well. God forbid the Palmetto should be forced to admit just *anyone*."

At that instant, the telephone rings atop Mr. Billings's fine mahogany podium. He lifts the receiver and says *Palmetto Club*, qua-vering voice. Then—*Yes, sir.* Then—*No, sir.* Then—*Right away, sir.*

He sets down the receiver and clears his throat.

"If you'll follow me, ladies," he says, and he leads us through the archway into the club, where the world-famous Bobby Blue Orchestra tunes up to the rhythm of a dozen popping champagne corks.

IRIS

When Ruth stumbled out of her bedroom and asked where Iris was going, Iris told her a lie.

"Just for a walk," she said.

Ruth looked her up and down, from the top of her dark, curling head, to her pink lipstick to her blue dress with the Peter Pan collar, crutches, stockings, leather slingback shoe, and plaster cast held an inch or two above the floorboards. When she returned to Iris's face, she wore that tiny smile at the corner of her mouth. Ruth tightened the belt on her purple silk kimono. "Is that so?"

"I need a little fresh air, that's all."

"Sure you do. What about a hand with those stairs?"

Iris hesitated. "All right."

Ruth lent her a steadying hand down the stairs and held the doors for her. Iris thanked her and started off down the sidewalk.

Ruth called after her, "Don't do anything I wouldn't do!"

✦ ✦ ✦

IRIS COULDN'T REMEMBER A time when Ruth wasn't the prettiest, the cleverest, the most athletic of the Macallister twins. It simply went without saying!

Although people said it anyway. They'd remarked on it all the time, when Ruth and Iris were growing up. The twins would sit side by side at the dinner table or on the beach or astride their ponies, and Ruth's blond hair would catch the light and just shimmer, or she would open her mouth and say something brilliant, or she would leap off somewhere gracefully and long leggedly, and Iris would be left behind with her frizzy curls the color of dirt, her tied tongue, her pale and chubby limbs.

A couple of months before the day that would mark the end of their old lives, Ruth and Iris had gone out sailing with their father and Grandpa Walker, who was their mother's father. (Harry had been forced to stay at home and polish the silver, on account of some misdemeanor.) Iris had always liked her grandfather. He didn't talk much—leaving most communication to the women in his life—but he was calm and thoughtful and seemed to find the same things funny that Iris did. He had been in the garment business and made a killing during the war, and he and Granny Walker had invested some of their spoils in a rambling, half-timbered, brand-new pile in Glen Cove, Long Island, so their daughters could learn to sail and play tennis and meet all the right sorts. And it worked! The oldest had duly married a nice stockbroker from a good family—Harry and Ruth and Iris were born—the stock market set records practically every day. Nobody could say that the Walkers' investment hadn't made a solid return, indeed.

Anyway, there they were, the halcyon end of summer of the halcyon final year of the Roaring Twenties. They'd been out cruising in Long Island Sound for a few hours, all the way down to Orient Point and back again. Ruth was an enthusiastic sailor—absolutely fearless. She shimmied up the mainmast and leaned out over the side as they heeled; she managed sheets confidently and relished the shivering of the sails as they changed tack. Her hair whipped in the wind; her bare skin glowed in the sunshine. As they approached the harbor, the breeze picked up, stronger and stronger until it was almost a gale. The boat tore through the water at a steep angle, foam flying from the bow, and Ruth screamed with delight. Iris sat paralyzed in the stern and prayed they wouldn't capsize. Next to her, Daddy held the tiller with a firm, delicate touch and told her not to worry.

Sure enough, they cruised right into the calm of the harbor a half hour later and moored without incident. But while they were loading up the car to drive back to Stoneywild—this was the name the Walkers had given to their infant estate—Iris happened to pass by Grandpa Walker just as he said to her father, "That's some girl, that Ruth of yours. Hope you've got yourself a good baseball bat."

Daddy had laughed. "She's a beauty, all right. Poor little Iris."

Iris hadn't stuck around to hear what Grandpa Walker thought of that, or maybe she just didn't remember. But she did remember those words *poor little Iris*. They had whacked her like an electric shock. True, she'd heard that kind of observation plenty of times before—pretty much everybody was dazzled by Ruth and felt only pity for Iris, if they noticed her at all. But she'd never before heard Daddy call her *poor little Iris*. Until now, Daddy had always treated the two of them with strict evenhandedness. Everyone else might exclaim over Ruth's beauty and brains and spirit and then turn politely to Iris and squint up his face with the effort of conjuring a compliment, but Daddy never failed to dole out his admiration in equal shares. So it shocked Iris to learn the truth. What he really thought of his two daughters.

As it turned out, of course, those were among the last words she ever heard from her father, so they echoed in Iris's head ever after—*poor little Iris*, the diminutive to Ruth's superlative.

SO MAYBE THAT WAS why Iris climbed laboriously down all those stairs and hobbled with her crutches and her plaster cast to the Vespri Siciliani to meet Sasha Digby for coffee. To Sasha, she wasn't *poor little Iris*. She was *dolce Iris*. Yesterday evening, he'd looked at Ruth as if she were loathsome, and he'd turned to Iris and kissed her hand. Iris would have hobbled ten miles to meet Sasha Digby for coffee, but luckily he chose the café with consideration for her injuries, and she only had to hobble a couple of hundred yards before she arrived there at ten minutes past eleven, a little breathless.

Sasha rushed out from beneath the awning to help her with her crutches. He almost carried her to her seat. He called the waiter and ordered her a cappuccino and a piece of olive oil cake, specialty of the house, and he beamed at her.

"I was afraid you wouldn't come. I thought it was too much trouble."

"Of course not. I need a little fresh air."

"Then I was worried about all those stairs."

"Ruth helped me."

"Oh, of course." The smile drooped a little. "Did you tell her where you were going?"

Iris hesitated for an instant before she decided that she would *never* lie to this man, *ever*. "No," she said firmly.

"Why not?"

"Because she thinks she should protect me, for some reason."

The smile ratcheted back up. "I can't imagine why."

"I'm not as innocent as I *look*, you know. I've read *Balzac*."

"I know. I saw you in the museum, remember?" He leaned forward. "Let them think what they want, I say. Let them underestimate you."

Before Iris could come up with anything to reply to *that*, the waiter arrived with the coffee and the cake. Sasha asked did she mind if he smoked. She said of course not.

"But *you* don't smoke, do you?"

"No."

"Why not?"

"I don't know. I never wanted to." The cappuccino was almost too hot to sip, but Iris tasted it anyway. It was so much easier to pay attention to coffee than to Sasha. He was so big and electric! And they were sitting so close! This was nothing like sitting together in the hospital. This was like a man and a woman who were interested in each other, meeting for coffee to find out just how interested they really were. Sasha's long legs stretched out past the opposite edge of the round table. His shoulder nearly touched hers. He wore a conservative suit of navy blue, probably the same one he'd worn at the Villa Borghese. His big, bony fingers struck the match and lit the cigarette that stuck from his mouth.

Iris liked the shape of his hand and the smell of strong Italian coffee and the proximity of his leg to hers. She loved his eyes, even though she wasn't looking at them.

"Tell me about Spain," she said.

"Spain? What about it?"

"Why did you go?"

He made a ribbon of smoke. "It was the thing to do, I guess. If you were a young fellow just out of college, impatient with injustice—"

"A Communist?"

"And if I was?"

"I'd say it sounds just like you. Filled with hope and idealism. Were you?"

He smiled. "Not a party member, no. But I had Communist friends, and I wasn't unsympathetic. Capitalism's a shambles, misery everywhere, that's obvious to anyone who thinks. And none of your capitalist so-called democracies gave a damn about Hitler."

"You must have been devastated about the pact. The Nazis and the Soviets."

He looked away. "I was disappointed, yes. But every country's got a right to protect itself, even the Soviets, and by then everyone else was just kowtowing to Germany. I guess Stalin did the best he could. I don't say I agree, I don't say I wasn't disappointed, but who gave in to Germany at Munich? Not the Soviets."

Iris looked at the side of his face and thought how sharp and noble his profile was. "Is that why you ended up in the State Department?"

"Oh, muddled my way in, really. Went to Spain, as I said, with the *Herald-Tribune*. Saw enough of war to make me think I should try to do something to prevent it, so I came home and crammed for the civil service exam. Spent a year in Washington before they sent me here, summer of 1939."

"Only a year? They must think highly of you."

"Or wanted to get rid of me."

"What about the war?" she asked.

"What about it?"

"What will you do? If Mussolini goes with Hitler, I mean."

"Not if. *When*."

"Well, then? What happens? You can't stay *here*, can you?"

Sasha set the cigarette in the ashtray. "Of course we stay. A neutral embassy plays a vital role in war. How else do we get all these Jews out of Europe? Embassy staff stays to the bitter end, it's part of the job. *You*, on the other hand."

"Me?"

"You and your sister. You'll have to evacuate."

Iris glanced to the side, where a man and a woman shared a little round table identical to theirs. The man wore a plain gray-green uniform and the woman sat so close to him, you couldn't see a single crack of sunlight between them. The man nuzzled her cheek and whispered something. The woman ducked her head and *just like that*—quick as a snake—he kissed her neck. Iris was mesmerized. She tried to keep her mind on the war.

"Ruth says Hitler's going to invade France any day now."

"She might be right. But Mussolini won't declare himself, not at first. He'll wait to see which way the wind blows."

"How do you know that?"

"He's a canny old bastard, that's all. Like all Fascists. They don't care about ideals."

To Iris's right, the man looked up from his lover's neck and winked at Iris. She tore herself away and glanced up at the side of Sasha's face. "But *you* do."

Sasha looked down and smiled at her. Probably he saw the

whole exchange—Iris mesmerized by the intimate couple, the man winking back.

"Maybe," he said.

SASHA INSISTED ON WALKING her back to her apartment and helping her up the stairs. It was all his fault, he said, because he should've taken her to coffee that day at the Villa Borghese. He should have worked up the nerve to greet her sooner.

"How long were you following me?" she asked.

"Since you walked in."

"I didn't realize I was so intimidating."

They paused on the landing between the first and second floors, so Iris could catch her breath. The stairway was shaded and cool. Sasha kept his hand under her elbow. "Harry tells me you're an artist yourself."

"Did he say that? I draw, that's all."

"Are you any good?"

She looked right up into his eyes and said, "I think so."

"May I see some of your work?"

"Right now, you mean?"

He glanced up the stairs. "Why not?"

Iris checked her watch. Ruth was supposed to have a gig at noon today, and it was ten past the hour. "Only if you have the time."

"I'll make time."

THE APARTMENT WAS EMPTY, thank God. Iris called Ruth's name, just to be sure.

"She's at a photo shoot," Iris said to Sasha.

"Of course."

The apartment seemed larger than before. The crutches echoed from the walls as Iris opened the window shutters to let the sunshine in. "Would you like something to drink?" she asked.

"Don't trouble yourself. I can fetch it myself."

Sasha disappeared into the kitchen and Iris swung herself into the armchair, which still stood like a throne in the middle of the floor. She propped up her ankle with a sigh. Sasha returned with two glasses of gin and tonic. He handed her one.

"It's very strong," she gasped.

Instead of taking the nearest chair, Sasha walked to the window and leaned his shoulder against the frame. His eyes seemed to disappear underneath his heavy brow. "You know, I don't think I've ever seen a pair of twin sisters less alike than you and Ruth."

"That's what everyone says. I take after my mother, I guess."

"And Ruth? She takes after your father?"

"No, she's more like my aunt Vivian. Tall and blond." Iris smiled. "Like you."

"Then I guess it's true, that we're attracted to our opposite."

Iris coughed on her drink. Sasha started toward her, but she waved him away and hoisted herself back on her feet. "I should get those drawings before they miss you at the embassy."

"There's no rush," he said.

She hobbled to her bedroom and pulled the sketchbook from her nightstand. When she turned around, Sasha stood in the doorway, holding his drink and hers.

Iris held out the sketchbook. "Be kind."

He set down her drink and took the sketchbook from her hand. "I am *always* kind, Iris."

Iris retreated to sit on the edge of the bed, sipping her gin and tonic. The mattress was old and creaked every time she shifted, so she sat still and looked around the room, everywhere except directly at Sasha, who leaned one elbow on the dresser and examined her sketches, one after another. He furrowed his brow and took his time. Whenever she glanced from the corner of her eye to his face, he was frowning. Her hands shook a little. She drank the rest of the gin and tonic in a gulp, so she wouldn't spill it, and tucked her other hand under her thigh.

"These are very good," said Sasha.

"Do you think so?"

"Yes." He pointed to Ruth's profile. "You've got the sense of her, not just the look of her. You can almost tell what she thinks of the book. And the potted palm, the proportions just right. Excellent."

"Thank you."

"It's *how* you look at things, you know. It's how you really *see* them."

He stared at her again with his technicolor eyes, as if to prove his point—as if Iris were the only person in the universe, the only person who mattered. Iris couldn't speak. Ruth would probably have had some clever reply ready, but then Ruth could never have drawn those sketches. It was one or the other, really.

Sasha set down the drawings.

The bedroom was not quite square, maybe twelve feet by ten feet. The door was open partway, but the stuffy air and the shuttered window made Iris feel that they were together in some kind of cave. This room, in which she'd slept for months, became a new room altogether. It even smelled different, because of the gin and tonic and all the cigarette smoke steeped in Sasha's clothes. He moved his arm, and Iris thought he was maybe going to fish out his cigarettes, but he only leaned his elbow on the dresser as he stared at her.

"Does your family understand this? How good you are, I mean?"

Iris shook her head.

"No, I guess they wouldn't. Your crowd—*our* crowd—you know who I mean—they *think* they have taste, but they only like what they're told to like. What's already been approved by some gallery or museum or the arts page of the *New York Times*."

"Some *man*, probably."

Sasha's eyebrows rose. "Yes, some man, undoubtedly. Nobody takes a woman's art seriously. Not even women."

"Of course not. It's too sentimental, isn't it? Too banal or trivial or domestic. Not *important* enough."

"What's *important*," Sasha said, "is what's important to *you*."

"Oh, that's easy to *say*—"

"No, I mean it. As long as *you* know you've done something worthwhile."

"But what use is that? If nobody else cares. If nobody else *sees*."

"*I* care." He set his fingertips on the sketchbook like a spider. "*I* see them."

He wasn't looking at the drawings, though. He was looking at *her*—so earnestly that Iris thought maybe he was looking at the ugly bruise on her cheekbone, or a smear of dirt, or some other mesmerizing flaw. She flexed her fingers around the empty glass. She had something to say, but she didn't know how to put it into words. There was nothing in the whole English language that could express what she was thinking.

Sasha turned his head away. He lifted her hairbrush and ran his thumb along the bristles, put it down and examined a lampshade—a book—he grunted when he saw the title, *The Good Earth*—approval or disapproval?—the cheap fountain pen on her desk. When he set the pen down again, it rolled right to the edge, and he caught it just in time, though his head had already turned in the opposite direction, toward the mirror above the dresser. Iris could just see the reflection of the left side of his face, and it startled her. He looked so old! Not like an old man, of course, but a man of *experience*. Worldly. A dozen years older than she was.

But—he was *nervous*! He was more nervous than he was in the hospital, when he all but *admitted* that he was in love with her—yes, she was sure of it, he was in love with her!—all because he was in her bedroom now, not a hospital room, and there was no nurse hovering by the door and no sister in the other room—nobody at all but the two of them.

His eyes met hers in the mirror and looked swiftly away.

A burst of joy rushed all the way to Iris's fingertips. Joy and—what's the word?—not so much confidence as *sureness*, the knowledge that she was *absolutely right*, that their meeting here in Rome, two American misfits who belonged to nobody else, bore the fingerprint of fate. She could say this to herself—*fingerprint of fate*—because she was a romantic and so was he.

It wasn't easy to stand up when you had a broken ankle, and your arm was already sore from propping yourself on crutches all morning and all yesterday afternoon, but Iris figured this was the most important thing she'd ever do in her life. And maybe it was. She made enough noise that Sasha turned around, a little alarmed. The room was small, remember, and it took only a step or two to reach him. She ran her fingertips along the line of that pugnacious, determined brow. She continued along the side of his face and the rim of his ear until her palm settled on the warm skin at the back of his neck. They kissed each other at exactly the same instant.

IRIS DIDN'T TELL HIM she'd never been to bed with a man before, and he didn't ask. Only afterward, when he lay shuddering on top of her, and she gripped his wet shoulders for dear life, did he whisper—humbly, wonderingly—into her hair, *Was I the first?*

She nodded.

He lifted himself on his elbows and stared down at her. His skin gleamed, his cheekbones were as bright as raspberries. His eyes were so blue, it was unearthly. Her damp stomach stuck to his damp stomach, how extraordinary. Inside her, he was perfectly still. She wondered vaguely if she would have a baby. Wasn't that what happened when you went to bed with a man? But the thought didn't frighten her. Nothing frightened her anymore.

Well? she whispered.

He dipped his head and kissed her lips. *You're very brave,* he told her.

Brave how? she wondered. Brave for not telling him she was a virgin? Or brave for going to bed with him at all, in the middle of the day, in the middle of Rome, when she was an innocent and they'd only just met?

She slid her hands southward until she reached the curve of his bottom, which felt to her as if it had spent its whole life just waiting for her palms.

Well, I'm glad, she said.

AFTER A FEW MORE drowsy moments, Sasha lifted himself away, opened the shutters, and walked to the bathroom. He returned a moment later with a damp cloth, which he handed diffidently to Iris, and picked up his clothes from the floor. She rolled laboriously on her side and watched him. Through the window came a draft of warm spring air, smelling of sunshine and metropolitan grime. She offered to knot his necktie, so he knelt on the floor next to the bed. When she was done, he picked up her clothes, folded them, and put them on the nightstand. Then he kissed her.

"I'd stay all afternoon if I could," he said.

"No, you'd better go."

"When will I see you again?"

"Whenever you want. But not here. I don't want Ruth to know. Not yet. She'll have kittens."

He winced. "No, of course not. How do I find you? Telephone?"

"Yes, telephone. I'll make sure to answer first."

Iris marveled at herself, so composed and assured, making arrangements with her lover. What a difference from an hour ago! Now she'd seduced a man. There was no question who had seduced whom—*she* was the one who unbuttoned his shirt—*she* was the one who drew his hands to the zipper of her dress. Objectively, she knew she was bruised all over, that she had a plaster cast on her left leg plus stitches on her forehead near her hairline. Still she felt utterly beautiful, absolutely irresistible. She idled her hand on his cheek.

"Damn it all," he said. "I want to see you again. Tonight. And the next night, and the next, and all the nights after that."

"Then Ruth will know for sure."

He swore again. "Can't you get away at all?"

She squinted. "I could tell her I'm going away on a drawing holiday. There's this class I've been taking at the American Institute.

I could say we're going to sketch monasteries in Tuscany or something."

"That's it. You could stay at my flat. I can't take any vacation myself, or they'd know something was up. But I'd come home early every night. I'd take the most lavish care of you. We'd have a week or more."

"Like paradise. But not until the stitches are out. And the cast."

"How long is that?"

"Four more weeks for the cast. Is that all right? The first week of May."

Sasha bent his head to kiss her hand. He'd brushed his hair wet, and the warm light from the courtyard turned his hair a sleek, dark gold. Iris thought how soft his hair felt as it fell on her stomach and breasts and thighs.

"All right," he said. "The first week of May."

RUTH

JUNE 1952
New York City

I first discovered Barbara Kingsley in the same way Columbus discovered America—while I was busy looking for something else. There was this party in Greenwich Village, some artist pal, low-down dive kind of crowd, and I was hoping to glimpse a certain on-again, off-again beau of mine and climb on again.

At the time, Barbara was doing some artist work—you know what I mean, sitting there nude on a stool to inspire a bunch of men and their drawing pencils—and she lounged on a sofa between a pair of girls, bearing a glass of gin and a bored expression. The bells went off in my head. I forgot all about Mr. On Again and bustled right up to her.

"Excuse me. Ruth Macallister." I stuck out my hand. She not so much shook it as curled her fingers briefly around mine. "If you haven't already signed with a major New York modeling agency, I'd like you to consider mine."

"You don't even know my name, Miss Macallister."

"What *is* your name?"

"Barbara Kingsley," she said.

"Well, Barbara Kingsley, I think you're about the most beautiful woman I've ever met, and I'd like to set you up with a photographer for some headshots. Our expense, of course."

The bored expression hardened into appraisal. She later told me that she was trying to figure out if I was making a genuine professional advance or a personal one, if you know what I mean, and being of a sapphic bent herself, she was hoping for the latter. (She didn't put much faith in white folks who wanted to sign her up as a model, which was perfectly fair, I guess.)

Anyway, I convinced her eventually that my offer was bona fide, no strings attached, and we proceeded with the usual formalities. But that look of appraisal was a warning, I thought. It was like that yellow colonial flag with the snake, Don't Tread on Me. Miss Kingsley might allow me to manage her career—and champagne and oysters with a few celestial bodies at the Palmetto Club certainly fell under the standard definition of a professional outing, if a sensational one—but take one step across that line and Barbara called the shots.

WHICH ALL GOES TO explain how I wind up losing my bet, after all. We remain at the Palmetto for less than two hours, just long enough to drink a case of champagne and eat five dozen oysters, before we part company with our glittering entourage and head uptown to Barbara's neck of the woods. Her cousin owns a club, she says, a joint where they play real live jazz, none of this watered-down midtown nonsense, and she'll vouch for me. I say all right.

I thought she was kidding about vouching for me, but sure enough, the doorman stops us on the way in and respectfully asks Miss Barbara what the devil she thinks she's doing.

"Aw, she's all right, Linus," Barbara says, and Linus sighs and waves us through. Barbara finds us a table right near the front. The orchestra's on a break, it seems, so we get to talking while they bring us some drinks and peanuts.

Barbara watches me light a cigarette and cracks a wee smile. "Well, that was certainly fine work, Miss Ruth. I'll bet they can see your halo shining all the way over in Brooklyn."

"Can't they, though. I call it two birds with one stone—flashbulbs popping for Miss Barbara Kingsley, the newest modeling sensation, and the Palmetto Club gets a lesson in human decency."

"And you get to feel like everybody's fairy godmother, handing out favors to black folk."

"What's wrong with that? So long as I use my fairy powers for good."

"Just don't let it get to your head, is all. God gives us all kind of ways to make others feel small."

"Say." I set down my drink. "That didn't bother you, back there. Did it?"

"Of course it bothered me. Like the man said, I don't want to be a member of any club that won't have me. I did it for the publicity, is all. And now I like it better right here among my own kind, where I know folks can appreciate me."

"You think I'm stuck on myself, don't you?"

She shrugs. "I don't know anything about you, Miss Macallister, except you're the kind of woman who likes to have her own way."

"Most men like to have their own way, and nobody faults them for it."

Barbara laughs and says that's true, sure enough, if by *most men* you meant *all men*, which is why she stays away from them generally. Speak of the devil. The orchestra then starts filing back to their instruments. Each man—they're all men, of course—holds a drink in one hand, full enough to make you guess it isn't his first. I jingle my ice and consider them as they tune and riff.

Barbara leans over. "Something on your mind? Besides *that.*"

What I mean to say is *Nothing.* What comes out is *My sister.*

"I didn't know you had a sister," she says.

"I think she's in trouble."

"What kind of trouble? Man trouble? Baby trouble?"

"Both, I guess, but those are just the root cause of her main trouble. I don't know for sure, though. I haven't seen her in twelve years."

"Twelve years!" Barbara chokes on her gin. "What kind of idiot child you be, Miss Macallister?"

"Now, that's not fair. Maybe my sister's the idiot."

Barbara shakes her head. "Don't matter. Blood is the only thing that counts in this world, boss lady. Don't you know that? I don't care what you done or what she done, you both need your heads knocked together. Ain't nobody in the world understands you like your sister. Ain't nobody ever will."

At that point, the orchestra swings into action, thank God, swallowing up all the other noise in the room. I don't want to continue that conversation and wish most fervently that I hadn't started it to begin with.

The trouble is, you can drown out a conversation like that and even stop it entirely, but you can't forget it. The words keep beating inside your head to the illicit syncopation of the music outside, until you're half convinced you might go crazy with them.

◆ ◆ ◆

A SPRING CHICKEN I am no longer, and by two o'clock in the morning my jaw splits wide open with yawning. Barbara tells me to hand over the five bucks, and I actually ask her *What five bucks?*, because I've lost count of the lime rickeys I've drunk to drown out the syncopation of Barbara's wise advice.

Our bet, she says, and *Oh right*, I answer.

I pay her the five bucks and pay the bill, too. Prepare to rise, and that's when Barbara puts her hand on my elbow.

"I'm guessing he's yours?" she says, nodding to a man sitting alone at a table in the corner.

I follow her gaze and squint. Big, wide-shouldered man, face too shadowed to properly see. But two things are perfectly clear, even to my addled eyes. Number one, he's a white man, as fair-haired and pink-skinned as they come. And number two, he's watching me.

"Hell's bells," I mutter.

BARBARA OFFERS TO FIND me a ride home, call me a trustworthy taxi or something, but I figure I'm not going to start being a coward at this particular moment. I march right up to him and ask if he's ready to leave now.

"Certainly," Sumner Fox says politely.

He pays his bill—I have the feeling he left a large tip—and takes my elbow like a gentleman. I don't look back, just sail between the last few tables and out into the lobby and then the open air of West 125th Street. Fox signals to a taxi waiting by the curb, a half block away. I waste an entire moment thinking I've been very stupid indeed.

But there's nothing underhanded about the way he helps me into the taxi and gives the driver my address before he settles on the other side of the back seat, acres of cloth between us. As I settle against the seat and watch the buildings skim by, I experience this feeling of levitation, as if we're actually flying instead of driving, but the sober part of my brain—if one can be said to still exist—knows this is only an illusion. I anchor myself to the pocketbook in my lap, which happens to contain Iris's missives, both of them, postcard and letter. I don't know why I carry them around with me like that. Maybe it's a talisman—maybe my subconscious is trying to figure out what I should do with them and considers it's best to keep the objects on hand in case of need.

The nice thing about two o'clock in the morning is you're not subject to the aggravation of New York traffic. We skim down Fifth Avenue, pausing only when some light turns red before us. I don't speak, and neither does Fox. Like me, he's looking out the window, contemplating the blur of facades. Only they aren't a blur to him, I'll bet. Sumner Fox likely drank nothing stronger than ginger ale, certainly not while on duty. He probably sees each building as an individual edifice—notices all the fine architectural details—will remember them tomorrow.

"So why'd you quit football?" I hear myself ask.

"There was a war on."

"Are those your real teeth?"

He laughs—actually laughs, for the first time—and turns to me. "Fellow named Greenwald knocked the two front ones out of me at the Dartmouth game."

"Was he sorry?"

"He was sorry afterward. Offered to pay for the dental work."

"I'll bet you scored your goal anyway."

"Touchdown," he says.

The taxi slows and turns left on Fifty-Ninth Street to make its way east. Across Fox's face, the city lights roll and flash. He stares right back, cold sober, which is about the most terrifying thing you can imagine. I don't flinch, however. Maybe I'm too drunk to focus, maybe I'm too drunk to care. The air is fresh for June, as clean as you can possibly hope for at the beginning of a Manhattan summer, and the windows are cranked down to allow this miraculous breeze inside.

"Let's stop here and walk," I say. "I could use the air."

Fox leans forward to the driver and says something. The taxi pulls to the curb at the corner of Lexington Avenue. My palms are damp around my pocketbook. Fox pays the driver and jumps out to swing around the bumper and open my door. For once, I don't beat the gentleman to it—not that I don't appreciate niceties, you understand. I'm just too impatient under ordinary circumstances, too eager to get on with wherever it is we're going. Tonight there's no rush, and I need the help. I need a steady arm to draw me from the taxi and set me on my feet on the good solid New York sidewalk.

WE DON'T SAY AN awful lot. Sumner Fox doesn't seem to talk much, as a rule. Nor does he touch me, except when I stumble, stepping off the curb at First Avenue. We turn down Sutton Place to the sound of the traffic whisking along the East River Drive, the horns and distant shouts and nighttime music.

"How do you like the city?" I ask.

"It's all right. It's like they say, it never sleeps."

"You strike me as a country boy, that's why I asked."

"I guess I like the country most. But I can appreciate what the city has to offer."

"I remember VE Day. That was something, Mr. Fox. Every stranger you met was your new best friend. Never kissed so many men in my life. I remember thinking when I went to bed the next day, there was no place I'd rather be on a day like that, celebrating a thing like that." I pause. "Of course, you were out in the Pacific, weren't you?"

"Yes."

I don't often curse myself, but I curse myself then. A Japanese prison camp, that's what Uncle Charlie said, though not even Ruth Macallister dares ask him for certain. I find myself wondering, out of the blue, where Iris was on VE Day. She must have been in Europe itself, some embassy or another. I suppose they celebrated, all right. She and Sasha.

A handkerchief appears before me. "Here," says Fox, and it's only then that I realize I'm crying.

"I'm so sorry. I'm afraid I've had a little too much to drink."

"I figured."

We walk on to my apartment building, another block down on the corner of East Fifty-Sixth Street. The doorman doesn't look at all surprised to see me. He trades a glance with Fox that looks like a question, and Fox makes the absolute briefest negative shake of his head.

I proffer the handkerchief. "Thanks for the loan."

"Keep it."

"I couldn't possibly."

He takes back the handkerchief, and in that instant I regret insisting. It seems so pointlessly rude.

"Why were you tailing me?" I ask.

"It's my job."

"To make sure I'm not in secret communication with my sister, maybe?"

"Something like that. But also to demonstrate, if I can, that you don't need to be afraid of me. I'm on your side. I'm on hers. She's not in any trouble with us, not if I can help it."

He says this sincerely, and I don't for a moment imagine he could be lying. I'm not saying my instincts about people are never wrong, but they're only wrong if some prejudice on my part interferes with their natural operation. My instinct about Sumner Fox is that he's a straight shooter. If I were going to trust any FBI man, I would trust him.

But I'm not going to trust an FBI man. I know what I know, after all.

"I appreciate the lift home, Mr. Fox. I do hope I didn't ruin your evening."

"Not at all. Take some aspirin and get some rest. And try not to worry so much about your sister."

"Who said I was worried?"

"You did." He tips his hat and steps back. "We'll find her, never fear. Good night, Miss Macallister. You've still got my card, if you hear anything?"

I pat my pocketbook. "Right here."

MY APARTMENT IS NOT the kind of shabby shoebox you ordinarily associate with single Manhattan career girls. If you must know, it used to belong to my parents. I grew up in this apartment and, since neither my brother nor my sister ever had any use for it, haven't set foot within its walls in years, I had it redecorated ten years ago according to my own taste. The room we once called a dining room has been converted into a library. Harry's room I kept as it was, because Harry's the kind of brother who might turn up at any moment after a decade's absence and expect his dinner kept warm and his scotch with ice. The room I once shared with Iris became a spare bedroom for theoretical guests, and my parents' bedroom now belongs to me.

But I can't sleep yet. How can I sleep with my nerves in such a fizzle? I run a bath and sink gratefully into the warm water with a cigarette and a glass of Alka-Seltzer. I instruct myself not to think about Iris, but when my eyes close, there she is. All this time I've banished her without effort, and now that I *need* her gone— absolutely *must* be clear of Iris for my own peace of mind—she won't leave me alone.

I have twenty-two years crammed full of memories of Iris, but she keeps appearing to me from her hospital bed in Rome, after the accident. She was a mess. Bruises everywhere, one eye socket so black and puffy you couldn't make out the eyeball within, to say nothing of the broken ankle and various bandages stuck upon her body, so that she resembled a half-finished mummy. She was asleep when I came in, but her eyes opened the instant I came to the bed. She smiled bravely because she didn't want me to worry. "I'm sorry," she sort of croaked.

Sorry!

I don't cry much, and I certainly wasn't in the messy habit in those years. What a waste of time—what a crummy way to spend an afternoon. But I came within a kitten's whisker of breaking down in that moment. Iris was *sorry!* She was *sorry* to have occasioned all this trouble. She took the blame on her delicate shoulders.

You understand, therefore, that Iris and I are not estranged because she failed me in some unforgivable way. Iris would never fail anybody. There is not one disloyal bone in her body, not one atom of her that would not sacrifice itself for your sake. People might call that weakness, but I've always envied her for it, if I'm honest with myself and with you. She will never stagger under the weight of guilt, as I do—she will know regret, which is the lot of all mankind, but not because she's done anything to hurt you.

BY THE TIME I rise from the bath, dripping and wrinkled, it's practically dawn. Saturday, thank goodness, so I don't need to trouble myself about work. I brush my teeth and spread the cold cream over my face and find a clean pair of pajamas in the chest of drawers. The air in the bedroom is warm and stuffy and humid from the bath. I open a window and pull back the covers, and as I begin the ascent into bed my toe discovers something flat.

I glance at the floor. Just under the edge of the bedframe lies the snapshot Iris enclosed in her letter.

I take my time examining them, these nephews and niece I've never met. Iris's kids. Their features are blurred, as if the photographer moved his hand at the exact instant of the shutter's opening. Still, you can gather in the grosser details. Their hair glimmers in various states of blondness, like their father, and their neat, old-fashioned clothes are exactly the kind of uniform I imagine Iris would dress them in.

My finger touches the small, glossy rectangle and traces the outline of a face, a tiny ear, a smear of hair so blond it might be white. A hand that clutches the fingers of the little boy who stands next to her, whose face seems to have been caught in the act of turning toward her to say something. A smocked dress that comes just

to her knees, and the plump little knees themselves, and the white
socks with the ruffle and the black Mary Jane shoes, like the ones I
used to wear when I was small.

My niece. And I don't even know her name. I didn't even know
she existed. She would have been born in Moscow, I guess, after
they defected.

As for the boy who holds her hand—the oldest of them, the
tallest. This would be their firstborn, the son they conceived in
the first mad dash of infatuation. I always knew he'd be the spit of
his father, and I believe I'm right. You can see it in the outline of
him, the way he stands, the hint of a strong brow, the probable blue
eyes. Aunt Vivian told me they named him after Sasha, but you
can't address a young boy as Cornelius Alexander, so they call him
Kip—or did. A mere tiny, secret bud in his mother's womb when I
last saw Iris—desperately in love, her whole heart stolen so that not
a single piece of it remained to forgive *me*, her sister.

I LIE IN BED for a bit, staring at the ceiling, while the early summer dawn colors the air. Until I realize I'm not going to fall asleep,
not now. I rise and pad down the gray hallway to the foyer, where
my pocketbook lies on the hall table on which I tossed it a few
hours ago.

I open up the pocketbook and rattle around in there until I
discover what I'm looking for—not the postcard or the tissue-thin
airmail envelope, but the small, rectangular ecru card with the
raised black type that said simply C. SUMNER FOX, and beneath it a
telephone number from a Washington exchange. Underneath that,
in precise letters, Fox had written *Empire Hotel, room 808.*

I carry the card to the telephone in the kitchen and lift the receiver. At twenty-six minutes past five o'clock, I dial up the Empire Hotel and ask the switchboard operator for room 808.

He answers on the second ring. "Fox," he says, like a voice you hear on the radio.

"Mr. Fox, it's Ruth Macallister. I'm so sorry to bother you at such a disagreeable hour."

"Not at all. Is something the matter?"

"Not as such. It's just that I've got a little confession to make."

"I'll be there in ten minutes," he says.

IRIS

MAY 1940
Rome, Italy

The first thing Harry did when he got his posting to Rome, he bought a three-year-old Ford Cabriolet convertible cheap from some young widow in Hemel Hempstead and had it shipped across the ocean. The car had belonged to her husband before he'd succumbed to sepsis acquired from a mosquito bite—just like President Coolidge's poor son, except that was a blister—and Iris thought the deceased must have been an interesting fellow, because the car was bright red like a candy apple and had an engine Harry described as *souped up*. Iris wasn't sure of the particulars, but *souped up* apparently meant *loud and fast*, such that you couldn't fail to notice this machine, whether it was parked along the street or zipping past you on some highway. It was a swell car, all right.

Iris loved going for drives in Harry's convertible. She loved the wind in her hair and the sensation of speed, and the snug, fateful feeling of hurtling down some stretch of highway in a vehicle beyond your control. She loved it more than ever now that Sasha was at the wheel, and she sat next to him, and somewhere ahead lay a crumbling house on a sunbaked hillside where she and Sasha would spend the weekend.

IF SHE HAD TO confess, Iris would've told you that she rather *enjoyed* carrying on a secret love affair right beneath Ruth's sharp, perfect nose. (Iris's nose was decidedly snub, although Sasha called it adorable.) The secret was part of the fun! They'd go out to dinner, for example, the four of them, and Iris and Sasha would carry on a little flirtation of the feet under the table; or else Sasha's hand would slide underneath her dress, and Iris had to keep her face absolutely straight while he fondled her right there in the restaurant in front of everybody, while Harry told some story about the Swiss consul. Or they'd meet at some diplomatic party—those officials and their wives, all they ever did was meet and drink—and Sasha would flirt outrageously with some woman on one side of the room, to keep up appearances, while Iris did her best to flirt with someone on the other side, until by some prearranged signal they'd steal out separately to meet in the fragrant, darkened corner of a courtyard or a hallway and kiss the daylights out of each other, or worse. Or they'd bump into each other *quite by accident* in the Vatican museum, say, or the ruins of the ancient Roman agora, or even the Villa Borghese again, and experience all the riches of Western civilization, which they later discussed over coffee or lunch or the pillow of Sasha's bed.

Best of all were the times when Sasha rang the telephone around eleven o'clock in the morning and asked whether the coast was clear, and Iris would say *yea* or *nay*, depending on the proximity of Ruth. If *yea*, then Sasha arrived in a taxi fifteen minutes later, and they spent the next hour or two in bed, or on the sofa, or really anywhere a person wearing a plaster cast on her leg can have sexual intercourse with another person without discomfort or outright injury. Iris learned to speak up boldly and ask for a pillow or a change of position or a load off, for God's sake. Sasha always complied. He was terribly considerate, if also insatiable. After the first hasty bout, he liked to stalk naked around the apartment, mixing drinks for both of them, while Iris lay back and watched him happily. She told him he was like a cat, always prowling except when he was sleeping. He'd drink a couple of gin and tonics, maybe three if he was especially thirsty, while they talked about everything, the state of the world, capitalism, communism, Spain, East Hampton, Schuylers and van der Wahls and Digbys, where they would go on holiday.

In fact, that was how they devised this weekend—Sasha lifted his head from the pillow one afternoon and announced he wasn't just going to hang around his apartment with Iris from Friday to Sunday, or run the risk of bumping into somebody should they venture outside. He had a friend who had a villa in Tivoli, he told her on the twenty-second of April—a friend willing to let Sasha spend the weekend there with whomever he pleased. Nobody at the embassy would know. He could borrow Harry's car without raising any suspicions, because so far as her siblings would know, Iris had already gone off on her drawing holiday with some friends from the American Academy in Rome. Why, it was airtight! Not even Agatha Christie could have devised a better plan.

Even the weather conspired with them. Seven consecutive days of rain dampened Iris's spirits in the last week of April, but when she walked out of the doctor's office on the second of May a free woman, except for a cane, which was really rather stylish, the clouds parted and the sun poured down, and Iris spread out her arms and knew that everything would work out *perfectly*.

The next day, a Friday, she packed a small valise with sundresses and toothbrush and Pond's cream and said good-bye to Ruth. Ruth stopped her at the door and asked if she was forgetting something?

"No, I don't think so. What am I missing?"

Ruth made a cynical smile and nodded to the desk in the corner. "Your sketchbook and charcoals, maybe?"

The cynical smile worried Iris all the way over to Sasha's apartment on Via Terrenzio, near the Vatican. She let herself in with the key he'd loaned her and fretted until he met her at the small trattoria around the corner for dinner at half past seven.

"You're worried about a *smile*, darling?"

"You'd have to know Ruth. It's this particular smile she wears when she knows something you don't."

"But she *doesn't* know something you don't."

"Be serious."

"Well, who cares, anyway? It's about time she knows about us, if you ask me. Harry, too. We can't go sneaking around forever."

"Oh? Just when do you plan on telling them, then?"

He reached across the table and took her hand. "We'll know when it's time."

NOW IT WAS SATURDAY, the fourth of May, and they were hurtling around some hairpin turn toward this ancient yellow-brown town nestled into the neck of the Sabine Hills. Behind them, the Roman countryside spread out in a quilt of new green fields. The sun beat down on Iris's head. The draft streamed through her hair and filled her lungs. The land was so beautiful, her eyes ached with it. She would remember this drive forever. She'd remember the smell of exhaust and of asphalt, and the delicate green scent of spring.

THE VILLA WASN'T MUCH, after all. It sat a mile from the center of town, up on the hillside overlooking the falls, and the view was the best thing about it. The privy was outdoors. The kitchen sink had a pump handle. Needless to say, there wasn't an icebox or a stovetop in sight. Iris wandered from room to room—hall, living room, snug bedroom, walls of pink stucco, dark, monastic furniture, old books, sunshine, dust—everywhere the smell of centuries—and declared she loved it.

"It's rustic, all right. Like camping," Sasha said.

"You're the camping type, are you?"

"I wouldn't say I'm the type, exactly, but my brother and I used to climb up around the Adirondacks in August, while Dad watched his horses run at Saratoga."

Iris clasped her hands. "Your father has racehorses?"

"Why not? Profit in pursuit of trophies."

"No. You're not going to ruin horses for me. They're noble and beautiful, I don't care what you say."

He stood in the middle of the pink stucco living room, blinking at the dust and at her. He opened his arms. "Come here."

Iris launched herself at his chest. Her feet flew through the air in a loop or two before he settled her back to earth. "Horses should do useful things," he said, "not race each other around some crummy dirt track for the amusement of the wealthy."

"And the gamblers. Don't forget all those poor people losing their wages at the pari-mutuel window."

"You see what I mean?"

She shook her head against his shirt. Her arms still looped around his neck; his arms circled her waist. She felt the thud of his heart and the tingle of gin on his breath. (He'd packed a Thermos for the drive.) "They're still noble and beautiful, and it's noble and beautiful to want to run fast. They can't help it. It's who they are."

He grunted—agreement or disagreement, who knew—and kissed her.

"Am I ever going to meet your father?" Iris asked.

"You only want to meet his horses. Admit it."

"I want to meet everything that belongs to you."

"My father doesn't belong to me. He'd say it was the other way around. You'd be much better off meeting my mother. She's a decent human being, even if she's a prisoner of her class."

"We're all prisoners of something, aren't we?"

"Is that so, Miss Macallister? And what are you a prisoner of?"

"Nothing!"

"That sister of yours, maybe?"

Iris was snug inside Sasha's arms. He wore a shirt of crumpled white linen that smelled of cigarettes and perspiration, warm human smells, and his hair was straight and loose and flopped over his forehead. His eyes were the color of summer.

She said, "My father killed himself in 1929, after the crash. He'd lost all our money, and his clients' money, and most of my grandparents' money. We were broke after that, but pretending not to be broke. Mama didn't take it well. She always liked to spend money. Closets full of clothes. She would take all these sleeping pills, things her doctor prescribed her. If it wasn't for Aunt Vivian marrying Charles Schuyler, we couldn't have gone to college. There was just no money, none at all. No father and no mother, really. So I guess I'm a prisoner of that."

Sasha frowned at her.

To break the silence, Iris said, "That's why Ruth and I—we're so different, but we share this thing. We're both prisoners of it. It holds us together, always. Does that make sense?"

Sasha swooped her up in his arms and carried her into the bedroom. The window faced south and the room was very hot, but Iris didn't notice the heat until much later, when they lay sweating on top of the sheets and she couldn't seem to get her breath back. She rolled off the mattress, opened the window, and returned to the bed to tuck herself back under his arm. He'd lit a languid cigarette in the meantime. She tugged at the fine gold hairs on his chest and asked what he was a prisoner of.

"Isn't it obvious?" he said. "You."

IRIS SAID SHE COULDN'T possibly cook anything inside that primitive kitchen, so Sasha headed into town to fetch supplies. His skin was cold and damp after an improvised bath from a bucket of water pumped from the kitchen. They agreed to bathe in the stream at the corner of the garden from then on.

When the roar of Harry's motor died away down the lane, Iris rose, washed off the sweat from her skin, and put her dress back on. Her hair tangled around her face, but when she looked inside her valise, she realized she'd forgotten her hairbrush, of all things. Sasha's valise lay open on the floor next to the dresser. She looked inside and found a hairbrush under a folded shirt. Under the hairbrush was a thick manila envelope, of the type you found in offices, bound with a loop of twine that fastened around a clip.

Iris brushed her hair in the scrap of mirror above the dresser. Over the past few weeks her skin had acquired some pleasing color. Her short hair was thick and shiny, frizz in submission—curls in order that looked like disorder—little glimmers of Italian sunshine starting to streak through. Her large hazel eyes—by far her best feature, she'd always thought—sparkled back at her, rimmed with wet black lashes. She looked like a child, she knew, so heart-shaped and rose-skinned, and she also knew that her innocent face and delicate, curving figure—in contrast to Ruth's—drove Sasha's obsession for her. But her small mouth bowed downward. She brushed her curls a little too aggressively. Why should Sasha bring work with him this weekend? He'd had *all week* to clear his desk for their holiday together.

Don't be childish, she told her childish reflection.

Then she set down the hairbrush and returned to Sasha's valise. Carefully she disengaged the twine from its clip and opened the flap of the envelope.

THEY ATE IN THE garden, on a small wrought-iron table and chairs, somewhat rusted. The garden was enclosed by a low wall of crumbling brick, and a gate at the back opened to the hills and the stream that rushed happily past. Sasha fiddled with the terracotta fountain, trying to make it work, but it was no use. He threw himself on the grass instead and stared up at the generous sky. Iris joined him.

"Tell me about your friend," she said.

"What friend?"

"The friend who owns this place."

He shrugged, inasmuch as you could shrug your shoulders

while lying in grass with your hands behind your head. "A friend, that's all."

"A girlfriend?"

Sasha squinted one eye at her. "A friend who happens to be a woman, yes."

"Was she your lover?"

"Why all the questions? Christ. Yes, we were lovers once. Are you satisfied?"

Iris rolled herself on top of his chest and set her chin on her linked fingers, just below the hollow of his neck. "Is she the same woman you met outside the Borghese, the day of the accident?"

"How—"

"I saw you from the window."

Sasha untucked his hands from behind his head and slid them under her dress. "Ah."

"Ah what?"

"Somebody's jealous."

"Of course I am. Aren't you?"

"No. I don't believe you can possess exclusive sexual rights to another human being. I believe we are all free agents, men and women."

"Oh, is that so?"

"Don't be grumpy."

"Grumpy? Me?"

"You're grumpy because you think I'm telling you I'm not going to be loyal. But that's not what I'm talking about. I'm talking about my parents. What I saw as a little kid, how what started out as a little jealousy turned into something monstrous. How it turned my father into a monster. And the more monstrous he became, the more she turned away, until whatever love they had for each other at the beginning was just a pile of spent ashes."

"How awful."

"But loyalty, that's different. That's voluntary. That's free will. I *choose* to sleep with you. Every time I kiss you, every time I go to bed with you, I do it because I want *you*, because you're the woman I want to sleep with. That doesn't take away *your* freedom."

"Do you mean I can take another lover, if I want to?"

"If you like."

"What if I don't want to? What if I only want to sleep with you?"

He turned them both over on the grass and unbuttoned his trousers. "I see what you're getting at. You want me to make some kind of proclamation."

"I don't care. Any man can say whatever he wants, I guess."

"What if I proclaim, Iris Macallister, in front of God and this goddamn grass under your back, that I happen to be crazy for you? Is that enough?"

"Not nearly enough. You don't even believe in God. Anyway, how do I know you're not crazy about that other woman, too?"

"Well, I'm not. I'm in love with only one woman in the world."

"You don't say! Which one is that?"

Sasha reached down and yanked up her dress. The sun made a halo of his hair. Iris settled her hips and lifted her knees—sucked in her breath—*ah God*—what a wallop!—all right, fair play, a bit of revenge, a bit of primeval possession, whatever he said about *that*. She dug her fingernails into his furious buttocks—he yelled out—but didn't miss a beat.

"I want *you* to say it, Iris. Who am I *in love with*?"

"*Me!*" she gasped.

"And who are *you* in love with—*madly*—*badly*—as you have never loved anyone in your life?"

She released her claws from his skin. "*You!*"

Sasha growled out some filthy, triumphant word and lifted himself on his palms to hammer her in earnest. Iris grabbed fistfuls of grass. She shut her eyes against the jealous fury of the sun in Sasha's hair. She thought of random things, like flashes from another life—bacon frying, a fiery October maple, racehorses—oh, Sasha's father, not random at all—it's too much, too hard, too much, too deep, too *much*—sweat dropped on her face—*too much*—how does he do it, how does he keep *going*—she couldn't stand another second—the world went tiny and gigantic, both at once—short, desperate strokes, almost there—almost—then *smash*—*finally*— and Iris hollered her rapture as loud as she wanted because only the sun and stones and Sasha could hear her—how divine.

A few more beats, and Sasha shuddered and arched his back and let out a soft howl. The crisis died woozily away and Iris's bones went slack. She heard the stream again, giggling at them. She wanted to giggle, too. Sasha swore and rolled off, panting.

"What's wrong? I thought that was *wonderful*."

"I meant to pull out, that's all. I don't have a rubber on."

"I don't care. I don't care if it happens. Do you?"

"It would be inconvenient."

"Well, it didn't happen the first time, did it? *I* think it would be wonderful."

Sasha stuffed himself back inside his trousers and buttoned them. "You do realize there's a war going on out there, don't you?"

She rolled on her side and ran her finger along the bridge of his nose. "But do you *care*, or not?"

"I don't want to put you in any kind of position, that's all."

"I'd say you've already put me in all kinds of positions, and I've enjoyed them very much."

Sasha tried and failed to suppress a laugh. "Fair enough."

"What about *your* position, though? That's what I'm getting at. What would *you* think, if it happens? Would you want me to get rid of it?"

Finally he turned his head and looked at her. His face radiated that gleaming flush she knew so well. True, he wore a rubber most of the time, but not *every single* time, and sometimes when he wasn't wearing a rubber he didn't—or couldn't—pull out. So Iris wanted to pin him down. She wanted to hear this from his own mouth, in case it did happen. Maybe *today*, who knew. Maybe it already *had* happened. What about last week, in the cloakroom of the British ambassador's residence? What a messy occasion *that* was, but these mistakes would occur when you didn't plan ahead. Just now, for example.

Iris patted his cheek, not quite a slap. A few blades of grass fell away from her fingers. "Well? What do you say to that?"

He trapped her hand against his skin and leaned over the inches of grass to kiss her.

"I say we cross that bridge if we come to it."

THE REST OF SATURDAY passed in a haze, and most of Sunday, too. Sunday afternoon, as planned, Sasha drove into town to find a telephone box, from which he would call Harry to say that he'd had car trouble and would have to stay the night while the engine was being repaired, so he wouldn't return to Rome until Monday. Foolproof!

Iris asked to go along, too. She was curious about the town—

she loved old buildings and the art inside them. But Sasha said no, he'd run his errands faster if he knew she was waiting for him.

"Errands? What errands?"

"You'll see," he said, kissing her good-bye.

So Iris just wandered drowsily around the garden, listening to the stream and to the songbirds, until she remembered her sketchbook. Of course, she'd had to pack it after all, under Ruth's knowing eye, and her charcoals, too. She headed into the house and the small, hot bedroom. Neither Iris nor Sasha ever took the time to unpack, and the sketchbook lay at the bottom of her valise, under all her crumpled clothes, forgotten. She dug it out and turned to leave.

But some instinct forced her to stop at the door. The shutters were closed and the room was dark, and the air still smelled of human sleep. Iris felt as if she'd lived an entire lifetime since they'd arrived here Saturday morning, had burst into this room and made ravenous love, and afterward she'd brushed her hair in the scrap of mirror above the dresser. She'd almost forgotten about that envelope in Sasha's suitcase, and what it contained.

But not quite.

Iris rested her hand on the doorframe and stared at her short, round fingernails. A little dirty, perhaps, even though she and Sasha had bathed in the stream together that morning, and Sasha had soaped and washed her thoroughly. But that's what you got when you spent the day outdoors. When you spent the day laughing and playing, walking and talking, drinking and kissing, rolling stark naked on the grass and the floor and the bed, away on your first holiday with the man you loved—the man who loved you.

Who *trusted* you.

Iris tapped her fingers against the wood and turned around. She bent over Sasha's valise, still on the floor, and opened the lid to rummage around.

She looked in the main compartment and the small one, the zippered pocket next to the lining.

The envelope was gone.

WHEN SASHA RETURNED, AN hour later, Iris sat on the garden wall and stared into the fallen sun. The sketchbook lay open on the bricks beside her, along with a bottle of wine. Sasha had done most of the drinking since they arrived, as usual—a bottle of wine at lunch and another at dinner, gin and tonic to quench the thirst in between—but this time Iris retrieved the bottle from the cellar, a red wine from Tuscany, easy on the palate, and drank it solemnly atop the garden wall.

Iris's first thought, when he walked through the doorway onto the grass, was how beautiful he looked. Did she think he was plain when she first saw him, at the Villa Borghese? You could argue that his features were not beautiful, sure, that his big ears and long nose and bony cheeks and *especially* that sharp brow were maybe coarse and not in perfect balance, as in a work of art. But the overall effect just dazzled her. His height, and his hair, and the ultramarine eyes. He walked straight up to her and put his hands on either side of her hips and kissed her. He smelled of sweet liquor, limoncello maybe, the kind that Italians drink as digestivo.

"Mind if I join you?"

"Suit yourself."

He pulled his cigarettes from his jacket pocket. "Something wrong?"

"No, not at all. Did you get hold of Harry?"

"He bought it. Swallowed it whole actually. Swore at me a little."

"And your errands?"

"What about them?"

"Did you get them all done?"

He was having trouble lighting his cigarette, which was odd because there was no breeze at all. At last the end flared orange. He closed his eyes as he inhaled.

"Because I was wondering, you know. Isn't everything closed on a Sunday?"

"Oh, yes. Of course it was."

"But you were gone so long."

"I had trouble finding a working telephone."

Sasha squinted at some point past Iris's ear, the hillside or something, while the smoke curled in extravagant ribbons around his face and hair. There was some difference to him, but she couldn't pin it down. Was he paler? Maybe. His face was so rigid. His mouth and his cheeks made small adjustments as he smoked the cigarette, but his eyes, his forehead, his brow were cast in wax. He lifted the cigarette back to his lips, and Iris noticed that his hand was trembling.

"What's the matter? Didn't the photographs please her?"

"What's that?"

"The photographs in the envelope. In your suitcase. I assume you were passing those along to that woman? The one I saw you with in the Borghese gardens?"

What was surprising was that he wasn't surprised. If his eyebrows rose a millimeter or two, they only expressed amazement at her tone, which—she'd freely admit—smacked more of jealousy than outrage. If he channeled all the pyrotechnics of his blue eyes into hers, he was only trying to figure out whether she really cared. Sitting high on the brick wall, Iris exactly matched his height. She didn't realize how *unequal* they were until now—older, taller, stronger, better educated, worldly-wise—why, Sasha had had every advantage, until this moment when she knew his secret.

"So you looked through my suitcase, did you?" he said, without rancor, and revelation arrived on Iris's head like the dawn.

"You *wanted* me to see it, didn't you? You left it there yesterday for me to find. Right there in plain sight, an open suitcase. That's why you told me to stay behind today. You *wanted* me to see it was gone."

He put his hand over her mouth.

"Before you say another word, I want you to know that I've never done a single thing—never passed along a single iota of information that would harm the United States."

Iris nodded. He dropped his hand and pulled on the cigarette.

"The Soviets are being left in the cold, that's all, because of ideological prejudice. Because the success of the Soviet system threatens the way we've always done things. The way that killed *your* father, Iris, the same way that corrupted *mine*. You know I'm right. I couldn't just sit back and do *nothing*."

Iris slung her arms around his neck. "I don't care about any of that. I don't care about politics. I care about *you*. I want you to trust me. I don't want you to keep any secrets from me. Whatever you're doing, I know you're doing it because you believe in it, and you're trying to make the world a better place, and I love you for it. But I can't stand it if you don't trust me."

"That's why I left my suitcase open."

"And that woman. She's your—your—"

"Don't worry about her."

"But she's Russian, isn't she? She's the one who—"

"I said, don't worry about her. Anything personal between us—her and me—that's finished. It's just business now."

"But you won't tell me anything else about it."

"I've told you all you need to know, all right? Because I thought I should be square with you, what I'm doing."

She leaned her forehead against his. "Why?"

"It's only fair. I could get into trouble or something. It's only fair you know you're jumping into hot water."

"I already knew *that*."

He breathed into her mouth and she breathed back into his.

"So we're all right?" he said. "You're still with me?"

The sun was dropping into the sea. Iris's heart pounded so hard, her chest might explode—not because she was scared but because she understood that everything depended upon this moment, this conversation, this decision. The entire course of her life *pivoted* around this point of vital contact, his forehead against hers.

When Iris nodded, Sasha's head moved too.

He let out a noise of exultation and crushed out his cigarette on the bricks and kissed her—unbuttoned her dress—kissed her neck and breasts—all the familiar rituals. He untucked his shirt and Iris fumbled with the fastening on his trousers. On this wall nobody could see them or hear them—the ancient Sabine Hills rose up behind them—the sun set in unspeakable splendor behind Sasha's head. The bricks left angry marks on the backs of her thighs. She discovered them the next day, when Sasha bathed her in the stream at the corner of the garden, before they returned to Rome.

By then she'd forgotten how his hands shook when he returned from meeting his Soviet contact in Tivoli, how full of nerves he was.

EARLY IN THE MORNING of Friday, the tenth of May, a ringing telephone woke Iris. Sasha stirred next to her and stumbled out of bed. The air was warm and dusky; she couldn't see any sunlight through the cracks of the blinds. She flopped on her back and listened to Sasha's low voice in the other room. Once he left for the embassy, she was supposed to return home to the apartment she shared with Ruth, cheerful and rested from her sketching holiday, and she didn't know how she was going to do that. She wasn't that Iris anymore. Her life was *here*, next to Sasha.

Sasha said clearly, *All right, I'll be there in half an hour*, and the receiver rattled into its cradle. His footsteps treaded the floorboards back toward her. She stretched her hands above her head in hopes of enticing him, but he just sat on the edge of the bed, naked and somber, and said, *Well, it's begun.*

She didn't need to ask what had begun. Nor did she need to ask why he wasn't surprised.

RUTH

Remarkably enough, the house telephone rings precisely eleven minutes after I hang up the line from the Empire Hotel—remarkably, because I can't think of a method other than rocket propulsion that could have made the journey in so little time. Like many of Sumner Fox's feats, it remains an unexplained miracle.

"Gentleman to see you, Miss Macallister," says the doorman, perfectly neutral because I tip well at Christmas. "A Mr. Fox?"

"Send him right up, please, Mike." I smooth my hair and tighten the sash on my dressing gown, because regardless of the gentleman's beauty—let's admit it, he has none—I've always believed in presenting an orderly face to the world, particularly when my nerves are as shredded as they are in this moment. Then I light a cigarette, pace across the room, stub out the cigarette, think better of it, and light another. You see what I mean.

At last, the doorbell. I fly from living room to foyer and fling the door open. Sumner Fox stands in his dark suit and dark tie; the hallway lighting makes his bony face look jaundiced.

"You should have checked the peephole first."

"For God's sake." I step back. "Won't you come in, Mr. Fox."

He's so wide, he practically turns sideways to fit his shoulders through the door. I lead him into the living room and ask if he wants a drink or something. He shakes his head no. I feel a pang of disappointment. My head's throbbing, my arms and legs have that heavy, sick feeling that combines the worst effects of a hangover and a sleepless night. What I need is a couple of aspirin and a Bloody Mary. Or is it the other way around?

"Sit, please," I tell him. "I want to make a few things clear."

He waits for me to sit first before he finds the indicated armchair and lowers his body onto it. As I said, he isn't especially tall— I would say he only *just* clears six feet, if he clears them at all. He's simply *big*. Even his thighs have a thick, meaty diameter, especially crammed between the arms of a chair like that, a hundred years old, built for men of elegant, aristocratic frame. He rests his hands on his knees and cocks his head a few degrees, to indicate I should begin when ready.

I knot my hands in my lap. "First things first. I am *not* snitching on Sasha Digby. What I'm telling you, I'm telling you so you can make my sister and her children safe. You can't take down a single thing I say and use it against her husband in a court of law, or whatever it is you mean to do with him, if you find them. If I agree to help, you leave him alone."

"I can't promise that, but I *can* promise this conversation is off the record, so far as our investigation goes."

"I guess that's fair."

"Is there anything else?"

"Yes. You go first. I want to know why you're here right now, instead of four years ago or next month. Something's happened to my sister, hasn't it?"

His thumb moves, rubbing the material on the side of his knee. "Yes."

"They're in Moscow. Four years ago, when they disappeared, they went to the Soviet Union."

"What makes you say that?"

I don't answer. He nods and stands to look out the window at the sunrise, which has reached a tremendous zenith. The colors illuminate his face. I wait for him to think things over, weigh the risks versus the possible return, calculate how much he has to give in order to get something worthwhile back from me.

Without turning from the window, he speaks.

"On the fifteenth of November 1948, as you know, Sasha Digby failed to turn up at his office at the American embassy in London. There was no answer at his home telephone, nor did anyone answer the door at the family home in Kensington. Diplomatic staff established that neither he nor any member of his family had been seen since the previous Friday. The FBI was then alerted, but discovered no leads at all, not the slightest confirmed trace of them."

"I remember it well. A couple of nice gentlemen turned up at my apartment building at Thanksgiving and gave me the third degree. So tell me something I don't already know."

"I can't do that," he says. "Not unless you tell me what you *do* know."

"Ah. Clever."

He turns his head to look over his shoulder. "Miss Macallister?"

I reach for the pack of cigarettes on the sofa table. "I first met Sasha Digby in Rome, right before the Italians entered the war. As

I'm sure you're aware, he was working at the US embassy as a junior diplomat, alongside my brother, Harry. He had just rescued my sister from a traffic accident outside the Borghese gardens, that's how I met him."

"He was previously unknown to you or your sister?"

"We might have been introduced at some party or another, but I didn't take any notice of him until I saw him at the hospital afterward. As I'm sure you can imagine, it was a harrowing day, and that night Harry and I took him out for dinner and drinks to thank him for what he'd done. Afterward, he came home with me and spent the night."

Sumner Fox doesn't show the slightest reaction to this information, not so much as an eyebrow raised in faint disapproval. "Go on."

"We were both a little off our heads, after what happened, and needed to let off steam. Never occurred to me that Iris had any kind of crush on him, nor he on her. He came by the next night, and the next, and that's when he told me he was spying for the Soviets."

"He *told* you that?"

"Just like that." I snap my fingers. "I think he was trying to impress me. You know, to show off that he wasn't just some stuffy diplomat. Also, he was drunk. He spent a lot of time drunk. I think that's how he dealt with everything, you know? Because men of his class, loyalty's just bred into them. I've always thought that *in his head*, he was able to justify spying on his own country because it would bring forward the revolution and make the world just and peaceful under worldwide communism, et cetera, but down below he was all torn apart because he's betraying not just the United States of America, but his own friends. The people he works with and drinks with."

Fox says nothing to all that. Just stands there at the window until I can't bear it any longer. I stub out my cigarette and announce that since the sun's officially up, I'm going to mix myself a Bloody Mary.

When I return, he's still standing where I left him, hands shoved into his pockets. He says he's underestimated me.

I plop myself back down on the sofa and light another cigarette. "Of course you did. You're a man."

"It won't happen again," he says grimly.

"Oh, don't kick yourself. It's perfectly natural." My pocketbook lies on the sofa table, next to the cigarettes. I reach for it—open it wide—draw out the postcard and the letter. "Perhaps I should have given these to you sooner, but I needed to know you were a man I could trust."

Fox looks greedily at my hand. I hold it out, and he plucks the papers free and frames his fingers delicately around the edges while he examines each one, first the postcard and then the letter in its envelope. If I didn't know any better, I'd say the expression on his face—such as it is—suggests something like relief.

"It's been opened already."

"No kidding, Sherlock."

He ignores me, of course—just lifts the flap of the envelope with so delicate a touch, you simply can't imagine those fingers gripping an object so vulgar as a pigskin. Holding the extreme corner of one side of the letter, he eases it from its wrapper like a whisper and spreads it out on the sofa table. He bends over the paper and reads Iris's words. Then he picks up the envelope and examines that, too, every letter and especially the postmark, before at last he looks up at me.

"Do you mind if I take this with me?"

"I certainly *do* mind."

"We'll return it once we've had a chance to examine it in the lab."

"In the *lab*? What kind of lab? Where is it?"

"I'm afraid I can't say."

"Now just wait a moment. I think you owe me a little more than that. I did as you asked—I gave you the postcard and the letter. I've got a right to know what this is all about. She's my sister!"

"With whom you share so close and affectionate a relationship you haven't communicated with her in a dozen years."

"That's neither here nor there." The cigarette's nearly burned out against my fingertips; I stab it into the ashtray on the lamp table. "She's written to me *now*, hasn't she? Which means I have a moral responsibility to help."

"Which does you credit, Miss Macallister, but I'm afraid I must ask you to be patient." He turns back to the letter and replaces the paper inside the envelope—all with the exact featherweight delicacy of touch with which he took them out in the first place. From his briefcase he extracts a rectangular sleeve. He puts the envelope and the postcard in the sleeve and the sleeve in the briefcase and snaps the case shut. When he's finished, he turns back to my amazed face.

"That's it?" I ask.

"That's all for now. Of course we'll return your sister's letter when we're done examining it."

"And then what? My sister says she needs my help. She's living in Moscow, for God's sake, in the heart of the Soviet Union, and something's gone terribly wrong. I know it has, and *you* know it has, or she wouldn't have sent me those messages."

"I suspect you're right, but before we can take any action, we've got to determine the nature of the trouble. Whether these are genuine." Fox lifts the briefcase. "We may need to call you in for further questions, Miss Macallister."

"*Questions?* I want answers!"

"In the meantime, if you receive any additional letters or other communication—telephone calls, parcels, messages delivered in person—I urge you to reach me."

His face, as he says all this, hardly moves at all. You would think his nerves have been somehow disconnected from the muscles of his cheeks and forehead. I become fascinated with his mouth, the only thing that moves.

"Of course," I say meekly.

"Thank you. I'll walk myself out."

"Oh, no you don't."

I scurry in front and lead him back down the hall to the foyer. As he passes one of the framed photographs, he stops and squints. "Is that the two of you?"

I follow his stare, although I don't need to remind myself what the photograph depicts. A pair of laughing, carefree women, one tall and blond and the other petite and brunette. Bright dresses, scarves tied in triangles over shining young hair. The blonde slings a protective arm around the brunette's shoulders. Behind them, the Colosseum.

"Yes. That was in Rome, right before she met Sasha."

"You were close."

"We were *different*, Mr. Fox. But we were sisters. We looked out for each other."

Fox straightens away from the photograph and continues down the hall. By now it's drawing close to seven in the morning and the fizz of discovery has died away. I'm unsettled and exhausted. I can't think. I sense a puzzle of a thousand pieces lying before me, and I can't lift one, let alone connect it to another. We reach the door. Fox opens it and turns to say good-bye.

"How worried should I be?" I ask.

For the first time, his face softens. His pale eyes ease around the corners.

"Miss Macallister, I can only promise I'll do my damnedest to see no harm comes to Mrs. Digby, so long as I'm on the case."

AFTER HE LEAVES, I finish my Bloody Mary and make some dry toast. There's no point in trying to sleep, but I return to my bedroom anyway and pick up the photograph on the nightstand.

You have to remember that my sister is an artist. Since we were children she would stare at a painting or a drawing, a statue or a photograph, and take in every detail, however small. She would remember things about people and places. She would pick up her charcoals or her watercolors or her oil paints, and what I noticed—when I was bothered to notice—was that *every stroke mattered*, every speck that appeared on the paper or the canvas had some purpose, like a novelist writing a book—*every word matters*—or a musician composing a symphony—*every note matters*.

So I study that photograph with the same attention to detail from which I imagine she created it. I squint at the children's faces and their clothing. Though the photograph is black and white, I can tell they're standing in front of some Arctic habitat, like the one in the Bronx Zoo. An animal stands behind the little girl. It has white fur, and it's preparing to slide into the water. A polar bear.

I set the photograph back down on the nightstand and walk to the hallway closet, where I pull down the suitcase from the uppermost shelf.

IRIS

JUNE 1940
Rome, Italy

Since the day Iris had returned from her week with Sasha, the tenth of May, the radio remained switched on almost permanently—except when Ruth and Iris were asleep—blaring out tinny news bulletins from the BBC that turned worse and worse as the days went by.

Ruth was so depressed by the news, she spent the first few days in bed, reading newspaper after newspaper, calling for endless cups of tea, and when she finally rose, she said enough was enough, it was time to book passage home while they still could. Iris said she wasn't going home until the government ordered her to, but Ruth had bought her a ticket anyway, second class, for the SS *Antigone* leaving Civitavecchia on the twelfth of June. The tickets sat in the desk drawer. Iris refused to open it.

To make matters worse, she'd hardly seen Sasha at all. He worked all day at the embassy, sometimes sleeping there overnight, and Iris missed him the way you would miss breakfast, lunch, and dinner if they were all taken away from you at once, as if she'd stuffed herself at a banquet and been told the next day she couldn't eat again, ever. In the beginning, he wrote her a couple of tender notes, but since then he hadn't sent her so much as a postcard, let alone telephoned her.

To be fair, she *did* warn him that Ruth's work had dried up and he shouldn't try to telephone, because Ruth rarely left the apartment except to buy food and newspapers. Iris had never held a job, anyway, which she now regretted because she hated all this spare time, and all the war talk had turned Ruth into a bundle of nerves, snapping at whatever Iris said or didn't say. The tension grew worse by the day. Iris felt this inarticulate scream in the air between them. To escape, she'd taken to wandering around Rome with her sketchbook, filling page after page with shadowed, moody drawings of policemen and beggars and soldiers, or else the ruins of civilizations past, the Colosseum or the Forum. She would sit on some ancient stone and contemplate arches and columns that once teemed with civic life, and the idea calmed her. What did Gertrude say to Hamlet?—*Thou knowst tis common, all that lives must die, passing through nature into eternity.* Why rail against the tragedy of the human condition? Wars came and went, they destroyed and then created anew. What difference did her small, inconsequential life make among all these dozens of generations, all of them living and loving and fighting and grieving?

One day in early June, she sat in a café near the Palazzo Venezia, drinking listless coffee, while a pair of Fascists argued at the table next to her. Iris took out her sketchbook. Until now, she hadn't paid much attention to those men in their angry black shirts. She would have liked to pretend they didn't exist, and anyway she felt no connection to them at all, like foreigners from a country she'd never heard of. Today she studied them from the corner of her gaze. She'd learned some Italian over the past several months, and she could pick out certain words, but the truth was, she didn't really care what they were saying. She didn't understand the Fascist creed to begin with; politics had never interested her. Still, they *were* people, weren't they? They were men who, for reasons of their own, believed certain things so passionately they were willing to fight for them. In that respect, were they so different from Sasha? Each believed with his whole heart that he was doing the right thing, making the world a better place. Iris took out her sketchbook. She filled in the two men with quick, bold strokes of her charcoal. She tried not to glance at them too often; she stamped the images on her mind and drew from that memory as long as it lasted, and then she dipped for more.

She was nearly done with the drawing when one of them caught sight of her catching sight of him and nudged his friend. They turned to stare at her, at the sketchbook in her lap, the charcoal poised above the page.

Iris flipped the sketchbook shut and looked around for the waiter. Before she could find him, a shadow fell over the table. She glanced up just as one of the Blackshirts snatched the sketchbook from her lap.

"Hey!" She lunged after the book and fell right out of the chair. In an instant she was up again, but the man was already ripping the pages from the book, two at a time, flinging them into the air. The white leaves fluttered and scattered and littered the sidewalk. Iris yelled, *Stop, you can't do that, somebody help,* but the other people in the café glanced over their shoulders and turned swiftly away, and the passersby pretended not to notice anything at all, although they took care not to step on any of the drawings.

A DOOR CLICKED OPEN somewhere above her, and the noise echoed down the stairs.

"Iris? Is that you?"

Iris stuffed the handkerchief back in her pocketbook and wiped her eyes on her sleeve. "Yes. Yes, I'm fine."

Ruth's footsteps clattered down the stairs. Iris couldn't find the strength to rise. Ruth whipped around the second-floor landing and paused.

"Oh, pumpkin! What's wrong?"

"Nothing."

Ruth hurried down the rest of the stairs and sat down next to Iris. "That bastard. I oughta knock his lights out."

"It's not—it's not— It's my sketchbook!"

"What happened? Did you leave it on a bus somewhere?"

Iris told her sister about the Blackshirts and the café, about all the charcoal drawings fluttering in the air to land on the dirty floor and the sidewalk, about all the people who pretended not to notice, who wouldn't help, even the waiter. How the two men had left, jeering at her, and disappeared down the street.

Ruth took a handkerchief from her pocket. "Here."

"And I'm pretty sure they didn't *pay*, either!" Iris said, blowing her nose.

"Fascist pigs."

"I g-gathered up the pages, but they're all d-dirty and torn and just *ruined*."

Ruth gathered Iris in her arms and spoke soothingly into her hair. "Another week and we'll be gone from here. No more god-damn wars and Blackshirts. I'll take you home and everything will be all right again."

Iris leaned her face into Ruth's shoulder, which smelled of cig-arettes and some kind of perfume. Her throat hurt, not because of crying but because of everything she couldn't say to her own twin sister—the whole story—how she didn't want to leave, she couldn't leave, she could not possibly leave one-half of her entire heart in Rome and continue to exist—it was a medical impossibility. The incalculably precious moments of Tivoli laid against her present despair. All those pages torn from her sketchbook, containing ev-erything that was beautiful inside her.

THE NEXT EVENING, THE eighth of June, Harry arrived at their apartment for dinner. He was exhausted. *Feed me*, Harry begged, and Ruth poured out the drinks while Iris dressed a chicken and scraped together vegetables for a salad. Harry sucked every particle of meat from the bones and sat back on the sofa with a bottle of gin. Ruth asked what was up, was it really as bad as people were saying?

"Worse," said Harry. "They'll be in Paris in a week."

"What about Dunkirk?" Iris asked. "The poor English soldiers."

"They got as many out as they could. It's a miracle, really. Paris is next. There's nothing to keep the Nazis out."

"Poor Paris."

Harry looked destroyed. His shirt hung from his bones. His cheeks were hollow, his skin pale and impoverished. Even his hair looked tarnished. Iris couldn't believe her eyes. Harry, the stalwart older brother, their protector from the vicissitudes of life, the man of the house! She wanted to cook him another chicken and watch him eat it. She wanted to comfort him, to hold him in her arms like a child. She wanted to ask him about Sasha. Was Sasha as ruined as Harry? As overworked and underfed and underloved?

"What about Italy?" Ruth asked.

"Any day now." Harry straightened and reached for the bottle to refill his glass. They'd been drinking it neat, not even bothering with tonic water. "Maybe before you leave. Say, that's lucky you bought your tickets already. Order's going out to evacuate."

"Evacuate?" Iris cried.

"That's right. Soon as Mussolini declares war, the order goes out from the embassy. All Americans out, no exceptions, except embassy staff."

"Can't we stay and volunteer or something?" said Iris.

Harry gaped at her. "Volunteer for what? The Italian Red Cross? Help out the Fascists?"

"Maybe you've got a position available at the embassy for me."

"Iris, don't be stupid," said Ruth. "We're leaving next week. It's all settled."

"It's not settled. I never agreed to go. You went out and bought that ticket without even asking me."

"I don't need to *ask*. We're going home, that's all. Christ. What don't you understand about *evacuate*?"

"They can't *make* us go if we don't want to. There's no *law*. Is there?" Iris looked at Harry.

Harry lit a cigarette and shrugged. "No law against being an idiot that I heard of."

"Anyway, Italy's not going to war against us. America's still neutral, last I checked."

Ruth shot from her chair and marched to the kitchen.

"What's all this about?" Harry said.

"Oh, it's just Ruth. She's in a big fat hurry to go home, for some reason. I don't get it."

Harry spoke slowly. "Well, she's not wrong, is she? I mean, why the hell are you so determined to stay?"

"I just like Italy, that's all."

"But Italy's going to *war*, pumpkin. You don't understand what that *means*. A country at war, it's not a place for tourists."

"Don't speak to me like I'm a child, Harry."

Ruth marched back out of the kitchen and planted her hands on her hips. Her face was all lit up. "You're *acting* like a child! Like an *idiot child*! What, you *just like Italy*? What about how I picked you up off the stairs yesterday, blubbering like a baby because some crummy Blackshirts ripped up a few of your goddamn drawings?"

"Hold on," said Harry. "*What* happened?"

"It's nothing! I shouldn't've been drawing the two of them like that."

"It wasn't nothing. You were scared as a wee rabbit, Iris, and if a couple of Blackshirts can scare you like that, you won't last a week once the soldiers start with the rape and plunder."

"Oh, don't be ridiculous—"

"For God's sake, Iris," Harry said, topping up his drink, "just go home with Ruth! Rome's not going anywhere. What's keeping you here?"

"I'll tell you what's keeping her. Some fellow."

Harry almost dropped the gin bottle. "Are you kidding me?"

"Ask her, if you don't believe me."

"Iris? What the hell's going on?"

Iris set her glass on the floor, walked across the room, picked up her pocketbook from the coat stand, and walked out the door. As she left, she heard Harry's plaintive voice posing some question to Ruth.

THE STREETS WERE WARM and wet with rain, so recently departed that the eaves dripped on Iris's hair and shoulders and speckled her dress. As if she cared! She dodged around pedestrians and raindrops, hurried down streets and around corners, crossed the Tiber as twilight settled over the domes and rooftops of Rome. She reached Sasha's apartment in record time, not quite half an hour, shivering a little from the evening breeze on her wet skin.

Iris loved the street where Sasha lived. It was one of those quiet, ancient side streets you sometimes found in Rome, tucked around the corner from some grand boulevard packed with shops and achingly fashionable shoppers. She loved the damp, sleepy air and the trees and especially the buildings, tall and pale and curiously austere, so that you couldn't help but imagine what rich woods and frescoed walls existed inside. The first time Sasha unlocked the heavy, iron-barred door and ushered Iris into the vestibule and the courtyard beyond it, she thought she had never been so enchanted. She told Sasha it was like a secret garden, a fairy palace. In the late evening when they returned from Tivoli, she and Sasha had tangled together in the shadows beneath an orange tree. Iris had fallen asleep and Sasha woke her sometime during the night to carry her upstairs. The memory hurt her ribs. She actually pressed her hand there, at the intersection of bone, as she pressed the button next to his name on the brass plate. She waited for a minute before she pressed it again, although she knew he wasn't there. Of course not. He'd be working at the embassy, working through the night, sleeping on the sofa. Nobody in the entire consulate worked harder than Sasha Digby, Harry told them. This used to make her so proud.

She rang the bell a third time and looked up and down the street. Night had arrived, everything was dark. A streetlamp gleamed against the wet cobblestones. Iris opened her pocketbook and pulled out one of the pages she'd rescued yesterday, a sketch of the façade of the Pantheon, ripped at a careless diagonal across the top. She turned it over and wrote a note to Sasha, which she folded twice into a small square and slipped into the letterbox.

When she returned home, Harry had gone, and Ruth was cleaning the dishes in her kimono. Iris stood in the kitchen doorway and said, "So what did you tell Harry?"

A cigarette dangled from the corner of Ruth's mouth. She didn't trouble to remove it, or even to turn in Iris's direction. "I'm not a snitch, if that's what you're asking," she said, and those were the last words either of them spoke to each other for three whole days.

THE NEXT DAY, RUTH started packing up the apartment.

She dragged the steamer trunks from their duty as sofa tables and opened them up. She sorted through clothes and books—discarded the unwanted into a pile she took to the convent around the corner. Everything that didn't belong exclusively to Iris got packed or given away. Harry took all the wine and gin and mixers; the Sisters of the Sacred Heart took all the rest. Ruth was ruthless. She was a virago of organization. While Iris reclined on the sofa—which, like the rest of the furniture, came with the apartment—and leafed through a magazine, Ruth marched from cupboard to drawer, kitchen to bathroom, and emptied every sign of their habitation.

The day after that, she cleaned.

Binding her head in a matronly scarf, Ruth put on her oldest dress and set to work with mop and brush and buckets full of soapy water. Iris watched her in amazement. Because they weren't talking to each other, she couldn't ask what had brought on this fit of domesticity. Was Ruth trying to scour the floorboards or something more elusive? All this ferocious hygiene, what did it mean? Ruth scrubbed silently on. The apartment took on the smell of lemons and vinegar. The radio scratched away on its shelf. At some point, Ruth stopped midstroke and lifted her head to listen. Iris folded up the magazine and walked to the radio, where she turned up the volume dial. A familiar Italian voice shouted into the bare, acidic stillness of the living room. Every time it paused for breath, some crowd roared to fill the void. To Iris's ears, it was a joyless roar. You'd have thought those Fascists would be ecstatic to go to war against the plutocrats, but they weren't. Something was missing. It was the roar of patriotic duty, not fervor. Iris thought of the two men in black shirts the other day and wondered if their voices made up some tiny part of that noise. She turned to the window and shut it, even though they couldn't actually hear the crowd from here. Mussolini would be speaking from a balcony in the Palazzo Venezia, which was over a mile away and thankfully out of earshot.

THE NEXT DAY, IRIS woke to the sound of Ruth rattling around the kitchen cabinets. She opened the shutters to the gray, warm sky, but the morning air didn't revive her. The same sick despair clung to the organs in her middle. The same ache inside her chest.

Iris put on her dressing gown and wandered into the living room. She checked the front door—no folded note, no envelope pushed under the crack. Of course not. She turned her head to hear the noise from the open doorway to the kitchen, where Ruth seemed to be making coffee, by the clink of the percolator lid.

All around her, the apartment was bare. Ruth's steamer trunk sat in the middle of the floor. Iris's trunk sat against the wall next to her room, waiting to be filled. Today was the eleventh of June, and the SS *Antigone* departed from the pier in Civitavecchia at noon tomorrow.

Iris walked to the kitchen and stopped in the doorway. Ruth was slicing bread for toast and didn't turn. The percolator made comforting noises nearby.

"Well?" said Ruth. "Out with it."

"I was wondering if anyone's called for me. Any letters or notes or anything."

Ruth laid down the knife and turned her head. Her face was unexpectedly soft and full of sympathy.

"I'm sorry, pumpkin. Not that I know of."

Iris nodded and walked toward her bedroom. She took hold of the handle of the steamer trunk and dragged it inside. She made her bed neatly and didn't think about the April day when she slept with a man for the first time on this bed and decided she was in love. She figured it was best not to think about these things as you packed your clothes and shoes and your dear little objects, preparing to leave that man a few thousand miles behind you. There would be other men. Ruth seemed to flit from beau to beau without any travails of the heart. Iris folded her underthings into a bundle and imagined having sexual intercourse with a man who was not

Sasha Digby. But this man continued stubbornly to be long and lanky, and his gold hair kept falling in his face as he made love to her. At least that face was blank. No eyes, no nose or mouth or chin—just a peculiar, blurred void that no amount of determined imagination could sketch in.

HARRY TOOK THEM OUT for a farewell dinner at their favorite restaurant. Ruth had insisted; Iris said she would rather not, but since she couldn't come up with a plausible excuse, other than fatigue—the truth was, they had eaten here with Sasha once—off they went in their best dresses.

Harry wasn't the most observant of men, and to be fair he'd been deeply distracted those past weeks, so it wasn't until dessert that he noticed Iris hadn't been saying much.

"Oh, our pumpkin's got the blues, that's all," Ruth said.

"Aw, poor Iris. You'll forget all about the bastard when you get home, believe me."

Iris looked at Ruth. Ruth shrugged her shoulders.

"Don't be silly," Iris said. "I'm just tired, that's all. I've been packing all day. I've forgotten about *him* already."

Harry raised his glass. "Good for you. Take my advice, go home and find a nice American kid to fall in love with. You can't trust these Italians anyway. Right, Ruthie?"

Ruth clinked her class against Harry's. "Don't I know it."

"Too bad neither of you hit it off with Digby," said Harry, lighting a cigarette. "I tried to lure him along tonight. No use."

"Oh? What did he say?" Iris asked.

"Too busy, he said. Poor bastard's been working night and day. Catches a few winks on the sofa and he's back at his desk. I don't know what they've got him doing, but it's just about killing him."

On the way home, Iris said to Ruth, "So you told Harry I was seeing some Italian fellow?"

"I didn't say one way or another. I just let him reach his own conclusions. I'm no snitch, but I'm not a liar, either."

Iris walked silently. Ruth rummaged in her pocketbook and lit a cigarette.

"Pumpkin, you're taking this too hard. He's a louse, all right? A dog in a manger. Do like Harry says. Find some nice, simple American kid when we get home. Some fellow who really appreciates you. I'll help you. I've got a good eye."

"Sure you do. A good eye for husbands, maybe."

"So what if I do? Let the other woman do all the work of breaking him to saddle, that's what I say. Picking his socks up off the floor. We'll go back to New York, we'll set up a household of our own, just you and me, and take our men on the side with a spoonful of whipped cream. What do you say to that?"

"Sounds like a swell idea," said Iris.

Their heels went clickety-clack on the sidewalk, and the old buildings slid by, smeared by centuries of soot and dirt. A clear, bright moon rose above the city. Iris tried to paste it all in her memory, her last night in Rome, but nothing stuck. The magic was gone. Like Iris, the streets were quiet with foreboding.

RUTH ORDERED A TAXI for nine o'clock in the morning to take them to Civitavecchia, twenty miles up the coast where the ferries and steamships docked. Iris remembered going to see *Tosca* at the Teatro Reale dell'Opera last winter, and how the chief of police, when he writes out the safe passage for Tosca and her lover, asks if she plans to leave Rome from Civitavecchia, and Tosca replies hopelessly, *Sì*, and you can tell by the uneasy music that something's wrong—they'll never reach Civitavecchia. That was how Iris felt right now. Except Ruth wasn't some wicked police chief. Ruth was her sister and confidante, the person she trusted most in the world, especially now. Ruth would take her to safety. Together with Ruth, she'd find a way forward.

By ten minutes after nine, the taxi hadn't come. Ruth thought he might be outside and hadn't troubled to ring the bell. "You telephone the taxi company," she said to Iris, exasperated, "I'll go downstairs and see if I can flag him down."

Iris picked up the telephone and called the taxi company. In her broken Italian, she tried to explain the problem, and what she understood was that they dispatched the taxi, signorina, and it wasn't their fault if he hadn't arrived yet. Maybe she should look outside?

Iris hung up the telephone and stared at the bare walls, the empty apartment, the closed shutters, the steamer trunks by the door. How was it possible that she was leaving, that these walls that had rung with joy and merriment were now like a tomb? Ah, well. That was life. You won some, you lost some. You caught some glimpse of the sublime just before you fell into the mire.

The telephone rang.

Iris jumped.

The taxi company, she thought. She picked up the receiver and said, *Pronto.*

"Iris? Is that you?"

"*Sasha?*"

"Thank God. Thank God."

"What's the matter?"

"What's the *matter*? Christ. I just came home to bathe and change, and there's this *note* from you. My God, why didn't you say anything? Why didn't you tell me?"

"I *did*."

"Don't you know I've been going crazy, wondering what happened with us? Why you never answered me or telephoned back or anything?"

"Answered what?"

"My letters! My notes! I called twice a day. I left message after message. Just ask Ruth. And now *this*? The day you're *leaving? By the way, Sasha, I'm going to have your baby?* Why not just rip my heart out of my chest and finish the job?"

Iris whispered, "I don't understand. I never received anything. I never knew."

The telephone line crackled static in her ear. She swiveled around to face the door, which Ruth had left ajar.

"Goddamn," Sasha said slowly. "The bitch."

"No. No. It's some mistake."

"Iris, *don't go*. Please. Just stay where you are."

"I can't. The steamship—twelve o'clock—"

"*Stay where you are!* For God's sake! Just trust me, won't you? I'll be there in twenty minutes!"

"Sasha—"

The line clicked and went dead. Iris held the receiver to her ear anyway. Maybe it would come back to life again—maybe some wise, impartial operator's voice would explain everything, like in the movies.

She heard the quick thump of footsteps climbing the stairs. The door flung open. Ruth said, "Thank God, he's here at last. Iris, could you . . ."

From the dead receiver came a buzzing noise. Iris set it carefully in the cradle. Ruth stood in the doorway, flexing her fingers against her crisp linen trousers. A couple of lines appeared across her forehead.

"I just want to know whether you saved the letters," Iris said. "Did you save his letters or did you throw them away?"

"Look, it was for your own good. You're a bunny, Iris, a baby bunny. You don't know from anything. No idea how it is with men like that. He's too complicated for you. He'll take over your life, if he doesn't break your heart first. He'll run around on you, *believe me*, you can't trust him, he'll—"

"Just tell me whether you saved the *goddamn letters*."

Ruth whistled the air out of her lungs and threw up her hands. She kicked the steamer trunk next to her—it happened to be hers—and crouched down to open it with the little key from her pocket. Iris watched her rummage around. It was like watching an actress in a film, or someone in a dream. Her heart smacked against her ribs. She couldn't even feel her fingers, they were so cold.

Ruth rose at last. Her right hand clutched a packet of envelopes. "He's a narcissist," she said.

"Takes one to know one."

"Not true. I've slept with one or two, that's how I recognize it."

"Give me the letters."

"Iris, you're such a sweetheart. You're so sweet and gentle. He's going to crush you. He's going to gobble up all that sweetness to try and make himself whole, and it's not going to work, and he'll blame you for it and make you miserable. I couldn't let him do it."

"Give me the letters."

Ruth held out her hand. "You'll note they're still sealed."

"How honorable of you."

"I was going to give them to you later. Once you were cured."

Iris put the letters in her pocket. "I should have known. I should have figured it out. I should've had the nerve to call him up myself. I should've had the guts to march right up to him and ask him what was going on. But I didn't. You know why?"

"Because you trusted me. You never imagined in a million years I would play such a mean, dirty trick on you."

"So I ask you, Ruth. Who's worse, you or him? Who's really using me to fill some hole inside?"

Ruth blinked and turned around to close and lock the lid of the steamer trunk. She wore a white linen shirt tucked into the beige linen trousers. A silk scarf secured her hair in a ponytail. She looked like she'd just stepped out of a fashion shoot for a travel magazine. When she straightened and turned bravely back to Iris, only her pink eyes gave her away.

"So are you coming with me, or not?"

"I'm going to have a baby," Iris told her.

"You don't say."

Iris folded her arms across her chest. Ruth glanced to the shuttered window and back to Iris, and it reminded her of the time Sasha stood in her bedroom, not quite certain of her, and the same confidence she felt then returned to her now.

"You're making a mistake," Ruth said. "You can still come home with me. We'll find a way. You and me, Iris. You still have a chance."

"Actually, I like my chances here."

"Then you really are an idiot." Ruth picked up her pocketbook and slung it over her shoulder. "So long, then."

"So long."

Ruth dragged her steamer trunk into the hallway and shut the door. Iris heard her call for the taxi driver—bark instructions—*bang bang bang* as the poor trunk made its way to the courtyard. Then nothing, not even the roar of an engine. Just the smell of vinegar and wood, the smell of an empty apartment.

Iris sat down on the lid of her trunk and waited for Sasha to arrive.

TWO

I am really two people. I am a private
person and a political person.

Of course, if there is a conflict,
the political person comes first.

—*Kim Philby*

LYUDMILA

Sometimes it seems to Lyudmila that her work is futile. No matter how many traitors she unmasks, no matter how many acts of subversion, no matter how many instances of heresy to the great faith, a hundred more spring to life before her eyes. There's always some note out of tune in this Soviet chorus, some person who puts his own self-interest ahead of the interest of the state. Sometimes it's the very person who sings the best and the loudest.

Trust no one.

Early on in her work—the beginning, really—she learned to strip away all sentiment from her judgment. When is it possible to feel and to think at the same time? *Never.* So as Lyudmila pursued all possible candidates for the ASCOT leak over the past year, she didn't regard past service to the Soviet Union, faithful or not; nor did she consult her opinion of the man's character. There are only *facts*—did he have access to the information suspected to have been leaked? Did he have the opportunity and the means to communicate it? But until recently, there were not enough facts to guide her.

No further ASCOT communications were intercepted. The agent seemed to have gone quiet.

Now she sits in her small, windowless office in Moscow Centre and contemplates a photograph. It was taken a year ago in Gorky Park, where a local team had intercepted a bundle of photographs and coded messages during a random search of an ice cream vendor. Under interrogation, the vendor admitted to operating a post-box for an agent whose name and identity he didn't know. So the KGB sent a surveillance team. They had taken hundreds of photographs that yielded nothing useful, so the photographs had been filed away. Lyudmila had discovered their existence almost by accident, a conversation in the corridor with a secretary in the Moscow counterintelligence section.

To any ordinary observer, the scene's perfectly innocent. A tall, gangly man buys ice cream for his family—a wife and three children, two boys and a girl—what is wrong with that? But Lyudmila recognizes this man. It's HAMPTON, the American defector. HAMPTON now works primarily as an academic, lecturing on foreign relations at Moscow State University, but he's also frequently employed by the KGB training program. He lives in Moscow with his three children and his wife, who (if Lyudmila's not mistaken) is shortly to deliver another baby. Lyudmila knows all this not just because it's her job to know what men like HAMPTON are up to, but because his two older children happen to attend the same school as her own daughter.

LYUDMILA HAS A DAUGHTER, yes. Marina was born at the end of 1940, nine months after Lyudmila discovered her husband in possession of a radio set, with which he regularly listened to broadcasts from the BBC and other Western sources. She was twenty-six years old and deeply in love, but it was her duty to report this subversive activity to the authorities and so she did. She kept the baby, however. She and her mother raised little Marina together, and the three of them were Lyudmila's whole family until her mother—weakened by wartime deprivation—died five years ago. So now it's only Lyudmila and Marina.

When Lyudmila arrives home from work, her head full of the ASCOT case, Marina calls to her from the tiny kitchen, where she's making dinner. "Coming, pet," says Lyudmila. She sets down her briefcase and takes off her shoes and her small hat and pads across the living room. Marina looks up from the stove. Her blue eyes are exactly like her father's, crisp and smiling, surrounded by wet black lashes.

"How was your day, Mama?" she asks.

"Good. What are you making?"

"Solyanka."

"Hmm. My favorite soup, is it? Have you been misbehaving at school again?"

Marina gives her a playful look. "Maybe."

They eat the soup together at the little table in the corner of the tiny living room. Marina does her homework and Lyudmila checks it carefully. Of course, there are no mistakes. Dmitri was an electrical engineer when he was sent to the gulag; he had been the smartest boy in school, when they were children. He also had a rebellious streak, which he passed on to his daughter.

"Mama," Marina says, once they're settled on the sofa—Lyudmila reading a KGB training manual, Marina reading Tolstoy for school tomorrow—"how old were you when you met my father?"

Lyudmila thinks for a moment. "I was twelve years old."

"Ah. The same as me."

"A little older."

"Oh, a few months," Marina says impatiently.

She returns to her book and Lyudmila returns to her training manual, but thanks to Marina's strange question she can't concentrate. She keeps thinking about Dmitri, and how he used to shield her from some of the other children, who teased her because she was so smart and serious and wore clothes even uglier and shabbier than the other girls. She thought he was just being kind, but when she turned seventeen he told her it was because he fell in love with her that first day at school, when they were both twelve years old.

THE NEXT DAY, LYUDMILA receives word of an unusual request from the American embassy. Mrs. Alexander Digby, who has a history of difficult childbirth, has apparently invited her sister to stay with her in Moscow, during and after the period of her delivery. The sister wishes to formally apply for two visas to enter the Soviet Union, one for herself and one for her husband, to whom she is newly married.

Lyudmila's skin prickles as she reads this report. She holds no truck with *sentiment*, but *instinct* is a KGB officer's most valuable asset.

She picks up her telephone and asks to speak to the head of the American section.

RUTH

I'll say this for Herbert Hudson. When I told him I needed four hundred dollars to fly to Europe and help my sister with her new baby, he didn't ask any silly questions, like why couldn't I sail instead, and when would I return. He wrote me a check and wished me bon voyage, then expressed his hope that the agency would remain a going concern in my absence.

That was Saturday afternoon at his place. By Sunday afternoon at five o'clock, I'm safely belted into my seat on the Pan Am Strato Clipper transatlantic service, scheduled to stop in Boston before continuing across the ocean to Paris and then to Rome. On my lap, the Sunday paper features a photograph of our party at the Palmetto Club on the front of the society page, in which Miss Barbara Kingsley is singled out as "*the* up-and-coming model in New York these days." I fed that caption myself to my old pal Joan on the social beat, and it gives me immense satisfaction—it always does—to see my words repeated back to me in sincere black and white.

Now, I don't know if you've ever been inside one of those new double-decker Boeing Stratocruisers, but I can't recommend them enough. For one thing, they're fast. We lift off from Idlewild bang on schedule at five P.M., and an hour later we descend from a thin layer of clouds to land in Boston to take on a few more passengers. You hardly even notice the change in altitude because they pressurize the cabin to sea level, and the noise of those four giant Pratt & Whitney propeller engines is no more than a droning annoyance. We land with scarcely a bump and roll to a magnificent stop near the terminal. The seating's all first class, as it should be, and I paid extra for one of those sleeping berths up front, since we won't land in Paris until the following afternoon and God knows I need a few decent hours of shut-eye. I settle back in my seat and peer idly out the window at the five passengers preparing to board. There's a young couple that looks as if they're headed on their honeymoon, bless them, all pink and bright the way you set off on adventures when you're just a baby. A couple of dour businessmen in pin-striped suits and fedoras, not entering into the spirit of things at all. A grand dame speaks in an animated way to the head stewardess, telling her exactly how to do her job.

They find their seats—the stewardess bolts the door. The propellers whine, the airplane trundles back to the runway. It's nearly seven o'clock in the evening and the sun is a molten pool to the west. I light a cigarette and stare out the window at America as it falls away below me. God only knows when I'll see it again.

I HAVEN'T RETURNED TO Rome in twelve years, not since I sailed away on that terrible day in June of 1940. The good ship *Antigone* was packed with desperate Americans and I had to share my second-class berth with a middle-aged artistic type of woman whose sum-

mer tour of Italy's Renaissance treasures had been cut short almost
before it began. I remember she was indignant about it all, as if
she'd traveled to Italy that spring with no expectation whatsoever
that her travels might be interrupted by a thing so inconvenient as
war. In fact, she hadn't wanted to go home at all—she'd kicked up a
real fuss, she claimed proudly—but since the Italians were putting
all the great paintings in storage and boarding up the museums,
there was no point but to capitulate as rapidly as the French had.
I found her complaints strangely soothing. She was one of those
people who was happy to talk about herself and her troubles to
a complete stranger and expected nothing more of you than the
occasional sympathetic noise. She said she would go back just as
soon as this awful business was over. Sometimes she asked about
me, and what I was doing in Italy, and I made up extravagant lies
about a love affair with a Russian émigré, a jealous Italian wife,
some extremely valuable jewelry, a discreet apartment decorated in
beautifully preserved Carracci frescoes, all of which she drank up
like punch. When we docked in New York she insisted on exchang-
ing addresses. I'm afraid I never answered her letter.

DINNER IS CATERED BY Maxim's of Paris and lasts seven courses.
I'm able to sleep a good six hours in my berth before being awakened by the happy, muffled cadence of the honeymooners consum-
mating their union in the berth below, the darlings. I put on my
robe and grope my way through the dimmed corridor to the ladies' dressing room. When I return and part the curtains to peer
through the little window, the first gray-green streaks of dawn
have appeared on the vast dome of sky outside, and I think what
a miracle it is that this disappearing sun should reappear so soon,

and how clever of man to rush east to meet it. Then I suppose I fall asleep, because I wake to a series of hard bumps, followed by the sensation of falling, like you feel on the downslope of a roller coaster. I sit up in my berth. The heavy drone of the engines continues without interruption. Another hard bump nearly sends me flying. Somebody screams. I hear the stewardesses hurrying down the aisle, hushing everybody with nice calm melodious phrases. One of them attends to us nervous souls in the sleeping area, sticking our little heads out between the curtains, all panicky.

"Is something the matter?" asks a woman across the aisle with the voice of Brünhilde. I believe it's the grande dame who boarded in Boston, all bosom and quivering neck—the one who will probably help pass out the life vests and prop up morale with her steadfast refusal to give her heirs the satisfaction of her passing.

"Just a little bumpy air, ma'am!" chirps the stew. "But I'm afraid we'll have to ask you to return to your seat and fasten the belt."

Everybody groans—we've paid extra for the berths, damn it, and I imagine those honeymooners were counting on another hour or two before breakfast is served—but we put on our slippers and trudge obediently to our seats.

The next hour is almost the most harrowing of my life. We pass through a storm, one of those North Atlantic gales, and I imagine the wind will surely rip the engines from the wings—will rip the wings from the fuselage. The man sitting next to me just turns the pages of his newspaper, utterly unconcerned. At one point, when the stews come through to pass out chewing gum and ginger ale—I take both—he asks me if I'm a nervous flier.

"Not usually, but I've never flown through weather like this."

"Don't worry," he replies. "The pilots are highly trained, and the airplane itself has endured numerous tests in weather far worse than this."

He's what you might call an ordinary man, so very ordinary that you wouldn't even notice him unless he spoke to you. Five foot eight, dark, neatly trimmed hair, unexceptional suit, unexceptional face—you know the type I mean. He seems to affect a trace of an accent, but I can't place it and don't want to be so awkward as to ask. We exchange a few more observations. He asks if I'm flying for business or pleasure, and I tell him pleasure. I say I'm visiting a friend in Rome and turn back to the window. When we land in Paris, he takes his briefcase from the luggage cabinet above our heads, tips his hat, and wishes me a pleasant stay in Italy, and I think no more about him. I don't think I could even recognize his face if you showed me a picture of it.

WE LAND IN ROME at the most beautiful moment of the evening, just before the sunset. By the time I make my way through immigration and customs and hail a taxi to take me to Orlovsky's apartment on the Palatine Hill, it's twilight. He's expecting me. I sent a telegram on Saturday night, and though I hadn't received a reply by the time I left for the airport, I didn't need one. He can't possibly refuse me.

All right, so those extravagant lies I told the nice lady on board the *Antigone* weren't *entirely* truthless. I first met Valeri Valierovich Orlovsky only a couple of weeks after arriving in Rome in 1939. He was, in fact, a Russian émigré. He could have styled himself a prince, if he chose to, but in his professional life he was simply Orlovsky. He'd arrived in Rome twenty years earlier, young and penniless, and apprenticed himself to a tailor. Now he was head of one of the great fashion houses in Italy. He had married a beautiful Roman aristocrat who went into rages whenever he got a new mistress and could only be mollified by diamonds of the first water, and his atelier was the most beautiful building I had ever seen. He kept a private studio on the piano nobile, decorated—he said—by those Carracci frescoes I mentioned earlier, although as I knew nothing about frescoes, then or now, I can't say whether he was telling the truth. They were mesmerizing, however. Whenever we slept together, I would stare for ages at those entwined nude figures that so mimicked our own and thought how erotic Rome was, how you simply couldn't *do* this back in New York City—sprawl with your lover on a studio couch in the middle of the afternoon and gaze at some ancient, obscene painting that was part of the wall itself.

This is the building where I direct the taxi. So far as I know, his wife has neither died nor divorced him (she's Catholic, and they have seven or eight children together at last count) nor yet murdered him herself, as I would have done. I admit, I feel a little anxious when I ring the bell. Will he meet me? Will he care at all? We parted in such terrible anger, after all.

But the door opens, and there he stands, a million years old. His hair has turned gray, his jowls now merge seamlessly into his neck. His famous black eyes glitter as he holds out his arms to me. "Bambina!" he says in his curious accent—Italy by way of old St. Petersburg, a residual disdain for definite articles. "I thought you would be married with dozen children by now."

I allow myself to be folded into his embrace. "Who says I'm not?"

"Your figure, bambina. So slim and beautiful still. And your skin, smooth like butter. But come inside. I brought out some good wine for you."

It's like I never left—like the past dozen years never passed. The vestibule is exactly the same, down to the single umbrella and four ivory-handled walking sticks in the wrought-iron stand. The little courtyard holds the same lemon trees—a few feet taller—and the same stone benches I recall. The staircase curves upward in the same spiral, the stone steps are worn down in the same shiny, dark divots. When he opens the familiar thick wooden door to the studio, every stick of furniture sits where I remember it. I stand next to the large, wide couch, which bears the same soft upholstery, and stare yet again at the domed ceiling, where the nymphs still gambol with their satyrs.

"You haven't changed a thing."

"Why should I? This way I am never old. I am always young man with beautiful young woman. Wine?"

"Oh, damn," I murmur.

"Is that yes or no?"

"Yes. I was just thinking about old buildings, that's all. Our fanatical need to keep them exactly as they were. I still live in my parents' old apartment in New York."

"But you have redecorated."

"Some of it. Not all."

He hands me the wine and nods. "Because if it stays as it was, they are not entirely dead, yes? Your childhood still there in walls."

"What I've always hated about you, Orlovsky, is that you understood me better than anybody. Next you'll be telling me you were actually in love with me." I clink my glass against his. "Cheers."

"But I was in love with you. I love each girl I sleep with. I love them with all my heart." He presses his hand against his chest, where this generous organ resides. "But especially you, bambina."

"Oh, of course."

"No, is true. You have quality, special quality in your spirit, I cannot find word in English."

"Don't bother. I'm not twenty-two anymore, and I'm not here to be seduced. We can be perfectly honest with each other."

"But I am always honest with you, bambina. When did I ever tell lie to you?"

I make a skeptical noise. "Shall we sit? I don't imagine we have much time. The princess will want you home."

"My wife? No, she is not so particular now." He half shrugs, half gestures to the couch. "We are both getting old, yes? More kind to each other. Forgiveness. You see, it is relief to let go of passions."

I sit not on the couch, but on the armchair next to it—a massive, ancient hulk made of unyielding dark wood upholstered in sumptuous bronze and green tapestry, which contains its own set of memories. I recall a few as I arrange myself, things I haven't remembered in years, and I wonder at my own youthful abandon. What happened to that gamine blond girl who so gleefully straddled a married man in a chair built for a Medici prince and made him howl like some kind of Siberian wolf? Does she still exist? Or is age and wisdom a permanent affliction? The wine surprises me. "Oh, you've finally gone native, have you?"

"It seemed patriotic thing to do, in time of war. Then I developed taste for it." He brushes his hand over the corner of the sofa nearest me and sits like an old man, stiff and deliberate, not altogether confident in his joints. My God, what the war's done to him. Twelve years, and he's transformed from a vigorous, distinguished, infinitely charismatic man enjoying a singularly virile middle age to this creaking roué. "You approve? Is some champagne in cellar, I think."

"No, I like it." I fiddle with the stem. I've realized it was stupid to come here right off the airplane, so tired and disoriented, not just from the marathon flight but from Rome itself. I lived here less than a year—why did it take such an outsized hold of my imagination? "I saw your fall collection. Marvelous. That tweed dress with the—"

"Bambina," he says sadly, "you did not come all the way to Roma to talk to old man about his clothes, did you?"

"No."

"Then tell me what you want. What this besotted old lover can do for you to make amends for his sins."

"I need your help."

"So I am guessing. What do you need? Some money? Some work for new model?"

"Nothing so simple, I'm afraid. It's my sister, Iris. I think she's in terrible trouble."

He frowns. "Your sister? Little brown mouse with luscious tits?"

"The same."

"What kind of trouble? She needs husband? My son Giovanni—"

"A *husband*? God, no. The husband's the trouble." I set the empty wineglass on the floor and lean toward him, bracing my folded arms on my knees. "I need your help to go to Moscow and rescue her."

LET'S RETURN, FOR JUST a moment, to those sins Orlovsky mentioned.

As I said, I have some moral advantage over Orlovsky, which I never intended to use. Moral advantage has its own priceless value, after all, a hefty solid weight in the column of your assets, and if you cash it in, you don't possess this credit any longer. You're no longer wealthy in the only currency that human beings really care about.

On the other hand, isn't it merciful to allow others a chance to pay their debts?

When I first met Orlovsky, he made no secret of his hatred for the Bolsheviks. Obviously Russia needed to reform, he said, needed to modernize its archaic ways and make way for the lower classes to escape the terrible poverty that was the legacy of serfdom. But the Bolsheviks were no more than brutes, he went on, whose vision of world Communist revolution was a grotesque and indeed opportunistic twisting of an idealistic political movement to achieve both vengeance on their ideological opponents and power—always power—for themselves. He was absolute on this point, that bolshevism was *corruption*, was a psychological pathology. I remember how he used to pace naked around the studio—pale and compact and somewhat paunchy—still ravishingly masculine inside his field of bristling energy. He waved his arms and told me stories about neighbor informing on neighbor, about a petty party official he knew who delivered an impassioned speech at dinner about Communist principles—*From each according to his abilities, to each according to his needs*, that kind of thing—when everyone at the table knew that he sent his wife to obtain goods at the special shops available only to party officials in favor with Comrade Lenin.

"Well, why shouldn't he, if he could?" I said, because I loved to bait Orlovsky—if I wound him up enough, he would turn on me like a tiger. "It's human nature to want more and better things than your neighbor."

"Because of the hypocrisy, don't you see!" he raged.

"That's human nature, too."

"They turn citizen against citizen in name of solidarity! Is diabolical! They want everyone to be loyal only to state—not to his mother or father, not to his child, not to his neighbor, not to God. Only state!"

So I told him to come over here and demonstrate his loyalty to his lover, and he turned on me like a tiger. Oh, it was the most passionate affair I've ever had, before or since. We were insatiable together, and the businesslike way he treated me during photo shoots and fitting sessions only made us more concupiscent in private. All through the winter and early spring we carried on, dirty as hell, until one day at the end of March, not long before Iris's accident, when he rolled off me, lit a cigarette, and informed me in a regretful voice—this after making love twice during the course of a rainy morning!—that his wife had put her foot down and said enough with this new mistress of yours, you're neglecting your family.

"So what does that mean?" I said.

"It means we must go separate ways for some period of time, bambina."

"For how long? A week or two?"

"Longer, my love. After baby is born."

I sat up. You see, for a peculiar moment I thought he meant *our* baby, the one I was about to reveal to him, once I worked up the nerve. I had it all planned out. Dinner with a nice Bordeaux, a lively tussle on the couch, and then the news dropped casually, as a compliment to his virility, *just look what you've done to me, you wanton beast.* And then of course *I don't expect you to leave your wife,* that kind of thing, *but we'll get a nice cozy place somewhere, she'll come to accept the arrangement.*

After all, you told me the marriage is only in name. You told me this.

"What baby?" I said.

"I did not tell you? Laura is having baby." He counted on his fingers. "November, I think?"

I smacked him across his bottom. *"I'm* having a baby, you son of a bitch!"

He was surprised and apologetic. He said it was an unfortunate coincidence, but he had promised his wife he would give me up, and he could not go back on his word to Laura—she would tear his balls off—and anyway theirs was a sacred union ordained by God. I asked what was our union, chopped liver? The idiom perplexed him so he didn't answer right away. But I didn't wait for him to puzzle it out. I saw at once that I had been an idiot. I put on my clothes and stormed out, which solved Orlovsky's problem rather neatly, now that I think about it, and after some dithering—naturally he wrote to me and offered money, naturally I ignored him—I consulted one of the other models and found a reputable doctor to perform an abortion. I know you'll hate me for that, but the situation seemed impossible to me. Aside from being unsuited to motherhood, aside from the practical difficulties, aside from my irrational, outsized fear of the physical travails, in what possible hell could I give birth inside some shabby Italian hospital at the exact same time the Princess Orlovskaya was giving birth inside the grand villa she and Orlovsky shared in the hills outside of Rome? I scheduled the procedure for the beginning of May, when Iris was going away on her dirty weekend with Digby in Tivoli—adorably, she told me she was headed for some kind of artist holiday—and after that I had no wish to remain in Rome at all, war or no war. I simply couldn't get out of the city fast enough.

SO YOU SEE, IN addition to the great moral debt Orlovsky owes me for acting like such a skunk, I know he's disposed to hate the Soviet Union with a passion peculiar to exiles. In former days, I even suspected that he did what he could to undermine the Communist regime from time to time, by passing along whatever interesting tidbits came his way. I don't know if this might still be the case—the espionage, I mean—but nobody changes his political views once his hair starts to turn gray. If anything, those views harden into obstinacy in the face of any contrary evidence. It's almost as if that entire painful episode with Orlovsky—which I refused to think about afterward, so that it took on the quality of a dream and I had to remind myself that it really happened—has perhaps found some purpose after all. The sacrifice of young love and nascent life wasn't for nothing.

Orlovsky is more skeptical.

"To Moscow?" he says, incredulous. "Do you know what you are asking?"

"Obviously there's some difficulty—"

"Difficulty? Bambina cara, is suicide. Do you speak Russian?"

"Nyet a word."

He smacks his forehead. "*Gran Dio*. What do expect me to do?"

"Please. I know for certain you've got contacts in the Soviet embassy." (This is a bluff—it's not *impossible* he might have a friend on the inside, but who can know for certain?) "I need a tourist visa and maybe a name or two, people who might be able to help me."

"You are nuts. Who is going to risk his life for strange American woman and her sister?"

"Then forget the names. I just need a visa. You can do that much for me, I know you can. You hate the Soviet system. And you *owe* it to me, Orlovsky. You *know* you do."

He gives me a tormented look and rises from the couch. I think about how he used to pace naked across that floor, raging at the Soviet Union and its barbarous occupation of the human spirit, and then make love to me over the arm of the sofa or the drafting table or the rug, or downstairs in the courtyard against the lemon tree, and it occurs to me that the one place we never had intercourse was a bed. Orlovsky walks to the table without speaking and lifts the wine decanter. Even in his torment, he's a gentleman. He returns to me and refills my wineglass first, and then his own. Instead of resuming his seat, he continues to the window overlooking the courtyard, and I don't know, maybe he's thinking of the past, too. Maybe he's thinking of all the places he loved me, and how brutally he stopped.

"I might know somebody," he says softly.

IRIS

At first, Iris thought the man had mistaken her for someone else. He was bloated and untidy, with handsome features tucked in a pasty face and a shock of waving dark hair. He stared at her from the corner of the room, where he leaned heavily against a bookshelf in the company of two other men and sipped at a glass of clear liquid.

The party was like every other party. Whenever they moved to a new posting—Zurich, then Ankara, and now London—Iris somehow expected, against all experience, some change of pace and company and mood, to go along with the change of climate and national culture, but diplomats were all the same, and diplomatic parties all followed the same unspoken pattern. Protocol, you might call it, but Iris secretly hated words like *protocol*. *Pattern* she understood; pattern occurred in nature. *Rhythm, rhyme, repeat*—those were all appealing, but protocol? Just an ugly, artificial human invention. Like this party.

The flat was typical of London. It was both grand and shabby and smelled of coal smoke. The ceiling was the color of tea and mysteriously stained. The wallpaper curled from the corners, and the plasterwork was liable to crumble from some noble design above your head and into your hair—or worse, your drink. Speaking of drinks. Those were all right, at least. They flowed abundantly from bottles of wine and champagne, bottles of scotch and gin and brandy and so on, mixed—if they were mixed at all—in straightforward, no-nonsense combinations. As for food, well. You might be offered tinned mackerel on crackers, or a square of rubber masquerading as cheddar cheese. But it was best not to think too much about what you were eating, Iris had learned. Three years after the end of the war, Great Britain was a cramped, bland, ungenerous land of ration cards and making do.

Iris glanced down at the tidbit between her index finger and her thumb—some kind of colorless, elderly olive stuffed with pink matter. The old Iris would've tossed it into a houseplant, but Iris was now a seasoned diplomatic wife, so she knew the trick of chewing and swallowing food without quite passing it over your tongue. Then she drank champagne to chase down the olive—not bad— and when she looked up again, the man was still watching her.

SHE FOUND SASHA IN the study, between a bookshelf and a fog of cigarette smoke. She heard his laugh first, deep and abundant, about three-fifths of the way to his usual state of drunkenness at these things. He held his whiskey and his cigarette in the same hand. He was chatting earnestly with two other people—a scarred, silver-haired man named Philip Beauchamp, a friend of hers and Sasha's; and a handsome blond woman in a snug, rustcolored turtleneck sweater over a long tweed skirt, unfamiliar. The woman sucked on her cigarette and examined Iris as she sidled up to Sasha.

"There's a man staring at me in the other room," she told him.

"Is there? I don't blame him."

"He looks a little unsavory, if you ask me."

"Seedy chap, eh?" said Philip. "Must be Burgess. Dark hair, pudgy sort, probably drunk?"

"I think so."

Philip nodded. "Burgess, all right. If he makes a nuisance of himself, swat him with a newspaper."

The woman in the turtleneck laughed. "Don't listen to him. Burgess won't make a nuisance of himself with *you*. Perhaps your *husband*"—more laughter passed among them—"but women only by consent."

Iris laughed, too, though she wasn't quite in on the joke. The other thing about the diplomatic service, everyone knew one another—not just the outward man, but all his foibles, his eccentricities, his past indiscretions, things that among women would be called *gossip*—all shared without words, like a secret handshake.

"Mind you, he's got a first-rate brain," said Philip.

"Oh, no doubt of that," the woman said. "First-rate. And always good for a drunken escapade, whenever one's in need of those things."

"Charming fellow, if you like his particular brand of charm."

"What if you don't?" Iris asked.

"Then you'll hate him," said the woman. "Oh, I *say*. *Speak* of the very *devil*."

Iris swiveled her head just in time to see him walking through the doorway, the man named Burgess, holding a cigarette and a highball *brimming* with gin in his right hand and a champagne coupe in the left hand. He made straight for the slight gap between Sasha and Iris and slid himself inside it.

"This is for you, Mrs. Digby," he said solemnly, handing her the champagne.

"Oh! *Thank* you."

"Guy Burgess. Foreign Office. Now, you mustn't hold it against me, but I suspect I see more of your husband than you do."

"Not true," Sasha said. "Though not entirely false, either."

"All matters of state, I assure you. You do like champagne, Mrs. Digby?"

"Very much."

"Then you won't mind if I steal away the old man for just a moment? Matters of state, you see."

"Not at all," Iris said, and it wasn't entirely a lie.

AFTER A MOMENT OR two of trivial conversation, the blond woman—her name was Fischer, Nedda Fischer—invented some excuse and left Iris and Philip to each other. Iris smiled. Philip smiled back. The effect was ever so slightly sinister, because Philip had encountered some terrible calamity during the war—exactly *what*, nobody could agree, and Philip *himself* wasn't going to talk about it—that had left the right side of his face scarred and pitted and not quite as mobile as the left side. Also, most of the ear was missing.

It was commonly accepted that Philip's hair turned white after the injury. Iris found the effect somewhat dazzling, next to his dark eyes and surreal face. They'd met at a party like this one, about a month or so after she and Sasha moved here from Turkey. Sasha had become incapably drunk and Philip had driven them home in his Morris Eight, and it was only later that Iris discovered what a sacrifice this was, because of petrol rationing. She wrote him a thank-you note, and they went out to dinner the following week, Iris with Sasha and Philip with some woman they never saw again. Sasha told her that Philip's wife had left him right after the war, had simply taken the children and moved to Canada, and was now dragging the divorce interminably through the courts because of Philip's money. Iris spent weeks calling him *Mr. Boh-shahm* in her best French accent before he took her aside and confessed that his surname was actually pronounced *Beecham*, English style, and their mutual embarrassment was so severe that they agreed she should simply call him *Philip*, and just like that, they became the best of friends.

Which explained why the smile they shared now was one of mutual relief, because the flinty blond woman had finally left them alone.

"Has this aunt of yours arrived yet?" he asked her.

"Not until next week. She's setting herself up in the Dorchester for a week to show the girls the sights, Tower of London and Buckingham Palace and everything, and then we head down to Dorset, thank God."

He made a little bow. "Delighted to be of service."

"Honestly, we're awfully grateful for the cottage. I'm so desperate for some country air, I could scream."

"Will your husband be staying long?"

"The first week, and then only on weekends. He says it's a good time to catch up on work, when everyone's off in August."

"Digby's got a reputation for hard work."

"It's very nice for his employers. Less so for his boys and his poor neglected wife."

"Ah, how are the boys? Relieved to be out of school at last?"

"They are absolute *terrors* at the moment. The woman in the downstairs flat came up this morning and very politely requested that they stop running up and down the corridor, because her chandelier was shaking dangerously. I'm at my wit's end without a garden."

"It's jolly criminal, this business of stuffing young families into these beastly so-called mansion flats. You'll recall I did recommend you find a nice detached house down in Surrey or even Kent."

"You'll recall I did my best to convince Sasha to take your advice."

They exchanged a look of understanding.

Iris drank her champagne and continued. "Anyway, all will be forgiven in August, if the three of us can survive that long. Will we see much of you?"

"That's all up to you, my dear. Generally I go down after Ascot and don't come up to London again until after Boxing Day. But I wouldn't dream of intruding on your summer holidays."

"You wouldn't be intruding at all. How far away is the main house?"

"About a mile, I should think. Enough we shouldn't be on top of each other."

"Oh, but I'd be delighted if we were on top of each other!" Iris said, without thinking. Philip turned a little red and started to laugh, and Iris clapped her hand over her mouth. "I didn't mean—"

"Of course you didn't. It's part of your charm."

Iris looked away and said, "What were the three of you talking about when I came up? You were awfully engrossed in each other."

"Oh, just business. These hearings in Washington, you know. The—what do you call it?—the Un-American Activities Committee. Such a typically American name. There's a woman testifying right now who claims to have run a Soviet spy network in the State Department for years."

Iris didn't flinch, though her blood ran cold. "Soviets in the State Department? That's nonsense."

"It's all these chaps, you know, bright young things who radicalized at university in the thirties, when the capitalist economies went to pieces. They very fashionably joined the Communist Party as students and wound up recruited by the NKVD, or whatever they called themselves back then, the Soviet intelligence service."

"But surely they all shed their illusions as they got older?"

"Most of them, of course. I daresay the Nazi-Soviet pact did for a great many. Stalin's thuggery, the famines. But it's like a religion, you know. To the true fanatic, everything and anything can be twisted around to prove what you believe in."

Was it her imagination, or did Philip stare at her with particular focus as he said this? Iris forced a smile, a hopeless shake of the head. "Well, I certainly hope it isn't true. I hate betrayal of any kind."

"Yes, you do," Philip said kindly, "which is why I confess I've been dithering a bit with you. Wondering whether to bring the subject up."

"The hearings, you mean?"

"Not the hearings. It's about your husband, I'm afraid."

Iris swallowed down the rest of the champagne. "Sasha? Goodness."

"Do you mind if we sit?" He gestured to the nearby sofa—a deep, worn leather Chesterfield flanked by a pair of mismatched lamp tables. Iris followed the direction of his arm and sat on the edge of the cushion, holding her empty glass. He sat next to her, against the back of the sofa, more relaxed, at a respectful distance but still close enough to be private.

"I hope it's not something serious," she said.

"You may kick me if I'm being officious. It's only because I consider you a friend, Iris, whom I admire very much. I wouldn't dream of coming between a man and his wife—"

"Goodness," she said again.

"—but I've watched your distress in silence for the past few months, and I feel the time has come for me to butt in, as they say, because it may do some good. I beg your pardon. I'll come to the point. We are all sinners, and I don't judge a man for his sins, and we all drink perhaps a little too much in these circles, yours truly among the guilty. But Digby—stop me at once if I distress you—seems to have, shall we say, passed some point of no return, in recent months." Philip peered into Iris's face. "Do you hate me?"

"No. I'd be an idiot to tell you it's not true."

"I suppose what I'm asking is whether there's anything I can do to help. Whether you're aware of how much, and how dangerous— There's talk of indiscretion, the kind of thing that can ruin a man's career."

"I'm . . . I'm so sorry."

"For God's sake, it's not your *fault*. Frankly, I think the man's a fool to go out drinking all night with the lads, when he's got a woman like you waiting for him at home, and the children, too— wonderful boys. And I wouldn't have said a thing—I didn't *mean* to say a thing, not a word, but—well, there's a story from a reliable source—the other night, at the Gargoyle—I'll spare the sordid details, but perhaps one might be wise to convince him to spend all of

August down in Dorset. Keep him away from chaps like Burgess and that sort. Good fresh air and family life, I think it would do him a world of good."

Philip stopped and caught his breath, like a man relieved of a burden. He looked at her anxiously, and Iris gathered herself, because she hated to see Philip so uncomfortable.

"Yes, thank you. I think so, too. I've been trying to convince him, really I have. Because of course—well, I'm not a fool. You're very kind, you've been so tactful, but I'm not a fool."

Philip reached into his pocket and gave her a handkerchief.

"You see I'm arguing nobly against my own interest, because I should very much rather have you all to myself," he said.

"You're too sweet."

"I hope I haven't been a bother."

"No, no! You've meant well, you've been so kind. I know how difficult it must have been to say anything at all—such an awkward— a terrible thing to have to say to a-a wife." Iris kept the sobs under control, just a dab or two at the corners, though what she really wanted was to lock herself in a closet and bawl buckets of humiliation.

"You're quite in order to throw your drink in my face and call me a bastard."

"I don't have any left, and if it had been anyone other than you, Philip, I might have."

"I shall take that as a very great compliment, my dear. Believe me, if it had been any other woman, I should have kept my mouth shut. But I feel certain that Digby must have many brilliant qualities in order to deserve such a wife, and I wish on nobody the pain of . . . of marital discord."

"Of course."

"There. I've said my piece. Shall I fetch you another drink?"

Iris rose. "No, thank you. I'm going to find my husband, I think."

Philip rose and took her hand, and for a moment Iris thought he'd kiss it, like some courtier from a hundred years ago. But he only pressed her fingers between his two palms and said softly, "I think that would be a very good idea."

She started to pull her hand away and paused. There were still tears in her eyes, and she was afraid to blink in case they might spill out. So she left them there, brimming, because she wanted to make something clear to Philip, though she wasn't sure why.

"You know, we were very happy once, Sasha and I. In Rome, when we first married, we were very happy."

"Well, then," Philip said, with the same sad smile, "maybe you should go back."

COULD SHE? COULD IRIS and Sasha ever go back to Rome? It wasn't the first time Iris had thought about this, but she knew the answer was no. The Rome of their early months no longer existed, because the two of them were no longer the Sasha and Iris who'd met and married there. And it had been wartime. The British embassy was closed, the French embassy was closed, same with the Belgians and the Dutch; the Italians and Germans were distracted by war. Only the Swiss remained in any significant numbers, and the Swiss were so busy taking on all the consular duties of the belligerent nations, they held no parties at all. In those early days, nothing stopped Sasha coming straight home as soon as he had finished working for the day, and he usually finished as early as he could.

They'd found a larger flat together, one with two additional bedrooms. The smaller one they decorated as a nursery. Iris had thought Sasha would be dismayed by her pregnancy, but really you couldn't have found a more eagerly expectant father. After the fifth month or so, he took to measuring her waist with a tape every evening when he got home, so he could tally the progress of their child, millimeter by millimeter. When he drank, he drank with Iris, and then not very much because the doctor said she should only have a glass or two of red wine or possibly beer, which promoted good lactation.

On weekends he would take her out of Rome, usually to the little villa in Tivoli, so she could breathe plenty of fresh air. He never said anything about marriage, and neither did she. Not until Christmas, when Iris was too huge to do much more than lie on the sofa like some sort of beached humpback, did Harry finally—and somewhat sheepishly—suggest some official recognition of their union. Iris had looked at Sasha and Sasha had looked at Iris. "I'm game if you are," he told her, gallant as he always was in those days.

After Harry left, Iris told Sasha they didn't *have* to get married if he didn't want to. Wasn't he against marriage on principle, after all?

"On principle, yes. But as a personal matter, I can't think of anything I want more."

Iris couldn't speak. She put her arms around his neck and kissed him.

"Besides," he murmured, "it's better for the child. Children want their parents properly married."

So they were married the next week by the ambassador himself, Harry as witness, and held a little champagne reception afterward for a very few friends. The next morning Iris went into labor and Kip was born twenty-six harrowing hours later—almost ten pounds of him—eight minutes before the end of 1940. Iris didn't learn until later that the doctor had taken Sasha aside at one point and asked him if Iris's affairs were all in order, and that Sasha was so drunk by the time the baby was born, he registered the birth as female—not by accident, but because he didn't actually remember.

IRIS FOUND HER HUSBAND in the foyer on the balcony with Burgess and the blonde in the turtleneck, smoking cigarettes and drinking gin. "I'm going to get my coat," she told him. "Meet you outside in ten minutes?"

She turned and walked away before he could react. Before she could see the expressions on the faces of Burgess and the blonde—those expressions she knew so well. *Oh, the old battle-ax.* Wives spoil all the fun, don't they?

Her raincoat hung from some hook in the hallway, identical to the others. She rifled through them all until she found hers, identifiable by her slim clutch pocketbook stuck into the right armhole, because she hated having to carry a pocketbook around a party. The coat was layered beneath a couple of others, and it took some effort to untangle them all. Somewhere in the middle of the struggle, a friendly American voice asked, "May I be of assistance?"

Iris jumped and turned. A man had appeared out of nowhere—a thick-shouldered, square-jawed, cleft-chinned all-American of a type Iris hadn't seen in years. He showed her some friendly white teeth and continued in a slow country cadence designed by God to soothe skittish horses. "Say, I didn't mean to sneak up on you."

"Not at all."

He reached up and removed her raincoat from the hook. Like a gentleman, he helped her into it, holding her pocketbook for her as she stuck in one arm and then the other. When she turned to thank him, he tipped his hat and wished her a good evening. She was still staring at the door when Sasha ranged up and asked her what was the matter.

Nothing, she said.

BY THE TIME SHE and Sasha arrived home in Holland Park at half past one in the morning, a light, miserable rain dropped from the sky. Sasha stumbled out of the taxi and told the driver to wait, he'd be back in a moment.

"You're not going back out again, are you?"

"Burgess and a few others. Gargoyle Club. I won't be long. I'll walk you upstairs," he added generously, as he gave her his arm to help her out of the taxi.

"No, you won't. You'll come upstairs with me and go to bed, like a decent husband and father. Tomorrow's Sunday."

"In point of fact, it's already Sunday."

"Sasha, please. Stay."

She put her hand on his chest and did her best to capture his gaze, the way she used to do, but his eyes were drunk and blurry and he looked right through her.

"Darling, just for an hour or two. Back before you know it."

"You know that's not true. Don't be an idiot, Sasha."

The taxi driver tooted the horn.

"Christ, Iris. It's just a drink."

"It's not just a drink. It's your life, it's your career! I've been hearing rumors—"

He seized her by the arms. "Rumors? What the hell are you talking about? Who's spreading rumors?"

"Nobody! Just people, they're talking about how much you drink, all these stupid, crazy escapades—"

He swore and let her go. He swung the taxi door open without another word and she wanted to scream after him, *What's wrong? What's happening? Why won't you tell me?*

But it was too late. The taxi roared off. Iris stood in the drizzle and watched the headlights spin around the corner onto Abbotsbury Road, off to the Gargoyle Club in Mayfair, a different world from this quiet suburban neighborhood of wife and sons.

THEY LIVED ON THE fourth floor of a block of mansion flats called Oakwood Court, just off the grounds of poor ruined Holland House. Like the Desboroughs' apartment, where tonight's party had taken place, theirs was grand and spacious and in dire need of decorative updating. During the winter and spring, it was impossibly cold. Because the block had been built at the turn of the century, it did boast certain *mod cons*, as the British called them, such as central heating and hot water. But the ceilings were so lofty and the air outside so dank and chill most of the year that Iris never felt really *warm* until June, no matter how many cardigans and mufflers she wrapped around her shivering body, and she would dream of Rome or Ankara. She would remember the hot sun and pungent blue sky as you might remember a happy childhood, all the unpleasant threads snipped conveniently away.

The porter went home at eight P.M. sharp and would not return until six in the morning. Iris crossed the small, deserted lobby and took the lift to the fourth floor. It was the old-fashioned kind, so

Iris had to open and close the door and the grille by herself. Her hands were shaking—her eyes stung with unshed tears. There were two flats on each floor, and the other one was empty. The family had moved out in January, suddenly and without explanation, and nobody had taken their place. Iris fumbled with the latchkey, tiptoed through the door, and shrugged off her raincoat. Mrs. Betts would be asleep in her small room off the kitchen; she'd have tucked in Kip and Jack at seven o'clock, and though they were good sleepers generally, parents could never be too quiet in the middle of the night, could they? Iris perched on the bench and wriggled off one shoe and then the other and sat for a moment—shoe in each hand—eyes closed. She thought of Sasha in his taxi, racing up the Kensington Road—no traffic, not at this hour—toward Mayfair and the Gargoyle Club. Iris had never seen the Gargoyle Club, but she had no trouble picturing it. Burgess and the others would be waiting for him, bottles ready.

Iris opened her eyes and rose from the bench. She stole in her stockings down the dark corridor and stopped by the door to the boys' room.

Now that Jack was nearly four years old, he slept in a real bed like his brother, all tangled up in sheets and blankets. Iris straightened them around his warm little body. He wore a soft, blue-striped union suit, his favorite. Mrs. Betts must have fished it out of the clothes hamper for him because Mummy and Daddy were away at a party. Iris smoothed his damp hair from his temple and imagined him sipping his warm milk, swinging his legs on the chair at the kitchen table next to Kip, while she and Sasha sat in their taxi and edged through the drizzle and the traffic toward the Desboroughs' flat in Eaton Square.

Kip, on the other hand. Kip lay like a vampire in a coffin, perfectly straight, nose pointed to the ceiling, blankets tucked around him. Kip was the sweeter one, the sensitive one, who shared Iris's artistic spirit but liked everything just so—soldiers lined up on the chest of drawers, clothes folded and ready for the next day—that kind of thing. Iris didn't understand, but she went along with it. Last year he'd decided warm milk before bedtime was for babies, so he drank cocoa instead and instructed Jack on the finer points of the milk mustache.

Sometimes, when the boys lay asleep like this, tranquil as they never were when awake, Iris would stare at them and not quite believe they were hers. Eight years! How could eight years pass so quickly, and yet seem like forever? Iris felt like a different person now. She'd lived an entire lifetime in those eight years. That sense of holy purpose she'd felt in Rome—that determination to belong to Sasha, whatever the cost, and his determination to belong to her—where had it gone?

Jack stirred under Iris's hand. She stepped back and held her breath, waiting for him to settle. In the shadows, she couldn't see his shape, let alone the colors of him—his pale hair, his round, rosy cheeks. But she knew they were there. She knew the essence of both boys in her marrow. Her second child, her baby born in Ankara as the Allies marched through Normandy. She had suffered two miscarriages between Kip and Jack, and Jack's birth had been even more harrowing than Kip's. Nearly thirty-six hours before they wrestled him out into the world, and all that time Sasha was away on some special mission, she didn't know where, because she'd gone into labor two weeks early.

No more babies, Sasha had said, when he stood by her bedside a week later—home at last—pale and disheveled—and Iris had agreed.

But that was history. The fear and agony had faded, as they'd faded after Kip, and now Iris stared down at Jack, so small and yet such a *little boy* now, all traces of babyhood slipped right through her fingers, she felt the familiar stir in her belly—the clutch of longing.

She turned and slipped out the door and down the hall to the bedroom she shared with Sasha. The door was closed—she pushed it open and turned her head away from the empty bed.

The dressing room connected the bedroom to the bathroom. Iris laid her pocketbook on the dresser—wriggled out of her dress—hung it in the wardrobe. She sat on the stool and removed her stockings and slip, found a nightgown to slip over her underthings. Before heading into the bathroom, she emptied out her pocketbook, so she could put away her lipstick and compact.

But the lipstick and compact wouldn't fall free. Something else lay on top of them at a particular angle, trapping the objects within. Iris stuck her fingers between the lips to dislodge this thing, which turned out to be a calling card. She pulled it out and held it to the light.

On the face of the card, the name c. SUMNER FOX appeared in raised black letters. Underneath, in smaller type, was an American telephone number with a Washington exchange. On the back, in sharp, masculine handwriting, someone had written *In case of need,* followed by a telephone number in Mayfair.

RUTH

I wake the next morning to a noise both obnoxious and distantly familiar. I take in the plaster walls and wooden beams of a small, white room, and for a moment I have no idea where I am, or even *who* I am. Then I remember I'm in Rome, in the attic of Orlovsky's old atelier, and that noise is the particular noise of an Italian telephone ringing its head off.

The bedroom is tiny and hot, designed for servants, and the telephone's on the floor below. I experience a moment of crisis when I stagger into the hall and lose my way to the staircase. The telephone keeps ringing. At last I stumble through the doorway of the studio and find it. "Hello?" I mumble.

"Good morning, bambina. Have I wake you?"

"What *time* is it?"

"Half past ten o'clock."

"Half past *ten?*"

"Never mind," Orlovsky says soothingly. "Is good to sleep. And I am working on your behalf this morning."

"Oh? What have you done?"

"First put on your dress and have coffee. You remember café, end of street?"

"Yes, but—"

"Meet me for lunch. I explain everything there."

"Why can't you just come here?"

"Because I have loose ends, bambina. Lunch at half past noon, is okay?"

"I don't have time for lunch!"

"You must eat, however. So we meet and have lunch and discuss things in rational manner. Good-bye."

He hangs up, and the once-familiar noise of an Italian dial tone buzzes in my ear. I set the receiver in the cradle and attempt to collect my thoughts, which are still mired in the confusion of deep sleep. I had no right to sleep like that, just as I have no right to eat a leisurely lunch in an Italian café with a man who was once my lover. I need to get to Moscow—I need to find Iris with an urgency that's only grown stronger during the night, as if some part of my brain has turned into a ticking clock.

But Orlovsky's right. I must eat—I must sleep—and anyway I can't do anything until we find a way inside the Soviet Union.

I head upstairs and open my suitcase.

"YOU LOOK MUCH BETTER," Orlovsky tells me, when the waiter's opened the first bottle of wine and poured our glasses.

"You, on the other hand, look worse. What's happened to you?"

He shrugs. "Life. War. You know we lost two sons—"

"Oh, damn. I hadn't heard. I'm so sorry."

"War kills the young, this is fact of life. Laura prayed to God, but I am not believer. I believe in fate, that is all." He sips his wine and offers me a cigarette. We spend some time lighting up, enjoying the first drag. He waves away the smoke that gathers between us and says, "Enrico died in Albania. Mario at Palermo. So Giovanni is now our only son. Five girls and one boy. His mother spoils him."

"Of course she does." I'm now filled only with pity for Orlovsky's wife. Still, I can't resist adding, "But at least she had the new baby to comfort her."

He looks at me in surprise. "But you did not know this? Baby died two days after he was born. His heart, doctors said to us. He had weak heart."

"Oh, God. What a heel I am."

"No, it is I who am heel, bambina. It is I who am brought to learn humility before will of fate. I thought I was tremendous man. I have wife and children and beautiful mistress, all because I am great fellow, I am like God. Whole world moves in magnificent circle around me. I am immortal!" He pulls on the cigarette. "So fate strikes me down. One by one, my children die. Is greatest agony man can endure. Why not kill me instead? No, fate tortures me first, because I am proud, because I play with hearts of women like you play with cards."

"That's not true. That has nothing to do with it. Your children didn't deserve to die because of you. You didn't deserve for them to die."

"Ah, you are generous with me, bambina cara. Always you are generous."

The conversation's become morbid, and the wine turns sour in my mouth. "What about your daughters? Are any of them married?"

"Yes, Elvira and Renata, they marry nice Italian boys. I have two grandchildren, girl and boy."

I lift my glass. "Cheers to that, anyway."

"And my little Donna, she is spending summer in Russia with my parents, near Sochi. You know Sochi?"

"It's by the Black Sea, isn't it?"

"Yes. Is beautiful there, like resort. She will come home tanned and happy, with Russian boyfriend." He shakes his head. "Is terrible burden, children. Always they take your heart with them, wherever they go."

"I wouldn't know. But my sister has a fourth on the way, I hear."

"Ah, yes." He stubs out the cigarette. "Let us talk about your sister for a minute."

The waiter returns at that instant and refills the wine. Orlovsky orders fish; I order lamb. When he departs, Orlovsky lights another cigarette and says, in an undertone, "I have spoken to person who can help you."

"Someone at the embassy?"

"You understand, you cannot simply dance into Moscow and find your sister and dance home again. Do you know what is the KGB?"

"It's the Soviet spy agency, isn't it?"

"Is more than that. Is everywhere. When you step off airplane— no, before. When you *buy ticket* to Moscow, they are watching. Listening. You go nowhere, *see* nothing, *say* nothing that KGB does not know."

"Then I'll just have to find a way around them."

Orlovsky lays his palm on the table. His eyes blaze, although he keeps his voice at the same low monotone, so we might be speaking of the weather. "Oh, you are so clever! Like me, you believe you can outsmart fate—you can outsmart KGB. You know nothing! They will kill anybody—innocents—because to KGB man, all is in service to revolution, to world communism. So you find sister—by some miracle of God—so you visit sister? They take sister to Moscow Centre. They do interrogation—KGB interrogation, they study how to do this, they are scientific—they maybe even torture her, if they want confession. Maybe they take her son, they say we will kill your son unless you confess."

"That won't happen. I'm an American citizen, I'll go to the US consulate and kick up such a fuss—"

"*This* is your plan? Your plan to cause major diplomatic *incident*? You think Soviets care what American newspapers think? I tell you now, they will lie. They will say, oh, this woman is spy—she is agent of American intelligence. They will insist on their lies until gullible people of America—yes, gullible people of *entire world* believe them. Ruth Macallister, she is terrible spy, *she* is guilty one. Then what happens? You disappear. Nobody ever know what happen to you."

"That's not true. The United States would never let that happen to one of its citizens."

"Bambina. Bambina cara. Let me explain to you. United States government cannot help you if you do this idiot thing and go to Moscow. You are too small—Soviet Union too big. Soviet Union will kill anybody—it will kill millions brazenly. Stalin killed millions in Ukraine, did you know this?"

"*Millions?* That's impossible."

"Not impossible. Starvation. He creates famine so people starve, so they have nothing left but Soviet state."

"How do you know this?"

"Because I listen." He touches his ear. "Friends. Family. They have to whisper, they cannot shout this or some nosy neighbor denounce them, their own children denounce them. If you are not good little Communist, if you do not recite daily catechism—and catechism sometimes change with no warning, so you must pay attention—then comes knock on your door." He knocks twice on the table with the hand holding the cigarette, which by now has burned almost to a stub. "Do you see? In this terrible war—this war between communism and liberal democracy—communism will win, because it does not care how many lives it devours."

I make a hushing movement with my hand, because the waiter has just arrived with our lunch. Anyway, Orlovsky's become overwrought with his daily catechisms and his starving millions. I already know what evil looks like; I've seen the photographs out of Dachau and Auschwitz and Bergen-Belsen.

We eat our lunch, just like any couple. The restaurant is only half full and the other diners are mostly young people, tanned and happy and unscarred, too young to have fought in the war. Naturally, Orlovsky *would* choose a place like this. He loves young, beautiful people, especially women. His gaze flicks around the room without even noticing what he does—resting on that face, those legs, this bosom—subconscious, pleasurable assessments. The waiter clears away the plates and brings tiny cups of espresso. Over the rim, I notice a man sitting at a table in the corner, reading a newspaper. I can't see his face, but he has a slim build and long, elegant fingers that grip the edges of the newspaper.

I return my attention to Orlovsky. "If you think it's such a terrible idea, why are you helping me?"

"First, because I know I cannot stop you, and if you must go, you need all help I can find you."

"Second?"

He smiles a wan, toothy grin. "Because I am Russian, bambina. I cannot resist lost cause."

WE WALK BACK TO Orlovsky's atelier in the hot sunshine. There's a whiff of sewage in the air, and my dress sticks to my back. As we stroll down the sidewalk, flashes of memory return to me—things I haven't remembered in years. The tobacco shop on the corner, where Orlovsky once stopped to buy cigarettes, and the tobacconist mistook me for his daughter. The florist where he used to buy me flowers, and the mysterious palazzo a street away from the atelier that always intrigued me, because it was so austere on the outside, like a medieval fortress, and not even Orlovsky knew whom it belonged to. As we turn the corner and stop on the curb to allow a taxi to race by, I catch a glimpse of a slim man ducking into the shelter of a doorway, holding a newspaper under his arm.

When we cross the street, I look over my shoulder. But nobody's there, after all.

WE REACH THE ATELIER. Orlovsky unlocks the iron-studded door. He ushers me inside first, and as he turns to follow me, he seems to look both ways, up and down the sidewalk, before he steps into the vestibule and closes and locks the door behind him.

"When do we meet this friend of yours?" I ask.

Orlovsky replaces the walking stick in the stand and puts his hand to the small of my back. "Is here already. He said not to waste any time."

"Good. I agree."

I say this bravely to stifle a tremor of panic. We climb the stairs, which spiral upward in a pleasant medieval way. The damp, cool smell of the stones wafts by. I find myself wondering who he is, this contact of Orlovsky's, and what he does. Is he some kind of double agent nested inside the Soviet embassy? A disaffected Italian Communist?

All these possibilities whirl through my mind as we reach the first floor and walk down the hallway, at the end of which lies the studio that runs the width of the courtyard below. None of them comes close to the truth. The man who looks up from the drafting table, who scrapes the chair back and stands politely, is a man I already know.

"Miss Macallister," says Sumner Fox. "You'd better take a seat. We've got a lot of ground to cover."

IRIS

At half past six the next morning, the boys burst into the room and jumped on the bed.

"Mama! Daddy! I lost a tooth!" Kip said.

Next to her, Sasha groaned and rolled on his stomach. Iris's head throbbed. She must have drunk more champagne than she realized last night. She glanced at Sasha—out cold—and sat up painfully. "You lost a tooth! Where?"

He showed her.

"There was blood all over his nightshirt and Mrs. Betts put it to soak!" Jack announced.

"The tooth or the nightshirt?"

"The nightshirt, of course! You look awful, Mama."

"Not as awful as Daddy," she said.

"Does this mean we don't have to go to church?" Kip asked, bouncing a little.

Iris swung her feet to the floor and stared at her toes.

"I don't know, darling, but I guess we'd better start breakfast, just in case."

◆ ◆ ◆

EVEN THOUGH SASHA WAS an atheist, the family went to church most Sundays, a habit they established when they moved to London. Sasha said it was important for the boys to have a proper religious education, so they could disavow God from a position of confidence when they were old enough to reason things out for themselves. Besides, you met a lot of important people at church on a Sunday.

So Iris rolled out of bed and trudged to the bathroom to make herself a little more human. On the way back to the bedroom, she picked up Sasha's discarded clothes and hung them in his wardrobe. Sasha himself hadn't moved. He sprawled on his stomach, hair in disorder, perfectly naked—thank God for the blankets. There was just enough light that she could see his face, so relaxed it was almost angelic, relieved of all its sins. Iris remembered what Philip had said last night—the hearings—and wondered why Sasha hadn't said anything to her about them. Because he wasn't worried about anything this woman might reveal in her testimony, or because he was?

She tucked the blanket around him and headed down the hall toward the kitchen, where the boys were making the usual joyful racket—take that, Mrs. Bannister in the downstairs flat—as Mrs. Betts flitted around the room getting breakfast. Jack spotted Iris first.

"Mama! Mrs. Betts said I could have hot cocoa with breakfast! Because it's Sunday!"

"That sounds like an awful good idea."

"Good morning, Mrs. D," Mrs. Betts said cheerfully. "Coffee's in the pot."

Iris sat in the chair next to Jack and reached for the coffeepot. "You're an angel."

"I've gone ahead and laid out their suits for church. Master Kip's going to need a new jacket soon, he's grown that fast. I do believe he'll be tall, like his father."

Mrs. Betts had come to them through some reference at the embassy. She was about fifty, extremely slender, with blue eyes and graying blond hair she kept tidy in an old-fashioned bun. She'd previously worked for a large, wealthy, traditional English household, and Iris couldn't break her of certain habits, like calling a seven-year-old boy *Master Kip*. Still, she appreciated the efficiency with which Mrs. Betts approached her job. Some of the other wives complained about the help—this was a common pastime, apparently—and how you couldn't get a housemaid to cook or mind the children, or a cook to clean the parlor or wash the laundry; ask for a housekeeper and you'd get a woman who expected to run the other servants, not to do any real work herself. But Mrs. Betts did. Iris considered the family lucky to have her. Mrs. Betts could get away with murder and keep her job, but she only asked for a half day off every week, Sunday morning to Sunday afternoon, so she could visit her mother in Clapham.

She was untying her apron right now.

"Breakfast is all laid out in the dining room as usual, Mrs. D. Anything else before I'm off?"

"No, thank you, Mrs. Betts."

"You're certain of that? You're looking a bit pale, if I may."

Iris looked up. Mrs. Betts had folded her apron over her arm, and she gazed down on Iris with an expression of motherly concern.

"I'm all right, thank you. The party went a little late, that's all."

"So it did. I believe I heard Mr. D arriving home at seven minutes past five."

Iris turned back to Jack and urged a mouthful of egg. "I appreciate your concern, Mrs. Betts, but I'm really quite well. It's part of Mr. Digby's job to attend these functions."

Mrs. Betts made a noise of disapproval. "Well, I'll be off now. Oh—good morning, Mr. Digby."

Sasha's voice rang from the doorway. "Good morning, Mrs. Betts. Off for your half day, I guess. Coffee?"

"There's Mrs. D pouring your cup this instant. Pale though she is." With this parting shot, Mrs. Betts swept out the door and clattered down the hall.

Sasha kissed the top of Iris's head. "I suppose it's my fault you're pale?"

"She's just a mother hen, that's all."

"So she should be. Somebody needs to look after you when I'm not around. Boys? You're looking after your mother when Daddy's at work, aren't you?"

Kip looked up from his magazine. "Yes, Daddy."

"I helped Mama make the bed yesterday!" Jack cried.

"That's the ticket. Good boy." Sasha plopped into the chair and reached for his coffee cup. A cigarette trailed from his left hand. He wore a creased dressing gown and his hair was rumpled like a pile of old straw; he smelled of bed, of perspiration, of booze, of worry. It was a smell Iris had come to associate with him ever since the war ended, as if the absence of a real enemy had evaporated his vital spirit. On the other hand, here he was—up and out of bed, drinking coffee with his family when any ordinary man would sleep the entire morning off. So there must be *something* left of him still, right? The man she loved.

Iris handed him the cream. "Church today?"

Sasha looked at his wristwatch and swore.

+ + +

THEY ATTENDED SERVICES AT St. Barnabas, just around the corner on Addison Road. As Sasha pointed out, the Anglican church was just about the same in character and temperament as the Episcopal church in America, in which both of them had been raised, so their immortal souls shouldn't be materially damaged by the experience. Iris had asked him what exactly he meant by *immortal soul*, since he didn't believe in God, and he told her to be a good wife and not ask so many questions. At the time, she thought he was only being ironic.

Iris wasn't sure whether she believed in God or not, but she experienced the Sunday services at St. Barnabas in a different way than she used to experience church at home. For one thing, when Iris was a child, they hardly ever went to church, rallying themselves for Christmas and Easter and weddings and funerals but not for the ordinary, quotidian rites. Churchgoing was a social obligation, undertaken against your personal inclinations, not a spiritual wellspring. When Iris *had* attended church, she hadn't paid much attention, and when she did pay attention, the words floated past her ears like a pleasant music.

Now Iris had Kip and Jack, and raising children seemed to have unplugged some emotional drain inside her. When the priest offered her the wine and said *The blood of Christ, the cup of salvation*, she sometimes had to hold back sobs. Ridiculous! Then he laid his hand on Kip's blond curls and said, *Christ's blessing be upon you*, and the tide of desperate gratitude nearly choked her.

Why? She wasn't religious. She didn't give much thought to Christianity once she stepped outside the church and went about her daily life. If she did, she would typically question the foundational tenets of faith, not confirm them. Sometimes she thought it was the *idea* of salvation that moved her. She didn't feel *saved*, exactly, but the older she got, the more she felt the terrible weight of all the hundred faults and mistakes—sins, let's call them—she was liable to commit in a given week, and it nearly broke her with gratitude just to *imagine*, for an instant, that somebody knew them all and forgave her for them.

On this particular Sunday, however, Iris suffered from too much champagne and too little sleep the night before. Drag herself to church? Not on your life. Her sins could wait until next week, when they'd be properly ripened.

But Sasha insisted.

"Are you nuts?" she said. "You must've drunk half the gin in London last night, you and your pals. You look like death."

"What's that supposed to mean?"

"I mean you're hungover, that's all. You need aspirin and coffee, not God. Anyway, it's almost nine thirty, and you haven't even shaved yet."

He threw down his napkin and rose from the table. "I'll shave now. Have the boys ready in twenty minutes."

"Oh, but Sasha—"

"We're going, all right? That's all there is to it."

She watched him storm out of the kitchen and turned to Jack, who sat awestruck in his chair, nibbling a toast soldier while his brother studiously flipped the page of his magazine and dragged his cocoa cup to his mouth.

"And for this I married an atheist," she said.

WHILE SASHA BANGED AROUND in the bathroom, Iris put on her lilac Sunday dress and forced Kip and Jack into their navy sailor suits, neatly pressed. They left the building at nine fifty-four, leaving just enough time to hurry around the corner under the shelter of an umbrella for the ten o'clock rites at St. Barnabas, the second and longer service of the morning. Privately she thought Sasha was more suited to St. Mary Abbots up Kensington High Street, which was larger and grander and more High Church than low, lots of ceremony and incantation and that kind of thing, but he seemed to prefer the convenience of a smaller neighborhood church.

The bell tolled gloomily, calling the faithful, or whatever they were. Sasha lengthened his stride and Kip, holding his father's hand, stepped up his pace—her small determined boy. Iris held tight to Jack's hand so he didn't fall behind. When she glanced at Sasha, she saw he'd nicked himself shaving, and the cut was beginning to bleed again. She reached into the pocket of her raincoat for a handkerchief and fished it out just in time to catch the trickle before it landed on Sasha's shirt collar.

At the touch of the handkerchief, Sasha flew around, throwing out his elbow. Kip stumbled and nearly fell—Iris cried out and stepped back. She clutched the handkerchief with his blood on it.

"Mama, what's wrong?" said Jack.

Sasha looked at the red stain, then at her. His eyes were bloodshot. Probably he wasn't even hungover, just still drunk from the night before.

"What's the matter with you?" she exclaimed.

"Nothing. Nervy, I guess. I didn't hit you, did I?"

"No."

He took the handkerchief and shoved it in his pocket. "I'm sorry," he said. He picked up the umbrella, which he'd dropped on the pavement, and took her arm with his other hand. St. Barnabas loomed nearby, soot-stained and Gothic. In another minute they reached the steps. They trudged up and through the open door just as the organ prepared to lurch into the processional. Sasha folded the umbrella and turned left, as usual, to walk up the side aisle to the pew where they always sat, without fail. The church only filled at Christmas and Easter, and their seats were still empty. Iris filed in silently behind Sasha—settled the boys—picked up her hymnal.

The first time they went inside this church, Iris was pleasantly surprised. Instead of the usual gloomy Gothic nave, obscured by pillars and arches, the space was wide open and full of light. Sasha said this was because the weight of the roof was supported entirely by the external buttressing. Well, whatever. Iris loved this openness because it allowed her to glance around as the hymn droned on and observe her fellow worshippers. She recognized some families from Oakwood Court, although she didn't actually know any of them, except for the woman who lived on the second floor of their own block and had two small children—a boy named Peter, slightly older than Jack, and tiny, dainty Gladys, who was about a year younger. Their last name was Peabody. Mrs. Peabody caught Iris's glance and smiled back, a little sternly because they were in church and supposed to be singing a hymn.

Or so Iris thought. But Mrs. Peabody *might* have looked stern because Jack, at that very second of connection, was slithering under the pew. Iris caught him just in time and discreetly dragged him back upward.

As she straightened, she saw Sasha take a piece of paper from his hymnal and tuck it into his jacket pocket, singing lustily as he did so—*Bring me my bow of burning gold, bring me my arrows of desire.*

The nick was bleeding again, but this time Iris didn't try to stop it.

SINCE THE LONG-AGO DAY in Tivoli, when Iris confronted Sasha about the envelope in his suitcase and the woman he used to meet in the Borghese gardens, they'd only once discussed the subject. That was in December of 1941, after Pearl Harbor, when the US embassy in Rome was hastily closed on account of war, and they'd moved back to the United States in an almighty hustle. On the promenade deck of the steamship bound for New York one stormy afternoon, staring nervously out to sea for the possibility of German submarines, Iris had looked around to make sure nobody could hear them and said to Sasha, "I suppose this makes your work a little easier, doesn't it? Now that we're all fighting on the same side?"

He'd looked down at her incredulously. "What work?"

"I mean what you were doing with the envelopes and the . . . the woman you used to meet."

He hadn't answered at once. They were leaning on the railing and little Kip, only a year old, lay snug in his perambulator, bundled up in blankets and fast asleep. Iris remembered how taut Sasha's face looked. He'd worked without sleep for days, rolling up all the affairs at the embassy, and now he seemed to have fallen out of the *habit* of sleeping. He would go to bed long after Iris and wake up earlier, and during the night, if Kip stirred, he told Iris to go back to sleep, he would take care of the boy. So he was tired, but he wasn't exhausted; it was the insomnia of the newly awakened, of somebody too thrilled with the possibilities of life to waste valuable minutes unconscious.

"Listen," he'd said at last, "I was wrong to tell you about that. You should just forget we ever had that conversation."

Iris was devastated. "I don't understand. Don't you trust me anymore?"

Sasha had turned and gathered her up against his thick, damp overcoat. "Darling, I trust you more than ever. You mean more to me than ever, a thousand times more. It's why I can't say a word to you. Not even if it kills me to hold back."

"You need to talk to somebody," she said. "You can't do this all alone."

"Just forget I ever said anything. Forget you ever knew anything. That's all."

Iris had stared at the perambulator, which they'd set next to the rivet-studded steel wall, sheltered from the wind, brakes on. She remembered thinking she should try harder. She remembered thinking this was one of those moments in a marriage, a crossroads, and she was taking the cowardly fork. If she were brave and clever—if she were Ruth, for example—she would insist he spill the beans and then become some kind of partner to him in all this. She would show him that she believed in what he believed—that she would do all she could to help him bring about an end to war and injustice.

Instead, she'd just said, "What if something goes wrong?"

Sasha had brushed back her hair and kissed her forehead. "Then you'll tell Kip his father was trying to make the world a better place, that's all."

And from that day to this one, Iris had put the whole matter out of her head, as something beyond her control. Soon after arriving in Washington, they were dispatched to Zurich, then Turkey, and now London, and Iris had never seen the slightest clue that

Sasha was, or was not, anything more than an ambitious member of the US diplomatic corps, working his way up the service through hard work and brilliance.

Until now.

THE SERVICE LASTED OVER an hour, and it seemed even longer. Sasha kept fidgeting and looking at his wristwatch. When at last the congregation was dismissed, Sasha hustled them out of the pew and through the door. Iris heard someone call her name as they descended the steps to the wet pavement outside. Sasha tugged her arm, but she turned around anyway to see Mrs. Peabody waving at her, little Peter on one side and Gladys the other.

But Sasha was already hurrying them up Addison Road. His hand still gripped the sleeve of her raincoat. As soon as they turned the corner into Oakwood Court, she shrugged it off.

"What on earth was that about? Why couldn't we stop?"

"For God's sake, I don't have time to dither about after church." He didn't pause; if anything, he lengthened his stride as they approached number 10 on the right. Despite the drizzle, he hadn't put up the umbrella. It poked out from under his elbow as he struggled to light a cigarette.

She tagged along behind, Kip on one hand and Jack on the other, calling over his shoulder, "But they're our neighbors!"

"We've got friends enough already."

"*You've* got friends! I haven't got anybody. Just women *you* know. Women like that blond number last night."

Sasha spun around. He wore a trench coat, dark with rain, and his wet fedora. He was terribly pale and thin, she realized, as gaunt as a cadaver. "What the devil do you mean by that?"

"Nothing. I just—nothing, of course."

He tried again to light the cigarette, covering the match with his hand. From the corner of his mouth, he said, "You have no idea, Iris. No idea."

"Of course I don't. You don't tell me a thing. You come and go and sneak notes out of hymnals—"

"What's that?"

"I saw you. I saw you take that note out of the—" She glanced down at Jack, who dangled from her hand and jumped in an adjacent puddle. Kip had already wandered away to stand against the wall of the building, affecting an air of utter boredom, hands stuffed in the pockets of his suit like a sailor on leave whose trousers had been sliced off at the knee.

Sasha lit the cigarette at last and blew out a large cloud of smoke into the damp air. He stared at the treetops over the walls of the nearby park. "Iris, go inside. Take the boys and go inside out of the rain, all right? I'll be home in a bit."

"Home in a bit? Where are you going?"

He handed her the umbrella. "Out."

Iris opened her mouth to demand where, but he'd already turned to hurry up the pavement toward Abbotsbury Road, leaving her standing by the entrance to the building with an umbrella in one hand and Jack in the other.

WITH MRS. BETTS GONE, THEIR footsteps made lonely, clattering sounds on the parquet floor of the apartment. Iris made the boys take off their shoes and raincoats. Jack ran off down the long hallway to his room, shouting something about an airplane, while Kip wandered into the living room and slumped on the sofa, where he picked up a battered paperback from between the cushions. The light was dim and gray, not July at all. Iris wandered to the window overlooking the entrance to the block, where the Peabodys were coming up the sidewalk. (The *pavement*, she reminded herself.) Mrs. Peabody's arm linked through Mr. Peabody's elbow, and a child skipped from each of their outside hands. Mr. Peabody's damp, pink face turned toward his wife; he seemed to be laughing at something she'd said.

Well, Sasha had warned her, hadn't he? He'd told her at the beginning that the life of a diplomat wasn't an easy one, that you would move to one city and make a certain set of friends, and then a few years later you moved a few hundred or a few thousand miles away and had to start all over again, and how could anybody form a real friendship that way?

It doesn't matter, she'd told him. *I'll have you. You're all I need.*

SASHA RETURNED JUST BEFORE dinner came out of the oven, a beef roast that would be made into soup, into hash, into sandwiches as the week went on, because meat was still rationed here in England, almost three years after the war had ended. His face was weary and he smelled of whiskey. After dinner he helped Iris bathe the boys and put them to bed. He read one of the railway stories, the one where Henry stops in a tunnel, speaking in all his funny voices.

Once the boys were tucked in, he took a long bath and then disappeared into his study until almost midnight. Iris was still awake in bed, reading a book. She didn't say anything when he passed by, into the dressing room and the bathroom, brushing his teeth and so on. When he climbed into bed, one leg and then the other, she set the book on the nightstand and said, "Is it about these hearings? In Washington?"

"Following the news from America, are you?"

"Somebody mentioned it at the party last night."

He was holding something in his hand, which he gave to her. "This fellow, maybe?"

It was a handkerchief, crumpled, bloodied in one corner—the one Iris gave him to stop the blood on his neck. Iris stared at it, bemused, until she noticed the monogram in the corner, plain black letters, PBH.

"Oh, it's Philip's! How funny. I must have put it in my coat pocket last night."

"And what were you weeping about with Philip?"

Iris set the handkerchief on top of the book on her nightstand. "I don't remember. Some silly thing. I might have had something in my eye."

"You don't need to *lie* to me, Iris. I'm not going to play the jealous husband, if that's what you're thinking."

"Oh, Sasha. You can't be—*Philip?* He's very dear, he's awfully kind to me—"

"I'm sure he is. He's giving you a cottage, isn't he?"

"And you just said you weren't going to play the jealous husband. Anyway, the cottage is for us—the entire family, you included. And Aunt Vivian and the girls."

He made a little groan. "I'd forgotten about Vivian."

"You'll love her. You need to get away from London, Sasha, you really do. All of this—the war's over, you should be settled now, you should be happy in your work. Put all the past behind you."

He started to say something and changed his mind. He lay on

his back, staring straight up at the ceiling—a little like Kip. Iris turned on her side and put her hand on his chest.

"You didn't answer my questions about the hearings."

"Don't worry yourself about that."

"But *you're* worried—"

"Just shut up about it, all right? There's nothing you can do."

"Do about what? Sasha, you have to tell me. If something happens to you—"

"If something happens to me, you clam up. Do you hear me? You don't know a thing. Nothing ever happened, you never noticed anything, saw anything, you're just the nice dumb housewife they think you are."

Iris sat up. "How dare you. How dare you. If I am—if I *am* just a housewife—it's because of *you*, because I've given up everything I dreamed of doing, all for your sake. Ruth was right—"

Sasha sat up too and clamped his hand over her mouth. "Christ, shut up! The neighbors!"

"I don't care!" She snatched his palm away, but when she spoke again, she whispered. "I haven't drawn a single thing since Jack was born. Not a sketch or a painting. When was the last time I spent the afternoon in a museum? By myself, I mean, actually *looking* at what's on the walls instead of chasing after children? I've given it all up for you and the boys."

"*You're* the one who wanted another baby."

Iris felt as if he'd struck her between the ribs. For a moment, she couldn't even breathe.

"Iris, I'm sorry—"

"Never mind. You know what? Never mind. Go ahead and— and do your cloak-and-dagger act, if it makes you happy. Go ruin yourself for a lost cause." She fell back on the pillow and rolled on her side, away from her husband. "I'll just be home raising our sons."

"It's not a lost cause. It's the most important cause in the world."

Iris closed her eyes.

"Someone's got to do this. You don't understand—I'm working to *end war*, end all this terrible injustice; look what capitalism's bought us, the means to destroy the whole world! I want to bring about a revolution that—"

"You want to feel important, that's all. It doesn't matter how. Communism is just what fell in your lap at the right moment. It might just as easily have been—I don't know, Hinduism."

"If you really think that, you're an idiot."

Iris sat up again and pointed to the door. "Go. Go sleep on the sofa."

"Oh, for Christ's *sake*—"

"Go."

Sasha stared at her in the light from the lamp on her nightstand. For an instant, she wavered. His blue eyes were wide and hurt, his hair askew. He looked more like a wounded animal than an angry husband. For once, he smelled of nothing but soap and toothpaste and warm, scrubbed skin. He was clean and perfect—uncorrupted. She heard the words again in her head—*You're an idiot*—yet even in the full vortex of fury, she saw his beautiful face and the small, beloved fragments of his beautiful soul—*her Sasha*—and thought, *Just apologize, just say you're sorry, God knows I'll take you back, I'll always take you back.*

But Sasha couldn't hear Iris's thoughts, or he didn't care. He climbed out of bed, took his pillow and the spare blanket folded at the end, and walked out of the bedroom.

◆ ◆ ◆

SASHA ALWAYS LOCKED HIS study door when he was out, but Iris knew where he kept the key—behind the frame of the mirror above the mantel in the dining room.

The next morning, after Sasha left for work, Iris unlocked the study door and slipped inside. Her husband was not an immaculate man. There was always something slightly askew about his dress, even if you couldn't quite pinpoint what was out of order, and his study was no different. Except, perhaps, that you *could* pinpoint the mess, because it lay all around you—the stacks of unfiled papers, the books shoved in odd corners of the bookshelves, the broken lampshade sitting upside-down next to the lamp. The morning sunshine speared through the window and struck a framed map that hung off-kilter on the opposite wall. Mrs. Betts was only allowed to clean the room while Sasha was inside it. He liked his privacy, he always said, and until now, Iris was happy to let him enjoy it. Wasn't it better not to know?

She didn't have much time. Mrs. Betts would be whipping up the hot cocoa this moment, and Jack would drink it in the kitchen, legs swinging, asking the housekeeper questions that she'd answer as she finished washing up the breakfast dishes. But Jack's three-year-old powers of attention were not vast. He might drink half the cocoa and slide off the chair in search of new amusement, probably prodding his brother—currently slumped on the sofa in the drawing room, reading his book—and Iris would have to take them both to the park or something. So she didn't waste time idling about the room. She went straight to the file cabinet and found it locked, as she expected. To hunt for the key would be time wasted. She turned instead to the desk drawers. There were two on each side—

both drawers on the left were locked, and so was the bottom drawer on the right, but the top one slid right open.

Had he left it unlocked by accident, or did he keep nothing important there?

Iris rummaged around the interior. It seemed to be the place where Sasha dropped everything that didn't have a place—matchbooks and pens, rubber erasers and half-eaten chocolate bars, a pair of scissors and a small pot of glue, a compact flashlight from which the batteries had been removed. Underneath an A-Z London road atlas, she found a pair of snapshots. She took them out and examined them.

The first one was of her. Iris held it close and squinted at the blurred figure, wearing a dark, dowdy swimsuit she recognized as the one she hurriedly packed into her suitcase when she first left New York for Rome, age twenty-one. She was amazed. The Iris in that photograph was so gamine and perfectly formed! You didn't notice the dowdiness of the swimsuit at all, just the miniature grace of the figure inside it. How had she ever been so doubtful of her appeal? Her short dark hair curled on her neck, her breasts stood out firm and round beneath the swimsuit. Her arms stretched wide on either side, like a crucifixion, but instead of agony she wore an expression of delighted love, as if she were welcoming the photographer into an embrace.

For the life of her, Iris couldn't remember Sasha taking that photograph. But she did recognize the setting. A couple of weeks after Ruth left for New York, once his workload diminished a little, Sasha had taken Iris away to a resort on the Amalfi Coast for a short holiday—to celebrate, he said. It was a honeymoon in all but name. He booked a luxurious room overlooking the beach, and the days passed in a haze of champagne and salt and sunshine. One afternoon, when they returned from a few hours' frolic in the sea, Iris discovered vases and vases filled with night jasmine, because she had told Sasha at breakfast that jasmine was her favorite flower. Even now, when she smelled jasmine, she thought of making love to Sasha in a hot, luxurious hotel room. God, that was a lifetime ago. To think the baby inside that flat stomach was Kip! She touched her own joyful, innocent, monochrome face and picked up the other photograph.

Now this. Who on earth was this? Another woman, a dark-haired woman in a plain uniform, casting an expression of resigned amusement at the camera, or the person behind it. Her arms were folded against her chest. She had a tall, rangy look to her, and her face seemed familiar, though Iris couldn't place her. Her eyes were pale, almost certainly blue. She wasn't beautiful, but she had a wide-faced, intelligent, animal look to her that snagged your attention. Iris stared at the snapshot, trying to place her. Wouldn't she remember a face like that?

Iris turned the photograph over, but nothing was written there, no caption or note or date, no label of any kind, nothing at all to betray the identity of the subject. Of course, it had to have been taken during the war. The woman's hairstyle, the plain uniform. Sasha and Iris had lived in Zurich for much of the conflict, and Sasha was away so often. She knew he wasn't simply working for the embassy, though she never asked what he was doing, or what he was working for. She wouldn't have dreamed of that.

From the other side of the study door came the sound of Jack's voice, piping a question, and Mrs. Betts's low, gentle voice answering him. Iris glanced at the clock; five minutes had passed already.

She shoved both snapshots back in the drawer. As she pulled her hand back, the tips of her fingers bumped against some hard object.

She drew it out.

She'd never seen one before, but she knew what it was—a slim, rectangular box about the size of a man's index finger, made of some light, silvery metal, probably aluminum. When she pulled on both ends together, the box slid apart to reveal a couple of buttons and dials and a tiny, round lens.

A Minox camera, Iris thought. So this was what it looked like. It was even smaller than she imagined—a tiny, cunning device, easily hidden, made for one purpose only. Really, Sasha shouldn't have been so careless, leaving it in an unlocked drawer like this. Anyone could have found it.

From the other side of the door, Iris heard a shout, a pair of feet thundering down the hall—poor Mrs. Bannister in the downstairs flat—and an answering shout. Then Mrs. Betts's voice, shushing them, and another thundering journey back up the hallway.

Iris thrust the camera back in the desk, underneath the snapshots. As she closed the drawer, though, something felt out of place.

She laid her hand flat on the bottom of the drawer and looked at it from the front.

Was it her imagination, or was there an inch of space unaccounted for, between her hand and the place where the drawer actually stopped?

PHILIP BEAUCHAMP'S SECRETARY PUT her through right away. "Beauchamp," he said briskly, when he answered the ring.

"Philip, it's Iris. Iris Digby."

"Iris! So glad you've rung. I spent a miserable Sunday certain

I'd overstepped the bounds of friendship and I'd never hear your voice again."

"Oh! Don't be silly. I guess a girl needs a shoulder to cry on, once in a while."

"Well, this old shoulder stands ready for duty whenever you require it."

"You're too kind, Philip, and I hope I'm not imposing—"

"Ah! Have you a favor to ask me, I hope?"

"I do, I'm afraid. This cottage of yours. I don't suppose you'd be willing to let us move in earlier than planned?"

"I'd be delighted. How early did you have in mind?"

A muffled crash reached Iris, as of books tumbling from a shelf. "Just a moment," she said to Philip and put the receiver to her chest. "Mrs. Betts! Everything all right?"

A few seconds passed. Mrs. Betts called back, "Quite all right, Mrs. D!"

Iris lifted the receiver back to her ear.

"I'm so sorry, Philip. Would tomorrow be too soon?"

RUTH

For a moment, I don't understand why Sumner Fox should be standing there in Orlovsky's studio, when he's supposed to be back in New York.

Then I whip around and stab Orlovsky in the chest with my finger. "You bastard! I thought I could trust you!"

"You *can* trust him," says Fox. "I paid him a visit last night and explained the scope of the situation."

"The scope? The *scope?*"

"Miss Macallister, may I remind you that the operation to extract your sister from Moscow originated with me? That I may be privy to information I haven't yet had the opportunity or inclination to discuss with you?"

"*Bambina*, let me pour some wine," says Orlovsky.

"I don't want your damned wine. I asked you to find somebody who could help me get into Moscow—"

"But I did! I found best man for job."

"*He* found *you*, you mean."

"What difference, so long as you have best chance of success? Just because he is big, strong man—man you can't boss around so easily—"

"That's ridiculous."

Orlovsky looks away swiftly, but not before I notice the little smile at the corner of his mouth. I turn back to Fox.

"For all I know, you're here to sabotage me."

Fox swings around the side of the drafting table and props his big body against it. One leg crosses over the other. His hands curl around the thick wooden edge. He speaks slowly, as he always does, in that comforting tone of voice. "Miss Macallister, I have a confession to make, though I suspect you already know it. I've been handling the Digby case for some years. Before they defected, even. I happen to admire your sister a great deal. There is nothing I want more than to help her out of her present difficulty. So it seems to me that our purposes are not in the least opposed to each other."

"Well, you *would* say that, wouldn't you?"

"I say it because it's true. I haven't told you everything I know, because I can't. That's the nature of this job. But I have always conducted my affairs in as honorable a fashion as I can. To lay as many cards as possible upon the table, depending on how well I can trust the person sitting across from me. I would like to trust you, Miss Macallister, and I hope you can trust me. I don't believe I overstate the case when I say that your sister's life depends on it."

He's not a handsome man, Sumner Fox, as I've already explained. His wide, blunt face bears no more resemblance to the exquisite men I've signed to the Hudson Agency than an army boot resembles a custom Italian shoe. The ruff of hair on his head is an afterthought, so pale it's nearly white. His nose looks as if someone's nudged it gently to one side. The most you can say of his looks is that they're *arresting*—no pun intended—and yet I can't seem to look away from him. I stare into his colorless eyes the way you stare into a mirror. I badly want a cigarette.

"What makes you think you can trust *me*, Mr. Fox?"

He stares at me as if this isn't what he was expecting me to say. Then he reaches behind his back and lifts a manila envelope. His arm is remarkably long, like a gorilla's. He offers me the envelope.

"What's this?" I ask.

"What I was busy obtaining for you last weekend. You see, Miss Macallister, I already know a great deal about you. I hope that doesn't disturb you. I know that your father took his life in 1929, when you were eleven years old, and your mother died of cancer when you were twenty. You attended the Chapin School in Manhattan from 1923 until 1935, when you graduated and enrolled at Mount Holyoke College in Massachusetts, along with your twin sister, and earned a bachelor's degree in *geology*, of all things—"

"I like rocks," I say.

"—and then traveled with your sister to Rome, where your brother worked in the consular services department of the US embassy."

"Congratulations on your fine detective work, Mr. Fox. Those are all nice facts."

"Signore Orlovsky," says Fox, in perfect Italian, and without looking away, "may I beg you for a moment of privacy with Miss Macallister?"

"Yes, of course."

From the corner of my eye, I see Orlovsky bow—briefly—and walk out of the studio.

"Your Italian's a lot better than mine," I tell Fox.

"Language is a hobby of mine. May I continue?"

I don't especially want him to continue. I have a bad feeling about his continuing. Still, I shrug back as if I don't care. As if I'm curious to discover what he knows about me.

"During the course of your winter in Rome, you began a relationship with a Russian émigré and fashion designer by the name of Valeri Valierovich Orlovsky. The affair broke off around the third week of March, just before your sister's accident brought you both into contact with Mr. Digby."

"If you'll excuse me, Mr. Fox. I don't know where the hell you've been getting your facts, but I don't see that my private life is any of your business—"

He shakes his head. "I'm not interested in prurient details, and I don't care how you conduct your personal affairs. We are all different. We are all locked in struggle with our own demons. But I wouldn't be doing my job if I didn't make some effort to understand the psychology of everyone connected to this case, Miss Macallister. You asked me how I knew I could trust you, and I'm telling you."

"Jesus Christ."

He sends me a hard look. I presume that whatever tolerance he extends to my sexual history, he doesn't enjoy hearing the name of his Lord taken in vain. "At the beginning of May, you made plans to leave Rome. You booked a second-class cabin in the steamship *Antigone* for you and Mrs. Digby—then, of course, still Miss Macallister—but at the last minute, she elected to stay in Rome with Mr. Digby. You traveled home to New York, sharing your cabin with a Mrs. Slocombe, who recalled that you were subdued and—I quote her—*under the weight of some great sorrow.*"

"That's only because Mrs. Slocombe wouldn't stop talking."

"Two years after your return, you found a job as Mr. Hudson's secretary, taking over more of his duties following his stroke in the summer of 1944. The agency enjoyed great success under your administration. During the war, you organized your more celebrated clients to sell government bonds, and for propaganda efforts under the direction of the War Department. Just about everyone who's worked with you—clients, government officials, advertising executives, magazine editors, even business rivals—describes you as fiercely intelligent, honorable, tough but fair, and not above using your personal charisma to achieve advantage on behalf of the models you represent."

Sometime during the course of this disquisition, I find a seat on the wide, deep couch. I cross my legs and light a cigarette from my pocketbook, and my God, I have never needed one more badly.

"Throughout your adult life," he continues, watching my face, "you have conducted your private affairs with remarkable discretion. You donate significant sums of money to several worthy charities, but you choose to keep your contributions anonymous. Your social activities are chiefly undertaken with some business angle, such as fund raisers and publicity outings—your evening visit to the Palmetto Club last weekend, for example. You've taken pains to project an image of sexual sophistication, but in fact, since returning to New York, you appear to have had intimate relationships with only a handful of men. In rotation, like a baseball lineup."

"Now, there's a fascinating analogy. And what do you make of all this?"

"As a psychological evaluation? I'd say you're a person who, having suffered profound loss as a child, has erected various defenses to protect herself. The events in Rome only hardened your determination to separate heart from head, to speak in layman's terms. As a person of great natural loyalty, you fear betrayal most of all. Your trust is hard-won. You have, as a result, no close friends, and you don't wish for any."

I blow out a long stream of smoke and clap one hand against the other, holding the cigarette. "Well done, Doctor. Excellent investigative work. Must have taken years. All that without even having spoken to the patient and asked her opinion about herself."

"I'm afraid that wasn't possible."

"But you know, there's still something that my poor, traumatized, straitjacketed ego can't quite grasp. What in God's name does any of this have to do with my sister?"

Fox levers himself away from the drafting table and walks to the couch, where he takes a seat at the extreme opposite end from me and leans forward to link his hands between his enormous knees. "Because you asked how I knew I could trust you."

"You're nuts, you know that?" I stub out the cigarette and rise to my feet. "You come in here and tell me all about myself, like you've known me for years. It's the most condescending thing any man's ever said to me, and believe me, I've heard it all."

"I apologize. If you think I'm wrong about any of that, set me straight."

I don't know how to answer him. I'm angry, all right, mostly because he's probably *not* wrong about any of that, if I'm going to be honest with myself. I mean, it doesn't take a genius to analyze the mess inside my head, does it? But I don't like the fact that this fellow seems to have been following me around for *years*, speaking to everyone who knew me, going through paperwork, *spying* on me.

Drawing goddamn *conclusions* about me. And I never suspected a thing, the son of a bitch.

He rises too. "I understand you're upset. *Probably* upset," he adds swiftly.

"You've got that right, at least."

"As the sister of a woman married to a Soviet intelligence agent, you must have known you'd be subject to investigation."

"To be honest, the thought never occurred to me."

"If you want me to walk right out of this building, I'll do that. You'll never hear from me again."

I stare at his pale, narrowed eyes. He stares back at mine. The room is summer-warm, and the perspiration trickles down my back. I think of Iris in Moscow. How warm is Moscow in summer? I remember the two of us lying on the sand, Ruth and Iris, side by side, nine years old, while the sun scorched our skin and the thick hot nebulous summer air surrounded us like the womb we had once shared, and that was our bond. That was the love in which we existed together, the air we breathed in order to live.

"Or I can stay," Fox says quietly, "and explain how you and I can get your sister out of Russia alive."

I WAS THE ONE who discovered our father's body. Have I mentioned that? Leave it to Ruth to go nosing around where she doesn't belong.

They say the mind is supposed to block off terrible memories, in order to protect a person from having to experience them over and over. Well, I wish *my* mind knew that trick. I remember every detail, from the angle of sunlight through the window to the design on the bathroom tiles to the expression on my father's face, mouth open in a shocked oval, eyes open to stare in amazement at the ceiling, as if death wasn't quite what he expected. How his lips were the same color as his skin, because his blood had all poured out into the bathwater in which he lay. The nakedness of his body beneath the translucent red water, his delicate limbs, his bloated stomach, his penis floating above his dark pubic hair, all those human parts of him I had never before seen and now saw lifeless. Most of all, the smell of blood, as coppery as they say.

I dropped the magazine I had snuck into the bathroom to read. I crept out the door and closed it behind me and walked back down the hall to the bedroom I shared with Iris. We had two twin beds, but I crawled into hers and scooped her into my arms. She didn't even stir. I was the light sleeper, the jittery one. I always did the worrying for both of us. I remember feeling jealous of her, because she didn't *know*, and at the same time I didn't want her to know. I dreaded the coming of dawn, when her universe would shatter. I felt our barren, hard lives yawn eternally before us. I felt her heart beat and wished with all my might that we could die together like this and never know what the world was like without a father.

But no fairy godmother came to grant my wish that night. Sometime during those terrible hours, I fell briefly asleep, and then woke to the sound of screaming. Iris stirred against my chest and asked what was that. I stroked her hair and told her *Daddy's gone to heaven, darling.*

At the time, she thought she was dreaming, or else I was kidding, and maybe she was right. I don't believe in an afterlife of heaven or hell. I think we create our own, here on earth.

SUMNER FOX, ON THE other hand. No doubt he believes firmly in heaven and hell, angels and purgatory and the devil himself, to go along with the God he wishes I wouldn't curse. As a decent Christian, though, he doesn't seem to judge me for my failure of faith. He just stands there waiting for me to make my decision.

I nod at the manila envelope I left on the couch.

"All right. What have you got for me?"

To my surprise, he holds his eyelids shut for an instant or two, betraying relief. Then he opens them and reaches for the envelope.

"A little background, first," he says, motioning me to sit, which I do. Then he sits back down, a few inches closer than before, and removes some documents from the envelope. "We began formulating plans for the extraction of the Digbys as soon as we knew they'd defected—"

"*Extraction?* You mean like a tooth?"

"I apologize for the jargon. You see, we'd suspected Digby's involvement with Soviet intelligence for some time, and to be perfectly honest, his defection was a relief. We couldn't prosecute him on the evidence we had, because most of it was classified and highly sensitive, but we couldn't allow him to stay where he was, feeding them more information. And if the Soviets knew he was compromised, they might try to eliminate him, because they couldn't take a chance we'd turned him."

"Turned him?"

"Convinced him to work for us instead, as a double agent. Even if we hadn't, they'd be afraid he would break down under interrogation and compromise his handler—that's the KGB officer who ran him—or any other agents in the network. Instead they convinced him to defect. I expect he'd been such a valuable agent, they thought he might be some use for them at Moscow Centre. KGB headquarters," he adds.

"Yes, I know."

"Anyway, about four years ago, Digby started showing signs of breakdown. The Soviets had broken off the network, because of some high-level defections to our side that compromised a number of their agents in the field."

"You mean like Alger Hiss?"

"Hiss and others. You have to understand the degree of paranoia that prevails in Moscow Centre. Well, in Soviet Russia generally, but the Communist Party and the intelligence service in particular. On top of the usual backstabbings and betrayals you find in a revolutionary government, there was a series of purges in the 1930s that decimated the army and the NKVD, as the intelligence agency was then known—"

"Yes, yes. Orlovsky told me all the stories."

"Well, it left behind a legacy of fear. Nobody trusts anybody. So when Digby found himself adrift, cut off, his guiding purpose vanished from his life—well, he went off the rails. That was the summer of 1948. We were already on his trail at that point, waiting for him to make a move. I figured that if he broke down completely, we might be able to rescue him and possibly even turn him, risky as it was."

"But he disappeared instead," I say. "That was when he defected, wasn't it? In the autumn of 1948, when he vanished with Iris and the kids."

Fox fingers the edges of the papers in his hands. "One of our agents confirmed they'd arrived in Russia in November of 1948. Seems they were first taken to a sort of secure city outside of Moscow for a year or two, to make sure they were clean—that we hadn't turned him—and then he seems to have been given an academic job of some kind, lecturing on foreign affairs, probably doing some instruction work with the KGB."

"How do you know all this?"

"Local assets," he says.

"So what's changed? Why did Iris ask me for help? And what makes you think she wants to come back home altogether?"

Fox stands and walks to the window that overlooks the courtyard. In the manner of ancient buildings, the window is a small one, the stone walls thick, so you must stand close to really look out properly. He's still holding the envelope and the documents in one hand, while he sets them both on his hips. Someone's opened the window to allow in some fresh air, and the smell of lemons drifts up bright and clean from the lemon tree.

"A little over a year ago," he says, "as you might have heard, a pair of English diplomats disappeared from a pleasure cruise off the coast of France—"

"I knew it!" I exclaim.

"—both of whom had held a series of extremely well-placed and sensitive positions within the British Foreign Office. One was already under investigation as a spy for the Soviets. The other we didn't know about, only suspected. They successfully escaped through France and Switzerland and arrived safely in Moscow a few days later, and that's when we first saw signs of trouble."

"But I don't understand. If all three of them were loyal Soviet agents, what danger could Burgess and Maclean have brought with them?"

"We don't know." Fox turns to face her. "It could be anything. Whatever it was, their arrival seems to have precipitated some kind of crisis. Not long after, we understood that the Digbys were in trouble. Afraid for their lives, in fact."

"How did you learn that?"

"I'm afraid I can't be more specific." He holds out the envelope. I rise from the couch and take it. "I've spent a number of years draw-ing up various plans for a possible extraction of the Digby family—"

"Why?"

"What do you mean, why?"

"Why would you want him back?"

For a moment, he looks flummoxed. Then he says, "Because of the information he could bring back with him, of course. If he wanted out, of course we'd try to do it. The problem is *how*. It's not easy to get agents inside Russia—the Soviets are paranoid to a man. And now there's the additional complication of Mrs. Digby's pregnancy, which brings new and unacceptable risk to the original schemes. Then I read again what Mrs. Digby wrote to you, and I realized she might have been offering us a solution."

"You mean me? *I'm* the solution?"

"If you'd stayed put in New York, as I asked, I would have had the opportunity to discuss this with you there. Thank God our man was keeping a close eye on you. You might have compromised the whole operation if you'd managed to get any further along."

"What operation?"

"This one," he says. "In which Iris Digby's sister applies for spe-cial permission to travel to Moscow in order to care for Mrs. Digby during the weeks surrounding the delivery of her expected baby, an ordeal with which Mrs. Digby has a history of serious com-plications. Mrs. Digby will then be transported out of Moscow to receive medical treatment at a clinic in Riga, Latvia, in the com-pany of her family. On their way to this clinic, the family will ren-dezvous with a ship off the coast of Latvia, in the Baltic Sea. That's just the bare bones, naturally."

"Naturally," I say faintly.

"We'll go over every aspect of the operation. I want you familiar with all the details, the contingencies. Once we get to Moscow—"

"We?"

He clears his throat. For the first time, he looks away from me—at my ear, possibly, or else some point beyond my ear.

"We recognized immediately," he says, "that the complexity and potential danger of the operation—the knowledge of tactics and procedure—required an experienced agent to accompany and . . . well . . . and direct you."

"I see. And where on earth could they find such an agent? I can't imagine."

Fox turns back to look on me straight. "Can you live with that?"

I look down at the passport in my hand, which has my picture in it. "But how exactly are *you* supposed to get permission to travel to the Soviet Union? And how . . . how are we supposed to . . ."

My voice trails off, because I've just realized that the name printed inside the passport is not my own. Not altogether, at any rate.

"I'll be undercover," he says. "As your spouse."

IRIS

At noon on the first day of August, a horse and cart ambled up the long drive to Honeysuckle Cottage under a blazing sun.

"Welcome to the land of petrol rationing!" Iris called out to Aunt Vivian, who sat in front next to Philip Beauchamp holding the reins. The three small girls waved frantically from among the suitcases piled in the box.

"Absolutely *charming!*" Aunt Vivian called back. In the next instant she reached back for one of her offspring, a towheaded monster attempting to climb over the edge. "Pepper! Bad girl!"

Iris hadn't met either of the two younger girls, and Tiny—the oldest—was only a year old when Ruth and Iris left for Rome, just starting to toddle about and speak with an elegant lisp. Aunt Vivian, on the other hand. Aunt Vivian was her mother's younger sister, who'd parlayed her wit and her long-limbed, blond beauty into a marriage with none other than Charles Schuyler III, scion of one of New York's most prestigious families, an eligible bachelor if there ever was one. Everyone had whispered about what a *fine match* Aunt Vivian had made, as if this were the previous century and Aunt Vivian was some pert, pretty miss from the country, marrying above her station. Well, maybe she was. But Iris would always be loyal to Aunt Vivian. Say what you would—and people said plenty—Aunt Vivian had always stood in like another mother to Ruth and Iris, or maybe more like a worldly older sister.

Now she hauled the wriggling Pepper into her lap and gathered her pocketbook and hatbox while Philip set the brake and leapt off the box to help her down.

"Thank you," Aunt Vivian said in that impeccable voice, more lockjaw than the toniest Long Island heiress. She dropped Pepper on the grass like a sack of unwanted potatoes and turned to lift Little Viv out of the cart. Iris ran forward to help Tiny. From inside the house, the boys came thundering onto the drive and stopped dead at the sight of the three blond girls in their neat matching dresses and Mary Jane shoes. Kip scratched his head. Jack scuffed his bare feet on the gravel.

"Boys! Come say hello to your cousins!" Iris called out.

"My God," said Aunt Vivian, by way of greeting, "it's like the OK Corral. How are you, darling? You look wonderful, all pink and plump. You're not with child again, are you?"

"Of course not!" Iris gasped. She glanced at Philip as she returned Aunt Vivian's embrace.

"Good. Nothing spoils your summer like a bun in the oven. This must be Cornelius."

"Kip!" said Kip stoutly, holding his ground.

"Is that so? Kip it is, then." She shook his hand and turned to Jack. "And this is little John."

"It's Jack, you old biddy!" Jack shouted. "Ma'am."

"Jack! For shame!"

"No, he's absolutely right. I *am* an old biddy, as far as a three-year-old boy's concerned, anyway. Thank God the older fellows take a more liberal view. So this is Honeysuckle Cottage, is it? Very attractive."

Aunt Vivian shaded her eyes with her hand and took in every detail of the rambling stone house, the overgrown garden, the distant view of the sea. In her mind, she was probably calculating its worth—a habit the Schuylers would have considered unspeakably gauche, if they knew. Maybe they did. They hadn't exactly welcomed the courtship, after all. The Walkers might have done well in the postwar boom, but they'd lost most of their fortune in the Crash and Aunt Vivian shouldn't have stood any chance with one of the original Knickerbocker families, the very definition of old New York society. Lucky for her, though, Uncle Charlie was apparently afflicted with the romantic streak that was the downfall of many a Schuyler man, and he had fallen in love with Aunt Vivian at some party during the winter season of 1935. By June, he was absconding regularly from the Schuyler compound in East Hampton—The Dunes, they called it—to the Walker family home in Glen Cove, in order to improve their acquaintance away from disapproving eyes.

Anyway, the story went, Uncle Charlie's mother, who had been widowed several years earlier, began to panic around the middle of July and paid a call on the Walkers. In a scene right out of some cobwebby old novel, she told them she'd see the entire Walker clan blackballed if That Tramp didn't renounce her precious only child, the last legacy of her departed husband. So Aunt Vivian said all right, whatever you say, and the next thing you knew, the Walkers had taken ship on the *Queen Mary* (second class) for a European tour. They were in Florence by the time Uncle Charlie caught up with them, and in a dramatic tableau on the Piazza Michelangelo at either dawn or sunset, depending on whom you asked, while the rising (or setting) sun turned the tiled rooftops fiery orange, he went down on one knee, extracted a four-carat diamond ring from his pocket, and begged Aunt Vivian to do him the honor of becoming his wife.

Needless to say, they were married by Labor Day.

As for the dowager Mrs. Schuyler? Acknowledging she was outfoxed, she presented The Dunes to the new couple as a wedding gift—really sportsmanlike, when you thought about it—and moved down to Palm Beach, never to return. No doubt she was cackling into her bougainvillea right now, Iris imagined. That fiery dawn (or sunset) on the Piazza Michelangelo seemed to have long since faded.

Philip cheerfully unloaded the suitcases from the back of the cart and carried them to the door. Iris noticed him and called out, "No, Philip, you mustn't! Really, we can manage!"

"Oh, don't *stop* the poor man. Can't you see he's enjoying himself?"

"Don't listen to her!" Iris told him.

Philip, who had just delivered the last suitcase to the stoop, made an extravagant bow. "Delighted to be of service. Dare I hope you'll be settled in time to wander up to the main house for drinks this evening?"

"Drinks? Only if you insist," said Aunt Vivian.

"Very good. Around six, then? And if you're wondering about the children, they're having a jolly adventure in the mud puddles over by the flowerbeds."

✦ ✦ ✦

IN HER LETTER, WHICH had arrived around the beginning of
May, Aunt Vivian didn't explain why she was bringing her young
daughters—but not her husband—to England for six weeks, smack
bang in the middle of that time of year when Schuylers tradition-
ally migrate to the eastern end of Long Island. Iris broached the
question as she walked with Aunt Vivian down the beaten lane
across the meadow for drinks at Philip Beauchamp's house.

"He simply couldn't get away," Aunt Vivian said. "The firm's got
too much work at the moment. So I told him I'd just take the girls
and go without him, if he didn't mind."

"But what about The Dunes? It's so lovely there in the summer.
I don't know how you could stand to go anywhere else."

"Oh, the house is all right, but the *crowd*, Iris. I just didn't have
the stomach for it this summer. Besides, I figured I should give
some other woman a chance at the ladies' singles at the club this
year."

"That's sportsmanlike."

"Yes, I thought so." Aunt Vivian rummaged in her pocketbook
and offered Iris a cigarette, which she declined. Aunt Vivian lit one
for herself, put the lighter away, and said, "Anyway, Charlie has
been having an affair with poor Theresa Marshall's daughter—you
know who I mean—the orphan—"

"*Marie Marshall?*"

"That's the one."

"But she's just a young thing! She can't be more than twenty."

"Twenty-*five*, darling. You're awfully out of touch. I don't suppose you remember her much, but she's a real knockout now. I can't
say I blame him—I'd do the same, in his position—though I *do*

wonder what she sees in *him*." Aunt Vivian laughed bitterly. "But never mind. It'll all blow over. Tell me about this Philip of yours."

"Of mine?"

"I mean he must be thoroughly infatuated with you, if he's giving you a place like *that* for the summer."

"Oh, no. It's not like that at all. We're paying rent."

"How nice. Are cocktails with mine host included in the deal?"

"He's just being kind. We're all good friends, up in London."

"Speaking of which." Aunt Vivian flicked some ash into a clump of grass. "Where's your husband?"

"Working, of course. He comes down on the weekends. He's taking the train this evening—he should be joining us."

"How very— *Good Lord*."

Aunt Vivian stopped in the middle of the lane and stared at Highcliffe, which had just become visible around the bend. Iris followed her line of sight and laughed.

"Oh, didn't I tell you? Philip's quite rich. He's due to inherit some kind of title, I think. Sasha told me, but I can't remember what."

"You clever little devil."

They continued up the lane to what Philip apologetically called *the pile*. In fact, he apologized constantly as he led them from the entrance hall through the various staterooms—served as some kind of army intelligence headquarters during the war, he said, and they still hadn't put everything to rights—*intelligence officers rather like dogs in their personal habits—drank all the good wine and the vintage port, the bastards—should just deed the whole shambles to the National Trust and let them deal with everything, serve them right—right, here we are—invited a friend or two, as you see.*

Here was a pleasant, light-filled room with French doors open-ing to a wide stone terrace and the lawn, on which several cricket matches might be played simultaneously, if you didn't mind hur-dling the odd hedge or flowerbed. The *friend or two* was really five or six, dressed for the country, but Iris's gaze went straight to the blond woman in the lean, daring trousers and silk blouse, smoking a cigarette, caressing a damp gin and tonic in the other hand. She was the woman at the Desboroughs' party, the one talking with Philip and Sasha in the library—Iris recognized her at once—recognized also, like a puzzle piece falling into place, she was the woman in the snapshot that Sasha kept in his desk drawer, a per-fect match, except her hair was now a different color.

PHILIP WALKED THEM HOME around eleven o'clock. The other guests had left after an hour or two, and still there was no sign of Sasha, so Philip had persuaded Vivian and Iris to stay for dinner—roast chicken grown on the home farm—eat all you want, no ration book—plenty of wine to wash it down. Aunt Vivian did most of the talking. She and Philip got on like a mansion on fire. At half past ten Philip had glanced at the clock and suggested that perhaps Sasha had taken a later train and gone straight to the cottage?

"Oh, the poor man," said Aunt Vivian. "I'd forgotten all about him."

So now they tramped back down the lane, through the fragrant meadow that smelled of hay and wildflowers. Tonight the moon was new and invisible, but the stars were bountiful here in the coun-try and they dusted the tips of the grass with silver. Iris listened to Aunt Vivian chatter with Philip. She was flirting shamelessly—

probably planned to sleep with him, if only for revenge on her husband. The starlight glinted on his silver hair. His profile was pristine. He looked noble and wise, like a sage. His footsteps made no sound on the dirt.

They reached the cottage. Mrs. Betts had been looking after the children. She seemed surprised to see Philip—gave her report with many a nervous glance and then retired to her room. There was no sign of Sasha.

"I wouldn't worry." Aunt Vivian yawned. "I expect he went out with a friend or two."

"That's why I'm worried." Iris turned to Philip. "Before you leave, I was hoping to have a word with you?"

"Certainly."

Aunt Vivian gave Iris a wise look. "I guess that's my cue, then. Good night, chums. Don't do anything I wouldn't do."

Philip laughed and said he imagined that left a wide range of possibilities.

When Aunt Vivian's footsteps creaked up the stairs, Iris turned to Philip. "She's so outrageous. I apologize."

"Not at all. I worship your American characters. Shall we step outside? It's a rare evening out there."

He knew the cottage better than she did—guided her through the darkened sunroom to the French doors—knew the trick of opening the sticky middle one. The doors led straight onto the grass and a gentle salt breeze coming off the Channel.

"Come along. We won't be overheard," Philip said.

Iris glanced down the lane, where Sasha would be arriving if he were going to arrive. Nothing stirred. She walked on next to Philip, across the grass toward the sea cliffs.

"You're right, it's a beautiful evening. It's a beautiful place—magical—I can't thank you enough."

He made a diffident English noise. Some seagulls squawked out of the darkness.

"I wanted to ask you about Miss Fischer," Iris said.

"Nedda? What about her?"

"I found her photograph in Sasha's desk."

He stopped and said, *Ah*.

"She had brown hair instead of blond, and she was wearing a uniform. But it was definitely her. You can't mistake her face."

"No, you can't." Philip resumed walking. "What do you want to know?"

"I don't even know what to ask. But I thought—since she's a friend of yours—I don't know. Maybe you know how they might have known each other."

Philip motioned to the left and Iris saw a stone bench, hardly visible in the starlight. She sat and he sat next to her, stretching out his legs with a sigh. "Of course you should ask your husband," he said.

"I know. But he's not around, is he? And I'm asking you instead."

"You see, I don't know how to answer you."

"Then allow me to guess, and if I'm right, you can nod or something."

"That seems fair."

"I think Sasha may have been involved in some sort of intelligence operations during the war, when we were in Zurich, and Miss Fischer was a contact of his."

"You're very clever."

"I'd have to be stupid not to figure that out."

"Then why do you ask me?"

"Maybe I'm just wondering if you did the same thing."

"And I suppose I've just confirmed your suspicions?"

"No," she said, "I realized when you told me about the house being used for intelligence. I didn't think you'd let them take over the family estate unless they gave you a piece of the action."

He started to laugh. "How I love you Americans."

The air smelled of night blossoms, of jasmine and the nearby sea. The wind sifted through the boxwoods. Iris put her face in her hands.

"Oh, my dear. I'm sorry." Philip put a gentle arm around her shoulders. She turned her head into his chest for a moment or two, maybe thirty seconds—bliss. His shirt was unspeakably soft. Everything beneath it perfectly solid.

SASHA ARRIVED AT HONEYSUCKLE Cottage at half past eight o'clock in the morning, in a taxi from the station. He walked into the breakfast room with the kind of exaggerated care that meant he was still drunk, had probably gone straight to Victoria Station from the Gargoyle Club or wherever he was. Though he reeked of cigarettes, his clothes were remarkably neat, and he greeted Aunt Vivian with a civilized handshake.

"Welcome to Honeysuckle, Aunt Vivian. I'm awfully sorry to turn up like this. Had a work session that went late."

"So I see. *Vivian* will do." She squinted at his face. "I hope you don't mind my saying so, but you look as if you wouldn't mind a cup of coffee."

He smiled, and for a moment he was like the old Sasha, hair

swinging down onto his forehead, the bluest eyes you ever saw. "I'd be grateful," he said.

AFTER HE'D DRUNK TWO cups of coffee, wolfed down half a dozen eggs on toast, and charmed the children, Sasha headed upstairs to bathe and change. Iris followed him. He spotted her in the mirror above his dresser while he unbuttoned his shirt.

"Go ahead. Deliver the lecture. I deserve it."

"Where *were* you? That's all I want to know."

"Out. With friends. That's all you need to know."

"I was worried."

"Were you?" He tossed the shirt in the hamper and stripped off his undershirt, his drawers. "I figured Beauchamp would be keeping you company."

"What's that supposed to mean?"

"Nothing." He started out the door to the bathroom, where the water was already running into the tub, nice and warm.

"You can't go out in the hall like that! The girls!"

He swore and snatched a dressing gown from the hook. Iris sat on the bed and put her face in her hands. She heard the opening and closing of the bedroom door and lay back across the bed to stare at the simple plaster ceiling. Outside the window, the children played some noisy game on the lawn, and Iris marveled at how easily they'd come together, these cousins who didn't even know each other—how deep and instinctive is the human need for connection.

She lay there for some time, even though duty tugged her downstairs. She felt paralyzed, unable to move, let alone rise and do all the mothering things. She couldn't confront Sasha about Nedda Fischer, because she'd have to tell him how she came to see the photograph in the desk. She wasn't even sure she wanted to. What was the point?

The door creaked open. Sasha's voice, a touch ironic—*Still here?*

"Tell me about Zurich," she said.

He moved to the dresser. "Zurich? Why Zurich?"

"You weren't just working for the embassy, were you?"

"No. I was seconded to the OSS, under diplomatic cover. Liaising with our agents in Germany. Assisting the escape lines, that kind of thing. I assumed you knew."

She sat up. "How should I know if you didn't tell me anything?"

"Because you couldn't possibly think I'd spend the war stamping passports, for one thing." He had a towel wrapped around his middle. His cheeks were pink and smooth; his hair combed back wet from his forehead. He took a cigarette from the pack on the dresser and lit up. "For another thing, I wasn't exactly home every evening at five o'clock, was I?"

"You were so happy in Zurich. I always wondered why."

"Because I was doing something worthwhile. Fighting the right side."

"Is that all?"

He sucked on the cigarette. "And I had you. And Kip. What more could a man ask for?"

"It's funny, because I was miserable in Zurich. I had all those miscarriages, and you were hardly ever home, and the war was going badly."

He stared at her a moment and turned to the window, where the children screamed around the lawn. "All's well that ends well, I guess. We ended up with Jack, didn't we, and we won the war. And now you've got me around all the time, a nice well-trained husband."

"No, you're not. You're a drunken, irritable, unreliable husband who's probably having an affair."

Sasha spun around. "What the devil? Who's having an affair?"

"With that blond woman. Fischer. She keeps popping up, doesn't she?"

"Damn it, Iris. I told you, it was over long ago with her. I—"

He bit off the sentence cleanly, like the snip of a pair of scissors. Iris stared back at him. She took in the instant of panic, the flexing around the eyes, replaced almost—but not quite—immediately with a look of bored irritation that was the screen for something else, the search for something to say.

"You're talking nonsense," he said.

"She's your contact. Your handler." Iris spoke slowly, because it was so much to understand—*everything*—the history of the past eight years—of her marriage, of Sasha—all rewriting itself inside her head.

Outside the window, a cloud shifted. Sunlight poured through the glass and turned Sasha to gold. His hair, his skin. The angle of the light had some strange effect on his eyes, turning them an extraordinary pale green. He didn't move, not a flicker. One hand held the towel in place at his waist.

Iris waited. He had to tell her—he had to say the truth or not. She wouldn't do him the favor of dragging it out of him.

"*Was*," he said, in a voice so low, Iris strained to hear it. "She *was* my handler, in the beginning. She recruited me."

"I'll bet."

"She arranged for the Zurich posting, the diplomatic cover. Because Germany was important, it was important that we had some strategic advantage in Germany, so that we knew what the Americans were up to."

"*We?* You mean the Soviet Union."

He didn't answer.

"She doesn't sound Russian," Iris said.

"Her mother's Russian. They used to spend summers there, when she was growing up. At her grandfather's dacha. So SIS hired her as an intelligence officer, because she was fluent."

"But really she's working for the Soviets."

He turned away to stub out his cigarette in the ashtray on the bedside table. "Was. It's all finished."

"Finished? Why?"

"Never mind. I've already told you more than I should."

"Do you mean you're not spying anymore? What about the note in the hymnal? All those urgent meetings?"

"*Never mind,* I said!"

"You said once that you wanted to tell me. You used to trust me."

"Would you just *shut up* about it? *Christ.* The less you know, the better. Don't you understand?" He whipped around. "What I told you about Nedda, do you understand, you never heard it."

"Of course not."

"Your pal Beauchamp, all right? Not a word, not a goddamn hint. Do you understand? *Do you?*"

"Are you still sleeping with her?"

He banged the wall with his fist and yelled, "*Do you under-stand?*"

The door sprang open. Kip rushed in. "Mama! Are you all right?"

"Yes! Yes, darling, I'm fine." Iris stood just in time to take his small, hard body as he hurled himself into her middle.

"Then why are you crying?"

"Because Daddy's a beast," said Sasha. "If you'll excuse me, I'm going to get dressed in the bathroom. Seems to have got a little crowded in here."

AUNT VIVIAN LOWERED HERSELF on the picnic blanket and stretched her long legs out in the sun. "You haven't asked me about your sister yet."

"No, I haven't. Grapes?"

"Have you got anything stronger?"

"Champagne."

"Much better."

Iris poured a glass for Aunt Vivian and another glass for herself—she was on her third—while Aunt Vivian lit a cigarette and squinted in the direction of the children, who were busy teaching Philip Beauchamp and his dog—a scruffy black Labrador—how to play baseball. Pepper was pitching, Kip was catching, Philip was poised at the plate with a cricket bat and an expression of extreme concentration.

"Why, she's very well, since you ask," said Aunt Vivian. "She's working as a personal secretary to the president of some company or another, I can't remember the name. Something to do with fashion models."

"How nice."

Striiiiike! yelled Tiny, the umpire. (Tiny was always the umpire—she never met a rule she didn't like—while Pepper and Little Viv were natural anarchists.)

"What's that? No, she's still not interested in marrying anybody. She likes keeping her beaux on their toes, the little minx, and frankly I don't blame her. They're a damned nuisance, husbands."

"I'll say."

Aunt Vivian leaned closer. "What's that?"

"I said, they're perfect dears, once you get used to them."

A loud, splendid crack echoed off the boxwoods and the walls of the house. Philip dashed off toward first base, limping slightly, followed by Raffles the black Labrador. Jack, playing all the bases and the outfield, got up an instant too late to catch him at second base.

Safe! shouted Tiny. Jack threw down his cap and stomped on it.

"Tell me something," said Iris. "What happens when you get back to New York?"

"I'll take him back, of course. I won't put the girls through a divorce." Aunt Vivian finished her champagne and reached for the bottle. "It'll burn itself out. That Marshall girl will come to her senses and realize that once I'm out of the picture, there's no excitement in it. He'll be begging me to take him back, and you know I don't come cheap. Diamonds, at least."

"But it won't be the same, will it?"

"No. But marriage never is, is it? You go through stages, like acts in a play. Act One, you fall in love, and the birds twitter and the bees go buzz, and you'll never love somebody else as long as you both shall live, amen. Act Two, enter the baby carriage, and all of a sudden he catches sight of a pair of firm young tits and figures life is short. Act *Three* . . ." Aunt Vivian narrowed her eyes at the ball game, where Little Viv had come up to bat against Pepper, and Philip Beauchamp seemed to know more than an Englishman should about taking a lead off second base.

"Act Three?"

"Act Three, you realize there's no point letting the husbands have all the fun."

Pepper released the ball, and Philip took off toward third base. Iris rose on her knees. Little Viv whistled her bat through the air—*Striiike!* yelled Tiny—Kip hurled the ball toward poor Jack, who ran with all his might to cover third—caught the ball, a miracle—tagged a sliding Philip Beauchamp at the very instant he touched base—

Out! called Tiny.

"She's not pulling any punches, is she?" said Sasha.

Iris whirled around. Her husband stood at the edge of the picnic blanket, carrying a smoke and a glass of whiskey in one hand and his briefcase in the other. He wore his suit with a fresh shirt and tie. He set down the briefcase and finished the whiskey.

"You're leaving?" Iris said.

"Something's come up. Headed back to London. Awfully sorry to miss all the fun, but it looks as if Beauchamp has matters well in hand."

Iris scrambled to her feet. "But how will you get to the station?"

"I've called a taxi."

"That's going to be awfully expensive."

He leaned forward to kiss her cheek. "We'll try again next weekend, shall we? Give the boys my love."

"Give it to them yourself."

"I'm afraid there isn't time. Vivian? Good to see you."

He picked up his briefcase and walked back across the lawn with the exaggerated care of a man who'd already washed down his eggs with a few sides of whiskey. As Iris watched, stunned and empty, a small car, red or possibly orange, pulled up to the drive from the lane and stopped. Iris couldn't see the driver, but she was pretty sure that car was no taxi.

Sasha reached the vehicle and opened the front door. He swung his long body inside and the car took off in a spurt of gravel.

Iris turned back to the game. Her fingers trembled against the sides of her legs, so she folded her arms across her middle. The air smelled of cut grass and sunshine. Little Viv stood at home plate, preparing to swing. Philip Beauchamp stood near the batter's box, holding a salmon-pink cricket ball in one hand, staring right past Iris at the car that disappeared down the lane.

LYUDMILA

Lyudmila has never traveled outside the Soviet Union. She does not even possess a passport. To travel overseas is to bring attention to yourself, and anyway she has plenty to do in Moscow, stamping out the sparks of counterrevolution before they can catch flame.

Still, the enemies of the Soviet state flourish throughout the world, so she's developed a network of overseas agents to act as her eyes and—occasionally—her deputies. Mere hours after identifying Mrs. Digby's sister as one Ruth Macallister of New York City, Lyudmila has a tail put on the woman, just in time to catch her departing New York on a Pan American flight to Rome. When the airplane departs from its scheduled stop in Boston, one of Lyudmila's operatives accompanies her to Paris. A local tail in Rome picks up Miss Macallister there, where the new husband—a Mr. Sumner Fox, who caught a later flight—meets her at the atelier of a Russian émigré aristocrat.

There's something fishy about the husband. Lyudmila can't

quite put her finger on it. The marriage checks out—some decadent American resort in Rhode Island in May—certificate, marriage registry, all paperwork in place. But why don't they travel to
Rome together? Why Rome at all? And why do they meet at the
place of business of a Russian counterrevolutionary, of all people?

Today is Thursday. Mr. and Mrs. Fox are due in Moscow in
three days. Lyudmila's telephone rings—it's the head of the American section. He wants her to join him in his office this instant.

VASHNIKOV WAS AGAINST LYUDMILA's plan from the beginning. He
said it was too risky, too much potential for sabotage, and for what
gain? Lyudmila told him she had evidence of a Western counterspy
active in Moscow at the highest level, being run out of London.
He asked to see this so-called evidence. She refused on grounds of
security, but really because she doesn't trust him—which isn't personal, remember. Lyudmila does not trust anybody, except Marina.

She doesn't like him, either, although she doesn't like most people. At one time he was a handsome, trim, dark-haired man—they
slept together once or twice, a decade ago—but now he's run to
fat, and his face is always red, and his teeth are yellow from cigarettes. Like her, he's never traveled outside the country, but in his
case it's because of incuriosity and general laziness. He was given
this plum job of head of the American section because he's very
good at claiming credit for other people's successes, such as Lyudmila's. This is why he reluctantly gave permission for the plan to go
forward—not because he likes it, but because if it succeeds, he'll get
the recognition. If it doesn't, Lyudmila will take the blame.

"All right," he tells her now, pushing a manila file folder toward
her. "You have your visas and special permissions. You can have

Kedrov to mind them, and a driver. They will stay at the National, suite 807."

Lyudmila nods. Suite 807 is exceptionally well covered with listening devices.

"You understand that Digby is irreproachable. He was one of our most valuable assets in the West, until he was unmasked through no fault of his own."

"Then this operation will confirm your trust in him."

He grinds his teeth and lifts his cigarette from the ashtray. "I have looked into Fox's background. All clean. He works as a lawyer in Washington. At university he became famous playing American football, which means he cannot possibly be working in any form of intelligence work."

"Why not?"

"Have you *seen* an American football player? They are like oxen. Oxen in a china shop. Besides, this one is famous. His face alone disqualifies him."

"In short, the ideal cover. What about the war?"

Vashnikov glances down at the papers on his desk. "He flew torpedo bombers in the Pacific. Spent two years in a Japanese prison camp."

"So he knows how to resist interrogation."

"You see an ominous sign in every star, Ivanova."

"I am a realist. If you will excuse me, I have many details to arrange before the Foxes arrive in Moscow."

She rises from her chair. Vashnikov remains seated, staring at her speculatively while he flips a pen between his thumb and forefinger. He turns his head to smoke from the cigarette in his other hand—a gesture of dismissal.

Lyudmila walks to the door and pauses with her hand on the knob.

"What about Mrs. Digby?" she says. "Is there any news of her health?"

Vashnikov shrugs and stubs out the cigarette. "She's still pregnant, if that's what you mean."

"Good," Lyudmila says, and walks out the door.

DOWNSTAIRS, SHE COMPOSES A cable and takes it down herself to the cipher room. It's addressed to a KGB operative called SALT in Odessa, who has done excellent work for her before.

URGENT APPREHEND FEMALE ITALIAN NATIONAL IN SOCHI NAME DONNA ANNA ORLOVSKAYA AGE 15 CURRENTLY RESIDENT HOME OF GRANDFATHER SERGEI ORLOVSKY ADDRESS KAMANINI STREET STOP DETAIN UNTIL FURTHER NOTICE STOP

RUTH

My first glimpse of Russia occurs between some clouds as we approach the airport in Moscow. I've been peering out the window for some time, hoping for any open seam in the almost unending blanket that's covered the landscape since we took off from Berlin, while I smoked cigarette after cigarette until even my tolerant husband made a gentle cough from the seat next to me.

The aircraft is called a Lisunov something-or-other, but it's really an old DC-3 built in Russia by license from the McDonnell Douglas Corporation, on account of the Soviet Union being our ally at the time. I haven't flown in a DC-3 in years, but here it is again, the particular timbre of the propellers droning in my ears like a childhood memory. Actually, I find it comforting. Everything else around me is incomprehensibly foreign.

No, I lie. Inches away sits Sumner Fox, who's somehow taken on all the familiarity of a long acquaintance in the short, packed days we've spent together. Was there ever a time I haven't known him? I now recognize the smell of his shaving soap and the way he chews his meat, the vibration in his voice that signals impatience and the note that means he's amused. I know he's not strictly tee-total but only drinks wine on occasion, that he doesn't smoke or swear but sometimes looks as if he wishes he did. I know he has an extraordinary facility for language. He mentioned, in an apologetic way, that he'd learned Russian in two months, including the Cyrillic lettering that I still couldn't make heads or tails of. He also speaks Italian, French, Spanish, German, Arabic, Urdu, Mandarin, Persian, and—of course—Japanese. (He stressed that he was only *proficient* in Mandarin and Urdu, not fluent.) As for Latin and ancient Greek, he picked them up as a schoolboy and studied classics at Yale. I told him the rhyme *I* learned at school: *Latin's a dead language, as dead as it could be. First it killed the Romans, now it's killing me.* He smiled and said he'd heard that one before.

The airplane seat is too small for his shoulders, but he's wedged himself in gallantly and crossed his legs to keep them from straying against mine. Early this morning we flew from Rome to Vienna and then Vienna to Berlin, and at Schoenfeld Airport we boarded this Aeroflot for the final stretch. Now the clouds open up at last, just as we plunge through them and hurtle toward the airport, which is east of the city center. I peer eagerly at the roads and buildings and fields below me, but they don't seem any different from the landscape outside New York or Rome or any other big, sprawling metropolis. There's nothing that says this is incontrovertibly the Soviet Union, no Communist shade coloring the country. The grass is green, the clouds are gray, the cracks of sky are blue. The runway's the same dirty slate as every airport runway, rising up to meet us with a solid bump that rattles my teeth.

I look at Fox, and maybe I wear an expression of terror on my face, because he leans forward and kisses me on the lips, and his mouth tastes like the mouth of any other man, the particular taste of kissing, except that it isn't.

AS WE SAT TOGETHER in the studio over the course of two days, going over every possible detail, cramming months of training into a few spare hours, Fox told me that I should remember one thing above all: the KGB was always watching. There would be watchers at the airport, as soon as we presented our passports and visas and alerted the authorities that Mr. and Mrs. Fox had arrived as the particular guests of the Soviet people, who had graciously allowed sister to visit beloved sister as a gesture of goodwill between our two countries. (Some very clever diplomats have been at work on our behalf, you see.)

There would be watchers on the airplane, he went on. The driver who guided us around Moscow in an official car would report back to Moscow Centre. There would be watchers in the lobby of the luxury hotel where we would stay—a hotel designed expressly for visits from foreigners, of course. The hotel room itself would be bugged—the telephone, naturally, but also the bedroom and the bathroom, the closet, maybe even the bed. We could not risk a single candid conversation, in other words. We would have to speak in code instead. So if I mentioned my aunt Vivian, for example, that would mean I thought I had been poisoned. (Apparently the Soviet intelligence service was fond of poison.) If one of us made a reference to elephants, that meant we should abort whatever activity we were attempting. Foreign language not being a strength of mine, I abandoned my attempts to learn some rudimentary Russian and focused my mind on memorizing this code instead, because Fox told me it would likely save our lives at some point, when something went wrong. As it would. Something always went wrong.

Above all, we must act at all times as if we were a married couple, recently wed. According to the story put forth by the US diplomatic service, in arranging for our visit together, we met each other at a New Year's party six months ago at the Yale Club, where Fox was given some kind of award for athletic accomplishment for the glory of the university. (That last part is actually true.) That night, we fell madly in love and married quietly in May—a marriage certificate was duly submitted to the Russian authorities, to demonstrate that Fox's presence was on the up-and-up—in a small weekend ceremony in Newport, Rhode Island, close family only. This was because Fox had been married before, another fact that turned out to be genuine.

"You're not serious," I said.

"No, it's true."

"So what's the story?"

He put on that granite expression of his. "We married right after college. I went away to fight in the war and didn't return for years. She fell in love with someone else."

"That's not very nice."

"At one point, they told her I was dead," he said grudgingly, as if this was a piece of information he didn't like to share.

I stared at him a moment, trying to think of any question I had a right to ask.

"Did you have any children?" I said finally.

He shook his head. "No."

And apparently this was all I need to know about that, because he wouldn't reveal any more, other than her name: Constance.

"Well, that's ironic," I said.

✦ ✦ ✦

WHERE WAS I? RIGHT. Fox kisses me on the lips, as a new husband should, and squeezes my hand. His palm is perfectly dry, the nerveless bastard. I myself am trembling, a fact of which I'm sure he's aware—hence the peck and the squeeze. The plane slows and then spins nimbly around, preparing to trundle to the terminal. Fox leans his mouth to my ear and murmurs lovingly, "Don't worry so much."

Easy for him to say. He's done this kind of thing before, I feel certain. Marriage, obviously, but also operating undercover. I have all kinds of questions I know he won't answer—questions I don't really want to hear answered, I suspect—and that ought to make me feel secure. He knows what he's doing! All I have to worry about is the cover story. I think it's strange, for example, that he's using his real name. Won't the Soviets know Sumner Fox works for the FBI?

Unlikely, he said, because he's always worked under a code name, per standard tradecraft. And his employment records plainly indicate that he works for a corporate law firm in Washington, not the FBI.

What if they investigate? I wanted to know. What if they ask around and find out we didn't meet at the Yale Club on the first of January, that nobody in Newport knows anything about a wedding between Mr. Sumner Fox and Miss Ruth Macallister?

He said they'd filed all the paperwork with the town hall in Newport, for one thing. Hudson's been briefed, he'll cover for us. Vivian's been briefed about the beautiful wedding at dawn on Bailey's Beach, how she cried buckets of tears, how Tiny and Pepper and Little Viv were my bridesmaids and all kinds of rubbish, and nobody lies quite so convincingly as Aunt Vivian.

"How the hell do you know so much about Aunt Vivian?" I asked.

"As I said," he answered placidly, "we've been working on an extraction plan for some time, just in case."

All right to all that, but I still feel as if I'm missing something, and I tell myself that's the reason for the bad behavior of my nerves, which usually perform so well in moments of high excitement. The airplane comes to stop outside the terminal. I catch a glimpse of a pair of men in dark suits, watching the workers in their boiler suits wheel the stairs into place. The stewardess opens the door and a moment later, the two men duck through the hatch and scan the interior.

"Mr. and Mrs. Fox?" says the man on the right, who has light brown hair and a pointed face like a rabbit.

Fox lifts his arm. "Right here."

He holds my hand as we make our way up the aisle—we sat in the third row—and out the hatch into the hazy sunshine of early evening. The terminal building looks right out of America, all pale beige stone and clean, rounded art deco lines. At the bottom of the stairs, the men in boiler suits have already taken our luggage from the hold. They carry the suitcases to a large, clumpy black car that sits near the door to the terminal, engine running. Fox keeps a snug hold of my damp hand. My shoes click on the asphalt. I'm wearing a dress, which is not my usual costume, and I can't get used to the way the skirt swishes around my legs as I walk.

We reach the car. One of the men opens the back door. Fox puts his hand to the small of my back and ushers me inside, then swings around to the other side and slides in beside me.

◆　◆　◆

AS WE HURTLE INTO Moscow, I can't tear my eyes from the scenes around me—the road signs with their strange letters—the building, building everywhere—gray, featureless blocks that seem to merge into each other, so you can't tell one from another. I remember reading the desperate newspaper dispatches from the Battle of Moscow, ten years earlier—how the brutal cold and the brutal fighting nearly broke both armies, Soviet and German, and yet you wouldn't ever imagine all this annihilation to see it now. Life goes on—the country rebuilds in ambitious, gigantic projects that rise from the ancient earth.

We don't say much, just hold hands and look out the windows. I glimpse people in flashes—walking down sidewalks, queuing up outside shops, sitting on benches to scatter crumbs for pigeons. When the car turns a corner and scoots to a stop outside the façade of an enormous fin de siècle building, I have to shake myself free of a trance.

To stand before the National Hotel in Moscow, you would never imagine you had traveled deep inside the beating heart of world communism. You would think yourself transported to maybe Paris before the calamity of war, everything that was decadent and cosmopolitan, chock-full of the aristocratic and the celebrated and the just plain rich—just picture the shining Packard limousines and the furs, the glimpses of ankles in white stockings, the black silk top hats and the swirling capes, all thronging in and out of these revolving doors, staring between the curtains of these pedimented windows. Inside the lobby, a man's waiting for us. Like the men at the airport, he wears a dark suit. He seems about forty years old, starting to bald, medium height and stocky. His wide, Slavic face stretches to an expression of welcome.

"Mr. and Mrs. Fox!" he exclaims, in supple English. He steps forward and holds out his hand. We perform the rituals. "My name is Yvgeny Kedrov, of Soviet Foreign Office. On behalf of Soviet people, I welcome you to Moscow."

I mumble some thanks and noises of gratitude, although I'm frankly distracted by the gigantic classical statue next to me, one of four holding up the walls. I don't object on principle to the mere strips of marble fabric protecting the modesty of these figures—on the contrary, I am all in favor of the human form—but the fellow's scarcely swathed stone privates hover just above my head.

I realize Mr. Kedrov is attempting to address me.

"Your journey, was it comfortable?" he inquires.

"Charming."

"Yes, thank you," Fox says. "But I'm afraid my wife is exhausted. I don't suppose we could rest for an hour or two before we start all our engagements?"

"Yes, of course. Your room is prepared. We have taken liberty of providing some refreshment for you. Won't you follow me, please?"

It seems odd to head straight up to a hotel room without checking in, but Fox falls right in step behind Mr. Kedrov and pulls me with him. Behind us, the men carry our suitcases discreetly to the service elevator, where—Fox has already warned me—they'll be carefully searched and repacked before being brought to our room. I hope they hurry. My dress is damp with sweat, and I can't wait to change clothes.

NOW, I HAVEN'T ASKED who's paying for our accommodation—the Soviet taxpayer, the US taxpayer, or we Foxes ourselves—but the bill will surely be monstrous. Kedrov leads us into a suite of parlor and bedroom and opulent bath. The balcony offers a view right over the red turrets of the Kremlin itself, by which I presume they mean to remind us to behave ourselves. I allow Fox to take the full force of Kedrov's observations and instructions while I wander through the rooms, test the wide, voluptuous bed, examine the wardrobes. I return to Fox and loop my arm through his. I tell him this place reminds me of Paris. (Paris happens to be our code for *I need to speak to you alone*.)

Instantly Fox's face takes on an expression of deep concern. "Darling, you look awfully tired. Do you need to lie down?"

I nod, the way I imagine a sweet, exhausted wife would nod, and Kedrov takes the hint and bustles away, but not before bringing the tea service to our attention. He waves his arm to the table before the sofa, where an enamel tray offers teapot and curving, elegant cups and plates stacked with pastry. After he leaves, Fox extracts his arm from mine, motions to his ear then to the four corners of the room, and says, "How are you feeling, darling?"

"Like I could use a nice bath and a rest."

"Some tea?"

"That would be lovely. I'll pour so you can have a look around. Where *are* those bellboys with our luggage?"

"Elevator must be slow," says Fox. He starts to move around the room, examining walls and objects and windows. I sit on the sofa but I don't pour any tea. I stare at the pot and the cups and the creamer. Instead of the delicate pale roses and leaves of an English tea service, they're painted in vivid lapis with gold rims.

I wonder what kind of tea service Iris has. I wonder what she looks like now. I wonder what she'll say to me, whether she still hates me, whether she wrote that letter in ink or bile. For the first time, I consider why Iris would reach out to *me*, of all people, when she needed help. What on earth made her think I would answer the summons? Yet I did.

Fox arrives back into the room.

"Something the matter?" he says softly.

I shake my head. He approaches me, anyway, and sits on the sofa by my side. The springs gasp and settle. He takes one of my hands and folds it between his own, and he speaks in a low, husky lover's whisper, so the microphones won't pick up his words.

"Don't be afraid. I won't fail you, Ruth."

I swallow back a laugh. Sumner Fox, *fail* me? That thought hasn't crossed my mind in days. The man can speak a dozen languages, for God's sake. He survived a Japanese prison camp.

But I nod anyway. It's easier than telling him what I'm really afraid of.

He says, a little louder, "Let me pour you some tea, sweetheart."

WE HAVE DINNER DOWNSTAIRS with a couple of undersecretaries from the American embassy whose unenviable job it was to smooth out the diplomatic details of our visit. I can't be certain whether they're in the know—*initiated*, to use the jargon—although I suspect not, because they talk without irony about facilitating understanding between the two countries at this sensitive time and so on. Lay it on thick. Even assuming the KGB is listening in, they seem awfully earnest. Everyone except Fox drinks too much. We part in the lobby at one in the morning. When they disappear into the revolving door, Fox leads me by the hand to the elevator, as if he isn't sure I can find it on my own.

Once in our suite, I drop the hand and hurry to the dressing room. The chambermaid has unpacked our suitcases and laid out our toiletries in the bathroom. I brought a silk negligee of the kind a bride would wear, and I shimmy it on now and brush my teeth and slather on the cold cream. When I'm finished, I step into the living room and tell Fox the coast is clear.

By arrangement, I'm to sleep on the giant bed in the bedroom, and Fox on the sofa nearby, covered by a blanket. For the record, I *did* protest. I said that as Fox was twice my weight, he should have the bed—my God, think of the embarrassed explanation should the delicate sofa come to grief in the night. But Fox only regarded me gravely and said that he wouldn't sleep a wink in that case.

So I climb alone onto the giant bed—some kind of elaborate relic of the Russian Empire, or else a convincing reproduction. The chambermaid has already turned back the heavy brocade bedspread, and a piece of chocolate lies on the pillow. I eat the chocolate even though I've already brushed my teeth. I hear faint noises from the bathroom, rushing water and so on, and a moment later Fox appears in a pair of silk pajamas that hang strangely on him.

I point to the walls. "Hello, handsome."

"Hello, yourself."

I pat the mattress next to me. He walks across the gilded room and lowers himself on the bed. He doesn't exactly move with the fluid grace you might expect of an athlete, but then he never has. I haven't asked him about the prison camp. I've always thought there are things nobody wants to talk about, especially to a woman you hardly know. He has a slight limp to his walk, which you only notice if you pay close attention, and the motion of his left hip isn't quite what it should be—again, too subtle for the casual observer, but by now I'm no longer a casual observer. He lays his hands on his knees and looks sheepish.

"What an evening," I say. "I think I might have had a little too much wine. I'm just so nervous about seeing my sister. It's been years."

"Nervous? You?"

"Yes, nervous! You've never had a twin sister, or you'd understand."

"I wouldn't worry. She wouldn't have asked you to come if she didn't want to mend fences, would she?"

"Or unless she's that worried about the birth. Do you think she'll be all right?"

"I'm sure they have terrific doctors here. She'll be fine. And you'll be here to help her."

I lay my head on his shoulder and pat his thigh. "Darling, thank you again for coming with me. Putting your work on hold like this and everything. You're the best husband a girl could ask for."

"Well, what else was I supposed to do for my best girl? I couldn't let you travel halfway across the world without me, could I?"

At this point, I should reveal—if you haven't guessed already—that we're not exactly speaking off the cuff. During our many long hours of preparation, we sketched out conversations like this, for the edification of anyone listening—it might not *convince* them, Fox said, but it would give our story a little more credibility. We had to pull it off right, though. We had to make it sound natural. No scripts, no set speeches. Spontaneity, that was the ticket. Did I think I could manage that? I said I thought I could.

What I don't expect is how naturally Fox carries off the act.

"Mmm," I purr, as if snuggling into his chest. "You'll love Iris, darling, even though she's not a bit like me."

"No? But I love every bit of you!"

I giggle, which is no stretch, believe me, as drunk as I am. "She's sweet and quiet and never puts a foot wrong. Never has too much to drink!"

"Aw, I don't mind that. I like a girl who likes a good time."

"Oh, Sumner, stop! I'm so awfully tired."

"*How* tired?"

"Tired enough to go right to sleep. Do you mind?"

"I sure do. A husband has his needs, you know."

"So does a wife, but not after a day like today. Now be a good boy and kiss me good night like a gentleman."

"Good night, darling." He kisses me, a little noisily, so I almost laugh. I put my arms around his neck and pull him down with me, so the bedsprings squeak.

"Oh, don't be naughty! I really can't!" I cry.

His shoulders shake. He rolls me over.

"Darling, *please*. Rain check?"

"Oh, all right. As long as I can cash it in tomorrow, with interest." He makes a noise like a dog with a bone. When he looks up, he's smiling this grateful smile—relieved—a wonderful and unguarded expression that transforms his face, and I realize this is the one part of the operation he hasn't planned out, or even allowed himself to consider, and I've come up trumps, haven't I? I mean, you couldn't have finessed that scene any better if you tried.

"You're the most considerate husband in the world, and I'm so glad I married you."

Fox winks a pale eye. "Sleep well, buttercup."

He reaches out to flick off the lamp and rise from the bed. I feel him move about in those un-Foxlike maroon silk pajamas that make me smile, just thinking about them. He gathers a pillow and blanket. As soundless as a cat, he walks back across the rug to the chaise longue next to the wall, where he arranges himself without a single creak.

IRIS

Over drinks in the library of Honeysuckle Cottage, Iris worked up the nerve to ask Philip Beauchamp about his children.

"I have three. Two girls, Dorothy and Hannah. A boy, Philip. He's the youngest. A bit of a surprise. We hadn't been trying for another. They are magnificent, of course. Above average by every possible measure."

"Children always are. Do you see them often?"

"Not any longer, I'm afraid. My wife took them to Canada with her. They're supposed to spend summers with me, but I'm afraid it didn't work out this year."

"Why not?"

He swirled the sherry in his glass. "She had some excuse, I forget what. I don't mean to speak against her. It was a disappointment. I'm taking leave in September. Sail over and see if she'll let me—if I can visit with them for a bit."

"It's outrageous. The government should do something. To keep a father from his children, it's terrible!"

"The government takes the view that young children are almost always better off with the mother, which I imagine is quite true in most cases."

"But you're a *wonderful* father. I can just tell—the way you play with the boys and with Aunt Vivian's girls. I think it's *wonderful* the way you pay attention to them. God knows they—" Iris bit off the end of the sentence. From the kitchen came the faint, happy noise of the children helping Mrs. Betts with the dinner—certain kids more helpful than others. Aunt Vivian stretched out on the chaise longue, deep in conversation with a neighbor of Philip's, some army major who saw action in North Africa and the Italian campaign and loved to talk all about it with pretty women. Iris sat with Philip on the sofa next to the bookcases. They were filled with old, musty Victorian novels that Iris read after the children were in bed, and the house was quiet, and there was nothing to do but commiserate with Aunt Vivian and wait for the telephone to ring with some drunken, incoherent confession from Sasha, or else the policeman who'd found him on a London park bench at six in the morning.

"We do write frequently," said Philip. "She's been good about that."

"But naturally she reads your letters first, before handing them over."

"One must assume so."

Iris laid her hand on his knee. Philip turned his face away.

"If you'll excuse me a moment, I think I'll have a smoke outside before dinner."

A HALF HOUR LATER, Iris found him beyond the lawn and the shrubbery, all the way near the sea cliffs. He stood with his hands in his pockets and stared over the Channel waters, pink and purple with sunset.

"You almost had me for a moment," she said, "and then I remembered you don't smoke."

"Ah, foiled again."

"Dinner's ready, if you're ready to come in."

He held out his elbow. "Shall we?"

Iris took his elbow with her hand, but she didn't turn back to the house. "Philip, I'm so sorry. I wish I could help."

"Iris—"

"I hope—I've been worried—I hope it doesn't *hurt* you, seeing all of ours all running about—"

"No! God, no. The opposite. I can't tell you what it means to me. Your taking me in like this, like a stray uncle."

She couldn't help it. She lifted her hand and found his mauled ear, the scars on the side of his face. "Not like an uncle at all," she said.

The scars were softer than she expected—like touching a palm, lightly calloused. Philip didn't flinch, even when her finger traced the ridge of mangled cartilage that was once a perfect ear. He lifted his fingers and touched the back of her hand.

"Do you know something, you're the only woman who actually looks at me. Straight at me, I mean, not sideways."

"I *love* to look at you."

Where did those words come from? Some other Iris must have said them, some Iris she didn't even know. The real Iris adored her husband, in spite of all his flaws and his anguish; the real Iris never *dreamed* of looking at another man. The real Iris kept her husband's secrets. The real Iris was loyal only to Sasha, and the things that

Sasha was loyal to; she understood that he did what he did—drank what he drank—because he was torn apart.

But this Iris seemed equally real. *This* Iris felt as if some wound in her chest was knitting together right now, under the sweetness of sherry on Philip Beauchamp's breath—like the scent of home, the smell of something that's loyal to *you*.

She put her arm around Philip's neck and rose on her toes. She caught his stutter of hesitation on her lips and kissed it away. From the house and the driveway drifted the sound of voices, but she was too busy kissing Philip Beauchamp's suddenly fierce mouth to notice or care what the rest of the world was doing right now, the real world she still belonged to.

THEY RETURNED TO THE house in the near darkness. Iris was too confused to say anything, to think ahead to what this meant—that she just kissed Philip Beauchamp desperately on a sea cliff and might be in love with him. She was just plucking up the courage to ask him whether this meant anything, would they kiss each other again, when Philip stopped and dropped her hand.

"What is it?" she whispered.

He stared at the driveway, steaked with light from the windows, and the car parked in front of the door, and Iris's ears finally picked up the pandemonium taking place indoors.

"It looks as if your husband's come home."

AUNT VIVIAN HAD TAKEN charge. She greeted Iris with a perfectly natural "There you are! Did you find the wine you were looking for?"

To which Iris answered coolly, "I'm afraid we've already drunk the last bottle. Philip's going to run back to Highcliffe to get some more. Aren't you, Philip?" Then she turned to Sasha, who was wrestling Kip and Jack on the living room floor, while Aunt Vivian's army major lounged on the sofa and a bloated, dark-haired man poured himself a drink at her liquor cabinet. "What a lovely surprise," she said.

Sasha looked up between the thrashing limbs. "Hope you don't mind, darling! I've brought a friend down for the weekend. I see Davenport's made himself at home, in my absence."

"Charming family you've got," said Major Davenport.

"You remember Guy, don't you, Iris?"

"Mr. Burgess. How lovely to see you."

Guy Burgess turned to face Iris. (*Saturnine*, she thought.) He grinned and saluted her with his drink. "Sorry to turn up uninvited! I'm afraid your husband jolly well *insisted* I needed a spot of fresh air to clean me out."

"He's very wise that way. But I'm afraid we don't have any spare bedrooms, now that my aunt and cousins are here."

"Don't we? I must have miscounted," said Sasha. "Hope you don't mind the library sofa, Burgess."

"Oh, I can make myself comfortable anywhere, I assure you." He sniffed the air. "Is that dinner? I'm famished."

PHILIP BEAUCHAMP NEVER RETURNED to Honeysuckle Cottage that night with bottles of wine, but only Iris noticed. Everyone else was too busy laughing at Sasha and Guy, who took turns with the jokes and the anecdotes, the impressions of various stuffy politicians and uncouth Americans, until the conversation turned— this was Aunt Vivian's doing—to Whittaker Chambers.

Guy Burgess turned pale. "He's a bloody Judas."

"Don't you mean *liar*, Mr. Burgess?" Aunt Vivian said innocently. "I mean, surely it's not *true* about this Hiss fellow and all the others."

"I amend. *If* it's true, then he's a bloody Judas."

Sasha reached for the wine and refilled his glass. His face turned the familiar raspberry pink of his deepest rage. Iris looked back and forth between the two of them and thought, *Of course.* Fellow travelers. She tried to remember where Guy Burgess worked—was it the British Foreign Office?—my God.

"Hiss," said Aunt Vivian. "*What* a name. I mean, it's too perfect. Snakes, you know."

Iris looked at the clock and said, "Goodness, it's far past bedtime. Children, up you go and into your pajamas, chop chop. Brush your teeth. We'll bathe in the morning."

THEY GAVE UP AROUND midnight, Iris and Aunt Vivian, and went to bed while the men continued their drinking and carousing outdoors. Iris stared at the ceiling for an hour or two. Songs and dirty laughter. At last she rolled on her side and fell asleep, only to be woken by Sasha as he climbed clumsily into bed and scooped her into his arms.

"I'm a beast," he told her.

"I know."

"I *do* love you, you know. You and the boys. I'm crazy about you."

"Funny way of showing it."

He turned her on her back. He was stark naked, warm and damp-skinned and salty-fresh, like he'd gone swimming in the sea.

"I can't tell you unless I'm drunk. It doesn't work. I'm only happy when I'm drunk."

"Were you swimming?"

"Yes. Best way to sober up, a nice cold swim in the sea."

He kissed her. She stiffened her lips, but he persisted until she yielded. As they kissed, he reached down and pulled her nightdress up and up, until he had to break off the kiss to pass it over her head. Then he moved down to kiss her breasts, and she gave up—stopped fighting this thing, whatever it was, this chemistry still lingering between them, even when she was furious at him. Anyway, he didn't stink of cigarettes and sin—he was like a sea creature, all washed clean, and she hadn't slept with him in weeks, and she was hungry for something, for any man at all. His wet hair fell on her skin. They mated like animals, a wrestling match, tangling and rolling and biting. She made him *pay* for it, by God. In the end, they lay panting, Iris on her stomach and Sasha a dead weight atop her, all four hands gripping the headboard for dear life. Why did they do it like this? Why couldn't they have tender intercourse anymore, like two human beings who loved each other? He rolled away, and his long limbs caught the moonlight from the window. His nose made a sharp, elegant triangle against the dark wall. For the longest time, until she drifted to sleep, he was her beautiful Sasha again, the father of her children, her warrior, her paladin of peace.

IRIS WOKE AT DAWN to the shrill noise of all the world's birds outside the open window. Yesterday was hot; this morning, the sky was cloudy and restless. Sasha lay asleep on his stomach, one arm thrown across her ribs. She untangled herself and slipped out of bed. She ached all over; when she looked in the mirror, she saw red

smudges scattered across her breasts and stomach and thighs. She
put on some clothes. When she returned to bed to stare at Sasha,
she was pleased to see she'd marked him, too. His mouth hung
open a little. His hair splayed across his forehead. Iris wondered
how he looked after he went to bed with Nedda Fischer—whether
they made love like this, snarling and snapping—whether they discussed Marxist theory afterward, among the tangled sheets—the
dialectic and all that, the class struggle as the basis of all history—
the inevitable revolution—all the things Iris didn't care about.

She wondered if she should tell Philip Beauchamp what she
knew—whether that would be an act of patriotism or of vengeance.

DOWNSTAIRS, THE COTTAGE WAS still quiet. Not even Mrs. Betts
had risen to put order to all the chaos. Iris found Burgess sprawled
asleep on the library sofa, covered by a horse blanket; Major Davenport lay on the floor half ensnared by a raincoat. Neither was
wearing a shirt; God knew if they had anything on down below.
The room stank of male perspiration and of stale cigarettes. Iris
picked up the empty bottles of gin from the weary Oriental rug
and threw them in the trash. She put on her sturdy leather Oxford
shoes and slipped out the kitchen door.

The air was speckled with fragile golden light and the dew
coated the meadow. Iris inhaled the smell of wet hay, the new
clean green morning. She started on the lane, toward Highcliffe,
then veered down a path that angled to the sea. Like the birds, she
couldn't settle. She tried to tie together Sasha and Nedda Fischer
and Guy Burgess, but the threads kept dropping as she picked
them up, because Sasha was at the American embassy and Burgess
worked for the British Foreign Office and what about the Fischer

woman? The SIS? How did they all tie together, how did it work? Sasha said it was finished. Why? Because the war was over, fascism was vanquished? Why did they still see each other, then? Why did they get drunk and trade messages and rush off?

Iris stopped in the middle of the path and held her hand up against the sun, which had broken between a pair of clouds to illuminate the world. Through her fingers, she spied some tiny movement to her left and turned her head. Along the edge of the meadow, on the other side of the wooden fence, a gray horse galloped hard, urged on by a taut man in tweeds and tall shining boots and no hat. The sun flashed on his silver hair. Iris made herself small in the grass. She watched the horse pound toward the fence, which must have been four feet high at least, and soar over it in a neat, perfect arc. They galloped on toward the cliffs. A foreboding took hold of Iris—the sea—something terrible! She held her breath and marveled at the beauty of the animal, his giant stride, the expert stillness of the man riding him. Her lungs almost burst with fear—with awe—no, don't!—*turn*, for God's sake!—

The horse bent around the curve in the cliff path, the way you might swing your body around a pole. The pair of them—silver horse, silver man—tore away into the sunshine.

Iris wanted to call after him. She wanted to shout *My husband is a traitor, your trusted Fischer is a traitor, Burgess too, maybe Davenport, who knows.*

But she didn't. Her husband might betray secrets, but loyalty was the stuff of Iris's bones.

RUTH

When I open my eyes, the curtains stand open to a bright northern summer morning, and the chaise longue is so immaculate, you'd never guess a two-hundred-pound man slept upon its cushions. The other thing immaculate is Fox himself. He's bathed and shaved and stands now in his American sport coat and slacks as bright as a new damn penny. Even his breath is sweet, though his voice is a little too stiff, in my opinion.

"Rise and shine, sweetheart. Car arrives in half an hour."

"Go to hell," I mutter and spring out of bed.

Thirty-three minutes later, he ushers me into the back seat of the same car that drove us here from the airport the previous evening. I can't say I shine, as instructed, but at least the hurry and bother have distracted me from my anxiety. I cross one leg over the other and watch the hotel spurt away. Fox, ever thorough, riled up the sheets and punched the pillows before we left, to make it look like a newlywed couple had spent the night in them, but a knot tightens around my stomach anyway. I hate the idea of some chambermaid reporting back on our sheets and the cleanliness of the bathroom. I hate the way you can never be alone.

I hate that this reunion with my sister is as unnatural as my union with Fox, and it means about as much.

I'M SURPRISED WHEN THE car swerves out of traffic and pulls up at an apartment building across from a large park, because the building seems old and shabby, the kind of place that was once the kind of smart, elegant residence where smart, elegant people lived, but has now fallen into neglect. Shouldn't the Digbys be living in style, as heroes of a grateful Soviet republic?

Mr. Kedrov travels with us in the passenger seat, next to the driver. During the drive, he occasionally turned to us and reminded us of things we'd already been told, like—*Now, remember family name is Dubinin, to protect privacy!* And—*Car will be waiting for you outside at two o'clock!* He now springs out, while Fox opens my door with his usual dispatch. Once I'm free, he keeps his fingers wound with mine, as if he's worried I might bolt at the last minute. Or possibly just to keep up the act of a tender pair of newlyweds—who knows? We step inside the lobby. There's no doorman on duty, no porter. Mr. Kedrov proceeds to the elevators and presses a button. He rolls back and forth from his toes to his heels and chuckles at the closed metal doors of the elevator, which looks as if it was added years after the original construction. He mumbles something about the Dubinins having moved in a few months ago, when an apartment became available, because of the expected new arrival.

"Is that so? Where were they living before that?" Fox asks, in the manner of a man making conversation.

"When they first arrived, we found them beautiful housing in resort, not far from city. They learned Russian language and sent boys to Soviet school. Is quieter there," he adds, frowning, and jabs the elevator call button a few more times.

I think I see a sheen of sweat at Kedrov's temple. Maybe Fox notices it too. I dig my fingers into Fox's hand and absorb the whip tension of his body alongside mine.

At last the elevator doors open with a jerk and a clang. The morning sunshine happens to be pouring through the lobby windows and door, which makes the cab seem darker than it really is. Kedrov motions us both inside. Fox urges me first, a perfect pantomime of old-fashioned courtesy. But Kedrov doesn't join us in the elevator. He stands by the door and holds it open with his hand until we've both turned, then he reaches inside and presses one of the numbers on the panel. They're Cyrillic, of course, so I can't tell which one it is, although I know the Digbys—the Dubinins, I remind myself—live on the fourth floor. He says, "Apartment 412, they are expecting you!" before he releases the door.

We jolt upward. Fox takes my hand—I don't know if he's acting on habit by now, or whether he wants to comfort me. Either way, I *feel* comforted. How much harder it would be to face her alone! Especially with Digby by her side, and their children, and an additional child crammed inside her womb, about to enter the world at any moment. I wonder why Kedrov didn't come up with us, keep an ear on things, and I remember there's no need. The Digbys' apartment must contain more microphones than a Hollywood sound stage.

The elevator takes an eternity, not nearly long enough. The cab halts with a bang and a jerk. The doors open. Fox urges me out and holds my hand as we walk down the hallway. I wear a nifty navy blue jacket over a white silk shirt and a blue silk scarf patterned in gold horseshoes for luck; light tan slacks and comfortable Oxford shoes; my hair a little longer than I like it, brushed back from my face, waving softly beneath my small, plain hat. I consider myself smart and modern; Iris will think I look mannish and severe. I long for a cigarette and a double scotch. Instead I have Fox's hand wrapped around my gloved fingers. Ahead of us, a door opens and a tall, angular man steps out, thinning hair sleek and gold under the hallway light. He waves at us.

"Hullo there! Welcome!" says Sasha Digby.

I'M NOT PREPARED FOR the fury that whips through me at the sight of him. I've almost forgotten about Digby as an actual man, a breathing human being, because he's lived so long as a villain in my imagination. But you can't just *hate* a person in the flesh, at the moment he presents his frail humanity to you—the thinning hair, the skin that's taken on lines and texture, the anxious blue eyes that want so badly to please you—to be forgiven. So the hatred transforms in an instant to anger.

Still, I disguise it well. You never saw such an actress! I hurry forward to clasp both of Digby's hands and *mwa* the air next to each cheek. "Sasha! My God, twelve years! I never *dreamed* we'd meet again *here!*"

"Nor did I, nor did I!" He turns to Fox and holds out his hand. "Sumner *Fox*, by God. I thought Iris was kidding me. Sasha Dubinin."

"Dubinin. Pleasure." Fox shakes his hand, man to man.

"Come in, come in. *Iris!* They're here! I can't tell you how much I appreciate your coming out like this. I know it's hell, a trip like that, visas and diplomatic clearance and every pesky thing. I hope nobody made any trouble for you."

"Not a bit," Fox says. "Smooth as butter. I couldn't believe it myself. Once the wheels went in motion, why, there was no stopping them rolling forward."

For some reason, we still stand outside the apartment door. I suppose we're all a little nervous of going in to face what's inside. But a space falls after Fox's last words, in which there is nothing else to say, so we all turn to the apartment's interior and perform the exact same pantomime as downstairs at the elevator a moment ago—Digby waving us both in, Fox urging me a half step forward with a hand that just caresses the curve of my spine.

Then I'm inside the foyer, and a small, delicate woman appears— heavily pregnant, dark hair, anxious face—*Iris*.

"Ruth? Thank you *so* much for coming."

I don't know how it is. I don't know why I do it, what force urges me forward. Something primeval, I imagine. My feet move by themselves. I open my arms at the last instant and cradle her shoulders and head—my stomach rams the mountain of hers—her dark hair fills my mouth. I have to spit it out to speak.

"Of *course* I came, pumpkin."

I WOULD LIKE TO say that we then settle down on a sofa somewhere and trade tender reminiscences until the cows come home, but an instant later the children tumble down the hall and that's that. I mean, the noise *alone*. The kids fire questions at me, Iris asks if I want tea or coffee—vodka, I call out—Digby tells Fox what a fan he was, something about a game against Harvard—there's no time at all for awkwardness. We wind up on a sofa fully half an hour later. The children get bored and wander off to somebody's room to play a game.

"Not Monopoly, I presume?"

Digby laughs. "No."

Now, the first thing I notice about Digby, once we're all arranged in this shabby living room of theirs, is that he drinks coffee instead of vodka, and he smokes a pipe instead of a cigarette. The second thing I notice is that he actually looks remarkably well, for a traitor—older, like I said, but still pink and healthy, not even so much as a fatherly paunch. The room in which we sit is lined with books. Digby's talking with Fox about his work, how he's writing a comprehensive study of American foreign policy since the First World War, teaching a class or two at Moscow University—that kind of thing, he says.

That kind of thing. Doesn't *that kind of thing* include delivering lectures to intelligence officers at the KGB? The *nerve* of him! But of course he spoke—like we all do—to the microphones listening silently in their hidden corners. Back in Rome, Fox had assured me that Digby wanted out of the Soviet Union. But as I sit and listen to Sasha rattle on about his life in the Soviet Union, it seems to me he's awfully cool. He's as cool as ice. Probably you have to be, doing what he did. But the Digby of Rome—the ardent Bolshevist delivering secrets to the Soviet Union because he believed so passionately in world communism—wasn't cool at all. He was a drunk. He argued his politics out loud, where anyone could hear them. He spilled his secrets to women, just to get them into bed. He'd only gotten worse after the war, by all accounts.

This Digby seems . . . well, happy.

I turn back to Iris and ask how she's feeling. How much longer

until the baby flies the coop? She puts her hand on her belly, the
way expectant women do, and says any day now.

"You look well. You look exactly like one of those women who
gives birth in the hayfield and gets right back up again."

"Well, I'm not," she says, a little cold. "I'm not at all. God knows,
I wish I were."

I open my mouth to ask what seems to me a logical question—
namely, why she keeps having them, in that case. But Digby rises
from his chair and wanders over to put his hand on her shoulder,
and I suppose he knows what I'm thinking.

"The trouble is, she forgets. They get to be a couple of years old
and she wants another one, and I haven't got the heart to say no."

"I don't think it's your *heart* that can't say no," I tell him crisply,
and for an instant nobody says anything. Then Digby bursts out
laughing.

"They're a lot of trouble, all right, but they have a way of re-
minding you of the future, and what's important. And they're a hell
of a lot of fun, too. Why—"

As if on cue, the youngest—her name is Claire, I've been told—
toddles charmingly into the room in her yellow dress and makes
straight for her daddy's leg. He bends down so she can whisper in
his ear. The expression on his face is so earnest, so devoted to what
she's telling him, it stops my heart. Then he rises and takes her
hand. He says solemnly, "If you'll excuse me a moment. Claire and
I have something important to attend to."

Then he walks away, hand in hand with his adorable daughter,
and I think maybe *that* was it. Maybe that's what focuses his mind
and makes him so cool when an absolute ice calm is called for—he
has his daughter to think about, her safety and her future, and his

only true loyalty is to her and her brothers and the woman who's given them to him.

AFTER LUNCH WE TAKE the elevator downstairs and visit the park across the street. The day's turned so sunny and warm, a perfect summer afternoon. I ask Iris if she's up to walking so far, and she says of course she is. In fact, exercise is absolutely *vital* to a healthy pregnancy, and anyway a good long walk might bring on her labor.

"But don't you want to wait until the last possible minute? Since it's such a trial to you?"

"The opposite. I want it over with. I want to look the dragon in the face so I can stop dreading him."

She gives me a particular look when she says this, which no microphone could have picked up, and turns to help little Claire with her shoes.

"And no more after that, I hope?" I ask.

She's busy with shoelaces and doesn't answer. But when she climbs to her feet, wincing, she says quietly, "Honestly, I'd hand you the gun myself."

And I am left wondering on which Digby I'm supposed to fire it.

THE MEN TRAMP ON ahead with the boys, while Iris and I walk with Claire. To my surprise, the little tyke picks up my hand and swings along next to me. She calls me *Auntie Wuth* as if she's known me all her life.

"Well, of course she does," Iris says. "I talk about you all the time. The trouble we used to get into when we were little. You would always take the blame for me."

"That's because nobody would have believed you'd caused the trouble yourself. That innocent face of yours."

She cuts off a laugh. I look at her face and notice she's wincing, though she keeps on walking in that rolling waddle of pregnant women.

"Everything all right?" I ask.

"Just the usual. I don't think it will be long."

"Good, because I don't think I can hold out much longer." I cast a glance around us and see nobody near, except for a man in a dark suit who lingers on the path behind us, about thirty yards away. I speak in a soft voice. "I don't know how you could stand it, all these years. The listening ears."

She laughs gently. "I do appreciate your coming, Ruth. I mean that. After all these years, out of the blue. I don't know how we'd manage without you."

Without warning, Claire wheels in front of me and holds up her hands. I stare at her, perplexed. She gazes up soulfully with her mother's face, shaped like a heart, fringed with her mother's dark hair, and waggles her fingers.

"My God, she looks exactly like you," I tell my sister.

"That's a blessing, anyway. Are you going to pick her up, or not?"

"Pick me up!" Claire says, right on cue.

"Oh, *that's* what this means." I waggle my fingers back at her and bend down to hoist her on my hip. She's lighter than I thought, as if her bones are hollow, like a bird's. She snuggles her arms and legs around me and rests her warm head in the hollow of my shoulder. Her hair smells of honeysuckle and childhood.

"Tank you, Auntie Wuth," she says.

So distracted am I by the unfamiliar sweet warmth of Claire's body, I don't think to ask Iris what she meant. Why it should be a blessing that a child looks like her mother instead of her handsome father.

IN FACT, SOMETHING ELSE nags me, and I realize what it is just before the second intermission of *Boris Godunov* at the Bolshoi Theatre that evening, where Kedrov takes us as a cultural surprise. An extraordinary and moving performance, of course, in the most sublime surroundings. The bass in the title role is as big and fearsome as a Cossack. We sit in a gilded box with a couple of Politburo types and their wives, who don't speak English and whose names I don't remember. Kedrov sits on one side and Fox sits on the other, murmuring the occasional translation in my ear. My agitation increases by the moment. I sit there in an agony of impatience until the curtain drops, the lights illuminate. I snatch Fox's hand and attempt to sweep him off for a moment of private conversation, but Kedrov steps between us, smiling his emollient smile, and insists we accompany him for a tour of the costume archives.

By the time we return to the hotel, the hour is just past midnight. A trace of gardenia perfumes the air, and a tray of caviar and chilled vodka sits on the sofa table in our suite. How nice. I kick off my shoes—unzip my long evening gown and kick that off, too—drag Fox straight into the bedroom—tug off his bow tie—purr, *Let's do what we did in Paris.*

"What did we do in Paris?"

"Don't you remember *Paris*, darling? I'll *show* you."

He catches on quickly. When we're both in bed, covers over our heads, I whisper, "Something's fishy over there, and I think you know it."

"Your sister?"

"No. Him. He's *happy*. He's not going anywhere."

Fox catches his breath. Our tent grows stuffy. I throw back the covers, suck in some oxygen, and moan, "Oh! Oh! Yes, *oh God!*"

Under the blankets again, I roll him over and bite his neck, so he shouts out the name of his Savior. Then I whisper in his ear, "I'm right, aren't I? *She's* the one who wants out. Which raises the question."

"What question?" he gasps.

Stuffy again. I sit up and straddle him—tear the buttons off his crisp white formal shirt—*oh, yes I do*—because I want him off guard, you see—I want him to act and sound like a man making ferocious love to his wife—I want him to let slip something he'd never slip otherwise. His pale hair bristles against the white sheets. His hands find my hips. His eyes shut tight against the sight of Ruth Macallister wearing nothing but her creamy satin slip.

"God, yes, *yes! More!*" I howl. I roll him on top of me—not an easy feat, he weighs a ton—and draw the covers back up.

"What's in it for you?" I whisper. "Why all this trouble for a housewife and her kids?"

"Not now!" he hisses back.

"Yes, *now*! Or I'll—"

And I guess I'll never know whether he does what he does next for my sake, for himself, or for the United States of America. Does it matter? He starts with a kiss, a real one. I kiss him back—why not? Down below, he's just as formidable as you might expect, an advantage he wields so tenderly, so patiently, I fly a little out of my mind at one point and possibly confess a few things you shouldn't confess to any man, even in bed. Afterward, he carries the caviar into the bedroom and feeds it to me in tiny spoonfuls. Allows me a little vodka to wash it down. Before we sleep, we do it all over again, and I imagine we leave those invisible listeners in no doubt of one thing, anyway, the authenticity of our connection, which might perhaps save our lives—who knows?

AT FIVE IN THE morning, the telephone rings. Fox untangles himself and answers it grimly. He returns with the news that Iris went into labor in the middle of the night and was taken to the Botkin Hospital in central Moscow, where she's now calling for me.

IRIS

AUGUST 1948
Dorset, England

The men had concocted a plan to sail to the Isle of Wight and meet some friend of Burgess's who was throwing a sunset party right by the water. Aunt Vivian and Iris were invited; the children had to stay home with Mrs. Betts—it was *that* kind of party. What sailboat? Iris wanted to know. Not to worry, Burgess assured her, he'd already chartered one from a chap in Bournemouth who would sail it for them, too.

Iris hated sailing. She was not reassured.

Still, she and Aunt Vivian set about packing a robust and mostly alcoholic picnic for the journey. The restless sky had turned to drizzle, so the children stayed indoors, where Burgess drew them caricatures—he was really a clever artist—that left them in stitches of giggles. When the charm of that amusement faded, he and Sasha and Davenport gave them horsey rides all around the house, neighing and pawing and rearing and racing, culminating in the Honeysuckle Guineas around the drawing room, all furniture moved to the middle (Burgess won, piloted by a shrieking Little Viv).

Eventually someone looked at his watch and said *Good God, we're going to be late.* Pandemonium. Sasha and Davenport pushed all the furniture back in place, on Iris's orders. Aunt Vivian put on lipstick and changed her clothes. Iris scurried around the kitchen and the pantry chasing last-minute necessaries—napkins, champagne glasses, a knife for the cheese, a first aid kit because of knives and champagne—while Burgess did the necessary work of soothing Mrs. Betts's frayed nerves after all this commotion.

As a result, they were almost an hour late making their way down the cliff path to the rendezvous. The schooner captain was understandably cross. He asked them whether they understood about tides and wind and how they were subject to change according to the time of day, and that he couldn't possibly think of nipping up the Solent now—they'd have to tack around the entire damned island to reach Abingdon's place.

Burgess looked at his watch and shrugged. "What's another hour among men of honor?"

THE JOURNEY STARTED OFF well enough, after that dodgy beginning. Sasha and Davenport—both reasonably experienced sailors—helped the captain cast off, while Burgess opened a couple of champagne bottles. The rain lifted. Everybody came out from the shelter of the deckhouse and sprawled comfortably near the bow, drinking champagne and nibbling sandwiches. Iris lay on her stomach and stared at the gray-green water, rising and falling, until she realized she was getting seasick.

"Stare at a fixed point on the horizon," Sasha said helpfully, so Iris stared at the white chalk cliffs of the island ahead of them and took long, slow breaths of the salty air, until her insides righted themselves.

Behind her, Aunt Vivian talked to Burgess about silkworms. Davenport came to sit beside Iris and sympathize. "Rotten show, seasickness. My brother's a navy man, doesn't bother him a bit. Cigarette?"

"No, thank you."

He took one out and stuck it in his mouth. "Like Beauchamp, eh? Chap's so chilly, he's never required a smoke in his life." He cupped his hand around the end of the cigarette and lit it carefully in the draft. "Intelligence man, you know."

"Yes, I'd heard."

"Had you? Well, so much for official secrecy and that."

"*You* just told me, didn't you?"

"Yes, I suppose I did." He blew a long cloud of smoke into the draft and lowered his voice. "They say Beauchamp pulled off stunts you wouldn't credit. Dropped him into France, you know, to stir up trouble. I knew a chap who ran a few of them. Told me one story that made my hair stand on end."

"What happened?"

"Oh, some village in the occupied zone—not sure where, exactly. Beauchamp's radio operator happens to be some local girl. Possibly he's sleeping with her, c'est la guerre and all that, one doesn't ask awkward questions. Anyway, the girl's just been taken by the local Gestapo, put in some jail in the next village for questioning. I expect you know what that means."

"They torture her, don't they?"

"Yes, and if that doesn't work they'll drag in her parents, too, and torture them right in front of her, and by the end of it she's singing like a canary, as you Americans say, and when she can't sing any more they put her on the train for the prison camps."

Davenport paused to suck on his cigarette. Iris couldn't speak, couldn't even ask what happened next. The sun had begun to set behind them, and it turned Davenport's hair a fiery shade of red.

"Now, it so happens they've got a plane coming in two nights hence, a supply drop. They fly in on this ruddy old airplane called a Lysander, dark of the moon, collect the reports and drop off radios and money and cigarettes and that kind of thing. And sometimes personnel, too. Land some fresh agents and cart away the ones that have cracked up or had their covers blown. So Beauchamp's got a plan. He's going to rescue this girl from prison and take her to the rendezvous and put her on that plane for England."

The cigarette was finished. Davenport dropped it in the sea and lit another. "You understand it's his bloody *radio* operator, his ears and mouth, and who knows what she's told the Germans by now. Besides which, someone has to keep an eye out for the Lysander, you know, guide her in with the flashlights, make sure there's no ambush. So Beauchamp heads out to spring this girl out of Gestapo hands and tells his junior to stay. Junior does as he's told, heads out of that basement and finds a barn, moves somewhere else the next night, and on the third night he heads out to the landing site nice and early, makes his recon, no Germans. Settles back and waits. Finally he hears the plane. Big loud propeller noise, *rackety rackety rackety*. He takes out his flashlight, signals them in. Ship's coming to land. Gunfire."

"But you said there weren't any Germans!"

"Oh, I expect they dug in, too, biding their time. By now it's too late to signal the plane, so the chap takes out his gun and runs toward the commotion." Davenport paused and closed his eyes, while his thumb jiggled the cigarette up and down. "Long story short. Not only has Beauchamp sprung the girl out of prison, he's rounded up her parents, too, because the Nazis would've taken them next, shot them in the village square *pour encourager les autres*. Beauchamp takes down the four or five Gestapo waiting at the landing site, all by himself, while the junior hustles that girl and her parents onto the Lysander and waves them off to Blighty."

"My God," whispered Iris.

"Quite. Of course that means neither Beauchamp nor his junior can get on the plane themselves, there isn't room, and two hours later they run smack into a patrol, the same Gestapo patrol sent to find out why their men hadn't returned from the landing site, and the pair of them wake up on a train to Mauthausen."

"That's a prison, isn't it? A German prison."

"Austrian, technically. But the damned thing is, Beauchamp springs them out of the prison camp a few months later, along with a few other men, and tracks down some resistance escape line into Switzerland." Davenport patted his jacket pocket, as if he'd forgotten something. "Though I'm afraid I haven't heard the details about that one."

"How do you know all this?"

"Friend of mine, as I said. An old school chum. I say, I wouldn't mind a little more champagne, would you?"

Iris wouldn't have minded the entire bottle. She told herself it was the seasickness that made her legs wobble. She turned back to Aunt Vivian and Burgess, who had somehow moved from silkworms to the atom bomb. Burgess claimed to think it was immoral.

"You only think it's immoral because we've got it, and you don't like Americans," Aunt Vivian said.

"Not true. I don't dislike *all* Americans. I quite like *you*, Mrs. Schuyler, even though you entertain some bloody stupid ideas."

"Besides, you weren't a fighting man, were you? You spent the war sitting pretty at your nice safe Foreign Office desk. Ask Major Davenport here whether he'd like to be fighting hand to hand on some Japanese island right now."

"I jolly well wouldn't," said Davenport cheerfully.

"There you have it. War's an immoral business to begin with, Mr. Burgess, you can't get around that. It comes down to how many of yours do we kill so you don't kill ours."

"*But!*" Burgess waved his cigarette. "But the women and children, Mrs. Schuyler! The awful consequences of radiation! How could a civilized nation *do* such a thing?"

"What about Burma? What about the poor Chinese? I'd say *somebody* had to give Japan a little of their own medicine."

"Well, I can't bear it," Iris said. "I still can't think about it."

Aunt Vivian sent her a pitying look and poured more champagne. "Anyway, it's done, and at least the damned thing is safely in our hands, as a deterrent to future war."

Sasha smacked his fist into his palm. "But that's the trouble! No single country should have the means to destroy the world. Who can stand against us?"

"My God, would you rather see the Soviets with the bomb?"

"Well, why shouldn't they?" Sasha said recklessly, sloppily, red-faced, and Iris realized he was drunk.

"Sasha—" she started.

"The Soviets have only done what they've had to do. If you want to make an omelette—"

"Digby, you ass." Burgess, sharp voice. "Have another drink and be quiet."

Sasha's pink face turned pinker. He stared at Burgess for a moment or two—flung his half-finished cigarette over the edge of the schooner—staggered to the champagne and found an open bottle.

THE MOOD WAS RUINED. The sun set, the Isle of Wight passed laboriously to port. The captain kept swearing at the tides and wind—Iris didn't understand, she'd never liked sailing—and when Aunt Vivian offered advice, he swore at her, too. Sasha got drunker and drunker and brooded over the side of the boat. Iris tried to talk him out of it, but he snarled back and she retreated to Major Davenport.

Nine o'clock passed, then ten. The air grew chill and damp, and they hadn't brought any coats. Iris sat on a cushion and wrapped her arms around her chest until Davenport gallantly offered his jacket. Sasha wanted to know what the hell was going on, why hadn't they reached Abingdon's place by now. He turned to Burgess, who reclined on the neat teak boards of the deck, smoking endless cigarettes and eating all the potted shrimp.

"*You!*" Sasha said. "This was your goddamn idea."

"Seemed like a jolly sort of lark at the time. How was I to know about tides?"

"You pretend to know everything about everything else."

Burgess shrugged. "Can I help being such a bloody clever chap?"

"Clever, my ass."

The champagne was finished, all eight bottles. Burgess produced a bottle of gin. Aunt Vivian and Iris gave up on the weather and trooped into the tiny deckhouse, followed by Sasha, who slumped on a bench and closed his eyes.

"Iris, my dear," said Aunt Vivian, "I'm beginning to think your husband's some kind of Communist. You don't suppose he's an old friend of Mr. Chambers, do you?"

Iris glanced at Sasha. His eyes were still closed, his hands linked at the junction of his ribs. Her brain was too fogged by champagne and by the incessant cigarettes to think properly. "I doubt it," she said.

"You're sure about that?" Aunt Vivian looked at Sasha. "What do you think, cousin? Communist spies in the State Department?"

"Don't know what you're talking about."

"I'm talking about this Chambers fellow. Ever meet him?"

"Oh, stop. He's drunk, can't you see?"

"Frankly I think Mr. Chambers is a very brave man. I imagine the assassination orders are going down from Moscow Centre as we speak. I hope he's got a decent bodyguard."

"Fucking rat," muttered Sasha.

"I beg your pardon?"

"Sasha, don't—"

Sasha struggled upward. The boat made some lurch and sent him spilling onto the deck—he staggered forward and caught himself on the edge of the small table—his eyes blazed. "He's a snitch. Sell his soul for what? Approval from women like you—rich and idle—bigots—bluebloods—no idea what's going on among regular people—"

"I imagine I know a lot more about regular people than you do, Sasha Digby. I was a typist when I met Charlie, and your kind never forgave me for it."

"Not because you were a typist. Because you married him for his money."

"Stop it!" said Iris. "Both of you, just stop."

"And *your* mother married for money, Sasha, and her mother before her. Every woman does—she has to."

"Because the system's corrupt."

"No, because humans are corrupt. We are all of us selfish, ignorant beasts, loyal only to ourselves and our own kind, interested only in getting a leg up on others, whether it's money or status or moral virtue. That's why we've got religion, to discover our better angels, and in the absence of religion I guess you've turned to communism. All right. I mean, you've got to believe in something. Some people are just born zealots. But you're wrong, my dear. Argue all you want, but you're wrong, and what's worse is that you'll never admit it. Like that fellow who combs his last remaining hair over the top of his head and tells himself he's not bald."

Sasha turned and hurled the bottle of champagne through the deckhouse window.

THE CAPTAIN DUMPED THEM ashore at the nearest possible landing, about a mile from Abingdon's place by the water. They argued for nearly an hour about which direction to take, until Aunt Vivian settled matters by saying she would follow an army major over a diplomat any day, and anyway Davenport was the most sober.

Sasha was quiet. Iris would almost have said contrite, except her husband was never really *contrite*, was he? She walked alongside him to make sure he didn't say anything else, didn't expose himself any more than he already had. Burgess kept up a merry conversation with Aunt Vivian and Major Davenport as they picked their way along the shingled beach, carrying the picnic basket between them.

"Buck up!" he called back to Sasha and Iris. "Nearly there! Can't wait to see the look on old Abby's face when we turn up at last."

"Oh, he'll be delighted," said Aunt Vivian. "Everybody wants a gang of drunken louts to turn up at his home at two o'clock in the morning."

Sasha said to Iris in a low voice, "I want her out of the house as soon as we get back."

"Sasha, she's my aunt. And the girls!"

"She goes or I go."

"You're hardly ever there to begin with."

He reached into his jacket pocket and tore out a packet of cigarettes. He was down to the last two. He jiggled them a moment and took one out and lit it, and when he smoked it was as if he were sucking life into himself.

"She doesn't mean what she says, you know. She just likes to stir people up."

"She's exactly what I'm fighting against. Don't you see? That kind of ignorance and . . . and willful selfishness . . . that individualism that's got no regard for the common good—"

"Not now, Sasha. For God's sake."

"Chambers is a rat, a goddamn rat. He's going to get people killed. Innocent men killed, just for believing in something."

"Please, Sasha—"

Burgess cupped his hands around his mouth and shouted a halloo. "There we are! Thank God. Abby! Abby, old boy!"

"He can't hear you, you sod," said Davenport.

Iris squinted into the distance and didn't see much, just shadows next to the moon-speckled Solent. "I think everyone's gone to bed."

"Nonsense." Burgess jogged heavily ahead. Davenport shrugged and followed him, then Sasha chased them both down the narrow, rocky strip of shore.

Iris ranged up next to Aunt Vivian. "Can you see anything?"

"There's a house there, all right, but I don't see a single light. This should be good."

Iris squinted harder and discovered the outline of a large, rectangular, symmetrical building, maybe Palladian, right on the brink of the water. The moonlight glinted white on its edges and corners. There seemed to be a terrace of some kind. Already the men had reached it. Iris caught their movement up some steps—heard their drunken shouts for the owner.

"God help us," she said.

They'd left the picnic basket on the shingles near the terrace steps. Aunt Vivian perched on one side and Iris on the other. More shouting. A spotlight flashed on, illuminating the terrace. Someone cried out—stumbled—a couple of thumps—a howl of pain.

Iris leapt from the basket and ran to the steps. Guy Burgess staggered up, clutching his head. Blood streamed out between his fingers.

"My God, he's hurt!" she screamed. "Somebody get help! Aunt Vivian, the napkins!"

Aunt Vivian opened the picnic basket—rummaged around until she found the napkins—bounded triumphantly to Iris and Burgess, who lurched away.

"S'fine—s'fine—"

"You're not fine, you're bleeding to death—my God—hold still—"

Iris stuck a napkin to the side of his head. The blood soaked right through and she told him to sit down, for God's sake. He sat. Above her head, there was more shouting, a new voice. Abingdon, in his dressing gown, roaring like an elephant.

"What the devil's going on here? Burgess?"

"He's fallen off your step," said Davenport. "Haven't got a doctor about, have you?"

Abingdon swore. "Lay him out on the chaise—that's it—Christ, what the devil d'you think you're doing, turning up at this hour? Everyone's long gone, you bloody fools!"

Iris grabbed another napkin and Davenport supported Burgess to some kind of chaise, like a deck chair. Burgess shouted out obscenities.

"We've got to use your telephone," Sasha said to Abingdon.

"Who the devil are *you*?"

"Chap from the American embassy," said Davenport. "I say, that's an awful lot of blood."

Iris was starting to get woozy from the coppery smell of Burgess's blood. She handed the napkin to Aunt Vivian and stepped to the edge of the terrace, where she vomited onto the shingles. When she looked up, she saw another man bounding up the steps, followed by a man in a constable's uniform.

"What the devil's going on here?" said the constable.

"It's a private matter, damn it!" said Abingdon.

"Caught these drunkards coming up the beach! Trespassing on the terrace!" yelled the other man.

"For God's sake, Houlihan!" Abingdon shouted. "If I wanted you to call the constabulary, I'd have done it myself!"

"It's my duty to protect this property, sir, and by God—"

"Oh, shut up, you idiot!" Sasha yelled.

"Shut *up*? I'll not be told to *shut up* by some bloody *American*!"

Sasha lurched forward, grabbed the baton from the constable, and started to beat Houlihan about the shoulders.

Burgess shouted to Davenport, "For God's sake, take him down!"

Davenport made a lunge for Sasha and the baton, but Sasha had several inches on him, to say nothing of all that pent-up drunken fury. He roared in rage and turned on Davenport. They crashed to the stone terrace together in some kind of struggling, punching tangle—not unlike last night's lovemaking, Iris thought loopily—then she screamed and reached for Sasha's shoulder. He rolled away from her, right on top of Davenport.

A sickening crunch escaped one of them.

Davenport howled in agony and went limp.

ABINGDON LET IRIS USE the telephone, not because he was any less angry but because he wanted them gone. They carried Davenport into the nearest room and laid him out on a sofa, where Sasha sat beside him, apologizing and berating himself. She dialed the operator and asked for Highcliffe. The operator asked her name and she said simply, "Iris."

A moment later, Philip Beauchamp's voice came down the line. "Iris! What's the matter?"

"I can't even begin to tell you. I don't suppose you've got some kind of motorboat handy, have you?"

The thing about Philip, he didn't ask why, or how. He gathered the necessary details and told Iris he'd be there as quickly as he could. He showed only a single sign of humanity—or maybe this matter-of-factness was itself one giant example of humanity—

when Iris, by now on the brink of tears, thanked him for his kindness.

"All you ever have to do is ask me, my dear," he said.

IRIS, SASHA, AND AUNT Vivian returned to Honeysuckle Cottage just as the sun cracked pink above the eastern horizon. Aunt Vivian climbed the stairs without a word and found her bedroom. Sasha had already downed most of a bottle of gin from Abingdon's private stock, and Iris had to support him up each step—not an easy task.

For once, shame had silenced him. Davenport declined to press any charges. He was at the hospital now, having his leg set, while Burgess and Philip Beauchamp dealt with the telephone calls and paperwork, to ensure there was no international diplomatic incident. There was nothing left for Sasha to do but sleep off the champagne and the gin and the shame and then figure out how to salvage what was left of his career.

Iris guided him into the bathroom first and told him to use the toilet, to change his clothes. She left to fetch his pajamas from the dresser and handed them through the crack in the door. As she turned away, she heard him vomit.

Eventually he staggered to the bedroom. She rolled him into bed and threw the blankets over him. Though she was exhausted, she didn't climb in beside him. What was the point? The children would be up soon, and anyway he stank of vomit and piss and gin and shame. Instead she turned for the door. The sound of her name stopped her.

"What is it? Do you need something else?"

Sasha stared at her with bleary blue eyes. His cheeks were streaked with tears. "I need to tell you something."

"Tell me tomorrow."

Sasha shook his head painfully and beckoned her close. "Can't wait."

Iris trudged back to the bed. He crooked his finger and she leaned a little closer, though the stench of him turned her stomach.

"Well?"

"I slept with Ruth."

Iris's head jerked. She stepped back. "*What* did you say?"

"The night you were in the hospital, after the accident. The first night. And the one after that. Maybe another time? I can't remember, sort of blurs together now. Not sure why, it just happened."

For some reason, Iris didn't feel anything at all. The night had numbed her—so many shocks—this was just another one. *It just happened*, he'd said. Maybe it was a dream. She tilted her head and stared at him as if he were a foreign object in her bed, a bug or something.

"It was *you* I really wanted," he said. "If that makes any difference."

Iris lifted her hand and slapped him once on the cheek. His head snapped back and he smiled at her, pleased. She slapped him again and walked away—returned to the bathroom and cleaned up the mess—he'd aimed for the toilet, at least, and mostly succeeded—while she ran a hot bath.

AUNT VIVIAN SLEPT UNTIL eleven, and Sasha stayed in bed until nearly three in the afternoon. The weather had turned drizzly again, and Philip telephoned just after lunch to update Iris on Davenport's condition.

"He'll be all right," Philip reassured her. "Spiral fracture of the left tibia."

"Whatever that means."

"It means he'll be all right. Your husband can thank his stars he attacked a military man who knows his duty. He's not pressing charges, nor filing a report. I've received assurances from Abingdon and the local constabulary."

"You're an angel. I can't even begin to thank you."

"Believe me, I'm not doing it for Digby's sake."

Iris lowered her voice. "I don't deserve you, Philip."

"You've got me anyway. Let me know how you're getting on, all right?"

Iris hung up the phone and returned to the study, which had been put to rights without comment by Mrs. Betts. Jack asked whether Daddy was sick, and Kip said, "No, stupid. He's just drunk."

"*Kip!*" Iris exclaimed.

Tiny put a consoling arm around Kip. "My daddy gets drunk, too."

"Well, I'm never going to get drunk. I'm never going to touch a drop," Kip said.

Aunt Vivian snorted. "Funny, that's what they all say."

At last Iris heard her husband stirring. The water ran in the bathroom—footfalls and thumps and clatters—doors open and shut. She went up to check on his progress and found him standing in front of the dresser, concentrating on his necktie. He looked remarkably well for a man recovering from the bender to end all benders—skin pink, hair brushed back wet, trousers and shirt correctly buttoned.

"Was it true about Ruth?" she asked.

He gives the tie a last tug. "Yes. I'm sorry. I never meant to tell you."

"You're going up to London, aren't you?"

"Yes."

"Good. Say good-bye to the boys. They'll miss you."

Sasha turned from the dresser and looked down at her. He'd always looked down at her from that height, her spindly husband. He lifted his hand to touch her, but she slapped it away. He sighed and walked past her to pick up his briefcase and walk carefully down the stairs. She listened to his voice, talking to the boys, and stared out the window toward the sea.

AT LAST, THE HOUSE was still. The boys were in bed, and so were the girls. Mrs. Betts had retired to her room—God only knew what she thought of all this, because she didn't let on—and Aunt Vivian was reading a book in the library.

"I'm going for a walk," Iris said.

"Good for you. Take as long as you need. All night, if you want."

Iris studied her aunt's blue eyes, her blond hair pulled back from her elegant cheekbones, and she thought how much Ruth looked like Aunt Vivian, while Iris resembled their mother.

"Thank you," she said.

She walked out the kitchen door and into the cool, clear night that smelled of hay. The clouds had moved on, the stars sprang from the black sky. A slender moon lit the path before her. When she reached Highcliffe, she circled around back and rapped on the French door that led from the study, where Philip always sat at his desk in the evening. He looked startled to see her.

Then his face relaxed, as much as a face so ravaged could express tranquility.

RUTH

JULY 1952
Moscow

The hospital's like any American hospital, not that I have much experience of hospitals. Actually, it reminds me of the one in Rome, where Iris lay in that bed with her cast and bandages and her mournful expression. Bare white walls, doctors and nurses who don't speak your language, a sense of panic that nobody really knows what they're doing.

And lo! There's Sasha Digby in the waiting room, looking destroyed. He sits hunched on a chair, hands plunged into his hair. "How is she?" I ask him.

"It's my fault. I'm a beast, aren't I?"

"It takes two."

"She wanted another one so much. How could I—but I should have—"

"Don't beat yourself up. She'll be all right. She always pulls through."

Fox is all business again. He finds the nurse for us. Even though he has to pretend he doesn't know more than a few words of idiot tourist Russian, he's at least able to communicate who we are and why we're there, before Kedrov comes rushing down the hallway.

"Mrs. Fox! At last."

Funny, he seems genuinely concerned. I presume he's just worried about the blow to Soviet prestige should this American woman die in childbirth in a Communist hospital. I follow him down the white corridor to Iris's room at the end. Along the way, I catch glimpses of other patients, other rooms, all of them serene and private, and it's only later that I learn this is a special hospital for party officials and their families.

I've resolved to remain calm. After all, our plan depends on a difficult labor—the more difficult the labor, the more plausible our actions. During our days in Rome, Fox and I studied Iris's medical history, the likely complications, the points at which intervention might occur.

But nothing prepares you for the sight of your sister lying gray-faced and sweating on a hospital bed in the throes of a mighty contraction. Nothing prepares you for the *sound* she makes when the pressure reaches its zenith. I hurtle to the bed and snatch her hand. I demand to know why they haven't given her something to numb the pain. They don't understand me. Iris gasps, "I don't want it! I don't want to go to *sleep!*"

"I won't let them do it, pumpkin. Trust me."

The contraction eases. When Iris catches her breath, she looks wanly at me and says she's sorry.

"My God. Don't be *sorry* at me. What do you need?"

The nurse says something to me in Russian. I gather they don't want me here—a woman in labor isn't allowed to have guests who might, by their pity, soften her too much for the task at hand. I look the nurse square in the eye and tell her I'm not going anywhere. We glare at each other, mutually stuck by this inability to communicate in words.

I turn to Iris. "How much Russian do you speak?"

"Enough."

"Because I can get a translator."

"I don't need a translator. I need—" She bites herself off and digs her fingers into my hand.

An illogical idea takes hold of me as those fingernails cut tiny crescents on my skin—that whatever pain she inflicts on me somehow diminishes the share she endures. In my terror, I imagine this pain flowing like a current of electricity through her fingers into my palm, so that I can bear her agony and she can be free.

THE FIRST HOUR PASSES, inch by inch, and I don't see how either of us could endure another. But we do, hour after hour. At three o'clock in the afternoon, I leave to use the toilet and see how Digby's holding up. But he's not inside the waiting room; Fox sits by himself in a chair, nursing a cup of coffee. He shoots to his feet when he sees me.

"You look like hell."

"You should see the other guy. Where's Digby?"

"Went home to look after the kids. How is she?"

"She just keeps going, that's all." I lower my voice. "I'm not going to have to put on an act, you know that? I want her out of there. I want a doctor I can understand, a nurse with even a grain of sympathy—"

"What can I get you? Coffee? Glass of water?"

"Coffee. Please."

I don't know where he goes, some kind of cafeteria or canteen or something, but he brings back coffee that isn't half bad. I gulp it down black and hand back the cup. I've forgotten all about the night before. What we did to each other. What I felt and said. I've almost forgotten my own name.

BY SIX O'CLOCK IN the evening, the doctor's shaking his head and looking tragic, and a few more doctors gather to shake their heads and look gravely at one another. I can't exactly ask Iris to translate for me—she's too tired to speak, spends the minute or so between each contraction just lying there with her eyes closed—so I march over and ask if anyone can speak English.

One of them makes a shallow, affirmative inclination of his head. He's about sixty years old—tall and gaunt with wide cheekbones and cobweb hair. He looks at me as if he thinks I'm going to be trouble. I can't imagine why.

I speak as nicely as I can. "Can you tell me what's happening? Is my sister in danger?"

"We are talking possibility of operation," he says, in a heavy accent.

"You mean a cesarean section?"

"Yes." He makes a tiny circle with his hands. "Cervix growing too slow."

"But she doesn't want a cesarean!"

He gives me a withering look. "Then she dies."

"That's not true. She's had three babies before, all—you know—the ordinary way."

He shrugs. "Maybe this time different."

"Well, it seems to me that if the Italian doctors could do it, and the Turkish doctors, surely the Soviet doctors could figure out how to get this baby out of her without ripping her open."

Apparently, he's too old to care about this challenge to his national pride. He sets his jaw at me. "Is big baby."

"Well, I won't let you do it. I just won't." I march over to Iris. She looks up at me, glassy-eyed. "They want you to have a cesarean, but I swear to you, they'll do it over my dead—"

"Goddamn it, Ruth! Give me the goddamn cesarean!" she shouts.

THEY WHEEL HER INTO the operating theater and shut the doors in front of my face. I trudge back toward the waiting room, head inside the tiny, appalling restroom, and throw up yellow bile into the Soviet toilet. When I emerge, Fox is waiting for me with another cup of coffee.

"She'll be all right," he tells me.

"You keep saying that."

"Because she will."

I look down at the coffee. "I don't think I can drink this."

"You need something to eat."

"What if they need me?"

"They won't." He puts his hand on my shoulder. "It's safer this way, you know."

I lift my gaze to meet his. We haven't really looked at each other, not eye to eye like this, not since last night when he spooned caviar into my mouth, and I cradled his face in my hands and smoothed down the spikes of his eyebrows with my thumbs. For some reason I imagine I'll see his old eyes, pale and inscrutable, but I'm wrong. His face is compassionate and his eyes are soft. It's too much. I start to turn away, but he catches me. We stand there in the white, bright corridor for a minute or two, just resting against each other. His heart beats in sound, slow, mighty thuds against my ear.

"What are we going to do?" I whisper. "This wasn't the plan."

"It is now," he says.

TWO AND A HALF hours later, the nurse appears through the swinging white doors with the round portholes. I'm half asleep on a pair of chairs. My head rests on Fox's lap. I sit up as she marches toward us.

"Is boy. Four and half kilos."

"Holy moly," says Fox.

"What's a kilo?" I ask.

"Two point two pounds," Fox tells me. "He's a bruiser, all right."

"I want to see my sister. How's my sister?"

The nurse shrugs. She's memorized the English words for *boy* and *four and half*, and that's all. I look around helplessly. Where's Kedrov when we need him?

"Don't worry," says Fox. "If something had gone wrong, they'd have sent the doctor who speaks English." He stands up. "Wait here. I'll go telephone Digby and tell him the news."

The nurse has already turned to march back to the doors. I consider calling after her, but what's the point? Instead I slump back in the chair and stare at the clock. Somewhere in this building there's probably a window, where you can look out into the brilliant sunshine that is Moscow at nine o'clock on an evening in early July, and see all the people walking outside, all the lives going on and on—women who have given birth and recovered, baby boys who've grown up into old men.

Fox returns. "No answer. I'll try again in a few minutes. Congratulations on the nephew, by the way. I don't think I said that before. It's the best kind of news."

A nephew. What do I want another nephew for? I want my sister.

"Thank you."

He picks up my hand.

"Tell me about the war," I say.

"Why?"

"I want to hear how you survived."

There's a beat or two of silence. I sense him glancing around, assessing our surroundings. But Kedrov is gone. There are no watchers nearby, just four or five people scattered around the nearby chairs, wearing their pale, anxious hospital faces—the kind of expression you can't possibly fake. For the first time, nobody's listening.

"I was in the South Pacific," he says quietly. "Naval intelligence."

"I thought you were a pilot."

"No, that was the cover story. I was running some local agents out of Manila. Plane went down on our way to a drop, but I wasn't flying it. Floated on a rubber raft for a couple of weeks before a Japanese patrol boat picked us up. First they sent me to an interrogation camp."

"Is that where you got all those scars?"

"Some of them, I guess. But I was used to getting beat up in football. I didn't care much about getting hurt. The hunger was harder. Thirst. You would eat the bugs in your cell. You would lick the dew from the rocks. You had to work all day and eat maybe a bowl of rice."

"How could you stand it?"

"You just did. At first, I used to lie there at night and think about everything I would eat when I got back. I had it all planned out. I'd take my wife out to dinner at some hotel, seven or eight courses, soup to nuts, and when we were done eating . . ."

"Yes?"

"After a while, though, it got to hurting too much even to think about food, or anything else—any kind of pleasure. You woke up in the morning, if you slept at all, and you just made it through the day without thinking about anything. Until one day, the war ended and we were free."

"Just one day after another, right? That's how you did it."

"Yep. No past and no future."

"Then how did you find the will to live?"

"It's just there, Ruth. Life wants to live. Why does a rabbit run from a fox? Why does an amoeba—I don't know, whatever an amoeba does to live, as long as it can? Because the point of life is to live."

"Isn't that a circular argument?"

"Isn't everything circular? The earth spins on its axis, right? Revolves around the sun. Sun revolves around the Milky Way, that's what the astronomers say. Doesn't mean we're not getting somewhere, without even realizing. Then one day you wake up and realize everything's changed."

"What did you do after the war?"

"Well, first I came home and found my wife was about to have a baby with a friend of mine."

"Some friend."

"Then I went back to work."

"Why? After what you went through."

"A lot of reasons. First, because I was a bachelor again, nobody to depend on me. But mostly—I don't know, maybe it's me—the case takes hold of you, sometimes. It's all you can think about. You live and breathe and eat and drink it. You're in love with it. That's what gets you through the long hours, combing through transcripts and telegrams and passenger lists. You never know where you're going to find that missing piece of the puzzle."

"Or find yourself sitting in a Soviet hospital, waiting for a baby to be born."

He laughs and stretches. "I'll go try to telephone Digby again. Don't go anywhere, will you?"

I spread my hands. "Where would I go?"

IT'S FUNNY, THOUGH, HOW Kedrov disappeared. He was so attentive before. I stand and walk around the waiting room, just to stretch my legs, and look over the other people waiting. They glance back and avert their eyes. An elderly man, well dressed; a mother and child; a single, attractive woman, sort of sumptuous looking, whom I imagine to be somebody's mistress, because that's so much more interesting than the probable reality. Fox still hasn't returned. He must be talking to Digby. I glance at the clock—nearly half past nine—and return to my seat.

NEXT THING I KNOW, Fox nudges me awake. Somehow I've fallen asleep on his lap, all curled up, though I have no memory of his returning or my dropping off. I sit up too quickly and he catches me just in time. A nurse stands in front of us—a different one than before, younger and smaller, dark-haired, almond-eyed, so that I imagine some warlike Mongol ancestor pillaging his way across the steppes. She points to me, not unfriendly. "Come, please."

"Go ahead," says Fox. "I'm meeting someone for breakfast."

Breakfast. Christ, the dead drop. I've forgotten all about it. Some contact was supposed to make a document drop in some predetermined location—inside a hollow stump or a trash can, maybe, marked by chalk or other means, though Fox won't tell me exactly where—as soon as Iris went to the hospital. Of course, there's no way to abort this operation at short notice, and he can't just leave such an extraordinary package lying around for someone to discover.

But where the devil is he going to keep it? Not the hotel room, examined daily by chambermaids and who knows what else.

I shake my head to clear it. The nurse stares at me.

"What time is it?" I ask Fox.

"Just past six o'clock in the morning."

"Good Lord! Where's Digby?"

"That's an excellent question." Fox rises to his feet, pulls me up by the hand, and kisses me on the lips, because the nurse is watching us. "Give her my love, darling, will you?"

THEY TAKE ME TO see the baby first. He's lying in a bassinet in the nursery, and even I—with no experience of babies—can see he's a bruiser. The three infants nearby look so tiny and delicate, and here's this frowning, squash-faced, broad-shouldered behemoth, crowned by a tuft of pale hair. If I didn't know any better, I'd think Fox had sired him.

The nurse whips a swaddle around him, lifts him up, and dumps him in my arms before I can object. His eyes fly open, but he doesn't cry. He just stares up at me and works his mouth. I thought newborns' eyes are supposed to be blue, but his are no color at all, just opaque.

Already the nurse is motioning me to follow her out of the nursery. I trail along behind her. I'm afraid I'll drop the baby, so I hold on tight as we turn down a couple of corridors and somehow end up in Iris's old room, from which they wheeled her last night. She lies in her bed, wan and bloodless, but her eyes fly open when I walk in after the nurse.

"Brought you something," I tell her.

IRIS SAYS HIS NAME is Gregory, and who am I to object? That was our father's name. She looks at his shifting mouth and says he's hungry. She and the nurse exchange some words that turn terse. The nurse happens to be taking her blood pressure, and frankly I think it's unwise to provoke an argument at such a moment, but whatever the issue in dispute, Iris seems to prevail. The nurse flounces away with her collar and bulb, and Iris pulls aside the hospital gown and starts to feed the baby.

"They think it's barbaric to nurse your young. She wanted to get a nice bottle of scientific milk for me."

"I happen to agree with the nurse, but it's your baby."

Iris looks up and smiles. "Don't sass, or I'll name you godmother."

"Oh, that's rich. Put the child's spiritual welfare in *my* hands, why don't you."

"I just might, if only to keep you from bolting again."

"Me? You were the one who bolted."

I nod at Gregory, who seems hard at work. His tiny hands grip her breast and his mouth works frantically.

"Seems to be an expert," I observe. "His mother, too."

"Well, I should *hope* I know what I'm doing by now."

She's so weak. She hardly moves, except to keep the baby secure against her breast. I think of the freshly stitched wound beneath the hospital gown and the firm, fluent way she spoke to the nurse, not like the old Iris at all. She feels my stare and looks up.

"What's the matter?"

"Just thinking of something your husband said. How much you wanted another baby, all of a sudden."

"What, me? I'm just a housewife, remember?"

Something about her tone of voice sends my memory racing back to the night before last, and what I said to Fox—the question I asked—before he . . . *well*. Call a spade a spade. Before he distracted me.

"Just a housewife," I repeat.

"Speaking of which, what's happened to my husband? I would have thought he'd have arrived by now."

"There's been a delay, I think."

"Oh? What kind of delay?"

"Fox is on the case, don't worry. Probably the little nippers are misbehaving. I'll report back with all the news." I rise from my chair. "You just rest, do you hear? Let me do all the worrying, for once."

"Just like you used to," she says softly.

I lean down, smooth back her sticky hair, and kiss her forehead.

"Just like I used to."

I DON'T SPEAK A word of Russian, but I do have my sister's street address written down in both English and Cyrillic on a sheet of paper I keep in my pocketbook. I find my way outside—nobody stops me—and light a cigarette while I wait for a taxi. It takes some time, but one pulls up to discharge a passenger, and I hail it the same way I would hail a taxi in New York City. I give him the address and he doesn't ask any questions, just nods and takes off.

At this point, it doesn't require a seasoned intelligence agent to sense that something's off. I know it in my bones. It isn't just my nagging suspicions about Iris and Digby; it's Kedrov's disappearance—it's Digby's silence—it's the fact that nobody seems to be following this taxi as it speeds through the streets of Moscow to the Digbys' apartment building. Surely Fox and I weren't *that* convincing in bed the other night? What's happened to the fabled Soviet paranoia?

Or am I just too blind to see who's watching?

And maybe it isn't the wisest idea in the world to bolt across town in a Soviet taxi, either, but some peculiar inner urgency propels me to disregard such risks. I roll open the window and suck on my cigarette. The summer morning rushes past, the clear new sunshine speckled with pigeons. I wish to God I knew what I was doing.

I HAVE SOME RUBLES in my pocketbook, thanks to Fox's foresight. I pay the driver and walk into the lobby of the apartment building as if I own the place, which is the only way to walk when you're scared to death.

The elevator jolts and creaks and lumbers slowly upward, just as it did two days ago. When the doors clang open, I turn left and abandon all pretense of nonchalance. I find the right apartment—at least, I hope so—and knock hard. Wait, and knock again.

At last, I hear footsteps. Then silence, as the occupant stares through the peephole at me. The knob turns, the door opens, and there stands young Kip like the man of the house, unable to disguise his relief at the sight of me.

"Well, hello! I just wanted to stop by and bring the good news. Is your father here?"

"Y-yes. Come in, please."

I step through the door and look around the foyer. "Have you just woken up? Guess what happened in the middle of the night. Your mother gave you a new baby brother! His name is Gregory and he's absolutely enormous, and he can't wait to meet you."

I am babbling, which I sometimes do when my mind races around like this. I detect a sour smell in the air, and I almost don't want to hear what Kip might say to me.

"Dad's resting," he says.

"Oh? Would he mind if we woke him up?"

"Probably."

"Where are your brother and sister?"

"I . . . they're playing."

"Can I go inside and find them?"

I don't wait for Kip to give me permission. I proceed to the hallway and turn left into the living room, which is empty and disordered, sofa cushions piled on the floor, lamp turned over, large bottle of probably vodka lying empty on the scruffy rug.

I say something like *oh, dear* and duck back into the hallway. A giggle drifts past. I follow the noise and wrinkle my nose—the smell's getting stronger, also sharper—until I reach the source, behind a door.

I open it.

It's Digby's office, or so I assume—a tiny, reeking room that looks as if it's recently exploded. Books and papers everywhere, desk askew, chair upside down. On the floor lies Digby himself, facedown. I figure he isn't dead, because Claire's jumping up and down on a fallen cushion near his head—that's the giggling—and Jack rolls with suppressed laughter on the floor next to his feet, and neither of them seems upset in the least. I look at Digby and at Claire and at Jack and back to Digby. Claire jumps off her cushion and squeals with some unfathomable childish delight.

"Daddy's wet himself!"

MUCH AS I WANT to, I can't just leave my brother-in-law lying on the floor in a pool of his own urine. I manage to wake him with some gentle slaps and a bit of water. I run him a bath and shut the bathroom door to let Darwin have his way with the man.

I can't read the labels on the cleaning supplies. I fill a bowl with water and a bit of what seems to be soap powder and wash up the floor as best I can. Kip helps me. Of the three children, he's the only one who grasps the seriousness of the situation. I suppose that's as it should be. He's eleven and a half and his blond hair is darkening to a shade somewhere between those of his two parents. He has a sober, scholarly handsomeness to him. I make sure that Jack and Claire are playing quietly in the children's bedroom and bring Kip into the office with me.

"First of all, young man, I think you've done an excellent job looking after your brother and sister with your father unwell."

"He wasn't unwell. He was drunk."

"Well, yes."

"He used to get drunk all the time, back in England. Then he stopped when we came here."

"So what set him off, do you think?"

Kip looks at the floor.

"Is it a secret?"

"I don't know. Maybe."

"You know a lot about secrets, don't you?"

"Maybe."

"You don't have to tell me anything you don't want to. But I'm your mother's sister, all right? I'm here to do whatever she would do, if she were here. I'm a pretty good listener, if you don't mind my bragging, and I can keep a secret, too."

Kip looks up. "When Dad brought us home from school yesterday, someone had been inside the apartment."

"Like a burglar?"

"I guess. But he didn't steal anything. I couldn't tell, but Dad knew. Dad went into his office to make sure his things were all there. I thought he looked scared. And then he came out again and that's when he went down to the shops and came back with the vodka."

As I listen to this spare account, and stare into my nephew's serious dark blue eyes, I feel as if I'm looking at one of those trick drawings. You know the ones I mean. You think it's a profile of an old man, say, but then someone says, *Don't you see the beautiful young woman in the old-fashioned dress?* And the man's big nose becomes a bustle or something, and the curls of his beard become her tumbling hair, and even though the drawing hasn't changed—the strokes of pen remain exactly the same—you realize it's a different picture altogether than the one you saw first.

I fold my arms and look around me. I assumed the mess was the result of a drunken rage, Digby coming apart because of guilt while his wife struggled in the throes of labor. But now the scattered papers and open drawers suggest a different story. Digby's drunken binge speaks of another kind of despair.

Kip stands before me in the tiny room, wearing his drawn, pale face. He needs me to do something. He needs me to hold myself together. He needs me to take charge of this disaster.

"I'll tell you what. If you can do your best to tidy things up in the living room, I'll tidy things up in here. Then we'll put your father in bed for some rest and go visit your mother and your baby brother in the hospital, all right?"

For a second, I imagine he might hug me. Instead, he takes a deep breath, nods, and leaves the room. I light myself a cigarette and start to work. An hour later, I've put everything in order, more or less, but I haven't found anything you might call incriminating.

On the other hand, if the KGB's searched the place, they've probably already found it.

SOMEHOW DIGBY MANAGES TO wash himself up and stumble into the bedroom. I follow him inside. The scene reminds me of one of those photo spreads in *Life* magazine after a hurricane or a tornado or something. Clothes strewn everywhere. Lamps overturned. Pocketbooks emptied. The bed itself isn't fit for sleep—the blankets and sheets have been stripped, the mattress ripped open.

"What in the hell have you done?"

He doesn't answer, just wraps himself in a blanket on the floor and closes his eyes. I bend down next to him and shake his shoulder.

"For God's sake, you have a *son*! A new baby! What about *Iris*?"

"Go to hell," he mumbles.

I stand up again and give him a kick in the derrière—not hard, just enough to stub my toe. "Have it your way. I'm taking the kids to the hospital now. In the meantime, I suggest you act like a grown-up for once in your life and do the right thing."

"Go to hell," he says again, more clearly.

I DON'T HAVE ANY idea how I manage to pack three children into a taxi and return to the hospital. Thank God Kip speaks decent Russian. Every moment I look over my shoulder for a KGB tail, for some sign that we're being watched or followed, or about to be arrested. Then I close my eyes and pray they aren't onto Fox. That he knows his—what do they call it again?—his *tradecraft* well enough to find his way back to me.

We're blown, I keep thinking. *It's over.*

But if the KGB *has* already searched the Digbys' apartment—searched it yesterday—why haven't they arrested us yet?

We reach the hospital. I pay the taxi and herd the kids onto the sidewalk and through the doors, where Kedrov paces the entrance hall. For an instant, I think he might die of relief. Then his face turns stern.

"Where have you been, Mrs. Fox? We have been looking everywhere for you!"

"Me? I went to pick up my nephews and niece at their apartment so they could meet their new brother. What's wrong with that?"

"You should have stayed here. You are not familiar with Moscow and Russian language."

"But you'd disappeared! What else was I to do?"

"I was called away to attend to some small matter, for which I apologize." He seems to be struggling not to lose his temper. The agitation rolls off him in waves, and I wonder what he's afraid of. He looks back over the four of us and says sharply, "Where is Mr. Fox?"

I lie smoothly. "He's gone back to the hotel to rest. It was a long night, as you can imagine. Now, do you mind? The children haven't yet met their new brother, and I'm eager to see how my sister's doing after her ordeal. You know she had a terrible, *terrible* time, while you were off attending to your *little matter.*"

Kedrov flushes and stutters. Claire says, in a small voice, "Is Mama all right?"

"She's fine now, darling. It was just *very hard work.*" I look straight at Kedrov and say fiercely, "That's why they call it *labor,* you know."

Well, he's set back on his heels by *this* assertion of moral authority, which just goes to show that there's humanity in everybody. He leads us back to the reception area and speaks to the nurse at the desk and, a moment later, ushers us down the hall to Iris's room, led by the nurse. The nurse opens the door. Iris lies in her bed, propped up by pillows, looking remarkably more cheerful than I left her a few hours ago. She holds the baby in her arms. A man rises from the chair next to the bed.

And I'll be damned, but it's Sumner Fox.

LYUDMILA

Lyudmila's waiting for Vashnikov when he crashes into his office at a quarter past nine. He's so startled, he drops the cigarette he was lighting and leans down, swearing, to pick it up from the floor.

"What the hell do you think you're doing with my operation?" she demands.

He stands up again and looks innocent. "I don't know what you're talking about."

"You sent men to search Digby's apartment yesterday, while he was at the hospital attending his wife's labor."

Vashnikov walks to his desk, sets down his briefcase and cigarette, and hangs up his coat. "Where did you hear this?"

"It doesn't matter where I heard it. You wish to sabotage my operation, and for what? For what possible purpose would you let the man know he was under suspicion? Unless you *wanted* him to know it?"

Vashnikov sits back in his chair and smokes his cigarette, though she notices his hand trembles a little as he puts it to his mouth. "That's ridiculous. If I'd wanted to warn him, I would have done so in a more sensible manner."

"Then you *were* trying to find something. What did you find?"

He spreads his hands. "Nothing."

"So you admit you sent the men?"

"I admit nothing. But whether his apartment has been searched or not, I am absolutely certain that nothing exists to implicate Mr. Digby as this phantom mole of yours. Your entire operation is a farce, Ivanova."

"Oh? Kedrov tells me he was given orders to cease surveillance until further notice. Whose orders? And why?"

"Mine. I've encountered unanswerable evidence that Mr. and Mrs. Fox are, as they claim, an ordinary married couple of decidedly amorous inclination."

"What business do you have listening to surveillance recordings of my operation?"

"Why, I was called over by the specialists themselves to have a listen. You should endeavor to exert better control over your subordinates, Ivanova. This is basic KGB training."

Lyudmila stares at him a moment. He stares back with his dark, piggy eyes. But he's not unmoved. The tip of his nose turns an even brighter shade of red than usual, and his fingers flick the cigarette spasmodically above the brass ashtray on the corner of his desk. Lyudmila remembers—not altogether inconsequentially—what a terrible lover he was. Even in a convenient and merely physical transaction, the man should have some regard for his partner's pleasure, and he had none. After a couple of meetings, she rebuffed him. It simply wasn't worth the trouble of taking your clothes off, to sleep with a man like that.

"Tell me something, Comrade Vashnikov," she says, in a pleasant voice, "wasn't it *you* who put together that ring in Rome, during the thirties? You sent in ROSEBUD to recruit and handle agents."

For an instant, he looks stricken. "Yes. What of it?"

"*You* were the one who gave ROSEBUD permission to recruit HAMPTON. Now, ordinarily a handler is not supposed to sleep with her agent, but for some reason you allowed ROSEBUD and HAMPTON to develop a sexual relationship alongside the professional one."

Vashnikov shrugs. "It was a stroke of genius, actually. It was the perfect way to run HAMPTON. He was young and sexually inexperienced, he lacked confidence. She gave him what he needed, and in return, he gave her everything she asked for, and more. He was our most productive agent in Italy. He wanted to impress her, you see."

"But then he outgrew her. He met Mrs. Digby, married her, had children with her."

"ROSEBUD is a professional," Vashnikov says. "She made adjustments. She ran him effectively, even after his marriage."

"They resumed their sexual relationship in Zurich, however."

Vashnikov lights another cigarette from the stub of the first. "You are remarkably well informed, Ivanova. Have you been up late reading files again? I can think of far more interesting nocturnal pursuits."

"Don't be vulgar, Vashnikov. I ask this question because it seems to me that the relationship between ROSEBUD and HAMPTON went well beyond the objective, professional association we prefer to see between agent and handler, and perhaps that is the root of our present trouble."

"What does that mean? Are you saying I made a *mistake*, Ivanova?"

"I am simply saying that HAMPTON's loyalty is a matter of vital importance to your career, isn't it? You would hate for this protegé of yours to be proved a traitor. You would hate, for example, to realize that some vital piece of information you might have slipped in his ear—the identity, say, of some important American asset—is now in the hands of a spy. Is that the case, Vashnikov? Has HAMPTON laid his fingers on the most important name of all?"

"He *isn't* a traitor."

"Then we shall discover this fact in the course of my carefully planned operation. For your sake, Vashnikov, I hope he isn't. This escapade won't look good at the tribunal." She leans forward and puts her two hands on the desk. "Nor the fact that HAMPTON's change of loyalty seems to have occurred at the exact same time you arranged for his defection."

"This is pure fantasy. I'm surprised at you, Comrade."

She straightens and adjusts the arms of her gray jacket. "And Vashnikov? Any pair of professionals can engage in sexual intercourse together for the satisfaction of whoever may be listening. This is basic KGB training."

THE ORLOVSKY MATTER HAS taken longer than she expected. For one thing, SALT was not at his station—some operation he was involved in. Then the girl and her grandparents were away visiting a cousin or something. They only arrived back home late Sunday night. So it was not until Monday noon that SALT had the girl Donna Anna Orlovskaya in his custody, and—in the manner of Italians, Lyudmila supposed—she proved extremely difficult. She said they had no right to detain her—she would lodge a complaint with the United Nations. She wouldn't do as they asked. If they put her on the phone with Papa, she would pretend to be somebody else. They couldn't make her do anything! They couldn't make Papa do anything! Lyudmila telephoned SALT from a secure line—*She's been watching too many American movies. You have to show her that this is real life, not a movie.* Then she hung up the telephone and thought that this Donna Anna Orlovskaya sounded a lot like Marina.

But today—Wednesday—there's a fresh cable waiting for her in the stack on her desk, already decoded in the cipher room. It arrived at four o'clock in the morning from her operative in Rome.

ORLOVSKY CONFIRMS SUMNER FOX OPERATIVE AMERICAN
INTELLIGENCE IN MOSCOW TO EXECUTE PLANNED
EXTRACTION HAMPTON FAMILY FOLLOWING BIRTH
HAMPTON BABY STOP CLAIMS HE KNOWS NOTHING MORE
STOP AWAIT INSTRUCTIONS APPLY FURTHER MEASURES STOP

Lyudmila taps her pencil against her lip and smiles. Then she composes an answer.

APPLY FURTHER MEASURES STOP

IRIS

About an hour before dawn, Philip nudged her awake. He was a military man, so he always sensed the approach of sunrise, and Iris slept deeply because she trusted him to know exactly when to wake her.

By now, four weeks into the affair, they had established a comfortable habit. Philip would kiss her forehead and say something like *Rise and shine, my beauty*—to which Iris just snuggled a little deeper. So he'd tickle her and she'd laugh and roll on his chest and press some kisses on his face. The room would be dark still—his face just shadow. She would kiss them all, shadow eyes and shadow nose and shadow chin—precious shadow scars—kiss lower—he'd sigh and take hold of her hips—*well*. Afterward, they had time enough to lie for a few decadent minutes, skin against skin, stunned and panting, before Iris would crawl from his arms and out of the stately bed, across the worn rug to the bathroom—gather her clothes—steal downstairs hand in hand so Philip could walk her back to Honeysuckle Cottage while the first green streaks colored the eastern sky.

◆ ◆ ◆

SOMETIMES, AS THEY WALKED back to the cottage, Iris thought about the reverse—the night she had first walked to Highcliffe from Honeysuckle Cottage, the courage it had required of her. The strangeness of walking to a man's house with the fixed intention of committing adultery with him. In the end, it was easy. Philip had made it seem perfectly natural to climb the stairs to his grand-shabby bedroom, hand in hand—almost ordained. But there was more to their affair than bed. Philip came down to the cottage every day. He led the children to the stables where they took turns riding the three ponies. They had picnics and walks by the sea, sometimes swimming when the sun was warm enough. Just yesterday they'd all gone sailing in Philip's schooner—a glorious sun-filled afternoon—even Aunt Vivian laughed her head off. Philip had pointed out all the battleships and the French coast in the distance, had shown the children how to make proper knots, had caught a few fish that Mrs. Betts fried for dinner. When Iris had tucked the boys into bed, sunburned and exhausted, Jack looked at her earnestly and asked if Mr. Beauchamp could please stay with them in Honeysuckle Cottage instead of his big lonely house with all the empty rooms.

Iris had reported this to Philip last night, as their fingers tangled in the lazy aftermath of intercourse. Philip reflected for a moment or two and said that it was a logical question, and Jack was plainly a bright and sensible lad.

THEY DIDN'T SAY A word as they made their way down the lane toward Honeysuckle Cottage. They rarely did. Philip's hand was warm around hers. The nights were turning chillier now, and Iris could see her breath and Philip's merging in the air. By the time they reached the great elm and ducked behind the trunk to say good-bye, safe from curious childish eyes, the sky was streaked with pink and the sun was inevitable. Philip leaned back against the bark and drew her against him.

"Vivian's leaving tomorrow," she said. "I can't stay the night anymore."

"I know."

"I haven't decided about school yet. It will break their hearts to go back up to London, though, after all this."

"You know you can have the cottage as long as you want. The local grammar is excellent."

She kissed the tip of his nose. "We'll talk about it soon, all right? I have to speak to Sasha first. We can't just go on like this, nothing settled."

"Whatever you decide."

"You're so good," she whispered, "so good to me. I wish I could give you more."

"You've already given me more than I dared to imagine."

"This is so impossible, this sneaking around. We belong together, look at us."

"Shh. I'm a patient man. If it takes years, I'll wait."

She said impetuously, "I hope you've given me a baby. If we've made a baby together then everything will be simple."

"Not *quite* so simple—"

"Don't you remember what you said, our first night? You said you would give me whatever I wanted, whatever I wished for, and I told you I wanted another baby, a girl this time, and *you* said—"

"I said I couldn't promise a girl—"

"*—Nature being so fickle,* your exact words—"

"—but I would do my best for you."

"Which you certainly *have.*"

Philip grinned. On a face like his, the effect was wonderfully fiendish. Iris knew she should go into the house, but she couldn't bring herself to step away. This was not enough for either of them. There were not enough hours between nine in the evening and five in the morning to talk and laugh and read—drink champagne or brandy or cocoa and lie together in Philip's bed, fingertips waltzing with fingertips—not enough days in the week that Iris could steal over from Honeysuckle Cottage and steal back, a little more happy, a little more in love, a little more *herself.* Iris couldn't go back to the old way of doing things any more than she could reoccupy the body of the old Iris. Even now, just *thinking* about sleeping with Philip— *remembering* the night before—she turned her lips to his shirt and wriggled her tongue between a pair of buttons. Philip took her by the arms and pushed her sternly away.

"Enough of that. Sun's rising. Our time is up."

IRIS PRACTICALLY DANCED THROUGH the kitchen door, giddy as a new bride, just as the phone started to ring.

She made a dive and answered it on the second bell.

"Honeysuckle Cottage," she said.

An hour later, she was on the train to London.

IRIS WAS SHOCKED TO see the flat in Oakwood Court. When she'd left it nine weeks ago, every article was in place, every surface shone, the air smelled of lemons and wood. She'd closed the door with a sense of satisfaction and purpose and imagined—as the taxi sped to Victoria Station—some ritual return at the end of August, refreshed and suntanned and ready to tackle life's challenges.

Now she banged up the lift in rising panic. Guy Burgess had been so cryptic over the telephone, so smug and English, she couldn't tell if Sasha had committed some unspeakable criminal act or simply went a little too far at a friend's party, as he so often did. The door, when she rattled the knob, was unlocked. She pushed it open and stepped into the foyer, where she gasped in horror.

For an instant, she thought they'd been burgled—ransacked. The few framed pictures had fallen off the walls; the floor was strewn with broken glass. An empty bottle of gin rolled helplessly across the parquet. The air stank of vomit and decay.

Then she thought—*Sasha*!

Burgess had said he'd left him in the bedroom. Iris picked her way around the broken glass, the bottle, the shoes left in a tumble. She walked down the darkened hallway, past the kitchen and study and the boys' bedroom, the family bathroom—didn't look inside any of them. A stink of spoiled milk turned her stomach. The bedroom door hung wide open. Iris hesitated. She hadn't seen Sasha in a month, not since the catastrophic expedition to the Isle of Wight. She'd spoken to him on the telephone a few times—he'd called down to Honeysuckle Cottage to ask about the milkman and where do we keep the checkbook, she'd rung up the embassy so he could speak to his sons twice a week—but each conversation was veneered in politeness, an almost excruciating formality. Anyway, both times she'd tried to reach him last week, his secretary informed her that he was out.

Until now, she hadn't thought to worry. Not any more than usual, at least.

Iris gathered herself and stepped into the bedroom.

Sasha was not, as she expected, on the bed. He lay on the floor next to the bed, fully clothed, on his stomach. For a terrible instant she thought he was dead. She cried out and leapt toward him, and yes, for that single instant, everything was forgiven—she loved him—her Sasha! But when she touched his shoulder, he groaned. She noticed a foul, sharp odor. She turned him over and realized he was wet, he was actually lying in his own urine, soaked through the rug beneath him. His eyes fluttered open. He focused on her— smiled—closed his eyes again.

"I knew you'd come," he said.

"What's happened, Sasha? What have you done this time?"

"Can't remember."

She shook him by the shoulder. "Yes, you can! Burgess said you'd wrecked somebody's flat. Whose, for God's sake?"

He started to fall away again, so she gritted her teeth and hauled him upright, propped him against the bed. When she removed her hands, he remained sitting, so she rose and fetched a glass of water from the sink in the bathroom. She turned her face away from the unspeakable mess and set the water glass at his lips for him to sip. The stench made her gag, so she tried to breathe through her mouth. He sipped again.

"Whose flat, Sasha? You have to tell me. Was it hers?"

"Whose?"

"You know who. Miss Fischer."

He made a lopsided smile and shook his head. "No, no. Got it all wrong, darling. Always did."

"Yes, I realize that. Whose flat, then?"

"I don't know."

"You just—what? Some *stranger*, Sasha? I don't understand. Burgess said—I couldn't make him out—something about a smashed mirror—Sasha, *look* at me!"

Sasha, who'd been staring at the hollow of her neck for most of the conversation, now lifted his unsteady eyes to meet hers. "You look good, Iris. Really good. I guess that Beauchamp guy agrees with you."

"Stop it."

"No, I'm happy for you. 'Sgood. Take good care of you an' the boys."

"What are you talking about?"

"She's dead, my love."

"Who's dead?"

"Who d'you think? They got her, Iris." Sasha made a gun with his thumb and forefinger, squinted one eye, and fired it. "Nedda's dead."

THE TELEPHONE RANG JUST as Iris reached for the receiver. The sound shocked her, for some reason, and she couldn't decide whether to pick it up or wait for the caller to go away.

On the second ring, she lifted the receiver. "Digby."

"Iris? Are you all right?"

"Oh, God. Philip. I was just about to call you. The most terrible news."

"I know."

"I'm so sorry. I know you were friends."

"It's damned strange. Just shot on the street, point blank, nobody saw a thing. Scotland Yard's looking into it, of course. I assume that's what set him off?"

"Yes. He's still drunk. I can't make heads or tails of him."

"I can bring the boys up, if you want."

"No, no. I don't want them to see him like this. Have you learned anything on your end? About the flat, I mean, and what happened."

Philip sighed, and the noise amplified down the line, so it sounded like a gust of wind. "I'm afraid he's in a bit of trouble. They're trying to hush it up, but the girl won't cooperate, not that I blame her."

"Girl? What girl?"

"Just some young woman. From what I can gather, your husband and Burgess went to some kind of party at her flat—friend of a friend, she didn't know them—and became excessively drunk, started smashing the place up, police were called. Burgess is connected everywhere and somehow got them both off without charges, but that won't last, not if the girl keeps making a fuss."

"As she should," Iris said. "The stupid fools."

She didn't hear the footsteps coming up behind her, not until Sasha's hand reached out and took the receiver from her hand.

"Beauchamp? That you? Beauchamp, old boy! How are you? Yes, yes, it's me. Been having a nice time out there by the sea, fucking my wife? Goddamn good lay, isn't she—"

Iris lunged for the receiver, but he twisted away easily, used his height to his advantage.

"Stop! You drunken idiot! Sasha!"

"What's that? Pistols at dawn? God, no, old man. You can have her. I'm a goner, anyway, right? Big red bull's-eye, right smack—"

At last Iris snatched the receiver away. He stumbled and crashed to the floor.

"Philip? Philip? No, I'm all right, I'm fine, he won't hurt me. He's just drunk."

"Iris, I'm jumping in the car this instant, I'm driving up—"

"No, don't—"

"You're not staying with him. Iris, do you hear me? Iris?"

"I'm here. Look, I've got to take care of him, all right? I'll sober him up. He'll be fine, he'll be very sorry. We'll get him help. That's all he needs." She was crying, for some reason. "All he needs is some help. A hospital or something. Good-bye, Philip."

"Iris—"

She hung up the receiver and dropped on the floor. She lifted Sasha's sobbing chest and cradled him—smoothed his tarnished hair—they wept together.

"I'm so sorry, darling," she said. "I'm so sorry."

IRIS BATHED HER HUSBAND and settled him into bed in fresh pajamas. Maybe Burgess was smart, leaving him on the floor like that, so he wouldn't soil the bed. Although the sheets didn't seem to have been changed in ages, now that Iris examined them. Well, what more harm could it do?

When he was asleep, she cleaned up the mess. She started with all the empty bottles, then found the broom and swept up everything else on the floor. She threw out the spoiled milk, washed the dishes, wiped everything down with vinegar and hot water. Opened all the windows to let in the fresh September air. She put the soiled clothes to soak in the washing tub and sprinkled baking soda on the bedroom rug. Not spick-and-span, but it was a start.

Before she left, she checked on Sasha, who seemed to be sleeping peacefully. She put on her hat and gloves and took her pocketbook from the hall table. She made sure to lock the door when she left—she would remember that later. She took the stairs instead of the lift.

The lobby was cool and empty, except for the porter, who nodded at her with an expression she couldn't make out. When she stepped outside, she paused to adjust her gloves and hat, and as she did so, she looked carefully around—the other blocks, the sidewalk, the street, the garden in the center of the drive. The few people about were all in motion, hurrying in some direction, except for the man in the dark suit on the bench in the garden, reading a newspaper. He looked up just as she looked away. For an instant their eyes met, and Iris knew she'd seen him before.

If only she could remember where.

RUTH

The children shout and squeal with delight at the sight of their new brother. Gregory starts to bawl. Fox takes me gently by the arm and leads me to the small, dirty window overlooking the street below.

I speak softly, because I expect the room is probably bugged. "How was your walk?"

"Exactly what I needed."

I put my arms around his waist and lean against his shoulder, like a wife who's had a difficult day. I glance at the children, busy creating a convenient cacophony a couple of yards away, and turn my face to speak near his ear.

"Listen, I took a taxi to Digby's place."

"You did *what*?"

"I was worried. Something was off. Sure enough, when I got there, he was dead drunk in his own piss. Kip was taking care of everybody. Said there'd been a break-in."

"Anything taken?"

"Kip said no, but he was only talking about valuables. Digby wouldn't say. But he was a mess, Fox. An awful mess."

"But they didn't arrest him."

"No. They broke in while he was at the hospital and the kids were at school. Fox, I'm not taking them back there to that apartment. I wouldn't trust Digby with a dog right now, for one thing, and for another—what if the KGB comes back? I mean, God knows what they're capable of."

"No, you're right."

I wait for him to say something more, but he stares out the window and holds me gingerly in his arms, as if I'm a mannequin. He's warm and taut, and I haven't slept more than four hours in the past forty-eight, and for a moment there I nearly doze off, even though my brain hums like a live wire. I start to step back but he draws me close again.

"How soon can she be ready to go, do you think?"

"I don't know. She's just had surgery. Probably lost a lot of blood. I don't know if they gave her a transfusion or anything or how much pain she's in."

"Find out, all right? I have everything we need. Whenever you give the signal, we can start."

My heart thuds against my ribs—so hard, I imagine Fox feels it, too. He holds me snug, so our words stay within the glow of our mutual warmth. I turn my head a few inches, so I can see my sister and her children, who are still making a terrible ruckus, though she tries to shush them. But it's a merry ruckus. It's the family kind of ruckus that seems loud and contentious when you're in the middle of it, but when it's gone, you miss it like you miss the sun when it slips down the other side of the world.

✦ ✦ ✦

FOX SOMEHOW MANEUVERS JACK and Claire to the window to take in the glorious sights of Moscow through a dirt-streaked pane of glass. Iris gives the baby to Kip. I lean over her to adjust a blanket. "Fox wants to leave as soon as possible."

"Damn," she says.

I sit back down and look at her, and she looks at me, and it seems she understands exactly what's happened without my having to say a word. Like she's been expecting this—their cover blown. She nods at me, a soundless *Yes.*

"Are you sure?" I murmur.

"I don't think we have a choice."

I stand up. "All right. Act One, the bossy American woman."

POOR KEDROV. HE HAS the soul of a diplomat, not a KGB man. I lay into him with my best hue and cry.

"I want my sister out of this hospital *immediately*. It's *barbaric*. She needs a *natural setting*, where she can rest and recover in peace."

He answers me soothingly. "With respect, Mrs. Fox, best place for new mother is hospital."

"*Oh?* And by what authority do *you*—a *man*—presume to tell *me*—a *woman*—what's best for a new mother? Are you a *doctor*? Are you a *mother*?"

"Mrs. Fox, is impossible. She is too delicate to be moved."

"But not too delicate to give birth to a ten-pound baby, which is something I doubt *you* could have accomplished, Mr. Kedrov, let alone *survived*."

"Mrs. Fox, please—"

"Don't *Mrs. Fox please* me! I will *not* calm down and stay quiet.

I will *not* back down when it comes to the health and happiness of *my sister.* I will cause such a *stink* as you've never seen before in your life."

"Mrs. Fox, doctors agree that—"

"I don't give a *damn* what your doctors say! Do you know that nurse tried to tell my sister that some kind of *milk* mixed together in a *factory*—molecule by molecule—*God only knows* what's in it—is better for a *brand-new baby* than the milk from his mother's own *breasts?*"

The word *breasts* stings him.

"I-I—"

"Do you want my sister to have a nervous collapse? *Do you?*"

"Of course n—"

"I mean, I can just see the headlines now, can't you? 'Communist doctors kill American mother and her new baby—'"

"You're being unreasonable, Mrs. Fox—"

"*Unreasonable?* Oh, believe me, you haven't *seen* unreasonable, Kedrov."

All the while, Fox stands to the side, arms folded, the way you might watch a boxing match. I don't spare an instant to glance over and see his expression. I don't need to do that—I know what he must be thinking. Nobody likes a shrew, do they? A woman who insists on having her way. Oh, a *man* in my position would be hailed a great leader! Firm, decisive, independent, uncompromising. But a woman who stands up for herself and those she loves—well, that's plain mean and selfish, isn't it?

No doubt Fox watches my display of shrewishness with natural distaste. He understands I'm not just acting, after all. I *am* mad. I don't like being eavesdropped on, and followed, and told what I should do or say or think, or what's best for me. To wait my turn and obey, because it's all for the common good. To have my every infraction reported on—oh, the delicious thrill of reporting on someone!—like we're children in a kindergarten class, and the damned Politburo is the teacher. My God, it's *cathartic* to take it all out on poor Kedrov, who is—after all—merely the representative of that sprawling Soviet state.

And what does Kedrov do? He turns and calls in reinforcements—namely, the cobweb-haired doctor who speaks English. They hold a rapid, hush-voiced conference in Russian. Now I glance to Fox, who's trying to catch their words. We stand in an unoccupied room—this is not, remember, a maternity ward available to the general public—because my angry noise might disturb the peace, while the doctor and Kedrov stand in the hall-way, just outside the door. The walls are the same hopeless gray as elsewhere. The bed's been stripped, the window's streaked with metropolitan grime. The air smells faintly of antiseptic. I shrug my shoulders to Fox, as if to say *Well?*

He shrugs back.

The doctor turns to stare at me through the doorway. His fe-rocity barrels through the air to land in the middle of my forehead. His body follows in short, quick strides.

"There is excellent clinic near Riga, on Baltic Sea. You leave tomorrow by special train."

I shoot an astonished glance to Fox, who smiles back.

The doctor frowns down at me. From the look of him, I can't tell if he's onto us. Whether this is an act of subversion or plain coincidence. Does it matter? I throw my arms around his neck and kiss his bristly cheek.

"Thank you," I say in Russian.

And I pray to God to protect him when the truth comes out.

WE SPEND OUR LAST night in Moscow like the first, in a suite at the National Hotel. Dinner's brought up at eight o'clock by a waiter in a white uniform. Is it unspeakably bourgeois to tip? I'm not sure, but I feel certain I see something pass from Fox's hand into that of the waiter—a man about forty years old, wiry and stone-eyed— and he doesn't refuse it.

I'm too nervy to eat much, or even to speak. What's there to say? We can't discuss our plans. I try to make conversation about the baby, to muster the kind of relief and excitement I imagine I would feel about this upcoming stay in a clinic on the Baltic Sea, but every word seems so forced and unnatural that I give up.

"You must be exhausted," Fox says at last. "You should get some sleep."

"You, too."

"Going to be a big day tomorrow."

"Yes, it is."

We stare at each other helplessly.

"Some vodka, maybe?" Fox suggests.

"God, yes."

He finds the bottle and a pair of glasses and pours us each a shot. To my surprise, he swallows his drink as swiftly and expertly as I do, and I'm even more surprised when he refills us both and repeats the exercise. I slump back against the sofa cushion and so does he.

"Everything's going to be all right, isn't it?"

Fox touches my cheek with his thumb. "Yes, darling. Everything's going to be all right."

* * *

AT SOME POINT IN the night, I wake with a jerk. From the window comes the murky greenish charcoal of a midsummer's dusk in the far north—no such thing as true night—so it couldn't be later than three in the morning.

"Fox," I breathe, but he's already awake. His tension prickles me from the other side of the bed.

He knows, as I do, that someone else shares the room with us.

We stumbled to bed just before eleven. He wore his silk pajamas and I wore my silk negligee, but it wasn't the same as two nights ago, though I wanted him just as badly. For one thing, we were too sober—literally sober, despite two shots each of excellent Russian vodka, but also in spirit—and for another, our journey together had just rounded its final turn. We could not risk further attachment. We could not allow our magnetic poles to lock together, no matter how great the pull of attraction.

Still, it wasn't the same as our first night in Moscow, either. I wanted him near, even if I couldn't touch him, and I felt he wanted the same from me. He lifted the covers for me. I scooted over to give him room. He leaned in to kiss me and said clearly *Good night, sweetheart,* and I like to think he said it to me, and not to the microphone tucked into the frame of the landscape that hung above the headboard.

I then slipped into a profound and dreamless sleep, so that my present jarred wakefulness makes me feel as if I've been propelled into a new universe. At first, I'm conscious only of the faint electricity of the intruder, the way you sense the presence of a living creature even if you can't see or hear or smell it. I called out to Fox out of instinct, just now, not because I remembered he was there.

I regret it instantly.

Now the spook knows we're awake.

A few feet away, Fox moves his arm, inch by inch. The mattress stirs delicately. I wonder what the hell he means to do. Launch himself into the dark? I can't see anything but shadows and the faint light of the streetlamps outside the window through the crack between the curtains.

The room is so quiet, I hear the sheets move as I breathe. Fox feels fluid next to me, sliding too smoothly for sound, muscles coiling, cat ready to pounce. *Don't do it,* I think. *He'll go away in a while.*

Unless he won't.

The blood rushes in my ears. My eyes ache from not blinking. I'm afraid to blink—I'm afraid to move—to distract Fox—to attract attention—

A shadow streaks across the room. I shoot up in time to hear an *oomph*, a crash, a cry—the cry's mine—I jump out of bed and grab the lamp, yank it from the socket—a horrifying crunch of flesh and bone—*thump thump thump* as somebody bolts into the living room, *thump thump thump* as somebody chases him.

I run after them and scrabble along the wall for the switch. Find it, flip it on. Bright light fills the room, illuminating the dark-haired man who throws open the door and staggers out into the hallway. Fox dives after him. I dive after Fox.

"Don't! Stop!"

He whirls on me. His pale eyes blaze with something I can only call *bloodlust*—beyond fury or fight or hate—just the desire to destroy whatever it was that threatened us. I fall back a step and the flame dies in an instant. Blood trickles from a small cut on his cheekbone.

"What was *that?*" I gasp.

"Just a watcher, I think. Checking on us."

I open my mouth to tell him that wasn't what I meant, but he's already turned away to close and lock the door—as if that will make any difference—so I walk to the bathroom instead and run a washcloth under the faucet. When I return, Fox stands with his hands braced against the door and his eyes shut tight.

"Turn around," I say.

He turns. I wash the cut gently while he sets his hands on his hips and stares at the ceiling. "I'm sorry," he says.

"Sorry for what?"

"You shouldn't have come to Moscow. On our own like this."

"Of course I should. I'm not a child." I put down my hand with the washcloth and stare at his chin, which contains a tiny dimple, so small you almost don't see it unless you're up close. He looks down at me over the ridge of his cheekbones, wary, and comprehension comes upon me like the beam of a searchlight, smack between the eyes. "Christ Almighty," I whisper.

He shakes his head and lays his finger over my mouth. I pluck it off and wheel around. I'm too angry to look at him. My skin scintillates with fury.

"Ruth!" he calls softly after me.

"Go to hell!"

I stride back into the bedroom and slam the door behind me. Between the curtains, a smudge of dawn colors the air. I plug the lamp back into the wall and turn it on. No point in going back to sleep. I pull my suitcase from the top of the armoire and yank my dresses from their hangers.

The door opens.

"I wish I could explain," Fox says.

"Oh, I'm sure you've got all kinds of pretty explanations ready. What I want to know is how long were you going to keep all this from me? How long before you told me the whole story about yourself?"

"Ruth, for God's sake. Keep your voice down!"

"I don't care who's listening! Hello? Hello?" I cup my hands around my mouth and shout to the framed landscape above the bed. "We're having an argument, all right? Just like any married couple! Because you'll never guess! I married a dirty low-down lying bastard! He told me he had a job, a real job with a paycheck, and it turns out he quit! He's in business for himself!"

Fox takes me by the shoulders and turns me around—not rough, I'll give him that, but firm enough to hold me in place in front of him so he can say his piece, in a low, calm voice that only makes me madder. "Ruth, listen to me. I'll make it up to you. I've got—I've got money you don't know about. We'll be all right, okay? I've got things lined up, people lined up, as soon as we're out of Moscow."

I throw up my hands. "That's what they all say. *Oh, my luck's about to turn, I've got it all planned out, our ship will come in!* Well, I'll tell you what, buster. Until I see that sail coming into harbor, I'm not counting on a red cent from you. *Not a red cent.*"

"*Fine,* then!"

"Yes, *fine!*"

We stand there panting at each other. The cut on his cheekbone has begun to bleed again. I pick up the evening gown I wore to the Bolshoi and blot away the blood. The sunrise blossoms behind the window. I want to cry at the pinks and golds.

"I promise you, everything will work out," Fox says. "This outfit I'm working with, they know what they're doing."

"Oh, they do, do they?"

"Honest to God."

"Then I guess you'd better start praying right now, Mr. Fox, because if they don't? You and I are *splitsville*."

THE WORST THING IS, I can't even ask him the real story. Silently we pack our suitcases and wait for six o'clock, when we can call down and order coffee. I like to think they can't possibly doubt we're really married now, a fight like that.

The coffee arrives, hot and strong. I smoke cigarette after cigarette. Fox opens a window and I come to stand next to him, so our words float straight out into the cool summer morning.

"So how long has this been going on?"

"I don't know what you mean."

I prop myself on the windowsill and stick my head out. Fox joins me, a little awkwardly, because his shoulders are almost too wide to fit.

I speak softly. "This business of yours. When did you set it up?"

For some time he leans there silent next to me, heads stuck side by side into the open air. Kremlin across the street. Noise of traffic down below. Truth lies somewhere between us. Will he give it to me?

He turns his mouth to my ear and speaks in an intimate murmur, the way a lover would. "When I got out of the hospital, after the war. Hoover called me in. The Bureau was decrypting Russian diplomatic telegrams and he'd come to realize they had a high-level leak. Who or where, he couldn't tell. Needed someone to work on his own, outside the agency. Someone who'd spent the last few years in a prison camp on the other side of the world. Told me he wanted us to get an agent in Moscow, right in the heart, root out all the names. Gave me whatever resources I needed."

I absorb all this along with his warm breath on the side of my face, my neck. Turn my own mouth to his ear.

"Well? Did you find the leak?"

"A lot more than that. But not the man at the top. Not the last name we needed. And a little over a year ago, our Moscow agent dropped all communication. We were sick with worry. Then finally we got a signal. The extraction signal."

"And here we are. That's why we're here. To bring your agent home."

Fox lowers himself on his elbows and gazes down at the sleepy street below. The rising sun makes his hair sparkle. Bathes the red spires of the Kremlin across the street. I lower myself next to him so our forearms lie against each other. Right hand holds the cigarette, smoke drifting into the delicate light. Fox takes my left hand and squeezes it.

Trust me, he says.

IRIS

SEPTEMBER 1948

London

Iris took a taxi to the American embassy in Grosvenor Square and gave her name to the receptionist in the lobby. "Mrs. Digby to see Mr. West, please," she said, dignified yet friendly.

The receptionist's eyes went round. She lifted the receiver of her telephone. A hushed, hurried conversation took place, and when the receptionist looked up again, Iris could've sworn she was forcing back a smile.

"You may go straight up, Mrs. Digby. Fourth floor."

MR. WEST STOOD UP HASTILY when Iris entered his office. He brushed some crumbs from his tie and held out his hand. "Mrs. Digby. It's been some time. Welcome."

"Mr. West. Yes, I've been spending the summer in the countryside. Dorset."

"Do sit."

"Thank you. I expect you know why I've come to see you."

He sighed and took his seat. "Yes, this silly affair of Digby's. How is he?"

"Sleeping it off. As I'm sure you know, he's been under tremendous strain lately."

"Indeed he has. We're well aware of the *toll* the service takes, Mrs. Digby, particularly for a man as able and as hardworking as your husband. I confess, I am *very* fond of Mr. Digby. He's *just* the kind of man we need here at the embassy, and under ordinary circumstances, we *do* look the other way when—*incidents* of this nature occur. We give the man some leave, a rest cure in the mountains, perhaps." Mr. West glanced down at the papers before him. "And your husband's service has been *exceptional*. Honestly, I can't think why he wasn't given some sort of leave after his last assignment. His work during the war was extraordinary, *extraordinary*. A man wouldn't be *human* if he didn't crack up a bit, after a time like that. We *quite* understand, Mrs. Digby."

"But?"

Mr. West steepled his fingers over the papers. "But. The *girl's* the trouble, you see. She's making a real fuss. She's gone to the papers—we've had to pull every string. *Every string.* The kind of strings we like to keep in reserve, you might say, for incidents of a more diplomatic nature."

"I see. I don't suppose you could give me the name of this girl? Her address? I don't mean her any *harm*," Iris added quickly. "Not at all. I sympathize with her entirely. In fact, I thought perhaps a woman's touch might help, in this case. I can convey my deepest apology, maybe explain the situation, gain her sympathy for what Sasha's been through—"

He frowned. "This is really quite irregular. Under ordinary circumstances—"

"These are hardly ordinary circumstances, Mr. West." Iris

smiled and made her eyes grow. "I promise you, a woman's touch is *exactly* what's needed here. I can accomplish things in half an hour that all your diplomats couldn't manage in a *week*."

"I daresay." He sat back in his chair and appraised her. "You understand, officially speaking, my hands are tied."

"But *unofficially?*"

Mr. West reached for a pen, scribbled something on a piece of paper, and handed it to Iris.

"*Unofficially*—Godspeed, Mrs. Digby."

GUY BURGESS WAITED FOR her outside on a bench. He was eating something from a small tin, which he tossed in a trash bin when he saw her. Stood, wiped his hands on his trousers, made a courtly bow.

"I ought to slap you," she said, when she reached him.

"I protest. I've been your guardian angel. Sasha's, anyway. How is the old boy? Awake yet?"

"Was. I cleaned him up and put him back to bed in fresh pajamas. Just what the hell were you two doing last night?"

He made a motion with his hand. "Shall we?"

"Ten minutes, then I have to return home. I'm expecting a guest."

"Anyone I know?"

She hesitated, but there hardly seemed any point in holding back. "Philip Beauchamp. Not that it's any of your business."

"Ah. Won't Sasha be pleased."

"What have you got to say to me, Mr. Burgess? Some new escapade I haven't heard about?"

"No, I believe I've sworn off your husband, for the time being. He gets me into the most awful trouble."

"I'd say it's the other way around." Iris stopped to cross Oxford Street, taking care to look right instead of left. "It's about Nedda Fischer, isn't it? Somebody killed her."

"Nedda Fischer? Yes, terribly sad business. Awful show. On the streets of London, no less. One simply isn't safe."

"Oh, don't play games with me, Mr. Burgess. I don't have the time or the patience. I'm an American, remember? We like to play straight. Lay our cards on the table. I know what Sasha was up to, and I know what Nedda Fischer was to him, and I imagine you know, too."

"Haven't the foggiest idea what you're talking about."

"No, of course not. You know nothing about nothing. You just *happened* by Grosvenor Square at the *exact* moment I wandered out of the US embassy."

"Careful!" Burgess stuck out his hand just in time to prevent her stepping off the curb in front of a taxi. Iris took a deep breath while the taxi passed. They crossed the street and Burgess took her arm. "Let's step into Selfridges for a moment, shall we?"

"I said *ten minutes*—"

Already he was steering her through the revolving doors and into the department store, around the counters with their sparse selections of cosmetics and scarves and haberdashery—clothing still rationed—glancing every so often in a mirror. Iris protested at an escalator, but she couldn't make a fuss, could she? They swept off the top of the escalator and plunged into Gentlemen's Furnishings. Iris thought they could hardly have been more conspicuous.

"What I think," Burgess said softly, examining a silk necktie, "is that poor old Digby needs a little holiday, somewhere quiet. Somewhere he can't be found. Do you understand me?"

"I *understand* my husband's on the verge of a nervous break-down, if he's not there already. No thanks to you, I might add."

"Well, that's a matter of opinion, my dear. What do you think of this necktie?"

"Garish. Look, I really don't require your advice on the matter of my husband. I'm going to check him into a drying-out hospital of some kind, as soon as possible, and I'd very much appreciate *you* and your little *friends* staying as far away from him as possible. Good day, Mr. Burgess."

She started to turn away, but he snared her wrist under the edge of the counter. "And here I thought you were a nice little mouse," he said caressingly.

"Maybe your judgment isn't as sound as you think."

"Just remember to keep your mouth shut about all this, all right? You don't want your husband to end up like poor old Nedda. Do you understand me? That new lover of yours, especially. No pillow talk."

The funny thing about Burgess, he was really rather handsome beneath the bloat and the livery color. Iris imagined that when he was younger—at university, maybe—he was really attractive. Though the whites of his eyes had yellowed to ecru, they were alive with brains and charm—a man who might have *been* somebody.

"I understand perfectly," she replied.

"Excellent." He released her wrist and held up another necktie. "Too green?"

"Too shiny."

Iris turned and walked out of Gentlemen's Furnishings, down the escalator and out the revolving door to the busy street, where she hailed a taxi to take her home.

But when she climbed inside, the cab wasn't empty. A man in a dark suit and fedora sat on the other end of the seat, newspaper folded on his lap. He took off his hat and said, in a distinct courtly American accent, "Hello, Mrs. Digby. I don't know if you remember me, but I gave you my card at a party not long ago. Sumner Fox."

NATURALLY IRIS REACHED FOR the door handle, but it was locked. The taxi moved off down Oxford Street toward Marble Arch. Iris turned to Mr. Fox and said recklessly, "Would you mind telling me what the hell's going on? Are you trying to kidnap me?"

"Not at all. Just seeing you safely back to Oakwood Court. London seems to have become a little more dangerous over the past twenty-four hours."

"I don't know what you mean."

Fox looked at his watch and looked out the taxi window. He leaned forward and rapped on the glass separation; the driver opened the window and they exchanged a few words Iris couldn't hear. He sat back in his seat and said, in a kind voice, "Mrs. Digby, I work for a counterintelligence bureau of the US government. You know what that means?"

"Of course I do. You look for spies."

"In a nutshell. Now, I know you've been living overseas for some time, but I'm thinking you might perhaps have heard of what's going on in Washington right now? The hearings and whatnot?"

"I've heard something about it, yes."

"Earlier this summer, a woman named Elizabeth Bentley testified before the House Un-American Activities Committee.

Miss Bentley, if you haven't heard, used to run a network of intelligence agents on behalf of the Soviet Union."

"Yes, I know all that. I can't think why you've kidnapped a perfect stranger in a London taxi to bring her up to date on all the stateside news. Unless you think I'm connected to this woman in some way? A housewife who hasn't spent more than two months in America since the war started?"

Fox made a reflective noise. Iris thought this was the moment he'd take a pack of cigarettes from his jacket pocket and light one up, but he didn't. He fiddled with the hat on his knee and said, in his beautiful baritone drawl, "Miss Bentley first contacted authorities in November of 1945. Couple of months before that, a cipher clerk operating under illegal cover in the Soviet embassy in Ottowa put himself under the protection of Canadian officials and provided us with a great deal of additional information. As you know, agents are run under code names to protect their true identities. So it takes some legwork, you see, some investigation to follow all the clues and identify the possible suspects."

"Sounds absolutely fascinating."

"Oh, it's boring as can be, most of the time. Spending hours cross-checking lists of embassy employees and dates of arrival and departure, that kind of thing. But every so often, you experience what we call a breakthrough."

Iris curled her palms around the edge of the cloth seat to dry them. "Indeed."

"I won't bore you with the particulars, but a few months ago we were able to connect one of the code names provided by Miss Bentley with a fellow carrying out operations for us in Turkey at the end of 1944."

"Anyone I know?"

He smoothed the felt on his fedora. "Your husband, Cornelius Digby."

"That's impossible. My husband is a loyal American."

"And you're a loyal wife. I can respect that, Mrs. Digby, believe me. That's why there's a law that says spouses can refuse to say anything to incriminate each other. But I want to assure you that my intention is *not* to arrest your husband. For one thing—I'll lay my cards out—we don't have enough evidence, and what we've got we can't reveal in a court of law. For another thing, we've got reason to believe that the American intelligence service is honeycombed with men like your husband, *fellow travelers* as they call each other, who climbed on board the Soviet service in the 1930s when communism was all the rage. We also believe that one or two of those men sit at the very top, because every time we piece together a code name and connect that Soviet agent to an actual human being in our service, why—he slips the noose. Somebody tips him off. Or the other side of the coin—we send in an operative somewhere, maybe recruit a local agent—and within a month he disappears."

"So why are you here?"

"Mrs. Digby, you know what happened to Nedda Fischer. You know she was his handler. She ran him for years, until Bentley compromised the network and the Soviets dropped contact. That was in early 1946. Now the Soviets are cleaning house. Sometimes they just eliminate a cold agent, nice and clean, like they used to do before the war. But the more useful ones, the more important ones, they can arrange a defection."

"*Defection?* You mean to the Soviet Union? To live there?"

"That's what I mean. From what we understand, that's what

they offered to Miss Fischer. They approached her through Burgess, who's still connected to Moscow Centre, with some kind of plan to get her to Russia. But she said no. Seems she didn't like the idea of actually living under communism. She told them no, so they eliminated her, rather than take a chance she'd get picked up by our service, or the British, and reveal what she knew."

"Look, Mr. Fox, this is a very exciting story you're telling me. I think it would make a swell spy novel. But it's fiction, it's just not true. My husband—"

"Mrs. Digby, we're headed down Notting Hill Gate. We haven't got much time. The Soviets approached Miss Fischer, and it's dollars to doughnuts your husband is next, if they haven't already made the offer. He's got one chance to make this right, do you see? We need a man in Moscow. We need to find out the name of the fellow or fellows they've got on our inside. And we've got to do it outside the service itself, or the operation is compromised before it even begins."

"I don't have the least idea what you're talking about. If all this is true, why don't you speak to my husband?"

"Because he's a true believer, Mrs. Digby. He's a Communist through and through. He's not doing it for money, he's doing it to save the world, and I haven't got a chance of talking him to our side. You're the only one who can."

Iris knit her hands in her lap and stared out the window. The shops passed by—the dour side streets—the war-weary dome of the Coronet cinema on Notting Hill Gate. They started down the hill, poor bombed-out Holland House somewhere to the left, behind its brick walls and overgrown parkland. The air outside was dense and warm, like it wanted to rain but couldn't, and the atmosphere inside the cab was even more humid. The taxi slowed to turn left down Abbotsbury Road. The driver glanced in the rearview mirror, as if to ask Mr. Fox a question. Fox nodded his head, just barely. The taxi turned and trundled down the road.

"I realize you've got a lot to think over," said Fox. "I sympathize with your predicament, I really do. But it's a fix of his own making, you see? Digby did some extraordinary work for us during the war—saved a lot of men. His record in Switzerland is the stuff of legend. I mean that. But he's also carried our innermost secrets into the heart of the Soviet government, Stalin himself, and maybe the Soviets were our allies a couple of years ago, but you have to understand, *you have to realize* that what's shaping up now is the most fundamental clash of two different ways of life that we've seen since classical times."

"What do you know about classical times?" Iris said bitterly.

"If you *knew*, Mrs. Digby. If you knew what they're doing inside that country, it would turn your blood cold. If he doesn't defect, they'll kill your husband without a second thought. They will. And they'll kill you and your children, if they think it's necessary. And if he *does* defect as their man, why, you either stay behind in London and never see him again—your children never see their father again—or else you go with him and spend the rest of your life as a citizen of the Soviet Union. And I guarantee, you'll never set foot outside Russia again."

Oakwood Court loomed before them. The driver turned right and pulled around the drive to the entrance to number 10. The car stopped.

"You have my card, Mrs. Digby. We'll be keeping watch in the meantime. But I'd advise you not to wait too long. It's likely they've already made the offer, through Burgess."

For some reason, Iris felt reluctant to leave the taxi and the warm, confidential voice of Mr. Fox. There was something reassuring about him, thick and rawboned as he was.

She reached for the door handle. It opened without any difficulty.

"Thanks so much for your advice, Mr. Fox," she said, and climbed out of the taxi.

LATER, IRIS WOULD REALIZE that she first sensed something amiss in the lobby, because the porter wasn't there in his usual station. Maybe she thought he was helping another resident with a heavy package or something—maybe she didn't take conscious note of his absence. What happened next shocked her so deeply, she would only piece together the various memories—start to make sense of them—when the passing of time allowed her to examine them more objectively.

She would remember climbing the stairs instead of taking the lift—not because of some strategic decision but mere animal instinct. She would remember she was a little out of breath by the time she reached the fourth-floor landing, almost nauseated. She would remember the door was ajar, and feeling irritated at Sasha for undoing her careful work in locking it. She would remember realizing, in the next instant, that something wasn't right. The door wasn't unlocked, after all—the lock itself was broken—the fresh, splintered wood lay on the floor beneath it.

Still she pushed the door open, because she had to. She couldn't allow anyone else to discover what lay behind that door before she did. Where did she find this resolve? She would never understand. She heard a whimper just before she saw the bodies on the floor. It came from Sasha, sitting upright against the wall. He held a gun in his trembling hand.

Sprawled on the parquet floor were two men. The first one, in the foyer, she didn't recognize.

The second, in the hallway—facedown in a pool of blood—was Philip Beauchamp.

THREE

If I had the choice between betraying my country and betraying my friend, I hope I should have the courage to betray my country.

—*E. M. Forster*

LYUDMILA

Lyudmila always arrives early at Moscow Centre, just as soon as she's dropped off Marina at school. While the headquarters of the Soviet intelligence service is naturally busy at all hours, for some reason there's a lull between seven and nine in the morning, as the night shift transitions to the day shift, and Lyudmila can pass through the doors and up the stairs (she always takes the stairs) and down the corridors to her office without the friction of other human beings. She can make herself some tea and work quietly, quietly, at her small ugly metal desk in her small ugly room the color of peas, where she can hear herself think.

MARINA, OF COURSE, IS now old enough to make her own way to school. She can take the bus, or she can take the subway. She's always been one of those competent, independent children, probably because she has no father and no siblings, and also because that's just her nature—to think for herself. Lyudmila's grateful for this self-sufficiency, but it makes her uneasy. Sometimes it feels like a powerful bomb that might detonate at any minute, and then where would Lyudmila be?

So she and Marina make their way to school together. Lyudmila watches her daughter swing confidently—too confidently!—through the iron gates and then the doors themselves. Sometimes she hails a friend, which startles Lyudmila. These friends—who are they? How is it possible that Marina daily enters a world to which Lyudmila doesn't belong? Naturally she's seen all their parents' files. She knows their histories intimately. But it's not the same as friendship. How does Marina *trust* all these friends? How can she be so worldly and yet so innocent of human nature? It falls to Lyudmila to keep her safe. Lyudmila carries the burden of suspicion for both of them. Today Lyudmila stands a few extra seconds outside the school, even after Marina disappears inside. In a week, the term will end and Marina will go off to youth camp for the first time, and for some reason Lyudmila wants to hold on to this moment, to these last few days of Marina's last school year before the state starts to pull her away from Lyudmila and turn her into a good Soviet citizen.

Then she turns and makes her way to the familiar concrete block that houses Moscow Centre. Ordinarily she spends this time reviewing the day ahead, sinking her mind into the vast complex machinery of her job, but today—*today of all days!*—she can't seem to focus herself on the HAMPTON case, which has obsessed her so exclusively for the past month. Instead she thinks of the day she took Marina to nursery for the first time—the chasm that opened up in her chest at the sight of those round blue uncomprehending eyes watching her go. She remembers how she arrived at her desk that morning to discover the news, delivered in a few spare words on a slip of telegram, that Marina's father had died of dysentery in the Siberian labor camp to which he had been sentenced, just three days before he was due to be furloughed out to the army in its last-ditch defense of Moscow against the Wehrmacht.

NOW LYUDMILA SITS AT her desk and gathers her papers. She's set up a secure operations room in the basement, taking care to ensure that nobody else knows where it is except for a single secretary named Anna Dubrovskaya. She doesn't exactly trust Dubrovskaya, either, but Dubrovskaya's proved loyal on many occasions in the past—even under what you might call duress—so Lyudmila designates her as deputy while she's out of her regular office. It will have to do.

At eight o'clock precisely, the telephone rings on the table in the operations room. Lyudmila lifts the receiver. The line is secure, or at least as secure as Lyudmila can possibly ensure. On the other end is an operative at a telephone in one of the safe houses Lyudmila maintains for operations such as this one.

"Ivanova," she snaps.

"The birds left the nest this morning at a quarter past seven," the man tells her.

"Good. You must follow at a distance, do you hear me? He cannot know your man is there."

"Affirmative."

"You are not to allow anyone to interfere with the progress of that car, remember. You may take whatever measures are necessary, including lethal force, to ensure it remains unmolested. I will deal with the consequences."

"Affirmative."

A firm click comes down the line. Lyudmila replaces the receiver and sips her tea to calm her nerves. So far, so good. She opens a manila folder from her surveillance team, which contains the transcripts from the night before. She pulls them out. They're rough, typed out without much punctuation or spelling by a translator on a headset, and sometimes Lyudmila has to puzzle out their meaning. Still, having examined the transcripts of the past few nights, she knows she's unlikely to encounter any interesting information. She can tell, for example, that Mr. and Mrs. Fox are either exactly what they claim—a pair of newlyweds very much in love—or else very much aware of the microphones in the walls. She suspects the latter. The words and phrases are almost too loving, too cinematic. What husband is possibly so attentive to his bride's every need? What wife is really so enthusiastic about the act of intercourse? Lyudmila regards the typed lines before her with cynicism and a touch of salt, and without any expectation of surprise.

A moment later, she reaches for the telephone.

NO ONE PLAYS INNOCENT like Vashnikov, which is remarkable because he looks exactly like a pig. "This is shocking," he says. "I am surprised at you, Ivanova, for not ensuring they were better guarded. Anything might have happened!"

"We both know they were perfectly well guarded. We both know that your man ordered mine to stand down."

"You should have them arrested, for dereliction of duty and for lying."

"What were you looking for, Vashnikov? Perhaps something you didn't find at HAMPTON's apartment? Something you suspect Mrs. Fox might have collected for safekeeping?"

"An interesting theory, if the Foxes were not so entirely engrossed in fucking each other instead."

"You'll never be promoted head of the agency, Vashnikov. Your mind only goes in one direction. Never mind. I'll find out. Whatever it is, the Americans will be carrying it. And *my* men won't bungle the job."

She hangs up the phone. Someone knocks on the door immediately, as if waiting for her to finish.

"Come in," she says.

Dubrovskaya enters with a telephone message from Kedrov, who arrived on schedule at the hospital this morning to accompany Mrs. Digby, her baby, and her sister in an ambulance to Rizhsky Station, where a train will take them to Riga.

Lyudmila sits back in her chair and exhales with relief.

Now all she can do is wait, like a spider in the center of an exquisite web.

RUTH

JULY 1952

Moscow

Wouldn't you know it, the clouds push in around seven o'clock in the morning. From the back seat of the car I watch the gray stuffing creep over the summer-blue sky, swallowing all joy. How dismal Moscow looks without the sun. The lonesome turrets and bleak apartment blocks stand tragically still while the gloom overcomes them.

I turn to Fox and make some crack about the dying of the light. He doesn't even smile. Inside his jacket are the passports and identification papers and the gun he retrieved from the dead drop yesterday. I guess the weight of them killed his sense of humor. His face looks as it did the day I met him, sculpted by a blunt hatchet. The pale, colorless eyes reflect the world back like a pair of tiny mirrors.

At the hospital, the lumpy white ambulance waits in the drive, engine rumbling. I don't like all the fuss; some human instinct recoils against accepting this extravagant Soviet hospitality when we're only going to betray them with it. I hurry inside with

Kedrov. He wears the same dark suit as before, the same expression of pained diplomacy—diplomacy at all costs—diplomacy if it kills him. We turn down a couple of corridors until we reach the waiting room in the maternity wing, where Iris sits in a wheelchair, wanly holding Gregory, who screams bloody murder. Nearby, the English-speaking doctor scribbles on a clipboard. He looks up fiercely at me and nods.

"Have a good journey," he orders me.

"Thank you. You've been such a great help to her."

The doctor shrugs and turns away, and for a moment I stand there helplessly. I wonder what's the story of his life, and whether he has some inkling what he's doing and how he's helping us. Whether he will pay a price for what happens next.

I take charge of the wheelchair myself and push Iris down the corridors until we reach the entrance. Kedrov holds open the door. The black car's still there, right behind the ambulance, inside a fog of exhaust. Fox stands next to the rear door. When he sees us emerge, he walks over briskly. First, he bends down and kisses Iris's cheek, like an affectionate brother-in-law; then he straightens and kisses me on the lips, exactly the way a husband bids his wife farewell.

"Travel safely, darling. We'll meet you there in a few days."

I help Iris and the baby into the back of the ambulance, and Fox climbs into the back of the official car, and we roar off on our separate ways under the overcast sky.

FROM THIS POINT ON, I have no way of knowing where Fox is, or what he's doing. *Trust me*, he said to me, as we leaned out the window of the hotel room, eight stories above the subdued morning bustle of Mokhovaya Street.

I sucked the remains of my cigarette and pondered this question of trust, and how absolute our trust in each other must be, and on what basis? He'd deceived me from the beginning. You might argue that he'd *had* to deceive me—the less I knew, the safer everyone was—God knew I might sing like a canary at the first whiff of interrogation—but nonetheless, there was deceit. Even now he wouldn't tell me the whole story. Yet he wanted me to trust him with my life, and my sister's life, and the lives of her children and husband!

But I had no choice, did I? No other way but forward. No one else but Fox.

I withdrew my left hand from his and examined the gold band, the inside of which was actually engraved in tiny cursive letters with a dollop of biblical wisdom, Paul's letter to the Corinthians—

*Love does not delight in evil but rejoices in the truth * CSF to REM * May 5 1952*

—because Fox is nothing if not thorough, isn't he? I did not take the ring off and read out that verse to him. I didn't believe I needed to. I stared at it and he stared at it, and we both knew what was written inside, and that Fox himself had chosen the line. I finished the cigarette and crushed it out on the windowsill. We ducked back inside the hotel room and I turned to look at him.

"You know, people say marriage is a leap of faith," I told him. "But I figure it's more like a bet. I've put my money on you, Sumner Fox, for no reason other than a thing in my gut telling me I should. I'm hoping it wasn't just indigestion."

Fox started to laugh in big, hearty whoops like he might have used to do at Yale, after he scored himself a home run, or whatever it was. When he was done amusing himself, he wiped away a tear or two from those stone eyes.

"Now that's the girl I married," he said.

THE AMBULANCE RUMBLES AWAY down the road, turning and swaying. Kedrov sits up front, next to the driver, while Iris and I make ourselves comfortable in the back with the nurse. Outside the tiny window, Moscow passes by in drab gray flashes. I fuss with the baby so as not to think about Fox, and where he's headed, and what he'll do.

A black fly has found its way inside the ambulance. I'm not surprised—have I mentioned the bugs in Moscow? My God. You know how it is in these territories that freeze solid during the winter months. Our parents once had the clever idea to send us to some outdoorsy girls' camp on the shores of Lake Winnipesaukee in New Hampshire for the month of August, and it's a wonder I had any skin left by the time we went back to school. Anyway, the thing buzzes deliriously around Gregory's head, simply out of its mind with the delicious scent of newborn baby. I swat and shoo and look helplessly at the nurse. She shrugs her shoulders and checks her watch. The ambulance swerves and lurches and turns some hairpin corner, and without prior warning screeches to a stop. I expect we must have reached a traffic signal or something, but no. The front doors open and slam; the rear ones swing open. We've arrived in Rizhskaya Square, just outside the Rizhsky railway terminal, from which our train will depart in half an hour.

The nurse clambers out first and extends her hand.

"I don't think there's a wheelchair for you," I tell Iris.

"That's all right. I can walk."

"Are you certain?"

She rolls her eyes at me—just as she used to do when we were children—and takes the nurse's hand. I tuck Gregory like a football in the crook of my right arm and jump out ahead of her to take the other hand. Kedrov appears around the door, lugging a pair of suitcases—mine and Iris's. Iris turns back to the open doors of the ambulance.

"My bag, Ruth. With Gregory's things."

I search about the back of the ambulance and discover a small, soft valise, which I hoist over my elbow. Together we make a slow procession toward the Roman arches at the entrance of Rizhsky Station, which looks something like a church, only grimier. Behind us, a tram rattles along its tracks. A bus growls past. The air is thick with exhaust and cigarettes. I concentrate all my attention on Iris to my left and Gregory on my right arm, and I hope to God I won't let either of them drop to the pavement.

The train is short—only three carriages—and pulled by a steam engine, just like the old days. The boiler hisses and the air reeks of coal smoke. Kedrov leads us to the carriage just behind the engine and helps Iris climb the steps. We have a compartment to ourselves, a sleeper, more comfortable than I expected. The nurse takes Iris's temperature and blood pressure and makes some notes on her chart, which she hands to Kedrov before she steps, with an air of relief, out of the compartment.

"No nurse?" I ask Kedrov.

He shakes his head and looks out the window at the busy platform below us. Gregory squirms, opens his eyes, and starts to cry.

Iris unbuttons her blouse. "Poor fellow, he's hungry after all this."

Kedrov flushes red and bolts for the door of the compartment so quickly his mumbled excuse hangs in the air behind him.

The whistle keens good-bye. The train jerks forward. I turn to the window just in time to see the nurse hurrying back down the platform and out of sight.

WHEN FOX WAS A kid—difficult to imagine, I know, but imagine it anyway—he used to love magic shows, he said.

We were inside Orlovsky's atelier when he told me this. It was one of those blurred, hurried days before we left for Moscow, when Fox was attempting to distill a decade's worth of accumulated experience and tradecraft into a few simple lessons. This was one of them. He told me he would order those kits in the mail, the ones with the flimsy boxes with the sliding bottoms and that kind of thing, and he would spend hours and hours perfecting the tricks, until he could fool even his mother—who was, he told me gravely, no fool.

I said that was a nice story, so what?

Well, tradecraft is a lot like magic, he said. All those KGB watchers, you have to fool them into thinking they're seeing one thing, when another thing is actually taking place before their eyes. Now, how do you execute this sleight of hand? You distract the viewer with some other maneuver, some elaborate display of the left hand while the right hand performs the dirty work, or else you employ some sinfully attractive assistant to lure the attention of the audience while the magician makes the rabbit disappear.

Now, I admit, I thought as you did when he explained this. I flattered myself that I was the sinfully attractive magician's assistant, and Fox was the magician, and Digby was the rabbit. But I guess you could say that Fox was practicing a little illusion on me as well, which I began to understand during that first visit to the Digbys' apartment. Still—because the illusion fits comfortably with all my notions of Iris and myself and the world in general—the whole truth only really dawns on me as I sit in that train compartment, rattling through all the switches as we progress out of Moscow.

I remember something else Fox told me. I turn to Iris and ask quietly, "When Sasha does his training lectures, how many of the candidates are women?"

"None," she says.

Sure, you see women agents from time to time, Fox said. *You see handlers, couriers, that kind of thing. But not case officers. Not our side and especially not theirs.*

I said that was unfair, but Fox shook his head.

It's an advantage, he said. *You're invisible to them. If we split up, they'll run after me, not you. They'll figure I've got the football, because what kind of man hands off the football to a woman?*

The rabbit. The football. Whatever it is, it's sitting right next to me. Hiding in plain sight, while the watchers watch someone else.

I settle back against the seat and close my eyes. "It figures," I mutter.

But I don't fall asleep. I just lie there staring at my eyelids and pray that Fox knows what he's doing.

AS THE TRAIN GATHERS speed, out of the Moscow suburbs and onto the vast western plains, I keep an eye out for KGB watchers. We have lunch in the dining car, but among the other passengers I see nobody who takes much notice of us. Iris doesn't eat much.

She looks a little pale, but what do I know about the aftermath of childbirth? She says she feels fine, just tired as you might expect. Outside the window, the landscape rolls by, green fields and hills, speckled by lakes. The clouds break up a little, exposing a pure blue sky. Sometimes we come to some village or town, gray and spent. I don't know much about this part of the world, but it seems to me that the land has been trampled on somehow, that that past half century has left the people exhausted.

Only Kedrov eats heartily. He recommends various dishes for us, points out features in the landscape as we rattle westward. Riga is about six hundred miles away, a full day's journey. Occasionally I spot a car or a truck, trundling down some road, or a horse and cart, and I send out a prayer for Fox.

We return to the compartment. I pull out a cheap paperback novel from my pocketbook and pretend to read, while Iris, holding Gregory, leans against my shoulder and falls asleep. Gently I pry the baby loose from her arms. He doesn't even stir, just collapses against my own weary bones as if he belonged to me. The sun inches ahead of us. Kedrov's eyelids droop.

Behind us, Fox has either succeeded or has not—drives with the children in a KGB car along some highway behind us or does not.

Is alive or is not.

SOON AFTER WE CROSS the border into Latvia, the train staggers to a stop and the border guards come aboard to check our passports. Kedrov rises and speaks with them, shows them some papers from his briefcase. There are two guards—both raise their eyebrows and regard us curiously. Iris is awake, holding the baby. She has that wan, innocent, maternal look about her. Her eyes are huge and wet.

Her bones are tiny and delicate. The guards nod and duck out of the compartment—Kedrov straightens his jacket and sits down again, pleased with himself. A half hour later, the train lurches back into motion.

I glance at Iris; she makes a slight nod.

I stretch my arms luxuriously. "What time is it? I wouldn't mind a little tea."

Kedrov looks up from his newspaper. "Tea? Of course."

FOX SHOWED ME HOW to do it. He made me practice with sugar, over and over, until I had the timing worked out exactly right—the misdirection, the infinitesimal flick of the wrist, the expressionless face, the bright chatter that continues without a break.

Kedrov never suspects a thing. He drinks his tea and falls asleep right on schedule, as we pull into the station at Ogre, the train's last stop before Riga.

We leave our suitcases on the luggage racks above our heads. I sling my pocketbook over my elbow and carry my nephew and the soft valise with Gregory's things inside it; Iris takes my arm and leans on it heavily as we descend the steps to the platform. I make the signal for a cigarette to the conductor, who nods and promptly forgets us.

The sun still shines high and white above the horizon, even though it's well past seven o'clock. Iris and I walk down the platform steps so nobody can see us from the station house, which is on the other side of the tracks. When the train moves off, we cross the tracks and sit in the waiting room for an hour or two.

The building is small but not unpleasant. By the look of the red bricks and creamy masonry, it was built around the turn of the century with some aspirations to grandeur. High ceilings and pretty plasterwork, that kind of thing. I smoke a couple of cigarettes and try not to check my watch. Iris feeds the baby. She had a couple of biscuits with her tea but nothing else since her meager lunch, and her movements seem sluggish, her eyes unfocused. I take Gregory and tell her to lie on the bench and rest.

I pace the width of the waiting room, over and over, because every time I stop his eyes fly open. What do I know about babies? At one point I realize he needs a change of diaper. I rummage in the valise until I find the clean cloth and the safety pins and whatnot. I guess I manage all right. I didn't know what to do with the dirty diaper—I can't just put it back in the valise like that—so I head for the bin to throw it away.

Iris's eyes fly open. "What are you doing?" she calls out.

"Throwing away the diaper."

"No, bring it back."

She sits up and wads the soiled cloth carefully into a ball, which she puts in a separate pocket. I walk with her over to the ladies' room so we can wash our hands. The journey nearly finishes her entirely. We return to the benches. She curls up and closes her eyes. I pace the floor with Gregory and smell the brown hay smell of the fields outside, the reek of coal smoke and of steam. The station's empty, except for a ticket clerk who reads some book behind his glass window. Above his head, the station clock ticks and tocks.

At a quarter past nine, I hear the distant rumble of a car engine, more like a vibration in the air than an actual noise. I pause in my pacing, but miraculously Gregory's little eyes stay shut. The rumble becomes louder until it's a recognizable sound. I return to Iris and shake her gently. She looks up at me, uncomprehending. "Ruth? Are we late for the party?"

She seems flushed. I touch her forehead, but I can't tell if it's warm or not. My own fingers are so chilly, because the weather in Latvia—in midsummer—isn't what you'd call tropical. Already a cool, dry evening breeze whisks through the open window, even though the sun still burns bright in the western sky.

"Not yet, pumpkin," I tell her. "Come with me."

I help her up with one arm, while my other arm holds Gregory. She leans heavily on me as we walk to the door. The ticket clerk glances up, watches us for a second or two, then returns to his book. We pass through the doorway and pause on the steps. The station seems to be on the outskirts of town, and the nearby streets are quiet, except for a large black car creeping down the road that fronts the station. I stand where I am, supporting Iris with my arm. The sunlight glints off the car's windows. It looks just like the vehicles we saw speeding through the Moscow streets, big sleek black machines that Fox told me—under his breath—belonged to the KGB.

The car slows and stops. My heart might pound right out of my chest. Iris's hand grips my wrist. Every instinct screams at me to duck back inside, into the shadows of the waiting room, but I force myself to remain just outside the entrance, under the shallow portico—visible if you're looking for me.

An eternity passes before the driver's door opens and a man steps out. He wears a dark suit and a fedora atop his dark hair. He closes the door and turns to face us. His big shoulders strain the jacket of his suit, the sleeves of which stop a couple of inches above each wrist.

My knees start to buckle. I have to lock them to stay upright, and even then I wobble. But the man's already started forward from the car. He climbs the steps two at a time. I catch the flash of his pale eyes before I hand Iris off to him. He guides her carefully down the steps to the waiting car. I follow them, cradling Gregory in both arms.

"It's going to be all right," I tell my nephew. "We're going to be just fine."

LYUDMILA

JULY 1952
Moscow

When the secure telephone rings in Lyudmila's basement operations room, the caller is not the person Lyudmila expects.

"It's your daughter, Comrade Ivanova," says Anna Dubrovskaya, a little warily.

"My daughter! She's supposed to be in school!" The astonished words pop out before Lyudmila can stop them, and this failure of self-control shocks her further. She takes a deep breath and says, more calmly, "Connect her, please."

"Mama?" comes Marina's voice.

"It's two o'clock in the afternoon, Marina. Where are you?"

"I'm at Kip Dubinin's apartment," she says.

Lyudmila's so stunned, she thinks at first that she didn't hear Marina correctly. She thinks maybe she's heard certain words echoing from her own head, because she's so deeply immersed in this operation that she can't tell the difference between what's outside her head and what's inside. "*What* did you say?" she gasps.

"Kip Dubinin. Mama, you have to help me. He and his brother never came to school today, and somebody said he saw them drive by in some kind of KGB car early this morning—"

"*Who* said that?"

"It doesn't matter—"

"*Yes, it does!*" Lyudmila thunders.

"Well, I won't tell you!" Marina says, in her calm, defiant voice that reminds Lyudmila of Dmitri.

Lyudmila grinds her teeth together. It's a bad habit and she'll reprimand herself later, when she's finished with this daughter of hers—when she's cooled her mind and encircled these strange, impossible pieces of information and brought them under control. "Why," she says coldly, "are you at the Dubinins' apartment when you are supposed to be at school?"

"I told you. Something's happened to them. I just had a feeling in my gut, Mama, when Nik—when the person told me that he was sure he saw them in the back seat of a KGB car this morning, on the way to school. And then Kip never came to class, and he never came to lunch, and Oleg in second form said that Jack never came to class either. So after lunch I left—"

"You left school. *In the middle of the day!* What were you *thinking*, Marina?"

"I was worried! And I got to the apartment and the door was *unlocked*, Mama, and nobody was inside but everything was messy, like it had been searched."

Marina pauses. She seems out of breath, not from exertion but from emotion and from speaking too much and too fast. Now she waits for her mother to say something.

What on earth is Lyudmila going to say to her?

"Tell me, Marina. Why do you care so much about young Dubinin?"

Another pause crackles down the secure line. Only it's not so secure, is it? A line is only as secure as the connection at the other end, and the Dubinins' telephone is, of course, bugged. Lyudmila realizes this fact the same way a snowball hits your chest—hard and cold, enough to break your ribs. She wants to bite off her tongue. If only she weren't so occupied by the operation—if only Marina didn't surprise her like this—she should have grasped the danger instantly. Probably Vashnikov is listening this second!

Luckily, Marina was like any eleven-year-old girl when it came to discussing these matters with her mother.

"Mama, I don't *care* about him. He's just a boy at my school. But—"

"Never mind," Lyudmila says hastily. "We'll speak of it tonight, when you're home from school."

"I've already left school, and I'm not going back. I'm not doing anything until you tell me what's going on."

Lyudmila attempts a laugh. "Darling, so *dramatic*! Nothing's going on. I'm sure there's a perfectly logical explanation. Didn't his mother have a new baby? Maybe they've gone to the hospital today."

"Mama—"

"In any case, I'm at the office now, as you know. I *can't speak* about any personal matters."

Marina makes a tiny noise that might be disgust or understanding—who can tell with a girl that age? And why in the name of reason has her daughter developed a fascination with *this particular boy*? What contrary fate placed the two of them together at the *same school* to begin with? Lyudmila feels a headache coming on. Her fingers flex to grasp one of the cigarettes she gave up during the war, when cigarettes were needed for the soldiers at the front. She stares at the bare gray-white walls, the speckled linoleum that covers the floor.

"All right," Marina says quietly. "I guess I'll see you at home, then."

"Go back to school, darling. Everything will be all right."

"Yes," says her daughter.

Yes to what? Lyudmila thinks frantically. "Probably they started the summer holidays a few days early."

"That's not allowed," Marina says flatly. "Good-bye, Mama."

"Good-bye, Marina."

The line clicks and goes dead. Lyudmila replaces the receiver and stares at the smooth black handle. The world, which seemed so orderly and so satisfactory a moment ago, has now gone haywire. All because of some impudent scrap of an eleven-year-old girl.

All right, Dmitri, she thinks. *Have your revenge. Just remember she's your daughter, too.*

AFTER THAT, THE TELEPHONE goes quiet. Lyudmila resists the urge to pick up the receiver and ask Dubrovskaya if a message has come in, a cable. Of course, Dubrovskaya would bring down any message or cable instantly—she's perfectly well trained, she's as loyal as it's possible to be loyal within these walls.

Trust nobody, Lyudmila reminds herself.

She stands and sits again. She flips through the papers on the desk before her—the cables, the transcripts, her own notes, all arranged in chronological order to tell the story of this operation. She rearranges the position of a stack or two. She sips her tea, which has gone cold.

The telephone rings, jarring her. She snatches up the receiver. "Ivanova!" she snaps.

Dubrovskaya's voice, carefully neutral—"The head of your daughter's school is on the telephone for you. Shall I take a message?"

IT IS INVIDIOUS—*INVIDIOUS!*—TO SIT in this low chair before Comrade Grievskaya's desk as if one were a recalcitrant schoolchild. It's invidious even to be here *at all*, in such a moment, when she's supposed to be directing this operation that will possibly bring down the careers of several traitors to the Soviet people, if Lyudmila's suspicions are accurate—and they always are, in these matters. Lyudmila wants to scream at this woman—*Do you know I am a KGB officer in the middle of a major operation? Do you know I can bring down so much trouble upon your head, you'll wish I would just execute you instead?*

But she doesn't. There's something in the authority of a head of school that transcends even the authority of the KGB—the authority of the Kremlin itself.

Still. Her male colleagues would never find themselves in such a position, on such a day, in a chair specifically designed to make a person feel several inches shorter than the person behind the desk. They've never known these ritual humiliations. They have wives to deal with them.

Lyudmila starts with an offensive move, as she's been trained. "I'm well aware that Marina has been absent from school today—"

"Yes, Comrade Ivanova," says Grievskaya, "and we will address this infraction shortly. At the moment, however, I must bring a more serious matter to your attention."

She pauses to examine Lyudmila over the rim of her spectacles. Lyudmila swallows and glances at the clock. Half past three.

"Yes?" she says.

Grievskaya steeples her hands above the blotter on her exemplary desk. "For some months—since the winter holidays, in fact—we have heard reports of a group of students meeting in secret to exchange subversive materials and discuss their contents."

Oh, shit, Lyudmila thinks.

"Subversive materials?" she says, perfectly composed. "I don't understand. How do young students get their hands on such things?"

Grievskaya waves her hand. "We are not yet concerned with *how.* Right now, we are concerned with *who* and *where.* Until recently, we were unable to identify even a single member of this clandestine group. It seems they are bound by a vow of absolute secrecy, to which they have proved remarkably loyal, given their ages. But this morning, a certain piece of information came to us by chance."

Grievskaya plucks a sheet of paper from the blotter and hands it across the desk to Lyudmila, who takes it reluctantly, forcing her fingers not to tremble. She smooths it out before her. EMERGENCY MEETING, it reads. AFTER SCHOOL AT HEADQUARTERS.

Underneath those letters, a list of names—PETREL, BEAR, EAGLE, PEGASUS, LION, ELEPHANT, HORSE, RAT. All of them are crossed out except the last two.

"What's this?"

"It was found on the floor of the cafeteria after lunch. It appears someone had dropped it."

Lyudmila hands the note back to Grievskaya. "Well? What does this have to do with Marina? Her name's not on the list."

"No. These are code names, Comrade Ivanova. That is plain even to those of us not engaged in intelligence work. But one of our teachers has identified the handwriting as that of your daughter. Who, as we have already established, left school early today, without authorization. What is more, two additional students are absent without leave today—one of whom we have long suspected of subversive opinions—which suggests . . ."

Grievskaya's voice trails away. She looks expectantly at Lyudmila.

"Suggests *what*, Comrade?" Lyudmila says. "What do you imply? I see nothing but some ordinary high spirits among young people, which is regrettable but hardly subversive."

Grievskaya removes her spectacles and folds the arms together. She speaks tiredly, as one who's repeated this lesson too many times already. "Out of little acorns, oak trees grow. As you very well know, Comrade, whose business it is to fell these oak trees. Would it not be preferable to root out the acorns before they can secure themselves in the soil and begin to sprout?"

Of course! Lyudmila wants to scream. *Of course it's preferable*—everybody knows this—Lyudmila believes wholeheartedly in the necessity for rooting out stubborn, rebellious acorns as aggressively as possible.

But this is not an acorn. This is Marina! This is her *daughter*, a human being, not a goddamned *acorn*!

"I confess, I'm surprised that you would presume to deliver me a lecture on this subject, Comrade Grievskaya," Lyudmila says, in the silky voice she uses to interrogate suspected oak trees. "A little like the arithmetic teacher presuming to instruct Einstein on calculus?"

Grievskaya shrugs her shoulders. "I am giving you the facts, Comrada Ivanova. I'm confident you will know how to use them. You are, after all, the child's mother. You are responsible for her. Her character reflects upon your reputation."

"My daughter is the most brilliant student in her class."

"In a few days, school will close for the summer, and Marina will join the youth camp at Ekaterinburg, isn't that right?"

"That's correct."

"Then I will dare to offer you a piece of advice, Comrade Ivanova, because I have directed this school for many years, and I well understand how nature softens us and makes us blind to the true character of our offspring. Believe me, I am entirely sympathetic to your plight."

Rage boils up inside Lyudmila. She presses her lips together so it doesn't escape in some catastrophic eruption.

Grievskaya continues. "Here at my school, I prefer to address these infractions quietly, within the walls of my office, in conversations with parents. I find it's the most efficient and effective solution, when the child is so young and his character still so soft and easily corrected. As you know, however, youth camp is different. The children are old enough to have some responsibility for themselves. They will be expected to understand the consequences of their actions, and it is the duty of the instructors at the camp to report any subversive behavior *not* to the parents of the child in question, but to the Soviet state. Do I make myself clear?"

It would be so easy to lean forward and apply some pressure to a certain point in Grievskaya's neck that would render her unable to speak further. It would be so easy to return to Moscow Centre and make a telephone call or two that would ruin Grievskaya's life, if not end it entirely by the most agonizing means possible.

But despite the rage that still boils in Lyudmila's chest and stomach and sizzles its way to the tips of her fingers and toes, she comprehends that Grievskaya is not altogether wrong. In fact, she speaks the truth. Were Marina to be caught at the youth camp engaging in any kind of activity deemed contrary to the principles of communism, or subversive to the Soviet state, it would be a serious matter indeed. Lyudmila would not have the luxury of sitting in an office with the camp director to discuss some gentle measures to correct her daughter's character. Lyudmila would have to strain every nerve, call in every possible favor, to remove the stain on Marina's official record. And—knowing Marina—that wouldn't stop her daughter from doing it again.

And again.

Indeed, as Lyudmila sits in her chair and locks her gaze with Grievskaya's gaze in some kind of silent, powerful duel, a terrible future seems to open up before her—a future she has willfully ignored for the past few years, while Marina dropped hint after hint, offered glimpse after glimpse. Honestly, you couldn't blame Marina. Lyudmila can blame only her own blind eyes for this oversight.

She rises from the chair and holds out her hand. "Perfectly clear, Comrade Grievskaya. Now, if you will excuse me, I must return to my work."

WHEN LYUDMILA OPENS THE door to her office at Moscow Centre at a quarter past four, Anna Dubrovskaya jumps from the chair at her desk. Her sallow face sags with relief.

"Thank goodness you're here," she says. "Comrade Vashnikov has been asking for you for the past hour. He says he has some very serious news to share with you, and he refused to tell me what it was."

VASHNIKOV'S FACE IS GRAY and shiny, the face of a sick man. He even smells like a sick man—like sour sweat. "They've disappeared," he croaks.

Lyudmila doesn't need to ask who's disappeared. "Of course they have. Mr. Fox is an American intelligence officer, as I warned you, and Mrs. Fox is his accomplice. I am going to hazard a guess, Vashnikov. I'm going to speculate that Mr. Fox has overpowered your driver, has assumed his identity, and has taken away HAMP-TON and his children in a KGB car, which will not be questioned at any checkpoint or border in the Soviet Union."

"How do you know this?"

"Call it intuition, perhaps."

He stares at her. "You've planned this, haven't you? You've counted on it."

"Just because it's all unfolded as I said it would doesn't mean I've planned it. The only thing I've counted on is your incompetence, Vashnikov. Or is it your desire to protect your own hide, perhaps? Because it seems you did find a few items at the Digbys' apartment, after all."

Vashnikov pauses in the act of lighting a cigarette. "How do you know this?"

"Does it matter? I found out. It wasn't hard, Vashnikov. Your people have no loyalty to you at all—it's a pity. A one-time pad for coding, a Minox camera? All very incriminating. *If only* you'd found some papers, too. *If only* you knew just how deeply HAMPTON has betrayed us. You must be desperate, eh? Desperate to find a way to cover this up, instead of simply admitting your mistake and stretching your utmost nerve to discover where HAMPTON has gone and bring him to justice."

Vashnikov is quivering like a jelly. He puts his unlit cigarette and his lighter on the desk before him. His mouth flops open and closed like a fish gasping for water.

"I thought so," says Lyudmila. "Very well. I will clean up your mess for you, never fear. It so happens I know precisely where HAMPTON is going, and with whom. I'm headed there shortly myself, to lead the interrogation and extract whatever information he's taking back to his handlers. We'll discover just how much damage has been done by your prize defector, Vashnikov, just how many valuable assets have been compromised by your stupidity, and if you're lucky, Comrade Stalin will never know just how spectacular a failure you are. But please remember one thing, as you go about your business."

"Yes, Comrade Ivanova?" Vashnikov says meekly.

She leans forward and whispers, "*I know.*"

MINUTES LATER, LYUDMILA RETURNS to her office and tells Anna Dubrovskaya that she's been called away to attend to an emergency. She will communicate regularly to receive any messages. In the meantime, she will need Dubrovskaya to go immediately to Lyudmila's apartment and wait there for Marina, whom Dubrovskaya will look after with the strictest possible eye until Lyudmila's return.

RUTH

The children want their mother, naturally, but the last thing Iris needs right now is a bunch of kids crawling over her. She sits in the front seat, the passenger side, holding Gregory, while Fox aims the car swiftly down the highway. I've crammed myself in back with the other kids. Kip sits squashed against the opposite door, Jack next to him, Claire cuddled up to my side. She motions me down to hear a secret and cups her hands around my ear.

"Daddy'th in the twunk," she whispers.

"Is he, now? I do hope he's comfortable in there, poor dear."

Claire giggles and nestles herself to sleep on my lap. I stare at the back of Fox's neck and think how lovely it would be to fall asleep like that, in somebody's lap, so limp and trusting that she doesn't even stir when I lean diagonally forward and ask Iris how she's feeling.

"Oh, I'm fine. Just fine."

I place my fingers against her temple. The skin burns me, but then my fingers are icy cold, so what? I turn to Fox and whisper, "How does she look to you?"

He glances to the side. "Not good."

I swear and sit back against the cloth cushions. A soft thump occurs somewhere behind me, so at least Digby's still alive. I wonder if he went in willingly, or if Fox had to force him there by gunpoint or moral persuasion. Outside, the sun bathes the landscape in the golden glow of late afternoon, except it's almost ten o'clock at night. According to plan, we should be skirting around Riga by now, heading to some remote location on the coast where a small boat will be waiting to take us to safety.

"Who's in the boat?" I asked earlier, and Fox shook his head. The less I know, the better, remember? In case we're caught. In case I—a mere amateur at enduring physical discomfort—spill all the beans under interrogation. At all costs, we must protect the small, covert network that directs our affairs—the secrets of which repose in the feverish head of the woman in the front seat.

I place my hand on Claire's warm, silky head. She's only three years old, this niece of mine. Her brothers sit next to me—Jack dozing off against the back of the seat, Kip staring out the window, arms crossed. I can't see his expression, but I know he understands what's going on. He's no innocent, this fellow. He's still wearing his school uniform, because Fox had no way of supplying changes of clothing for everybody. The contents of the dead drop would have been limited to passports and papers and the elements of his own current disguise. And the gun, of course. Fox is relying on speed and surprise, and the KGB identification of the driver of this car, God rest whatever soul he possessed.

It will be all right, I tell myself. In a matter of hours, we'll be safe on that boat, and Iris will have all the doctors and medicines and rest she needs.

Fox will take care of us. Fox takes care of everybody. There
he is now, driving this car confidently along the highway, as if he
knows every road in Latvia like the pattern of lines on the palm of
his hand. And I expect he does. I expect he memorized that map
before he even left New York.

AT LAST, THE SUN starts to set. The golden light takes on a salmon
hue, and the streaking clouds seem to be holding their breath. I
think Fox is traveling on secondary roads, which are pitted with
holes and bumps and the scars of war. Claire is a dead weight in
my lap, and now Jack leans against my shoulder, mouth open and
drooling a little on my crisp navy jacket. I turn my head just in time
to catch Fox looking at me in the rearview mirror, before his gaze
turns back to the road before him.

"How much farther?" I ask softly.

"Not long. We're getting near the coast."

"But how many minutes?"

"About twenty."

Some words come to my lips, but I bite them back.

"How's Iris?" I say instead.

He glances at her. "Holding strong."

Which means she's alive, I guess. Her head leans back against
the top of the seat—her eyes are closed. Is her skin flushed, or do
the colors of sunset melt on her beautiful skin, that creamy wonder
I always admired and often envied? Nobody has a skin like Iris,
as flawless as alabaster, not a line or a crease, each emotion ebbing
and flowing along its surface. Now it's perfectly still. The baby lies
secure in his swaddle on the seat between them. He doesn't make
a sound. The only noise in the car—apart from the faint rasp of

respiration, from my soft questions and Fox's low replies—comes from the trunk, where Digby rustles and thumps like a man in a fever dream.

Well, let him thrash.

I look back at the rearview mirror, just in time to catch Fox watching me again. This time he holds my gaze for a beat or two, because we're the only ones left awake inside this peculiar world— even Kip dozes off against the window glass—and because it seems we might be in love.

AT LAST FOX PRESSES the brakes and turns off onto an unpaved road. The car lurches and wallows, waking everybody up. Grunts and groans float through the back of the seat from the trunk. Gregory starts to cry and Iris finds the strength to gather him up in her arms.

"Poah Thathdy," Claire says solemnly around her thumb, which she's stuck into her mouth.

"Poor Daddy," I agree.

"We're driving on sand!" Jack announces, and sure enough, when I look through the window at the blue-tinted world, that sliver of time between sunset and twilight, I see nothing but pale dunes and tall seagrass.

"You're sure this is the place?" I ask.

"Yes," Fox replies.

He stops the car and tells us to wait.

"Wait for what? I want to get out of here. I need some air."

"I'm just going to scout ahead for a moment. Could you pass me the flashlight under the seat?"

Claire wriggles onto the floor of the car and finds it for him. It's funny how the kids just trust him, this stranger who killed a man and then kidnapped them in a KGB car. I hope they didn't see him do the deed. No doubt Fox did his best to conceal it from them.

"Thank you," he says gravely to Claire. He opens the door and lights the flashlight, covering the bulb with his palm so it's not so bright. Before he leaves, he ducks his head back in and says to me, "There's a gun in the glove compartment if you need it."

DO I NEED TO mention that—among other things—Fox showed me how to fire a gun? It was the day before we left for Moscow. We borrowed Orlovsky's car and drove in bizarre zigzags through the city for an hour to throw off any possible tail. (Who's going to tail us? I asked, and Fox just shrugged and said you never know, you should always assume somebody is watching you.) At last, just as I was about to ask him to pull over so I could throw up my breakfast in the gutter, we zoomed out of the city and wound our way into the hills somewhere, until Fox decided we were far enough from any living thing and pulled over.

We used a tree for a target. I didn't know a thing about guns, but I'll be damned if I didn't have a good eye and a steady hand. Fox showed me how to aim it and fire it, how to load more bullets if I needed to. I said I hoped I wouldn't need to fire the thing at all, and Fox sat me down and opened up a couple of bottles of lemonade and delivered me this lecture on how guns were a last resort—they were like an admission you had failed at the finer arts of espionage. But if *he* failed, and *I* failed, then he sure as the devil didn't want me to die for it. He said this sincerely, and I believed him. Then we packed up our little picnic and went back to Rome.

Now we sat in the gloaming on a sand dune on the Baltic coast somewhere—and yes, I could find the Baltic Sea on a map, but only because I'd spent four years poring over those charts of Europe that appeared daily in the newspapers throughout the war. I pondered whether I should reach over the seat and retrieve that gun from the glove compartment, just in case, even though I hated the cold, lethal feel of a gun in my hand, the terrible foreboding that something might go wrong and I'd end up killing somebody, possibly myself.

I hear the echo of Fox's words in my head. *If I fail and you fail, I sure as the devil don't want you to die for it.*

But I'm sitting in a carful of precious children. I can't take that chance.

Outside the window, a light jogs toward us.

"Thank God," I whisper.

Fox comes right up to the rear door, where I'm sitting, and opens it. "Come out," he says.

But there's something funny about his voice, and when I look up, I realize this man isn't Fox at all. He holds a flashlight in one hand and a gun in the other, which he points at my head.

SASHA

He recognizes the woman across the table, though he can't remember where or how. Some debriefing, perhaps, when they first arrived in the Soviet Union? Or later—some lecture or training session? Or both. She's extremely attractive in an unremarkable way, like a woman in a magazine advertisement, each feature flawless and bland. She's not wearing cosmetics, not even lipstick, and her dark hair sits in a tidy knot at the nape of her neck. Not the tiniest emotion manifests itself on her face—maybe that's why it's so forgettable. An asset in her line of work, he reminds himself, and a skill he was never able to master. He always had to get by on his other strengths.

"Mr. Dubinin," she says in English. "Or should I say Digby? Welcome."

"Welcome to what? What the devil's going on?"

"It's funny, I was going to ask the same of you. This is not what we expected of you, Comrade, when we extended the arm of friendship to you and your family four years ago. We did not expect betrayal."

"I don't know what you mean. I've never once betrayed my loyalty to the Soviet Union."

She allows a hint of inquiry to dent the space between her eyebrows. "Then why are we here? In Latvia?"

"I was kidnapped. My family and I, we were kidnapped by some kind of enemy operative, probably CIA—"

"You did not go willingly? You were not, perhaps, in the *very act* of returning to the protection of the US government?" She takes some documents out of the folder at her elbow and lays them out before him. "These passports, identification papers—they are not for you and your family?"

"I've never seen them before in my life. I don't know where they came from, or who arranged it, but it wasn't me. It's someone trying to frame me, and I can't begin to imagine why. Where's my family? My wife and children? My wife's just given birth, she might be ill—"

"Don't worry about your wife and children, Comrade. Let us concentrate first on the matter at hand."

Sasha leans against the chair, although not very much, because his hands are secured in a pair of handcuffs behind the chair's back. "Whatever's happened, I'm sure we can get to the bottom of it."

"Yes, I'm sure of that," the woman says. "Because if we don't, I'm afraid we shall have to imprison you and your entire family as traitors to the Soviet people."

"What? That's nonsense!"

"I'm afraid so. You see, we have incontrovertible proof that you've been passing along vital and highly classified information about the KGB and its agents abroad for the past four years, in a counterspy operation named"—she looks down at some papers before her—"Honeysuckle."

"Honeysuckle? I've never . . ."

The sentence dissolves in his mouth.

"Yes, Comrade?"

"I've never heard of it. I have no idea what you're talking about."

The woman puts her elbows on the table and leans forward. "Think, Comrade. Tell me about ASCOT."

"The racecourse? I've been there."

"Don't play with me."

"I'm not playing. I sincerely don't know what you mean. I've spent the past four years tirelessly working on behalf of the Soviet people, who have welcomed me so warmly. I have never acted as a counterspy in the Soviet Union. Look at my records. Since coming here I've been grateful to be relieved of the burden of hiding my true loyalty. I've given up the booze, I've given up women, I've been a devoted husband and father. *Just look at my records.*"

He says the last words fiercely. Of course, he knows they've had him under surveillance. He's always accepted this state of affairs philosophically, as the price one pays to hold off the ever-present threat of counterrevolution. Until now, in fact, he's been glad of them. Let anyone doubt his true intentions in defecting! Let anyone say a word against him! In those dark and terrible days after Iris found him bleeding inside their apartment in Oakwood Court, having shot Beauchamp as an intruder, he had sworn that if Iris forgave him and offered him another chance, he would be true and loyal to the rest of his days. He would never touch another drop of alcohol! He would devote himself to Iris, as she had devoted herself to him. When she agreed to go along with him—yes, she would do it, she would defect with him, take the children and start over again with him in the Soviet Union!—he had worshipped her for it. He had loved and cared for Claire just as if she were his own child. And now this! *This* was how they repaid him! *Just look at my records!*

"Of course I have looked at your records, Comrade. I have examined every word, believe me. You've been an exemplary citizen, by all appearances. But there is also this. Discovered in the diplomatic bag of the American embassy in Moscow."

"You opened a diplomatic bag?"

"You know this is sometimes necessary, Dubinin. Don't play innocent."

"I have never in my life opened the diplomatic bag of another country."

"Then you have been derelict in your duty." The woman picks up the slip of paper before her and lays it before him.

ALL RIGHT, SO HE's lied to this woman. But he's only lied because he doesn't really know the truth, and it seems stupid to muddy the waters with speculation.

Sitting in that hospital waiting room with Ruth's husband—Ruth was married to *Sumner Fox*, of all people, *the* Sumner Fox, he just couldn't get his head around that—he had craved a drink very badly. He hadn't *wanted* to get Iris pregnant again, God no, not after Claire's birth—but she had begged him and he was only a man, after all, and there it was, another baby, sapping the strength from his wife and possibly sapping her life as well.

The funny thing is, he's never loved Iris more than he has since they came to Moscow. He might almost say that he never really loved her *until* Moscow—had never appreciated all the beautiful qualities inside his wife because he was too busy drinking, obsessed with himself and his own agony and the guilt and secrecy that tore his guts apart. Also, in Moscow there was no Nedda. No dazzling unpredictable bitch to pour his vanity into. Just her sublime creature, Iris, to whom he was actually *married*—who, in this newly discovered perfection, took on all the qualities he once imagined existed only in such great works of art as they had examined in their first moments together. You might say he'd gone from one extreme to another, from hardly appreciating Iris at all to idealizing her as a goddess.

Which made it all the more bewildering when, after leaving the hospital almost with *relief* at three o'clock in the afternoon to retrieve the children from school, he came home to discover a world he did not understand.

He knew at once that someone had searched the apartment. Among the first things you learned as a covert operative, you figured how to detect the signs of intrusion. Sometimes it was easy, as when the searchers didn't bother to hide their intentions and just ransacked the place. Other times they covered their tracks exquisitely well, so the subject wouldn't know he was under suspicion.

But even after four years as a private citizen, more or less, Sasha still kept these residual instincts. His eyes still traveled to the drawers, to the doors, to the rug, and examined them—not even consciously—for disturbance. He couldn't remember what, exactly, had told him all was not as he'd left it. He just knew. He told the children to wait in the living room as he went through the house, finishing at last in his own office, which he knew to be clean—there couldn't possibly be anything there to interest the KGB, and yet still he felt this terror as he took out his key and opened all the drawers and felt along the horizontal panel where, in another desk in another city in another lifetime, he had once cut a small hole on a false bottom to form a cavity, and in this cavity he would keep his papers and his one-time pad for coding and his Minox camera.

Of course, this was a different desk, in a different city, in a different lifetime, and the thought of carving a hole hadn't even crossed his mind, until now. Until his hand felt along the top of the middle drawer—right where the false bottom in his old desk drawer used to be—and encountered a square opening into a cavity that contained something peculiar.

A small electronic device he recognized as a one-way radio receiver.

DESPITE RANSACKING THE ENTIRE apartment in a kind of delirious tantrum, like a child, he hadn't found anything else. He had only this device that might have come from anywhere—he told himself—might have been left by a previous owner. Did he believe himself? He couldn't say. He didn't want to think about what it meant and who might have used it and for how long, and there was only one way to keep himself from thinking too much. He went to the liquor cabinet in which Iris kept a bottle of hospitable vodka in case of guests and he poured himself a glass, and when that was finished he went down to the liquor store around the corner and bought another bottle of vodka, and he had not stopped drinking until that bottle was empty and so was his head.

BUT NOW HE'S SOBER again. That's always the trouble, isn't it? At some point you return to sobriety and nothing's changed, except it's probably gotten worse because you were drunk and did drunken things. And in addition to the crashing almighty hangover he woke up with this morning, he had experienced the peculiar confusion and indignity of being urged into the trunk of a car by Sumner Fox—you couldn't argue with Sumner Fox, he was just too strong—because Iris was in danger. In danger of what? Fox wouldn't say. The kids just thought it was a terrific adventure, but they weren't in the trunk of the car. Sasha vomited twice, until there was nothing left to vomit. They stopped a couple of times and Fox, with a sympathetic face under a wig and hat, gave him water. They passed through some kind of border checkpoint, during which Sasha expected any moment that a guard would open the trunk and shoot him, but for some reason the guards asked no questions and waved them right through. Afterward Fox told him it was the border to Latvia, and they were going to pick up Iris and Ruth and the baby and go somewhere safe.

This is all he knows. This is what he's said to this KGB woman across the table from him—leaving out the part about the one-way radio—with all the conviction of truth, because he can't say for certain who put that radio receiver there, and when it was last used, and what it was used for. Every time his mind reaches out to touch that poisoned cup, he snatches it back. No, it's not possible. It's unthinkable! All those thoughtless conversations with Iris about his work, all those innocent questions she asked. All those papers he brought home with him, all those secrets he shared with her because she was Iris. They were devoted to each other. Her loyalty was so essential to his existence that he didn't even think about it—like breathing.

But the KGB woman stares at him with her cold eyes, so he looks down obediently at the piece of paper in front of him and says, "It's in code."

"Yes, of course the message is encoded. Unfortunately our

cryptographers have been unable to decipher it. It's the recipient who interests us. Do you see the address line, in plain English? The name Lonicera?"

"Lonicera? I don't know him."

"It is the name of the owner of the flat. It is also the scientific name for the genus of plants commonly known as honeysuckle."

"Honeysuckle?"

"Yes, it's a funny coincidence, isn't it? I understand you and your family stayed in a house with the same name, the summer before your defection. It was owned by a man named Philip Beauchamp, whom we know to have been employed by the British intelligence service during the war."

"Philip Beauchamp is dead. I killed him myself. It was an accident, of course—"

"Of course. These things happen. Still, it's a peculiar coincidence."

The woman stares at him without blinking. He stares back. He knows his gaze has some power—something to do with the particular shade of his eyes, which others find mesmerizing. It's a power he never realized until Nedda pointed it out to him, the first time she took him to bed. He wasn't a virgin, but he'd only slept with a couple of prostitutes, so it was a new and exquisite experience to lie among clean sheets afterward and talk and touch and kiss. She covered his eyes with her hands and said, *That's better.* He asked her what she meant, and she said that he could make her do anything with those eyes of his, that ultramarine color like the purest lake in the world. She murmured in her gravelly voice that she only had to *look* at those beautiful eyes and she *came off,* like *that*—she snapped her fingers. Of course, she was just speaking hyperbole, bed talk, but still. The idea of his magnetic gaze gave him confidence. He would never have dared to approach Iris without it.

Now he trains those eyes on this KGB woman—my God, he doesn't even know her name!—as if he's casting a spell, the old razzle-dazzle, except it doesn't seem to have any effect on her.

She looks, in fact, a little bored.

"Let us cut to the chase, Dubinin. As you Americans say."

"I'm not an American. I'm a Soviet citizen now, remember?"

She shrugs this away. "You have something I require—a full confession of your crimes, and a certain piece of information which we know you to be carrying to your Western handlers. I, on the other hand, have in my possession something terribly important to you—your wife, who is very sick, it seems, and your children."

"Is that a threat? You're threatening me with the lives of my family?"

"Of course not. The decision is yours. The power of life and death is in your hands." The woman spreads her own large palms before him. "I merely offer you the chance for redemption from your crimes, like a good Communist."

"I can't confess to a crime I haven't committed. I can't give you information I don't possess. You can torture me, you can do whatever you like with me, but I have nothing to say."

"Torture?" She raises her eyebrows. "Don't be dramatic. I don't torture people for information. Goodness, no. It's barbaric."

"No, you're exquisitely subtle, aren't you? Bloodless."

The woman cocks her head a few degrees. "You look as if you could use a little fresh air. Let's take a walk, shall we?"

OUTSIDE, THE NIGHT IS cool and clear, a taste of salt. Sasha has no idea where they are. Some military facility, probably. He sees the shadow of barbed wire against the horizon. A ghost of a watchtower from which a bright light flares and disappears. A few squat buildings pass by, barracks by the look of them. Already dawn is approaching. A yellow, hazy glow like enemy bombardment illuminates the sky to the east. The KGB woman is tall and matches his long-legged pace. Their footsteps crunch along the gravel path. A few yards behind them, a guard follows discreetly.

Sometimes, when Sasha recalls the things he did during the war, the careless way he dodged Gestapo and slipped in and out of buildings in the night—when he recalls the things he did before and after the war, the thousand tiny acts of subterfuge required to photograph documents without anyone noticing, say, or slip papers into your briefcase at night, or glance at the documents on a colleague's desk and memorize paragraphs in a few instants—the dead drops, the radio transmissions, the pass-offs, the hours crisscrossing cities to shake off surveillance, the endless ciphers, the hurried sex in cars and back hallways and safe houses—the memories seem to belong to another person. The old alertness returns to him now, walking between these silent buildings, but he can't summon the old energy. The rush of purpose is gone. In his veins he feels only dread, so cold it numbs his nerves. His arms ache from the handcuffs behind his back. He wants another cigarette. He wants a drink.

They stop in front of a low-roofed, rectangular building with no windows. A guard stands outside, motionless. The KGB woman nods to him—he steps aside. She opens the heavy metal door and says, *After you*, please.

Sasha ducks through the doorway into a small guardroom. Three metal doors line the opposite wall, each with a tiny barred window.

Sasha stops and asks for a cigarette.

The woman turns back to the door and asks the guard if he's got any cigarettes. The guard reluctantly hands her one from a battered pack, along with a cheap lighter. She lights the cigarette for him and sticks it in the corner of his mouth. Sasha smokes it for a moment, staring at the wall.

The KGB woman looks in one window, then another. She smiles fondly and puts a finger over her mouth. "Sleeping," she whispers.

Sasha doesn't want to look. He doesn't have the guts to see his children in a prison cell, his wife and newborn baby son in a prison cell. But he walks forward anyway. It's his punishment, isn't it? Too many sins to count, and they're all coming due at once.

He looks through the window and lets out a small, anguished noise at the sight of Claire, curled up in a cot with Kip, who sleeps with one protective arm over his kid sister. Their clothes are dirty, their hair is matted. On the floor next to them sleeps Jack, rolled in a blanket. He's lying on his back, and his mouth wears a strange, lurid grin.

Sasha can't bear it—he can't look away—he can't stand it another second—he can't move. The pain is like a magnet that holds him in place. Jack's pale hair—oh God! Claire's flushed cheeks, the trusting way she snuggles into her brother. How many thousand times has he held his daughter in his arms and kissed her sweet hair?

He tears himself away and leans his head against the cold wall. He never could wear the mask, could he? He never could keep it all inside. Not like this woman.

She stands there next to the wall, arms crossed. She could possibly order him to look inside the next cell, but she doesn't. She has all the patience in the world. She waits for him to creep there himself, to bring his face near the bars of the window and open his eyes.

But it's not Iris, after all. It's Ruth.

She lies on a cot, long and golden, eyes open to the ceiling, arms crossed behind her head. She turns her face and looks at him, without a word, and the expression of her eyes is so deadly that he jerks away.

"Digby?" she calls after him. "Is that you?"

"Yes."

"How's Iris?"

"I don't know," he gasps, over his shoulder.

Ruth comes to the window. "She's in the cell next to me. I called out but she didn't answer. Can you just make sure she's all right, please?"

He nods and steps to the third door and peers through the window before he can even prepare himself.

Iris.

She's asleep on a cot, on her back. The baby, wrapped in a swaddle, rests in the crook of her elbow. Her breathing is rapid and shallow; her cheeks are flushed. Her short dark hair tumbles around her face.

How many times has Sasha seen his wife asleep with a newborn baby? Hundreds of times. All the memories dazzle him at once, colorful and brittle, in constant motion like a kaleidoscope. He can't choose one.

He turns his head to the KGB woman and says, "She needs a doctor! She's not well, she had a cesarean section three days ago!"

"She needs a doctor! *Please!*" echoes Ruth. She's wrapped her hands around the bars of the window.

"Of course she'll have a doctor," says the KGB woman sooth-ingly. "As soon as our dear Dubinin agrees to cooperate."

"But I can't cooperate! I don't know what you're talking about."

"Jesus *Christ*," said Ruth. "Are you not even *human*?"

For an instant Sasha thinks she meant him. But when he looks in her direction, she's staring instead at the KGB woman. She speaks in a sore, frayed voice.

"You see what it does to your soul? *This* is what it makes you. It turns you into a brute with no soul, a stone for a heart, movements and classes instead of human beings. My sister is a *person*! She's beautiful and loyal and she saved my *life* when we were kids. I'm not kidding. I had a stomachache and she made my parents take me to the doctor and they got my appendix out just in time. And I never thanked her. She needs to live. *Please*. She needs a doctor. She's a human being!"

"That's up to her husband."

"My God! Who *are* you? Don't you have a sister, don't you have anyone you love? What if she were your own *sister*? What if she were your *daughter*?"

From Iris's cell comes the sound of a baby crying. Sasha turns and bangs his forehead on the window bars. "Let me in! For God's sake, let me hold him!"

Behind him, Ruth screams at the KGB woman. Iris stirs and turns to the crying baby in her arms. In his panic, Sasha can't even remember the name. The name of his own son! He bangs the bars with such strength, the door rattles in its hinges. The baby bawls his heartbreaking newborn cry. Iris shushes him. A pair of hands grasp Sasha by the shoulders and haul him away from the door. He shouts his wife's name, he sobs at each breath. He struggles against the arms that hold him, but they're massive arms and he's as weak as a kitten from the drive—his hands are handcuffed behind his back—he's helpless. The guard drags him outside and the door clangs shut. He falls to his knees. The prison hut is soundproof— all those desperate cries and shouts are cut off like a faucet. Sasha tilts his head to the sky and stares disbelieving at the gray pattern of midnight clouds. He has the strange feeling that his chest and stomach have been cut open and his entrails are spilling onto the ground before him.

"All right," he whispers. "I'll talk."

LYUDMILA

Once a man confesses to treason, it's easy to vacuum out all the details from him. He doesn't want to die! He thinks if he tells you everything, every last detail, the information will somehow weigh in his favor. This many names and dates, this many acts of betrayal, all added together—surely the sum equals one traitor's life. All you have to do is convince him to break. That's the hard part.

But Digby seems reluctant to reveal anything. He answers her questions haltingly, backtracks, puzzles through his memory. Lyudmila's beginning to lose her temper. It's nearly four o'clock in the morning and the sun's rising, pink and orange and gold outside the window. She didn't sleep on the airplane that brought her here; she's worked through the night. She sets down her pen and nods to the transcript typist on the machine in the corner.

"You are not being forthcoming," she says sternly. "I have kept my side of the bargain. A doctor attends your wife this minute."

"I thought you were going to set her free. I thought you were going to let her and the children go to the Americans."

Lyudmila's astonished. "Where did you get this idea? It's absurd! They are citizens of the Soviet Union! Why would the Americans want them?"

"They have family there. If I'm going to be shot, I want them with their family."

"It can't be done. It's likely the Americans have already given up and sailed off."

He frowns. "What about Fox?"

"Fox is a spy and has been detained separately. Listen to me. The information you have given me is all very nice, but it's not especially useful. What I need to know, first of all, is the identity of ASCOT—"

"I've already told you, I don't know that. I only knew him by his code name."

"Nonsense. You knew him in England. You and he set up Operation Honeysuckle together, possibly with the assistance of Fox."

Digby leans forward. "How do I know there's a doctor with Iris?"

"A doctor has been called for."

"How do I know that?"

"You have my word," she says.

He sits back again. "I'm not going to give you any more information until Iris and the children are safely in American hands."

"This is nonsense. If you don't give me any more information, you'll be shot as a traitor and your family sent to a labor camp for rehabilitation."

"You can't do that!"

"I have your confession, Comrade."

"I retract my confession!"

Lyudmila sighs. "You're making this so difficult. Why not simply give me the information? We both know you have it. We both know you love your wife and your family, and you don't want to see any harm come to them."

Digby just stares at her. He has the most remarkable eyes, a color so intensely blue it's difficult to look away. A good thing Lyudmila is so hardened by years of practice at interrogation. Oh, the pathetic pleas she's heard, the weeping and distress! You simply have to imagine yourself as a rock, millions of years old, impervious to wind and sea and sun and the intensely blue eyes of traitors to the revolution. You have to remember the great ideal for which you're fighting.

"You're going to send them to the camps, anyway, aren't you? Whatever I say, whatever I reveal to you, you're going to have me shot and they're going to disappear into the gulag. Whatever I—"

Digby stops in the middle of his sentence and looks to the door in surprise. Lyudmila's seen this trick before, however. She doesn't flinch. Only when a small, dry gasp penetrates the air behind her does she turn her head to glance over her shoulder.

A girl stands there, all by herself. She's wearing a rumpled school uniform and an expression of horrified shock. It actually takes Lyudmila a second or two to recognize that it's Marina.

She starts to rise from the chair. "Marina! How did you—"

A guard appears behind her daughter and grabs her by the arm. Marina turns her head and bites his hand—kicks him—he snatches her arm and bends it behind her back and shoves her to the ground.

"Comrade! Let the girl go this instant! What's the meaning of this?"

The guard has his knee in the middle of Marina's back. He looks up, panting, and says, "This girl just shot the guard outside the prison hut, Comrade! She was trying to free the prisoners!"

THE GENERAL STANDS BY the window and stares at the rising sun. He clasps his arms behind his back. Lyudmila can see how furious he is by the tic of one finger against the back of the other hand.

"I did not wish to allow this facility to be used for KGB purposes," he says. "The locals are not happy about our presence here to begin with. I agreed, because one does not refuse requests from Moscow Centre."

"Your loyalty has been noted."

"Has it?" He turns his head. His face blazes pink. "Why could this affair not have been handled in one of the detention centers near Moscow?"

"For strategic reasons—"

"Luckily the bullet missed his heart by a couple of inches. As it is, I must write a report on the incident. This is very grave, Ivanova. Very grave."

"Don't worry about the report."

"I don't worry about it with respect to myself, Ivanova. I've written such reports before. They are inconvenient, but my career has survived worse. No. The trouble is the child. There are witnesses. I can't obscure the facts."

"Of course not. She is to blame. She must face the consequences."

The general stares at her. The color begins to fade from his skin, the blood to return to its usual habits of circulation. He must be about fifty or so. Lyudmila knows his record. He made his name during the defense of Moscow, was transferred to Stalingrad, then led a division into Poland and then Germany as the tide turned. He's seen more bloodshed and more human misery than any single person should witness in a hundred lifetimes.

"You realize, of course, what those consequences are. To attack a solider, to shoot him. To attempt a prison escape. These are the most serious possible offenses. Her age and sex will not protect her. Nor can *you*, Ivanova."

"I understand."

He sighs. "Do you know how she found this place?"

"According to her account, she forced the information from my deputy at Moscow Centre, then boarded a train for Riga, then stole a motorcycle, upon which she conveyed herself here."

"Where did she learn to ride a motorcycle, at her age?"

"I'm not exactly certain."

"My God. She has the tenacity of a tiger. What a shame. What a *waste*." He shakes his head and fixes Lyudmila with his dark, sunken eyes. "It would have been far better for her if she had succeeded."

Lyudmila holds the gaze for a moment or two. Neither of them says a word. Through the window comes the ecstatic song of birds, greeting the morning.

AFTER LYUDMILA LEAVES THE general's office, she finds a guard to accompany her to one of the prison huts. Only one prisoner inhabits this one. There's no cot inside his cell. He lies on the bare floor, without a blanket, either asleep or unconscious. When Lyudmila enters the cell, he lifts his head and winces. She crouches next to him and sets her hand on his big shoulder, before she realizes it has been grotesquely dislocated. She pats his other shoulder instead.

"Mr. Fox," she says. "I have a proposition for you."

IRIS

The cell has no window, other than the small barred opening cut into the door, so Iris has no way of knowing what time of day it is, or how much time has passed since the doctor left. The guards stripped away her jewelry, including her watch. From the other cell, Ruth reports that she hasn't got a watch, either.

Still, it must be light outside by now. The day's begun, the endless summer day of the high northern latitudes. Somewhere outside these walls, a sun burns white and clear in a perfectly blue sky, and a briny wind rushes off the Baltic Sea to clean the air. Not far away, a fishing boat plies the waves, to and fro, waiting for a signal from shore that will never come. A man stands in the bow right now, a man who has been up all night with his binoculars, searching the shore until his eyes ache. His face will be knit with anxiety. Someone will bring him a sympathetic cup of black coffee, which he'll sip as he leans against the railing and clings to hope. ASCOT. She's known him by that name for so long, she's almost forgotten the real one.

The children are still asleep, she thinks. They haven't made a sound since the ruckus a few hours ago, when Sasha appeared out of nowhere looking like a straw-haired cadaver. Poor Sasha! Does he know the truth? Does he *suspect*, at least? He must. That expression as he looked at her—terror and betrayal—devastated blue eyes—Sasha never could keep his emotions from invading the muscles and nerves of his face. It was the expression of a man who has turned the pages of his own personal Book of Revelation and read the judgment written there. Iris's heart mourns for him. She looks down at the crook of her right arm, where Gregory lies heavily, lips parted, a tiny trickle of contented milk at the corner of his mouth. He looks shockingly like Sasha—at least, how Sasha would look as an old man, red face compressed into permanent grumpiness. His limbs are already long, his eyes are already blue.

But the action of gazing at her baby has already exhausted Iris. She feels a little better now. The doctor changed her dressing and tut-tutted and made her take aspirin and water. He said she needs penicillin. He doesn't have any. Penicillin is scarce and rationed mostly to party officials and their families. But he will see what he can do.

You've got to fight this, Iris tells herself. *You've got to get better. Gregory needs you. The children need you.*

Ruth needs you.

Once that KGB woman has squeezed what she can out of Sasha—unless Sasha breaks and tells her the truth, or as much of the truth as he can surmise—they'll execute him and then send Iris and the children to some labor camp, probably. If Iris doesn't get better, they'll put Gregory and Claire in an orphanage, or possibly adoption by well-connected party members. Iris imagines some

Russian woman, some wife of a Politburo bigwig, feeding Gregory a bottle and tucking Claire into bed at night. The image hurts so much that she allows herself to doze off, but not before shifting Gregory so that he's lying safely between Iris and the wall. Her last conscious thought is that she must ask the guards for fresh diapers.

SHE WAKES FROM HER confused, feverish sleep to the noise of Claire crying. Somebody's trying to soothe her—sounds like Kip. Ruth sings a song from the cell between them. Oh! It's the song she used to sing to Iris, when Iris couldn't sleep in the weeks and months after Daddy died. *You are my sunshine, my only sunshine. You make me happy when skies are gray.*

Gregory stirs and makes those little newborn noises that work up to sobs and then pathetic mayhem. Iris summons her strength and lifts him back into her arms. Ruth breaks off singing and calls her name from the other cell.

"Yes, I'm awake!" Iris calls back.

"How are you feeling?"

"Better."

The doctor left some aspirin behind. Iris swallows a couple of pills and carefully stands, so she can walk back and forth with the baby. His diaper's soaking wet, poor thing. When they bring food, she'll beg for some cloths. Anything will do.

THE DAY PASSES, INCH by inch, in a strange, nightmarish haze. The guards bring bread and water, and then—grudgingly, a little horrified—cloths for Gregory and also for Iris, whose womb still bleeds heavily. She tries to rest as much as she can. Not to think too much.

Ruth tells her that a guard came earlier with another prisoner, some school friend of Kip's. Iris doesn't catch the name—she doesn't have the strength—but she hears them talking. It's a girl. She tries to remember Kip's friends. She knows there was a girl among them, very pretty in a solemn, fierce way—dark hair, energetic eyes that seemed to catch every movement. What was her name? Possibilities float in and out of Iris's mind, but she can't catch one. Her world has shrunk to the tiny dimensions of her cell—to the minutes ticking by—the baby who needs all her attention. The air is damp and stale, but every so often a clean fresh salt draft whooshes in from the sea with one of the guards, and she breathes this wind like a tonic that will restore her to health.

IRIS HAS SOME IDEA that Ruth is keeping up the children's spirits. There are songs and word games, the same songs and word games that she and Ruth used to sing and play when they were little, so Iris keeps having these half dreams—hallucinations, almost—that she's ten or eleven years old, she's on the beach with Ruth, some hot and eternal summer's day on the shore of Long Island Sound. She hears the word *marina*, over and over, and in her mind they're rigging the sailboat for a long day on the water, and Iris feels the old, familiar unease that comes to her when she's out sailing, and the old, familiar envy of Ruth, drenched in sunshine as she scampers around the boat while Iris clings to her seat and tries not to be seasick.

THE CELL DOOR CLANKS open. Ruth rushes inside. *Iris,* she says.

Ruth, Iris whispers back.

You have to get up. They're moving us.

Where?

I don't know. Maybe a hospital for you.

Iris almost laughs, this is so impossible. Ruth hasn't lived inside the Soviet Union for four years—she still has hope.

But she summons herself and stands, with Ruth's help. Ruth swaddles up Gregory and carries him with her right arm; with her left arm, she supports Iris.

"Don't forget Gregory's bag," Iris says.

Ruth finds the valise and wrinkles her nose. "Why don't you just throw out the soiled ones? I'm sure you can get fresh cloths where we're going."

"You never know," Iris replies. "Where are the children?"

"They're already in the truck."

Truck?

It's one of those military convoy vehicles, noisy and hard. One of the guards hoists her inside. The children clamor her name—*Mama!* She closes her eyes and savors the feel of their young legs and arms, of Claire's soft cheek against hers. The truck smells of dirt and sweat and mildewed canvas and vomit but she doesn't care. This is all that matters, her babies, for whose sake she has done what she has done, so that they can live in a better world. Of course, that's what Sasha told himself, isn't it? You start out wanting to make the world better, and you end up destroying everything that was good.

The truck lurches forward and everyone falls silent. Through the cracks in the truck's canvas covering they glimpse the twilit world outside. It might be any hour from eleven until three in the morning—twilight never quite sinks into the absolute dark of night during these midsummer weeks—just this purpling sky, the faint stars, the hush, now broken by the roar and rumble of the truck and some other vehicle ahead of them.

Wherever they're going, it's not along some road. The truck sways and dives. In her mind, Iris returns to Long Island Sound and a sailboat under the hot sun. The terror of a vessel she can't control, obeying natural laws she can't predict. She hears an unfamiliar voice speaking Russian, a girl's voice, and she remembers the other prisoner, the school friend of Kip's—what was her name? How did she get here? It's all part of the dream, maybe.

The truck stops with a jerk. A pair of guards appear at the back and shout at them to get down, file out, line up. The Russian girl shouts back at them. But they don't have any choice—the guards carry fearsome rifles, which they point to the girl, then Kip, then Ruth. They have the decency not to point at Iris. One by one, everyone crawls across the bed of the truck and jumps to the ground below. Ruth goes before Iris. She hands the baby to somebody, leaps down, and holds up her arms to help Iris. Ruth is so strong, she catches Iris without a stagger.

Iris gives her the bag with the soiled diapers. Because what does she have to lose? If something happens to them, the bag will be thrown away. Nobody will look inside a baby's soiled diaper. And maybe the bag will survive even if she does not. Maybe someone will come looking for her, and find this bag, forgotten in the mud. You never know.

The guards shout some more.

"What are they saying?" Ruth asks.

"They want us to follow them."

Ruth puts her arm around Iris's waist and walks with her at the end of the line. They're walking on hard sand, by the feel of it.

Iris can almost hear the rushing of the sea in her ears, unless it's her imagination again. The voices bark in Russian to hurry along. They travel some hundred yards or so, then a guard orders them to stop and line up. They stop and line up. Iris turns to face the guards. There are two of them, holding their rifles, and a woman who stands a few feet away. The KGB woman. She stares at them coldly, one by one, ending with the girl.

"Where's Fox?" Ruth shouts at her. "Where's Digby?"

"This is not your concern," the woman says, in perfect English. "After a thorough investigation, you have been found to have committed treason against the Soviet people. The penalty for this crime is death—"

"*I hate you!*" the girl screams.

The woman turns her head and stares at the girl. Not long, a few seconds only, during which not a murmur interrupts the cool, dark silence of twilight.

The woman makes a signal to the guards, who shoulder their rifles and aim them at the line of prisoners, women and children, newborn baby in the arms of his big brother.

Nobody moves. Nobody makes a sound, not even Claire. The shock is too great, the knowledge of instant death paralyzes them all. Iris feels the universe shrink and expand around her. Her flesh anticipates the thud of bullets and the spray of blood. She sees—no, not her life passing before her, but everything all at once—Sasha and Philip, the children, Ruth, Harry, her parents, all gathered into a single soul, like a star. She croaks out a soundless NO.

The woman opens her mouth and says, "—*or exile.*"

From the beach behind them comes another sound—a voice.

Ruth turns first, then the children, then Iris. A pair of men brace themselves in the sand, about a hundred yards away, illuminated by a sliver of moon. Behind them, a large rowboat rests on the ebbing tide.

"Go," the woman says, in English.

RUTH

JULY 1952
Baltic Sea

The sun is just beginning to rise when we reach the fishing trawler.

Trawlers are the most unlovely things afloat, in my opinion—dirty white and clumsy as a gravid rhinoceros. But this one is perhaps the most beautiful craft I have seen in my life, all bathed in the fine pink otherworldly glow of a breaking dawn.

Everyone in the rowboat is stupefied, except the girl Marina. She sits in the stern and silently weeps. I only know this because I turned around once, during the journey across the fidgety, chopping waves, and saw the trails of tears along her cheeks. At one point, Kip tried to climb back and console her, but she shook her head and he stopped in his tracks. Sat back down and faced forward. I guess they understand each other, those two—like me and Fox.

The trawler is well out to sea, and it requires almost three hours of hard pulling on the part of those two sailors before we meet. All this time I've been pushing back any thought of Fox—or of Digby, for that matter—but especially Fox. It helps that my hands are full, keeping Claire from climbing over the side of the rowboat, trading off Gregory with Kip, checking anxiously on Iris, who curls at my feet, propped against the curving side of the boat, burning hot and restless, while Fox's image clamors painfully at the back of my head. Three such hours can make anything look beautiful.

As we approach, one of the sailors hails the trawler. I don't think it's necessary. A rope ladder already hangs down the side, and a man stands there as though he's prepared to dive in at the slightest signal. For an instant I imagine it's Sumner Fox, by some extraordinary miracle on a night of miracles. I can almost see his big shoulders—his rough face soaked in sunrise. But as we draw nearer, my imagination dies away. These shoulders are no more than sturdy; the face is not as broad or as coarse; one side is marked with terrible scars, where he hasn't got much of an ear left. He leans forward to catch the rope tossed up by the sailor, and his hair catches the light—pink and gold as the dawn itself.

One by one, the children go up the ladder and into the man's arms. The boys seem to recognize him—Jack makes a squeal. Marina climbs carefully and doesn't say a word of thanks. Then Claire goes up. He catches her tenderly and says something to her that makes her laugh. Her feet hit the deck and she scampers out of sight.

Now it's my turn. I clamber forward on the rocking boat and hand up the baby to this man. He scoops Gregory like a man who's held a newborn in his time—one hand supporting the head, the other under the bottom—and comforts him while I climb the rope ladder and stagger to the deck.

"You must be Ruth," the scarred man says.

Without the scars, he might be handsome—you can't tell.

Without the white hair, he might be a young man—again, there's no telling. He has the eyes of someone who has lived too much and too long, but the trim, taut figure of someone who lives ferociously in the present. The sunlight makes a nimbus around him and the baby in his arms. All this I gather in an instant, because there is not an instant to lose. I hold out my hands for Gregory. "I am."

You know, I don't think he even sees me, really. He puts the baby in my arms and says hastily, "Philip Beauchamp. You'll excuse me."

I step away from the opening on the rail. From below, one sailor supports Iris around the waist while she puts her hands and feet on the rungs of rope. The man named Beauchamp goes down on his knees and then his belly and reaches down to take my sister in his arms. He hauls her carefully to the deck and cradles her as you might cradle a child. The new sunshine coats them both. He pushes away some hair from her forehead and shouts out for the medical kit.

Iris looks for me. "The bag!" she gasps out. "Gregory's bag."

I look back at the rowboat, where the valise sits, forlorn and forgotten, in the very peak of the bow, because nobody wanted to sit near it—reeking as it does. Gregory stirs in my arms and lets out a lusty cry.

Because I am numb with sorrow, revelation steals over me quietly, like a thief.

Lord Almighty. The football.

And I laugh—giggles at first, then giant, hysterical whoops that shock Gregory into silence and cause everyone in the trawler to stare at me as if I'm crazy. Maybe I am. Are we not still surrounded by misery and death? Does my heart not groan in anguish for what we left behind? Still, I laugh. I can't seem to help myself.

Sumner Fox's final handoff, across the goal at last.

Before I fit the baby into the crook of my elbow and reach down with one hand to take the bag from the sailor, I kiss my sister on the cheek. She's the only one left in the world who understands.

FOUR

Every man is hung upon the cross of himself.

—*Whittaker Chambers*

IRIS

AUGUST 1952
Dorset, England

After breakfast every morning, Iris settles Gregory into the enormous Silver Cross perambulator and heads out across the lawn and the meadow until the Channel breeze comes out of nowhere to tumble her hair and wash her cheeks and fill her lungs. Then she sits in the grass with her sketchbook and fills the crisp, new pages with drawings.

The perambulator was a gift from Philip, along with the nurse who tends Gregory during the middle of the night so Iris can rest. To say nothing of Honeysuckle Cottage itself—dear, crumbling bricks and climbing vines, like coming home! Philip—reading her mind as always—said it would be easier for the boys if they stay in the cottage, in their old familiar bedrooms, instead of Highcliffe. Even Mrs. Betts has returned to their lives. Philip hired her to look after Honeysuckle Cottage when the Digbys disappeared, and between Mrs. Betts and Ruth and the nurse, everything runs to the beat of some invisible clock, so Iris hardly has to lift a finger. Even if she wants to.

"When you're strong again . . ." Ruth says, from the grass beside her.

"I *am* strong. I'm all better."

"Thanks to good capitalist penicillin. Anyway, you've earned a holiday. Who would've thought my little pumpkin could break up an international spy ring?"

The sea air is good for everyone, even Gregory. Iris peers over the edge of the pram to check on him. He slumbers on, motionless—two small, perfect hands on either side of his small, perfect head. Iris gazes in rapture at the tufts of pale hair, the apple curve of his cheek, the outline of his long, bowed legs under the blanket. A part of her wants to answer Ruth's argument—to explain that she was never really the little pumpkin of Ruth's imagination, that the sisterhood is not divided neatly into adventuresome Ruths and retiring Irises, that bravery is woven from all kinds of different fabric and maybe hers is actually the more tough, the more durable. But this story is so important to Ruth—the story of Ruth forever coming to the rescue of a delicate Iris—so she returns to her drawing and doesn't say a word.

"What are you sketching this morning?" Ruth asks.

"Oh, nothing much."

"May I see?"

Iris turns the sketchbook so Ruth can see the page.

"Nifty. It's Beauchamp's sailboat, isn't it?"

Iris fills in a shadow with tiny crosshatches. "Not bad, for a Philistine."

"You used to hate sailing."

"Oh, I don't mind so much as I used to."

"I guess it depends on who's sailing the boat, then."

Iris makes a small smile. The morning is cool and so extraordinarily clear, she can almost see the coast of France. But she hasn't stopped here to see France. She's stopped because this is her favorite spot, where the cliffs jut out a bit and the soft turf invites you to sit, and where she kissed Philip Beauchamp for the first time. Of course, Ruth doesn't know that. Ruth doesn't know a lot of things. In the pram, Gregory starts to stir. Ruth climbs to her feet and adjusts his blanket. She's transformed into this obsessively attentive auntie—making up for lost time, Iris supposes.

"It's a pickle, isn't it?" Ruth asks.

"What's a pickle?"

"Your husband. Beauchamp. And don't play dumb on me or anything. I'm not an idiot. You and Beauchamp—the two of you—I know he's Claire's father."

Iris lays her charcoal back in the tin. "*Ruthie,*" she says.

Ruth turns to face her sister. Hands on hips. "It's just like you, not to think things through. Everything's done by the heart, with you."

"And you, everything by the head."

"So maybe we're perfect for each other."

Iris tries to smile back.

"The kids will be fine," Ruth says. "You know that, don't you? They have each other. Even that Marina kid, she'll come around."

"And now you're an expert on children?"

"Well, they have *you* for a mother, the lucky tramps." Ruth shades her eyes and nods to the cottage. "And that terrific Beauchamp of yours. Arriving any minute to start up a round of cricket or something, I'll bet. They'll be fine. The question is you. Will *you* be fine, Iris Macallister?"

Iris studies the sketchbook in her lap. The sailboat is not quite right. It's supposed to be a surprise for Philip, and also a little joke between them—how he loves that schooner more than he loves her. But Iris isn't a born sailor. She hates the sea. How can you draw a sailboat if you don't have some intuitive grasp of the physics of sailing? Anyway, sailboats remind her of that disastrous expedition to the Isle of Wight. Sasha, drunk and angry. She had almost forgotten how terrible he used to be, because he became a different man in Moscow. He became this sober, loving husband and father, and all along Iris had betrayed him—coldly, without mercy—photographing his papers and harvesting his memory and taking his children out for walks in the park, during which she would drop her bundles of photographs and coded reports into a hollow tree, say, or that ice cream vendor in Gorky Park. Then, after Burgess tipped her off—never *realizing* he was tipping her off, poor old thing—the most coldhearted manipulation of all.

Even now, when she thinks of that terrifying year—boxed in, trapped, exposure possible any minute—that final cache of vital information lying hidden in the apartment, month after month—unable to communicate to Fox and Philip except by their old, prearranged signals—her audacious plan, Sasha's unknowing cooperation—Gregory growing at last in her womb, thank God, praying she wouldn't miscarry, praying they wouldn't catch her first—guilt, worry, desperation—she has to shake herself to understand she's still alive. The children are alive. She has won her terrible gamble. She has this beautiful new baby, and she has Philip, and Ruth.

And Sasha has nothing.

"We have to assume he's alive," Iris says. "One of the labor camps, maybe."

Ruth drops to the grass next to her and pulls the sketchbook away. "Don't you feel guilty for a minute. Not a single goddamn second. He brought it on himself, and even if he did the right thing in the end—well, he's only bought salvation for his own soul, maybe. It's not nearly enough to make up for what he's done to *you. And the kids.*"

"I know all that. You don't need to worry about me. It's just sorrow, that's all."

"You have room in your heart for that?"

"He's their father."

On cue, Gregory makes a series of desperate sobs that culminates in a howl. Ruth climbs to her feet and lifts him out of the pram to cradle him against her shoulder. Iris stares not at her son, but at the ring on her sister's left hand, a plain gold band. She first noticed it a week or so ago. She didn't say anything to Ruth, but she mentioned it to Philip. *Why don't you ask her?* he said reasonably, and Iris recoiled. *If she wants to tell me, she'll tell me,* she said, and Philip rolled his eyes just a bit and told her she was supposed to be a *spy,* for God's sake.

Iris decides to speak up. "What about Sumner?"

Ruth whirls to face her. "Have you heard anything?"

Her blue, terrified eyes tell Iris everything she wants to know. She breathes out a zephyr of relief and considers whether she should tell Ruth what she knows, or whether such a tender fact would only make things harder for her sister if—well, Iris refuses to consider the *If.* There's always hope, isn't there?

"No," she says. "But Philip's in close contact with the Americans. He'll give us any news, the instant he gets it."

Ruth turns away to face the sea. Over the edge of her shoulder, Gregory's red face stares amazed at Iris. She rises from the grass and comes to stand next to her sister, who vibrates with energy or emotion or something, Iris isn't exactly sure what. Like a dam struggling to hold fast against a weight of mighty floodwater. Gregory's clean, puppy scent gathers them together.

"You didn't have to do it," Ruth says. "You could have let Digby defect on his own. Washed your hands of him. You knew by then what the bastards were capable of. You could have stayed behind and married Beauchamp. You were already pregnant—you had the boys—you had every reason to stay safe in England."

"Wouldn't you have done the same, though?"

"God, no. Take the children and walk straight into the jaws of the lion? When I had a fellow like Beauchamp madly in love with me? You're crazy."

Iris runs her index finger along the perfect crest of Gregory's ear. "Ruth, I spent most of my life just trying to be safe. Trying to hide from what scared me. Letting other people control what happened to me. Then I realized the idea of safety itself is just a delusion. *Life* is risky. And hiding isn't *living*."

Gregory starts to drowse against Ruth's shoulder. His little head bobbles and rests against the soft green knit of Ruth's cardigan. His eyes lose focus. There's some connection between these two—the kind of atomic bond that would set most new mothers buzzing with jealousy, but instead gives Iris the same feeling she used to get when the priest at St. Barnabas laid his hand on the children's heads and said *Christ's blessing be upon you.*

Iris continues, "I remember sitting there by Philip's bed, day after day, not sure if he would live or die. I thought about what Sumner told me, about a mole right inside the American intelligence service, right near the top, and operatives and agents were dying because of him. I thought about how I had stood by Sasha so stupidly all those years, telling myself that he was only following his ideals. I realized I was culpable, just as if I'd pulled the trigger that nearly killed Philip."

"Good old Fox," Ruth murmurs.

"Anyway, I went back to Sumner and told him I would do it—I would convince Sasha to defect—but I knew he wouldn't turn on the Soviets. I would have to do it myself."

"I'll bet Fox loved *that*."

"He was skeptical. But I won him over. I said it was the last thing anyone would expect. I said I was invisible to them, just some silent woman pushing a baby in a pram. And I was right." Iris touches Gregory's cheek. "Mummy did it, didn't she? She found the bad man."

"Sitting there in Washington all along. The fox guarding the henhouse."

"Well, they haven't caught him *yet*. Still on the lam, the last I heard."

"They'll catch him. I'll bet the FBI has never hunted a man down so ferociously. Dogs after a rat. Of course, his wife claims she never knew a thing."

"And I'm sure everyone believes her, too," Iris says grimly.

"Except Fox. I guess you taught him a thing or two about housewives."

The breeze picks up a little, lifting the ends of Iris's hair. She's about to suggest they put Gregory back in the pram, head back to the house, when Ruth speaks up, a little raspy—

"What if they never find him?"

"Fox? Oh, darling, they'll find him—he'll turn up—he's indestructible—"

"No, I mean Sasha. I mean your husband." Ruth turns her head and looks at Iris over the tuft of Gregory's pale hair. "Or was it all an act?"

"It wasn't an act. Not completely." Iris pauses. "Anyway, he sacrificed himself for us, didn't he? In the end, he loved us more than them."

"Then what about Beauchamp?"

Iris stares at a fishing smack, all by itself on the choppy Channel, beating off the leeward shore. In the liquid morning air, she can see every detail—the pure white sail against the blue water, the fisherman untangling his net in the stern.

"He's the best man I've ever known," she says.

THEY PUT GREGORY BACK in the pram, but instead of heading back to the house, they walk along the cliff path, talking for once. The ice—not broken, maybe, but cracked in a few places. Iris gathers her resolve and brings up Fox.

"You know he's been in love with you for years," Iris says. "Since he first started investigating you."

Ruth's voice registers disbelief. "Did he tell you that?"

"He didn't have to. I just knew. Also, Fox was the one who suggested that extraction signal. That I send *you* a postcard when we were ready to leave."

Ruth stares at the ground as she walks. The tip of her nose is bright pink. "Anyway, it doesn't matter. They've got him now. They won't let him go."

"I wouldn't be so sure. He has more value alive than dead. Propaganda. Or a spy exchange—they do that all the time. They only really execute their own people." Iris glances sideways. "The best thing is to keep busy until there's news. You'll be headed back to

New York soon, won't you? You have your modeling business to run."

"Actually." Ruth kicks away a stone. "I got a cable the other day. It seems this new model of mine—name of Barbara Kingsley, you'd love her—she's become such good friends with my dear old boss, helping him manage and all in my absence, she's thinking she might do better behind the scenes than inside them."

"Oh? How do you feel about that?"

Ruth squints at some object in the meadow. "I'm thinking I don't know what I feel about anything anymore. Say, speak of the devil."

"The devil?"

"Beauchamp."

Iris turns her head. Philip angles toward them with the long, purposeful strides of a man who has serious news to communicate. Iris's heart drops into her stomach. Beside her, Ruth stops and puts a hand on the edge of the pram.

"What is it?" Iris calls out, when he's within earshot.

Ruth stands silent and colorless as Philip approaches. When he reaches them, she says in a harsh voice, "Is it Fox? Is he dead?"

Philip glances at Iris and hands Ruth the telegram in his hand. She snatches it and turns away to read it.

"Oh, Christ," she whispers.

"What's happened?" Iris says.

Philip stares at the side of Ruth's cheek. "They've found him in Berlin. Dumped on a side street."

"Oh, God."

Iris reaches for Ruth's shoulder. Ruth turns beneath her hand. Her eyes are wild, her skin flushed. She speaks in a hoarse whisper. "But he's alive. He's alive."

"*Alive!*" Iris exclaims. "Philip, what—"

"The Americans are flying out a medical team from Northolt at ten thirty."

"How far is Northolt?"

Philip looks at his wristwatch. "If we hop in the car this instant, I can drive you there in time."

"Will they let me on?"

"By God," says Philip, "they'd better."

FOR A MOMENT, IRIS and Philip stand to watch Ruth as she bounds to the cottage to collect her toothbrush and passport. Her gold hair flies from the patterned silk scarf around her head. In the perambulator, Gregory's eyes flash open. His mouth screws in preparation for a good yell. Iris puts her hand inside Philip's hand.

"Will he live?" she whispers.

He turns his troubled face to her and smiles.

"Fox? Of course he'll live. He'll live for *her.*"

"Are you sure?"

"Can you think of a better reason?"

In the distance, the sun flashes against Ruth's bouncing gold hair. Gregory lets loose with a lusty cry. Philip takes the handlebar of the Silver Cross perambulator to guide them back to the cottage.

AUTHOR'S NOTE

I became familiar with the Cambridge spy ring sideways, while I was researching something else. The more I learned, the more desperate I became to set everything else aside and write about *this*.

In Great Britain, their names are as synonymous with treason as Benedict Arnold's is in the United States—Kim Philby, Donald Maclean, Guy Burgess, Anthony Blunt, John Cairncross—and the flight of Burgess and Maclean to the Soviet Union in May 1951 is the stuff of legend. Recruited by the Soviet spy agency NKVD in the 1930s, when communism was fashionable among the young elites of Oxford and Cambridge, they graduated and duly entered the corridors of power, where they served up their country's vital secrets to the Soviet Union for the next two decades, using their influential positions and the cultural capital of an Oxbridge man—no Englishman could possibly imagine a traitor among the chaps he went to school with, college with, clubs with—to avoid detection. Eventually it all came tumbling down, of course, but not before Stalin was privy to all the British negotiating points at Yalta, not before the minutes and papers of the Atomic Energy Commission were delivered into Soviet hands, not before the secrets of the nuclear program allowed Soviet scientists to create their own weapons, not before countless brave intelligence agents had been unmasked, tortured, executed.

But it was more than that. These men sat at the top of the British intelligence and diplomatic corps. The nation's faith in its political and academic elites was permanently shaken, and the partnership between the US and UK spy agencies became a minefield of distrust and paranoia at the very moment that the West needed a united front more than ever.

Needless to say, this rich ground has been thoroughly plowed by historians and novelists alike over the years, and many a spy thriller owes its inspiration—directly or indirectly—to one or more of the Cambridge Five. But as I dug deeper into these men and their lives, I was less fascinated by the mechanics of espionage— the *what* and the *how* of what they did, the narrow escapes and unspeakable blunders—than by the *who* and the *why*. How could these intellectually brilliant men cling so willfully and catastrophically to their beliefs, even as the everyday evils of the Soviet state lay so plain before them? How could they betray their friends with such cold disregard? Consign women and men to their deaths without a second thought? How did this constant betrayal and secrecy affect them psychologically? And my God, what did it do to their families? The wives and children who bore the brunt of their inner torment? Were they unwilling passengers or fellow travelers?

These questions brought me to the marriage of Donald and Melinda Maclean, a fraught and complex partnership if ever there was one. At various points in their relationship, Melinda was his victim and his enabler, sometimes fed up and other times addicted, and easily the steelier of the two. Because the intelligence service dismissed her as a brainless housewife, she was able to facilitate Maclean's defection in 1951 while eight and a half months pregnant, then slip away to join him with the children two years later. It hit me that the spymasters and spy catchers on both sides were missing a trick or two, and this kernel of inspiration grew and transformed into *Our Woman in Moscow*.

Sasha bears a physical and psychological resemblance to Maclean, and certain scenes are inspired by real-life incidents that marked Maclean's deterioration into alcoholism and self-loathing—the farce on the Isle of Wight, for example, is roughly drawn from a disastrous picnic expedition on the Nile during Maclean's posting to the British embassy in Cairo. Despite these parallels, Sasha and Iris are fictional characters and the narrative itself arises from my own imagination. Maclean died of natural causes in the Soviet Union in 1983; Melinda returned to the United States permanently in 1979, though not before having had an affair with Kim Philby, who defected in 1963.

Meanwhile, on a personal note, my own grandfather was born in St. Petersburg at the turn of the century to a British father and a Russian mother. At the outbreak of revolution in 1917, he fled across Scandinavia to England and never returned. As I grew up in the shadow of the Cold War, it seemed impossible to me that Deo had grown up in Russia, speaking Russian as well as English, summering at his grandfather's dacha near the Finnish border. Of course, I never talked to him much about it, which I now deeply regret, but he and my grandmother had the foresight to write down their recollections in memoirs for the family. The fictional flight from Russia in *Our Woman in Moscow* might just owe its inspiration to Deo's flight a hundred years earlier.

For those readers interested in learning more about the Cambridge spy ring, I can enthusiastically recommend the exhaustively researched *Enemies Within: Communists, the Cambridge Spies, and the Making of Modern Britain* by Richard Davenport-Hines, as well as Ben Macintyre's thorough and intensely readable narrative of the Kim Philby case, *A Spy Among Friends*. For a gripping account of Donald Maclean's life and espionage career, reach for *A Spy Named Orphan: The Enigma of Donald Maclean* by Roland Philipps, which meticulously captures the complex psychology of Maclean and his tortured marriage.

A final technical note: the Soviet intelligence services combined, split apart, and recombined in dozens of different incarnations over the first few decades of Soviet history, each time with a different name. For the sake of simplicity, I refer to the pre–Second World War agency as the NKVD and the postwar agency as the KGB familiar to Cold Warriors, although it didn't actually take on this final form until 1954. My apologies to the historical sticklers for this narrative convenience.

I wrote much of *Our Woman in Moscow* during the intense stress of the coronavirus shutdown in the spring of 2020, while juggling the physical and emotional needs of my large family all gathered together for weeks on end. For her patience and understanding (and timely care packages of artisan chocolate) I can't thank my editor, Rachel Kahan, enough. In fact, the entire team at William Morrow came through like heroes during this abrupt change of plan and working conditions—Tavia Kowalchuk, Brittani Hilles, Alivia Lopez, and all my other champions in sales and marketing and production, you are so deeply appreciated! Special gratitude is due to my eagle-eyed copyeditor, Laurie McGee, who kept my timelines straight and my hyphenation in order. My warmest thanks as well to my superstar agent, Alexandra Machinist, and her assistant Lindsey Sanderson, for handling the business side of things so ably while I tangled myself in knots of Cold War history.

As for my dearest, loveliest lovelies Karen White and Lauren Willig, there are no words to thank ewe for all your support and encouragement during the writing of this book. Certain things only the three of us shall ever know. One truth we've proved for sure, though—friendship knows no distance.

As always, my deepest thanks to my family for your love and patience as I made my endless daily circuits from kitchen to laundry room to writing chair.

To my readers, whose kind messages and thoughtful reviews revived my spirits at every low ebb, I can't begin to express my gratitude. This book wouldn't exist without you.